Crimson
Shadows

Crimson Shadows

by

Trisha Baker

Crimson Shadows

Cover design by Lori Osif and Allan Gilbreath

Published by
Dark Oak Press
Kerlak Enterprises, Inc.
Memphis, TN
www.darkoakpress.com

Trade Paperback
ISBN 13: 978-1-941754-30-6
Library of Congress Control Number: 2003587084
First Printing: 2014

This book is printed on acid free paper.

Printed in the United States of America

Table of Contents

Prologue

January 13, 2000

"Blood, Father," the tinny voice of his son piped up from the other end of the room. Simon Baldevar looked up from his easel in annoyance.

Putting his paintbrush aside, Simon stood up and swiftly crossed the vast chamber but he did not move quickly enough to appease the baby that began weeping inconsolably. The child's shrill, inhuman cries would puncture mortal eardrums, but they had no effect on the vampire father, except the mild irritation any parent felt toward wailing, howling offspring.

"Hush," Simon said to his one-year-old son and the boy's silver eyes with their inhuman slits for pupils focused on his father with an expression of intense longing and furious need. It was merely the blood lust all vampires suffered when they needed to feed, but it was decidedly odd to see those savage emotions reflected in the eyes of such a small creature.

"Blood," the baby repeated and Simon had to suppress a turn of disgust at his son's appearance. When the boy grew hungry and wasn't immediately appeased, his skin took on the translucent quality of a deformed vampire, knotted red and blue veins marring the surface of his milky white skin and his eyes started to lose their pigment.

Mikal flinched, perhaps sensing his father's revulsion, and his cries escalated into a strident howl that put a crack in one of the tower windows.

"Enough," Simon said over the din, but the child paid no attention. "I shall bring you food, now be silent."

As he left the room to secure prey, Simon reflected he should feel some pride that Mikal already spoke and understood language with such a precocious grasp. So far the boy was

1

developing with amazing speed—his first words were spoken a scant eight weeks after he was born. When he wasn't consumed by blood lust and able to think clearly, the child was already learning how to read and write.

Mikal's physical growth also far exceeded that of mortal children. He was now the size of a three year old, though he remained underweight, as he had been from birth. No doubt that stemmed from the child's inability to digest any substances but blood and water. Simon worried at first that an all-blood diet wouldn't contain all the nutrients a child needed to grow properly, but Mikal's only deformity was his thinness.

Disdaining the spiraling stone staircase at the base of the tower, Simon used astral projection to enter the common room downstairs and found his servants idling about, though they made an immediate effort to look busy when their master appeared. They showed no surprise at his materialization from thin air for they had learned the hard way of their employer's supernatural abilities.

Simon's requirements for servants were strict. They must be destitute, have no family or friends to inquire at their disappearance, and no command whatsoever of the English language. He found them in a variety of places—Calcutta, Romania, the former Soviet Union, really any country with a thriving homeless population.

Simon had procured the wretched mass before him by inquiring in the native tongue of each sordid hellhole he visited whether the young (youths always supplied better blood than aging humans) homeless would be interested in employment in a foreign land. Once it was ascertained that no one would inquire at their disappearance, a group of five to ten was gathered up and shipped to the remote Scottish island on which Simon had chosen to rear his son. He'd owned the property since the eighteenth century when he ruthlessly displaced the residents so he'd have the island to himself.

Once his servants arrived, they had no choice but to watch helplessly as one by one of their number were dragged away, giving their final duty to their master by supplying blood to the vampire child, his father, and Mikal's nursemaid.

Once they got some inkling of their predicament, a few attempted escape, only to be electrocuted by the fence surrounding the property or blown to pieces by the various land mines scattered around the moors. Even if they did manage to flee the island, they had to brave choppy, icy waters and swim to the mainland. If they survived that near impossible obstacle, the nearest village was ten miles away, ten miles of freezing, mountainous terrain impossible to cross without supplies. And if the escaped captive should manage to cross paths with a passerby before Simon caught up to them, they had no words to convey their predicament because they did not speak English.

Simon was careful to speak no English before his prisoners; he did not want some bright soul piecing together even a few words that could aid in their escape. That was why he beckoned to one dusky-skinned female and said in curt, perfect Hindi, "Come with me."

The girl paled to a dull beige color but could not disobey the vampiric order. Sobbing, because Simon made no effort to dull her terror with a psychic command that would have turned her into little more than a catatonic, she slowly crossed the room, piteously begging, "Please not me, please. I clean well. I am good servant. Please. . ."

Simon ignored the entreaty, though her anguish and terror were making his own blood lust rise. The girl was quite right in her argument, she was a good servant—they all were. The human spirit and capacity for hope never failed to astonish him. All his prisoners maintained perfect order in the castle. They seemed to believe that if they behaved, if they proved their worth, Simon would not harm them as he'd done to their less fortunate counterparts. Of course, such hope was utterly foolish—the world economy being what it was, Simon would never run out of food for Mikal or free help to run his home.

The girl broke out into uncontrollable tremors as they climbed the stone staircase and Mikal's cries became audible to her mortal ears. Her knees gave out and Simon had to yank her off her feet, carrying her the last few steps. The increased closeness, throwing her neck against his mouth, proved too much temptation and Simon's blood teeth punctured her young, tender neck to drink of the warm nectar pouring down his throat.

How pleasant it would be to drain her utterly but his son needed the blood far more than he did. Reluctantly, Simon pulled away from the girl after only a few swallows, enough to take the edge off his hunger momentarily. After Mikal fed, Simon would secure his own meal.

At least now, the girl was more docile. She'd been drained of any fight, though there was still more than enough blood in her to sate Mikal. Throwing open the thick wooden door to the chamber, Simon heard his son's screams increase when his sharp nose picked up the human's scent.

Simon dropped the girl, semi-conscious and no longer aware of her surroundings on the floor, and plucked Mikal from his playpen. He set the boy down and watched him toddle toward the girl with the lightning fast determination of a hunting cat.

No longer did Simon have to hold his son up to a human while the boy fastened his small, pointy fangs to their neck or wrists. Now Mikal was capable, if the prey was prone and unable to defend itself, of feeding by himself.

Simon watched in fascination as Mikal's head, with its sleek cap of thick, dark hair, bent toward her neck and he began to feed. A few minutes later, Mikal's deformities vanished; his skin and eyes regained their normal tones.

While Mikal fed, Simon reflected on the child's vampiric progress. As of yet, the child had no ability to travel the astral plane like his father, but his telekinetic ability was growing quickly. Even better, he was learning to control it—no longer did Simon have to keep the child in a room with no moveable objects for fear he might harm himself.

Mikal's other major improvement from infancy was his eyesight. When Mikal was newborn, his eyes had been extremely sensitive to light... even a candle made him flinch and cry. But over the past six months, his pupils and retinas had strengthened. Now Mikal tolerated artificial light and Simon was sure the child, product of the first successful mating between two vampires, would one day be able to walk in sunlight.

"All dead," Mikal sighed and raised his blood-stained mouth from the girl. At first, Mikal hadn't understood death, had wailed and screamed when the blood supply ended, banging his feet and fists against the floor like any ordinary child in the midst of a temper tantrum. But a few slaps from his annoyed father and his own instinct had led him to abandon corpses quietly once he had all he could of them.

Simon nodded and picked the child up, using a damp cloth to clean his face and dressed him in fresh garments. Mikal made no effort to resist his father's ministrations but neither did he seem to welcome them.

As Simon held the indifferent boy, he remembered Mikal's mortal twin, Elizabeth, and his heart contracted painfully. How different the little girl was from her brother, so appealing in her innocence and helplessness. Elizabeth... how he missed her, longed to rear his mortal girl with her mother.

Simon glanced over at the painting he'd been working on of Meghann nursing Elizabeth. He'd worked on the piece for more than six months now and still wasn't satisfied. It was a fair rendering of a pretty young mother feeding her baby, but Simon was frustrated by his failure to capture the maternal radiance he'd seen shining in Meghann's eyes. Meghann had never looked as beautiful to him as she had that night she first held their mortal daughter in her arms, the night Simon had had to leave her and take Mikal far from prying eyes.

Simon knew these thoughts of his consort and Elizabeth were dangerous, that his yearning for them made him resent Mikal. Simon had to remind himself that it wasn't the boy's fault Meghann had borne twin children, one a vampire that must be sheltered from all that would try to destroy him and the other a mortal that must be sheltered from the brother who would surely grow to despise Elizabeth for not needing to be hidden from the world as he was.

While Mikal was raised in obscurity and Elizabeth was safe with Meghann, Simon's responsibility was to foster in his son the strength and cunning that would ensure his safety and someday allow him to leave this wretched highland backwater.

With that thought in mind, Simon began Mikal's lessons for the evening. "You must begin learning to capture the humans on your own, young one. I cannot always bring them to you."

Mikal listened carefully, his fully restored silver eyes concentrating on Simon with an attention span that belied his chronological age. "How do you get them, Father?"

Simon laughed, resisting an urge to swing Mikal into his lap, and stretched out beside him on the gray stone floor. From past experience, he knew the child would resist any gesture of affection. "We have many ways of luring the mortals to our side and making them bend to our will. But you are too young to learn the arts of mesmerism just yet. Until you are old enough to hold them with your mind, you must deceive the humans, play on the pity and adoration they will feel for any small, helpless child. Remember what I told you about weeping?"

Mikal nodded and immediately began a false sobbing of great piteousness.

"Not yet," Simon said and held up his hand, pleased when the child shut off his cries with the ease of flicking off a light switch. "I will go now and secure another human. Wait until you pick up the scent outside the door and then begin to cry."

Simon flew back downstairs and saw the appalled glances of his servants. The false sense of relief they'd felt when Simon took the Hindi girl vanished now that he'd come back for another of their kind. Would there be still more deaths before he chained them up for the day? Of course, they dared not protest for fear Simon might dispose of the whole miserable pack. He grabbed a pretty blond Romanian, thinking she would be a most delectable meal; Simon intended to feed off the lion's share of her blood.

Outside the great, thick door, a perfectly normal child's crying began and Simon saw the young woman's terror subside at the thought of a child more helpless than she needing her.

Simon opened the door and leaned against the doorframe, watching the girl run to Mikal, exclaiming in her Eastern European dialect, "Oh, poor little child, poor boy! What does this dreadful man do to you?"

Careful, Simon thought at Mikal, sobbing and holding his arms out to the girl in an appealing manner. *Don't show your blood teeth; keep your lips over them. Don't strike, too soon, let her kneel down before you lunge...*

Mikal followed his father's commands perfectly; only when the girl knelt by his side and her movement to scoop him up brought her neck within range of his mouth did Mikal bite her.

The girl let out a stunned scream and tried to pull away from Mikal but the boy had a firm purchase on her neck and began drinking greedily, quickly draining the girl's strength to resist. Shocked and in great physical pain, the girl slumped next to Mikal, her skin rapidly losing color as he fed.

"Well done," Simon complimented Mikal before he wrenched the child from the mortal girl and began feeding from a vein in her breast.

"Mine!" Mikal howled in outrage and actually yanked on his father's hair to try and pull him away from the prey.

Annoyed at being interrupted while he fed, Simon dropped the unconscious girl to the floor and pulled Mikal over his knee, administering a swift spanking. "Never raise your hand to me, boy. Next time my reprimand will not be so light."

Simon deposited the screeching child, now sobbing in earnest, in his playpen and returned to the mortal girl, deciding to finish her off by feeding from the femoral artery in her left thigh.

"Mine! Mine! Mine!" Mikal continued to howl, but Simon paid him no mind as he drank the girl's youthful, vigorous blood. Though Mikal was smart enough to climb out of the enclosure, Simon had enchanted the playpen with a magical barrier Mikal could not exit unless his father allowed it.

"What in the world is this racket?" a female voice demanded and Simon smiled up at Adelaide, his nursemaid during his mortal lifetime and now immortal nanny to his son. She'd been in her early fifties when Simon transformed her, still a handsome woman with salt-and-pepper hair and a buxom figure, her age betrayed only by a small webbing of crow's feet around her eyes and a slight hint of sag under her jaw.

"Good evening, Adelaide," Simon said and pulled a steaming washcloth out of a brazier to clean his face. "I trust you've fed this evening."

7

"I fed a few nights ago and I have not your insatiable appetites," Adelaide retorted, the strong Scottish burr Simon remembered in her mortal voice reduced by four centuries spent on various continents to a mere hint of accent. "Now tell me what you've done to that poor child to make him carry on so."

"The boy interfered with my meal," Simon explained and Adelaide raced over to the playpen to remove the weeping child.

"Hush now, lovey," Adelaide crooned, holding the child with an expert air borne of vast experience. Simon noted with amusement that Mikal merely looked bored at the soothing.

"She was mine," Mikal said accusingly to Simon, impatiently brushing Adelaide's hands away from his face.

"My son," Simon said and grasped the boy's chin between his thumb and forefinger, "until you stand before me as a man with the means to support yourself, nothing belongs to you. Everything you have is a result of my largess and I may give it or take it away as I deem fit."

"You great, dumb lummox!" Adelaide blazed and Mikal's odd eyes showed appraising interest at her fury. "You cannot speak to a child like that!"

"I may speak to my child however I wish," Simon said evenly and pulled Mikal from her, returning the boy to his playpen. Simon handed the child some picture books and raised his eyebrows at the speculative glance his son shot him. This was no sulky pout but the measuring look of an adult, saying plainly he would neither forget nor forgive this incident

"Excellent," Simon praised and rewarded Mikal with the rare treat of a bottle filled with blood from several different victims. "You have seen you must bow down to my will for now, but some part of you looks to gaining revenge in the future. You learn quickly, son."

Something that might have been a smile crossed the child's face before he began suckling noisily at the rubber nipple on his bottle while he scanned The Three Little Pigs.

"Have you not a brain in your head?" Adelaide demanded with the same loving exasperation Simon had heard in her voice over four hundred years. Normally Simon would not entertain anyone upbraiding him but Adelaide had a special place in his heart. As his birth mother had died when he was three, Adelaide was the only mother Simon had ever known. He'd never forget how she'd sheltered him from his cruel father and two elder brothers, demanding her young charge be educated in a manner befitting a peer of the realm. If not for Adelaide, Simon could only speculate on how different, and most likely worse, his life would have been.

"A rather well-functioning one," Simon answered her question and invited her to join him at the polished oak table he'd set up in an alcove by the stained-glass, diamond-shaped windows.

"I have reason to doubt that," Adelaide muttered and accepted the proffered glass of single malt scotch. "What do you think you are doing with your son? Do you mean to rear him to despise you as you loathed your father? I do not think I need to remind you how that father-son relationship ended."

Simon smiled, remembering that his first success with the Black Arts came the night he had a demon dispose of his father. "Mikal will not make an attempt on my life simply because I discipline him."

"What you are doing is not discipline! You are bullying that boy and I can already see the resentment building in him."

Simon slammed his drink down with a thud that reverberated through the spacious chamber and glared at his former nurse. "Bullying? Have you forgotten what that child is? Adelaide, Mikal is the only vampire to be born, not made. You know the power he'll have one day. When Mikal grows to manhood, he'll be able to walk in sunlight, and we may have that gift as well by drinking his blood. But that's only if he survives long enough to achieve his destiny. Do I need to remind you of the fools that will try to destroy him for no better reason than that he is my son, let alone that his own might will make them weak as mortals compared with him? Once Mikal leaves this isle, there is no corner of the world that will be safe for him. He must be bred to have the heart and mind of a warrior. Yes, I push him, and there is little room for coddling in his upbringing. Mikal must grow up fierce and hard if he is to meet the challenges his fate will set before him. I'll not have the boy turning into a timid milksop like the pathetic nothings mortals are churning out these days."

"What would you turn the boy into?" Adelaide demanded. "If you smash any softness within him, that means the child will have no love in his heart for anyone—including you. Have you thought on why he'd bother to keep you alive then, if the day comes when Mikal's more powerful than you and he feels nothing for you but resentment? Or do you truly think you're so omniscient no one can destroy you?"

"Why should Mikal resent me? Because I shelter him until he's old enough to fight for himself? Because I will teach him all I know, make him my apprentice as I've done with no other before him? You talk of the child needing sentiment and petting—open your eyes, Adelaide. The boy spurns any affectionate gesture of yours, does he not?"

"That is why you must tread a careful line with him," Adelaide replied, undaunted. "Mikal is cold and withdrawn by nature. Love does not come easily to him. Meghann felt the darkness within Mikal before you took him from her... she writes to me that she fears what it might metamorphose into. Meghann felt all that when the child was an infant; her feelings have grown stronger in the past year. Why are you blinding yourself, Simon? Can you not feel that unfathomable need for destruction and harm inside your son? Instill some kind of affection in that boy or he may well develop into what the mortals' term a sociopath."

Simon laughed heartily and poured himself a fresh shot, shrugging when Adelaide refused a refill. "Now l know you've been corresponding with Meghann—sociopath is a word only my little psychologist would use. Do you know she threw that term in my face to describe me when she tried to leave me? She recanted her views on my behavior, just as she'll get over these baseless fears about Mikal."

"Meghann left you because you refused to let go of your old-fashioned blather about masters and tried to dominate her," Adelaide said, referring to the forty years when Simon and Meghann were separated and she sought shelter with Simon's deadliest enemy, the vampire priest, Alcuin. It wasn't until Simon managed to slay Alcuin two years ago that he was able to reclaim

Meghann. "I warned you that no modern girl, especially one as vivacious and spirited as the woman you described to me, would accept being nothing more than your chattel. I was right then and I'm right now when I tell you to honor your vow to Meghann and raise him as she would if she was here."

"But Meghann is not here," Simon said calmly. "And that foolishness of what she wants for Mikal is the reason why. Meghann has a soft heart—wonderful for the raising of our daughter, but she'd damage our son with those idiotic notions of good and evil she picked up from Alcuin."

"Meghann is not a soft fool to be dismissed simply because she lacks your ruthlessness!" Adelaide snapped. "She was canny enough to get a stake through your heart and evade you for forty years. You love the girl, I'll grant you that, but you show her no respect and that will lead to the demise of your relationship. Simon, don't you understand Meghann will leave you for good when she learns that you deliberately raised her son in contradiction of all her directives?"

Adelaide did not even have time to register the white-hot fury in Simon's eyes before he lunged over the table and grabbed her throat, placing a Bowie knife to her heart. Any sudden movement on her part and the knife would impale her.

"We go back a long way, nurse," Simon said in a low, menacing whisper as his knife tore through her clothes and nipped her skin. "I respect you deeply and I care for you. But I will not hesitate to slay you if you breathe a word of any discontent you feel to Meghann. What Meghann does not know about Mikal's upbringing cannot harm her. She has Elizabeth to keep her content until we reunite. I don't mind your correspondence with Meghann; continue to write her if that is your desire. But there will be no details in your letters; you tell her Mikal is healthy and safe and that is all you write. I don't want Meghann spending the next eighteen years pining for a child she cannot have... it might distract her from caring for Elizabeth properly. Is that understood?"

"Yes," Adelaide said immediately, knowing the only thing that placated Simon in one of his fits was immediate compliance. She wasn't displeased or hurt at Simon's behavior—it would take a great deal more than some little knife and hot words to turn her against him. Adelaide knew Simon Baldevar far better than he knew himself. She'd known him since he was a wee, screaming babe in her arms and then the ambitious young man that made his own fortune before he found immortality. He hadn't done either of those things by allowing anyone to perceive weakness in him. No, Adelaide wasn't hurt but she was disturbed at how thickheaded and stubborn he was being regarding Mikal.

"Then we shall consider this unpleasantness disposed of for good." After he licked a drop of her blood off the knife, Simon helped Adelaide out of her chair and escorted her to the door. "I must take a business trip. After all, I have spent a year in this miserable, cold hovel and neglected my interests. The computer has assisted me greatly, but the time has come to inspect my holdings personally. Besides, Mikal will need more food soon. Go and pack my bags and inform the pilot I wish him to be at Heathrow tomorrow evening at nine o'clock sharp."

"How long will you be gone?" Adelaide questioned calmly and saw Simon's eyes gleam with respect at her nonchalant attitude. The others he transformed always either knuckled under his harshness or made fruitless plans to destroy him for his humiliation of them. They never understood that Simon was a hard but fair master. After a punishment or reprimand, his rage was forgotten and he treated the disciplined person as he had before whatever they'd done to displease him.

"Several weeks... a month at most. I leave Mikal in your most capable hands," Simon said with a cool grin that showed he respected Adelaide enough to believe she would honor her word while he was gone and not take advantage of his absence to contact Meghann.

"Simon, wait," Adelaide said before he could close the tower door. "I am writing to Meghann this night and I wish to enclose this for Elizabeth. She must know of her father if she is to love you."

"Adelaide," Simon said softly at the antique miniature painting she pulled out of her pocket. It had been painted in 1590, when Simon was almost thirty years old, three years before he transformed. "Good nurse, I know your intentions toward me and mine are beyond reproach that any action on your part stems from love. Send the miniature to Meghann that she may show it to Elizabeth."

Adelaide smiled and left the tower to carry out Simon's bidding, knowing the praise was as close as Simon would come to apologizing for his behavior.

She also knew Simon had only written to Meghann once since he left her, despite the many letters Meghann sent him concerning their daughter's progress. Some might view Simon's behavior as cold but Adelaide knew he simply couldn't bear a correspondence with Meghann knowing he couldn't see her. A clandestine visit to Meghann and Elizabeth was out of the question—part of Mikal's present security stemmed from the other vampires of the world believing that Elizabeth was Simon and Meghann's only child. The immortals felt nothing but contempt for the mortal baby and left her and Meghann alone, believing Lord Baldevar's seeming abandonment of them showed they were no threat.

Adelaide sighed; she knew what it had cost Simon to leave Meghann just when he'd finally gotten her to accept him again. She also knew Simon's intentions for Mikal were good, wanting the child to grow tough and capable, but couldn't he see that he was going to turn Mikal into a monster?

Adelaide was not scared of the death Simon had promised her if she went to Meghann with her fears. She would go ahead and inform Meghann anyway if she thought it would benefit Mikal, but she knew Meghann didn't have the same sway over Simon's mind as she had over his heart. Simon might not listen to her any more than he did to Adelaide.

Right now, Adelaide could see only one path available to her. Simon had to spend a great deal of time away from this island to protect his wealth and make sure his enemies did not forget his power over them.

When he was away, Adelaide would attempt to instill in Mikal the love and sensitivity Meghann wished her son to have. She would also work on easing Simon away from his current position that any softness would spoil the child.

If that didn't work, then God help them all for Adelaide knew very well who Mikal's first victim would be if she didn't find a way to stem the remorseless evil she sensed in the child—the vampire that made him what he was. And if Mikal was successful in slaughtering his father, then there would be no one in the world to check him or keep him from destroying everything in his path... no one at all.

Chapter One

Sixteen years later

Ellie Winslow slammed the glass door behind her and stalked down the mirrored hallway, muttering to herself in ominous tones while she waited for an elevator. She continued her one-sided conversation when the elevator arrived at her floor then made a swift descent to the lobby. One might expect sidelong looks from the other passengers, but this was New York and if a well-dressed young woman carrying a black leather portfolio wanted to talk to herself that was her business.

Ellie had just finished a job interview for a position as an intern-architect with results as disappointing and frustrating as those of the other five interviews she'd had this past week. Each one was an identical, galling experience—the senior architect who deigned to interview her would praise her portfolio, compliment her excellent grades at Cooper Union, smile approvingly at the enthusiastic letters of recommendation she'd received from her summer internship position last year and her thesis advisor, ask a few halfhearted questions about her goals and what she thought she could bring to the firm, then smile and send her on her far from merry way—never to be heard from again.

Ellie whirled through the revolving doors, thinking whoever designed this copycat chrome monstrosity should be beaten to death with his or her own drawing board. She knew the reason she wasn't getting hired anywhere, though none of the companies had dared say it aloud—they were holding her age against her. No matter how talented she was (and Ellie had no false modesty about her work), how many design competitions she'd won, no one seemed to want to hire a seventeen-year-old... even one who'd been accepted to Cooper Union on a full scholarship as their youngest student

Was it her fault she'd been born with a 175 IQ? Ellie thought wrathfully, feeling some calm return to her when she breathed in the crisp, cool air more suited to early fall than June. She decided rather than return home with her tail between her legs and endure yet another chin-up pep talk from Uncle Lee, she'd head over to Central Park for a while.

Scowling at the horse drawn carriages Ellie felt exploited animals, she headed toward the lake, purchased a nicely salted pretzel from a passing vendor and then slumped on a park bench, disdaining the grass because it would ruin the cream silk blazer and culottes-style skirt she'd chosen to wear for the interview.

Ellie chomped on her pretzel furiously, ruminating that this whole miserable job situation was based on nothing more than bad luck—something Ellie hadn't experienced much of in her seventeen years. She'd managed to find a position at a small residential architectural firm back in October, on the strength of her senior design thesis. But then in February, the CEO suffered a fatal heart attack and his widow promptly sold the firm to a large monolith that had no interest in hiring such a young architect.

Ellie's cell phone shrilled in her purse and she briefly considered not picking it up. But there was always the remote chance the caller could be offering her a job so Ellie fished the phone out of her bag. "Hello?"

"Ellie, this is Professor Barrett. I have wonderful news, my dear. I think I may have found a buyer for your design thesis. So tell all those uninspired fools that refuse to hire you that you've just netted a commission that easily equals the annual salary for an intern-architect."

"Omigod!" Ellie yelped, a radiant, delighted smile dissolving her sullen expression. "When? How? Who?"

"I was at a party last night," her thesis advisor explained. "I met a delightful man who told me he wished to build a beach house but he hadn't been able to find an architect who understood what he wanted—something eclectic and dramatic that jumped out at passers-by, something full of imagination and daring. Naturally, I thought of your house immediately and I told him a bit about it and you. I've set up a meeting for eight this evening at the studio. He simply couldn't break any of his business engagements to meet you earlier. I do hope that's all right with you, dear."

If Ellie had a one hundred five degree fever and two shattered legs, she would have said the night meeting was fine and she'd be sure to make it. "I'll be there. What's this man like? What's his name?"

"A charming British fellow... rather odd for one of that race to appreciate organic architecture. By the way, you have my permission to shoot the Earl if he tries to impose Chesterfields and floral chintz on your house. That's right, dear—you might have a genuine aristocrat living in your beach house if he chooses to buy the design. He's an earl... Lord Simon Baldevar."

"Lord Simon Baldevar?" A queer kind of stillness settled over Ellie, followed by a searing rush of feeling tearing into her with the impact of a nuclear explosion. Had her professor really uttered her vampire father's name so casually? No, it was not possible that after seventeen years of unsatisfied curiosity and waiting, Simon Baldevar was simply going to wander into her life as a prospective client. He'd left Ellie and her mother when she was only six weeks old, taking her vampire twin brother with him. Her mother and father had decided to raise their children separately so Ellie, their mortal baby, could have a normal childhood.

A normal childhood—what kind of starry-eyed optimism made her parents believe she, the child of vampire parents, could have anything resembling a normal childhood? Oh, it had been a happy enough childhood, interesting and diverting, but never normal.

How can you be normal when you grow up accepting as fact things most people consider mere fantasy? One of Ellie's earliest memories was holding her arms up and crying, "Do your magic, Mommy!" as her mother used telekinesis to lift Ellie up off the ground and spin her round and round their twelve-foot Christmas tree. How could a child be normal when she grew up counting the hours until darkness fell and her mother would rise from her daytime slumber? Worse, Ellie could never even acknowledge her mother to any of her mortal acquaintances and she had to be so cautious as to what she was allowed to discuss that Ellie eventually decided it would be easier not to discuss her home life at all. The one relative Ellie could speak of safely was her homosexual, adoptive father, Lee Winslow.

Even putting aside her vampire progeny, Ellie herself had never been an average child. She was considered precocious and ahead of the curve even in her exclusive school for gifted children, being placed in the third grade at the age of five and completing high school before she turned twelve. Being so much younger than her classmates assured Ellie's ostracism at school. She was only able to make friends with the rich children that made their summer homes in Southampton, careful to disguise her intelligence as they engaged in noncerebral activities like swimming, sailing, and horseback riding.

The lack of friends hadn't disturbed Ellie overmuch. She was a solitary person by nature, preferring the company of her sketches and erector sets to other children. Besides, Ellie would always consider her mother her best friend. How could she ever feel lonely when Meghann lavished so much attention on her? Nighttime had always been devoted to her mother and their excursions together.

Still, Ellie had always thought that the one person who might understand her feelings of exclusion from the mortal world, the world of normalcy and tradition, was Mikal. Only he knew what it was like to be almost a new species, the only living children of vampire parents. Had their parents ever thought she and Mikal might have needed each other and shouldn't have been separated?

Ellie had confided these thoughts to her mother and Meghann replied that she'd never have allowed Ellie to grow up in the kind of isolation that was necessary for Mikal's safety. It would have been lonely and dull to a degree Ellie couldn't even imagine, Mom told her. There would have been no art classes, no interaction whatsoever with anyone but her parents and her twin. Mom said she'd be damned before her daughter lived the life of a virtual shut-in. Such an existence might be necessary for poor Mikal, disfigured, as he'd been when he was an infant; mortals and other vampires alike would try their best to kill him if they found him and Daddy. "Ellie!"

"I'm sorry, Professor Barrett," Ellie said, her advisor's impatient shout cutting through the chaos in her mind. "What did you say?"

"No need to apologize; I know you're a bit bemused," the professor said indulgently. "I just asked whether you know Lord Baldevar... you seemed so surprised when I said his name."

"No," Ellie said slowly, her hands shaking so badly I nearly dropped the phone. "I don't know him." I only know of him. I know what my mother, Uncle Lee and Uncle Charles tell me about him. What I don't know is how he feels toward me. This absentee father had sent her lavish presents on Christmas and her birthday every year she could remember, and cards arrived on those occasions, too, cards that were informative and indicated some interest in Ellie's activities but nevertheless impersonal— not one of the letters mentioned love. Ellie wanted to believe the gifts demonstrated her father's love for her, but they could just as easily be a desultory gesture of obligation on the part of a creature that had no use for his mortal offspring. That was Ellie's deepest fear that she'd managed to disappoint Simon Baldevar simply by being born human. Meghann had always done her best to assuage these fears, telling Ellie her father loved her dearly but he wasn't overly demonstrative, the way Mom, Lee and Charles were.

"Well, you're about to know him very well," Professor Barrett said cheerfully. "See you at eight."

Eight! Ellie thought with sudden dismay. That was five whole hours away—what on earth was she supposed to do until then? Briefly, Ellie thought of calling Lee and telling him about this shocking development.

Lee . . . was her longing to meet Simon Baldevar somehow disloyal to Lee Winslow, her much loved adopted father who'd selflessly forgone transformation so Ellie could have a daytime parent and protector?

Ellie didn't think her eagerness to meet Simon detracted from the special bond she shared with Uncle Lee. How could she feel anything but profound love and respect for a man who'd not only

19

given up his chance at immortality for her but also his medical career? Lee Winslow had retired from active practice when Ellie was born and conducted private research in a lab at the house until Ellie was twelve. This way she'd always have someone available to take her to school and a thousand other daytime affairs because it was out of the question for Meghann to allow some mortal babysitter with sharp eyes and sharper curiosity into the house. Once Ellie was a little older, Lee opted to teach at the Columbia College of Physicians and Surgeons, still not going back to practicing gynecology for fear he wouldn't be available if Ellie had an emergency during the day and needed her parent.

Ellie treasured her daytime with Lee and the stop they always made at Carvel before heading home. Over a sundae, Ellie would chatter about her day to Lee, who always listened eagerly and cheered her accomplishments while providing consolation when she told him of her distance from the other children. Lee was the only mortal Ellie could be honest with, the only who understood her confusion at living in a house of vampires and then trying to fit into the mortal world.

But terrific as Lee was, Ellie had never been able to think of him as Daddy. That word and all the sentiment behind it belonged to the shadowy presence she felt in her dreams. Imaginings of warm, strong hands holding her while a soothing, deep voice song lullabies. Mom said she didn't think it likely she remembered her infancy and Daddy caring for her. But in their family nothing was impossible. When Ellie had that dream, she always woke up with a feeling of complete security and peace and a cry of longing on her lips. The unseen man and the tenderness he illustrated was Daddy and no one could take his place.

In five short hours, Ellie would find out if Simon Baldevar was the father. She sometimes woke up crying out for or if that dream figure was simply a fantasy her subconscious had produced from her longing and need.

"Good afternoon, Miss Scarlett."

"Mickey, you startled me! What a coincidence, meeting here. I didn't even know you were back in New York." Ellie smiled up at her on-again, off-again boyfriend, Mickey Hollingsworth, whom she hadn't seen in a few weeks.

"I only got in a few days ago," Mickey said and sprawled his long, lanky form next to her on the bench. "Why don't you tell me why you're sitting in Central Park looking as forlorn and abandoned as Oliver Twist?"

Ellie laughed and told Mickey the unhappy story of her job hunt, relieved to have a friend to talk to and take her mind off the impending meeting with her father. She and Mickey had met through friends at Cooper Union about six months ago and hit it off immediately.

Mickey, with his long black hair that always looked like he'd just tumbled out of bed, infectious booming laugh and self-deprecating sense of humor had fascinated Ellie when they met. Though he was only nineteen, Mickey seemed so much more mature and interesting than the boys Ellie mingled with at home who were only interested in drinking, sun tanning, fighting, and getting laid—in that order. As for the boys at Cooper Union, most of them were a lot older than Ellie and if they weren't fiercely competitive and jealous of her talent, they tended to treat her like an adored little sister—hardly surprising considering the flat-chested twelve year old she'd been freshman year. So Mickey, son of minor British gentry and another child prodigy who'd finished Oxford at the age of eighteen, and was now "a lazy layabout leeching off my trust fund" was a godsend to Ellie.

For his part, Mickey told Ellie he was fascinated with her "Scarlett O'Hara eyes" and "your impossible American devotion to work." After their first meeting, their relationship took on a comfortable pattern of long talks and other activities in whatever hotel or friend's borrowed flat, Mickey happened to be staying in when he visited New York.

At first, Ellie had thought she might be in love with Mickey and his quicksilver charm but a few months of now-you-see-me-now-you-don't romancing quickly disabused her of that notion. It would be fatal to fall for someone who refused to take anything, including himself, very seriously. But Ellie did enjoy his company so she continued seeing him when he came to town. She'd confided to her mother that she was seeing him just for fun and Meghann told her that was fine as long her heart was as divorced from the situation as she claimed.

"Sod it!" Mickey exclaimed indignantly when Ellie finished her story. "If those bloody fools can't appreciate you, they don't deserve you. Besides, you can start your own business with this rich buyer your teacher found for you. You never said his name."

"That's right, I didn't. . . Michael," Ellie retorted, using his real and loathed first name to pay him back for not telling her the last time he'd abandoned New York in favor of whatever city (and girls) took his fancy for two weeks.

"Cheeky today, are we?" Mickey returned. "What is it a bleedin' state secret, then? Who's your buyer—the King of England, the President, the Shah of Iran?"

"No one important," Ellie demurred, remembering her mother's admonitions that she never reveal her father's true identity to anyone.

"Your father has enemies," Meghann had said over and over. "Vicious, brutal creatures that would think nothing of harming you to get at him. And don't think you're safe because you say his name to someone during the day. You think vampires can't employ humans to spy for them? Never, never tell anyone the name Baldevar and tell me or Charles immediately if anyone says the name to you."

Ellie hardly thought Mickey a vampire spy but her mother's warnings weren't something she took lightly. And Ellie was far too wound up about their impending meeting to say her father's name aloud without all kinds of embarrassing blushes and stammers that would alert Mickey or anyone else to how special this particular client was to her.

"You're right," Mickey agreed cheerfully. "Your old client's name isn't important. What is important is whether you'll have lunch with me and then maybe come see my room at the Sherry Netherland."

Ellie shrugged nonchalantly though she privately thought Mickey might have just offered her only chance at relaxation. "I'm not hungry."

"No?" Mickey questioned, playing along with her.

"No," Ellie said firmly and then favored him with a cool smile. "I'd rather see your hotel room and skip lunch... if that's all right with you."

"No complaints here," Mickey smirked and triumphantly plucked up her portfolio. "None at all."

"How's that ravishing sister of yours?" Mickey asked as they crossed Fifth Avenue.

"Maggie's fine. You know, she really liked you." In public, Ellie used her mother's mortal nickname because it was close to the Mommy she'd been used to saying as a child. Ellie hated having to tell the world that her mother was her sister but what else could you do when your ninety-year-old vampire mother was never going to look a day over eighteen?

Ellie sighed, cursing the blasted sunlight that took her mother away from her. Ellie might be enjoying Mickey's company, but the person she needed to talk to was Mom. She was the only one who'd be able to understand Ellie's conflicting feelings about meeting her father.

When she first heard Professor Barrett's shocking news, Ellie felt a brief pique that her mother hadn't warned her of Simon Baldevar's impending visit but quickly realized Mom would never keep something like her father's homecoming a secret from Ellie. Most likely, this visit was going to stun Meghann just as much as it had Ellie.

"I'm glad I met with Maggie's approval," Mickey smiled and wrapped his hand around Ellie's waist, using the cover of her blazer to start a stealthy, insidious climb toward her breasts. "You know, I have a fine mate back home she might be interested in. We could double up together one night."

Ellie playfully slapped Mickey's hand away. "Maggie doesn't date much." Actually, Mom didn't date at all; she'd never made any attempt to see other men while Ellie was growing up. Ellie knew Mom used to date Jimmy Delacroix, another vampire and good friend of the family, but that had been over before Ellie was born.

Ellie sighed, remembering that Jimmy Delacroix was proof there was a darker side to her father's nature, aside Mom had only lately even hinted at. Simon, Meghann had told her, could be quite ruthless when it came to dealing with anyone he considered an enemy or simply beneath him... like mortals. Ellie and Lee Winslow being the sole exceptions to that rule.

Meghann had never approved of this behavior. In fact, she'd been so disgusted by it that she left Simon for over forty years before they finally reunited, Ellie and Mikal being the result of their reconciliation.

"Why did you go back with him?" Ellie had asked her.

"Your father's a complex man," was Meghann's response. "You have to understand he was born in different times, Ellie. Not that that's any sort of excuse but he doesn't have the same belief system we do. He grew up thinking his nobility made him superior to anyone born with a lesser rank than he had. In his time, a man of his stature could brutalize his servants or his woman and no one would think less of him for it. Becoming a vampire simply exacerbated that inborn elitism. Forget about making him treat mortals fairly; you don't know what I went through to get him to treat me as an equal. It took a great deal of argument and that separation for him to understand that if he wanted me to be his wife, he'd have to treat me the way I or any other woman deserves to be treated, as a treasured partner and not some cowering subordinate."

"And when he got that through his head, you went back with him."

Meghann had smiled at Ellie's astuteness. "Yes and because, though I don't think he'll admit it, you changed him, Ellie. Raising our children separately so you'd have as normal and happy a childhood as we could give you . . . Honey, that was the first truly unselfish thing I'd ever known your father to do. If anything can melt the stone around his heart and make Simon see that some of his . . . ways . . . are wrong, it's you."

Meghann would never say exactly what 'ways' so distressed her but Ellie knew they were at the root of Jimmy Delacroix's transformation.

From earliest childhood, one of her mother's strictest rules was that Ellie never mention Simon's name to Jimmy. All Mom would tell her was that while she and Simon were separated, Jimmy had been Mom's mortal boyfriend. Mom had never planned to transform Jimmy, saying a vampire's life wasn't for him. But Daddy got so jealous over Mom having someone else in her life that he hurt Jimmy terribly and it was either transformation or death so Jimmy became a vampire.

Ellie knew there were considerable holes in her mother's careful explanation that everything worked out well enough in the end, with Jimmy adapting to his new existence. Mom would never tell Ellie exactly how Daddy hurt Jimmy, just that Ellie should never mention Simon so Jimmy wouldn't get upset. Ellie had often wondered if maybe Meghann didn't want her to talk to Jimmy about Simon, not so much out of consideration for Jimmy's feelings, but because Mom was afraid of what Jimmy would tell her about her father.

"Get your head out of the clouds," Mickey said and tapped her forehead lightly. "We're here."

Ellie followed him into the small suite, acknowledging that the spectacular view of the park was worth whatever astronomical fees Mickey was paying for the room. Mickey handed her a scotch and soda and they soon found themselves rolling around on the king-sized bed.

Naked and doing her best to match Mickey's frenetic rhythm, Ellie wondered if there was something the matter with her... if she might be frigid. Or was Mickey a bad partner? Ellie had kissed and done a little more than that before she met Mickey and always thought sex would simply incorporate all that fondling with a few more intimacies. But when she went to bed with Mickey, the only thing she'd ever felt aside from the unexpectedly sharp pain of losing her virginity, was irritation at the unlubricated condom chaffing her.

Why did Mickey treat foreplay in such a perfunctory manner, giving her a brief kiss and cursory grope before he started pounding away on top of her? Ellie wondered while staring at the ceiling. Mickey didn't seem at all interested in her satisfaction. In fact, he seemed to have forgotten her entirely as he charged after his own release.

But maybe Ellie was being unfair, blaming her disillusionment with sex on Mickey. As evidenced by the awkward way he behaved once they got their clothes off, most likely he didn't have much sexual experience either. Maybe they could experiment together.

With a final grunt and harsh thrust, Mickey came, immediately rolling off her with a good-natured ruffling of her hair more suitable to a golden retriever than a lover.

"Got a cigarette?" Ellie asked, moving the white sheet over her body while Mickey removed the condom.

Mickey reached into his trouser pocket and tossed Ellie a pack of Galois and his silver lighter. "I bet that doctor father of yours doesn't know you smoke."

"I think he'd be more upset at this," Ellie gestured to their naked bodies, "than a little smoke." Actually, that wasn't true. Lee was appalled at her occasional cigarette and so was Mom, though she felt it would be hypocritical to chasten Ellie when she was a longtime smoker herself. As for sex, Ellie had gone to Meghann and Lee when she decided to sleep with Mickey; Lee wrote out a prescription for the pill after a long talk about responsibility and caution. Of course, Ellie insisted Mickey use the condom as well to protect against disease.

Ellie inhaled deeply and exhaled the smoke through her nose, watching Mickey wrap a thick cotton towel around his narrow hips. "Want some company?" In some of the lurid romance novels Ellie kept hidden in a milk carton under her bed, there were many erotic adventures to be had in the shower.

"No time, love. I've got a meeting with a band promoter in an hour—that's right, I forgot to tell you! Your Mickey isn't going to be completely useless Eurotrash any longer. The old father gave me a few dollars and I'm building my own nightclub."

"That's fantastic!" A few months ago, Mickey had confided that he had no use for the Oxford education his parents had forced on him, and his ambition lay in establishing the biggest, scariest, sexiest Goth club the world had ever seen.

Complimenting Ellie's talent, Mickey informed her he was a huge Clive Barker fan and asked if she could design an interior for his club that would resemble the underground labyrinth in the movie *Nightbreed*. Ellie, familiar with the book and movie, had given Mickey a few preliminary sketches of a structure that would resemble a large haunted mansion with a maze of careening rooms and dead ends to amuse his patrons.

"Fantastic for us both," Mickey smiled and took a few drags from her cigarette. "That beach house isn't going to be your only commission. I found a big old mansion falling apart on Long Island I can have for a song. Say, why don't you come with me tomorrow and take a tour of the site? You can tailor our original ideas to the house's structure, maybe draw up some blueprints."

Two commissions in one day—Ellie was on her way to her own business! "I'd be delighted."

"Shall we say noon tomorrow, then? I'll meet you at your house. Now I've got to hurry but you feel free to lie around, maybe order up some of the lunch I didn't have a chance to give you. Just shut the door on your way out." Mickey ruffled her hair again and bounded into the bathroom.

Ellie thought of ordering a sandwich from room service but the adrenaline excitement of the day suddenly wore off and she felt as weak and wrung out as a used up washcloth. Ellie glanced at the clock on the white and gold gilt nightstand—4:30. She had time for a nice, refreshing nap before she showered and changed to meet her father.

Ellie, coming out of a dreamless sleep, turned on her side and bolted upright with a panic stricken yelp when she saw the time illuminated on the small digital clock by the beside. Seven thirty—she hadn't meant to sleep so late! Now she was going to be late for her first meeting with her father.

Ellie grabbed her purse and hurried into the shower, shampooing and bathing in a matter of minutes. At the large marble countertop, Ellie appropriated Mickey's toothbrush and searched the medicine cabinet for aspirin with no luck. Apparently Mickey didn't suffer from headaches like the one swiftly closing in on Ellie's temples.

Ellie brushed her thick brown hair quickly, knowing she had no time to blow dry her shoulder-length, layered pageboy properly. Ellie finger-combed the waves as best she could and pulled her hair off her face with a white headband she found at the bottom of her purse. A pair of gold studs gave the simple style a little pizzazz.

Thank God she'd never needed much makeup. Ellie simply applied a bit of powder to her shiny nose, some coral toned lip-gloss, and matching eye shadow. After she dressed, Ellie gave herself a cool appraisal. The cream silk suit and burnt ochre sleeveless shirt looked good against her suntan. Her hair and makeup were neat if uninspired. Ellie sighed for the daydreams where she met her father wearing her most stylish clothes and her too thick, wavy hair was on its best behavior... no time for all that now.

7:50—Ellie liberated her car from the parking garage at Sixtieth and Second, then sped down to the Village, racing through yellow lights, cutting other drivers off and illegally cruising through bus lanes, all the while keeping her eye out for police cars. All she needed now was to get pulled over and ticketed. Forget her mother's annoyance at a fifth ticket in as many weeks, who knew what time she'd get to the studio if a cop wrote her up?

Ellie made it to Cooper Union without incident and actually found a parking space across the street from the school on Astor Place, a minor miracle that Ellie considered a good omen. Though she'd broken her neck to get down here, Ellie had missed the eight o'clock deadline . . . her wristwatch informed her it was now a quarter after.

Not willing to wait on the ancient elevator, Ellie sped up the stairs to the studio, flushed and out of breath by the time she reached the cavernous, seemingly empty studio.

"Hello?" Ellie called into the room abandoned for summer vacation. Quick tears stung her eyelids—had her father decided to leave rather than wait on a daughter that couldn't even be bothered to meet him on time? Or worse, had he never showed up at all?

Ellie started to turn and walk out the door when a whispery voice with a hint of a British accent said softly, "Elizabeth."

Ellie spun around and watched a tall, broad-shouldered figure step out from the shadows, careful to walk near the walls and avoid the dying sunlight pouring into the room from the broad bank of windows. Of course, Ellie should have realized he'd remain in the dark. Ellie knew a vampire wasn't truly comfortable being up and around in the summer until nearly nine o'clock.

Ellie felt rooted to her spot by the door; she couldn't make her legs move and take her to the man crossing the room in graceful strides. As he stepped closer, Ellie was able to make out his features better, see the brown tinted sunglasses he wore with an elegant dark blazer.

Mom had always claimed Simon Baldevar was the handsomest man she'd ever seen and now Ellie found herself agreeing wholeheartedly with the assessment Of course, Ellie had known what her father looked like, thanks to her mother's treasured Elizabethan miniature. It showed a solemn-faced man dressed in a black doublet liberally decorated with diamonds and rubies. Of course, there were some changes in the intervening four hundred years since the miniature was painted. The Van Dyke beard had vanished, replaced by a clean-shaven countenance that emphasized the same sharp cheekbones that greeted Ellie whenever she looked in a mirror. His chestnut hair had also changed from a Prince Valiant cut to a style

Ellie privately thought more suited to him, close cropped at the sides with an abundance of wavy curls on top.

But it wasn't her father's handsome appearance that struck Ellie mute. Rather, it was the dynamic energy radiating from him. Though accustomed to vampires and their mesmerizing auras, Ellie had never felt anything like her father's power. It was like he sucked all the energy from the people and things surrounding him so he became larger than life while everything around him grew dim and pallid.

Simon paused a few inches from Ellie, pulling off his sunglasses to reveal slanted eyes of a soft, gold color unlike anything Ellie had ever seen before. They dominated his face and burned with an intensity that held Ellie in their thrall.

"I. . . I'm sorry I'm late," Ellie finally managed to say to the formidable man who simply stared but didn't speak. What was he thinking? Did she please him? Did he like her?

Ellie immediately regretted her banal words. In her countless daydreams of meeting her father, Ellie had imagined a thousand greetings and never once was a feeble apology one of them. Simon must think his mortal daughter was a flaky, inconsiderate, tongue-tied idiot.

But Simon smiled at her, his warm, open grin shattering the wide gulf of absence and awkwardness between them forever.

"It is I that must apologize to you, daughter, for missing your whole childhood. Can you ever forgive me?" Simon held open his arms and Ellie ran into them.

"Daddy," she cried, not caring if the term was immature for someone her age. Simon Baldevar had always been Daddy to her, the secret nighttime Daddy she could never admit to, the provider of exquisite gifts and the dashing charmer of the stories Mom told about the man that swept her off her feet and transformed her so they'd be together for all eternity. "Daddy, you're finally here!"

"Finally here indeed, my daughter, never to leave again," Simon said, still hugging her tightly and Ellie finally felt the blissful security of her dreams engulf her in reality.

"You mean it?" Ellie said and looked up into his shining eyes. "You're here to stay? Is Mikal here, too? Mom doesn't know you're here, does she?" Was she going to meet not only her father but also her twin brother, whom she knew almost nothing about? Ellie, like Meghann, was hurt and dismayed that Simon and the woman who called herself Ellie's Auntie Adelaide provided them with such scant, bare bones information about Mikal... and that Mikal had never chosen to communicate with them at all.

For a brief second, it seemed like a pall was thrown over Simon's gleaming eyes and he said tersely, "Your brother isn't with me. And no, Meghann doesn't know I've returned—I wanted to surprise her."

"You sure will," Ellie said, and Simon laughed as he released her. "I mean she's going to be so happy to see you! She's missed you so much." Ellie knew better than anyone how much her mother had missed Simon. How many times had she come upon Meghann, sitting alone with Daddy's miniature and faint tear stains marring her cheeks?

"Just as I've missed her," Simon said softly and Ellie suddenly wondered if maybe he'd shed his own tears during their seventeen-year separation. Then his expression cleared again and he extended his arm out to Ellie. "Now, I believe I've been promised a design by a very promising young architect?"

"You meant all that?" Ellie said and happily led her father to her board. "You really want me to design a beach house for you?"

"Marvelous," Simon said, inspecting the watercolor sketch and model on Ellie's board. Ellie didn't think it was conceit to consider the design her very best work to date. She loved the organic-style villa that seemed to grow out of the jagged cliff it perched upon. The copper and bleached wood cantilevered structure resembled a hawk poised for flight with its outstretched glass wing soaring over the cliff edge so it hung suspended over the rocky, churning sea below.

"You have an immense gift, Elizabeth. I have no doubt about the impact you'll make upon your generation once you establish your own firm."

"What firm?" Ellie asked blankly and her father grinned broadly, revealing a dimple in his left cheek Ellie had inherited.

"The firm I intend to help you set up," Simon said. "Perhaps you could partner up with that Vietnamese boy you wrote about."

Ellie smiled at this indication her father had read all her letters and remembered her speaking of Huang Truong, a phenomenally talented young architect who shared Ellie's passion for private residences and prairie-style architecture. Huang, who'd graduated a year before her, was currently serving a sentence at Mead Mckim and complained bitterly of being chained to his desk with the tedium of drafting environmental impact reports or if he was blessed beyond belief, actually being allowed to assist on drawing a window or hallway. Ellie knew Huang would jump at the chance to form a partnership with her but...

"Am I such an unsuitable investor?" Simon questioned at her unenthusiastic silence.

"No, Daddy, it's just..."

"Just what?"

"I want to achieve my own success," Ellie explained just as she had when Mom offered her start-up money for her own firm. How could she make them understand how important it was to receive a paycheck that had nothing to do with them, to find a job where she was valued for her talent and not merely being their daughter? Ellie needed to prove she could stand on her own two feet with no assistance from her parents.

"Nonsense!" Simon exclaimed and gestured to her model. "Your firm will succeed because of your talent, not my money. Do not think I made this offer out of nepotism—go ask your mother if I've ever invested in a foolish venture. Besides, in our family, we do not work for others. I never called any man my superior; when your mother practices her psychology, she works alone. Why slave on behalf of someone else, Elizabeth? Why allow them to profit from your designs while you receive a mere pittance for your labors? Now if you want a businesslike proposition, I shall give you one. My money shall not be a gift, but a loan you pay back in a set amount of time, with the proper interest. Do we have a deal?"

Ellie smiled and remembered something else Meghann had told her about Simon. When he chose to be, he was the most charming man in the world and it was absolutely impossible to say no to him. "Okay."

"Wonderful," Simon said and embraced her lightly. "Shall we go home now, daughter?"

"I'd love to, Daddy."

"Daddy... I have adored that title since you first bestowed it upon me." Simon smiled and withdrew from his wallet a yellowed sheet of paper filled with a looping, childish handwriting Ellie immediately recognized. Blinking back sentimental tears, she reread her very first letter to her father.

Dear Daddy,

Thank you for all my birthday presents. The carousel is my favorite, it is very big and really pretty especially when you put on the lights. Mommy said it is a Rococo antique which means it is very old and expensive so I must be careful when I play with it and not break it. Mommy says it's not just a toy and I can keep it my whole life and enjoy it. I will, I really really like it, Daddy.

The painted horses are so pretty, Lee says there is a place called Martha's Vineyard where they have a real life carousel that looks just like this one and he will take me there in summer.

Mommy can come to because they are open at night and there are bright lights and music just like my antique toy.

I like real horses too. I have a pony. He is chestnut brown just like my hair so I call him Chestnut. Chestnut takes lessons just like me so we can learn how to ride and lives at East End Stables. I already know how to run and we are learning to jump.

Lee has a movie called Dark Victory. It has a very pretty lady who lives in a big house just like this one and she rides horses, too. I would like to grow up like that but I don't want to die of being cross-eyed like Mommy said happened to her at the end of the movie so now I am careful not to make faces or I might die but I think that is very silly and you can't really die of that Mommy was just being funny because Uncle Charles laughed really loud when she told me that. Do you think that is funny? Do you have a horse? Mommy says you like horses a lot and taught her how to ride after you got married. She says she didn't have a horse when she was a little girl like me because she lived in the city and there would be no place to put him, poor Mommy. But she said when you were growing up, your house was much bigger than ours and you had lots of land too. Is that true? When can I see your big house, Daddy?

Goodbye Daddy, I love you very much and thank you for my presents.

Love and kisses, Lady Elizabeth Baldevar

P.S. Mommy says that is my real name, that I am a Lady because you are a Lord but most of the time my last name is Winslow for Uncle Lee because he can't have a little girl of his own so I am your girl and his, too. Mommy says it is good to share. More kisses, Ellie. That is my nickname that everybody calls me and you can, too.

"Pretty miserable chicken scrawl and abominable structure," Ellie said about her first attempts at script, smiling ruefully at the rambling tone.

"You were only five—most mortal children have not even mastered their alphabet at that age," Simon replied. "But I was most touched by your greeting... Daddy. No one had ever called me that before."

"What does Mikal call you?" Ellie asked curiously.

"Father," Simon said flatly and his lips tightened into a grim line.

"Is there something wrong between you and him, Daddy?" Ellie could almost see a dark cloud form around her father when Mikal's name came up.

"I cannot discuss Mikal until your mother joins us."

Ellie nodded her acquiescence, thinking whenever the discussion took place it was not likely to be a pleasant one, judging by the clipped, brusque tone her father developed when speaking of Mikal.

As they walked out of the quiet school and onto the busy street, Simon turned to her and broke the uncomfortable silence that had developed between them. "Would you mind terribly waiting until fall to establish your firm, Elizabeth? I was rather hoping I could take you and your mother on what we used to call a Grand Tour of Europe. If I say so myself, you could not have a better tour guide than someone who's had almost five hundred years to seek out the best sights."

"Daddy," Ellie glowed, momentarily forgetting Mikal, and a few pedestrians raised curious eyebrows at this teenager calling a man who could only be in his early thirties Daddy. "I'd love to!"

"I rather thought so. What architect could possibly consider their education complete without a tour of the grandeur of Europe? Tell me where you'd like to start... Florence, perhaps?"

"York," Ellie said promptly. "I've been dying to see the Gothic cathedrals."

"But if you die, you won't get to go anywhere," Simon teased and she smiled at him, liking this warm, funny father of hers.

"My college instructor said some people actually believe the Gothic cathedrals came from alien intelligence because the work is so advanced and beyond the capabilities of the time. But Mom says maybe the Gothic style was the result of a vampire architect. Do you know anything about that?"

Simon laughed and shook his head. "I'm afraid those cathedrals were erected nearly two hundred years before my birth. Contrary to your mother's view, I have not existed from the beginning of time. But Meghann's theory is certainly a valid one. Shall we go home and continue this discussion with her?"

"Yes," Ellie smiled and accepted his proffered arm. "Let's go home, Daddy."

Chapter Two

"Mom taught me how to drive," Elizabeth remarked as she narrowly missed a collision with a taxi that attempted to cut ahead of the sleekly restored navy-blue 1965 Mustang convertible Meghann had given her for her sixteenth birthday.

"I strongly suspected she did," Simon smiled as his daughter attacked the thick Manhattan traffic with the controlled aggression and high speed that were hallmarks of her mother's driving style. "And who do you think taught your mother to drive?"

"You?" Elizabeth smiled back, relaxing in Simon's easy approval of her daredevil driving.

"Indeed," Simon said, pushing his seat back and stretching his long legs as far as possible in the car's small cabin. He smiled again, remembering the battered old jalopy and dark, deserted roads he'd taken Meghann on for her first driving lessons. There'd been none of the normal timidity and heavy-footed awkwardness of a new driver in Meghann; she'd taken to maneuvering the car about with nimble self-confidence from her first time behind the wheel.

How well Simon remembered those early nights in their relationship, roaring through the night at dizzying, exhilarating speeds, stopping only to pick up some transient mortal hitchhiker. Then there would be the exquisite pleasure of indulging their blood lust together and making love, filled with all the wild, antic glee feeding and driving brought to the surface.

Simon missed those nights and he missed Meghann—his bright-eyed, high-spirited consort who made the night so much more alive and interesting for him. But soon enough, as long as Elizabeth continued to gun the little car far past the posted speed limit, he would see Meghann again.

Elizabeth—Simon turned to his daughter, marveling on how much she reminded him of Meghann, chattering away at him as she guided the Mustang along the highway road reeking of exhaust fumes and banally conversing mortals. A great many of Elizabeth's mannerisms were her mother all over again—the quick, perfunctory glance at the traffic in front of her before she turned to meet Simon's eyes, her flashing, sunny grin... even the way she turned her radio to some dull baseball game, following the announcer's spiel with the same avid attention Meghann always displayed for the inexplicable sport of grown men chasing some ball around a large park.

But Elizabeth, though she'd inherited her mother's vivacious sparkle, was no mere carbon copy of Meghann. Simon could tell that simply by listening as his daughter described her consuming interest in architecture, talking of her early facility for drawing and the construction sets that were the only toys to truly engage her interest. When she spoke of her work, Simon could see Elizabeth applied her talents with a careful, focused attention and cool logic quite foreign to Meghann's intelligent but tempestuous nature.

Elizabeth's analytic mind and artistic hands were a reflection of his own talents, Simon realized, smiling at this first sign of himself in his daughter. What a marvelous young woman his daughter had grown into—combining Meghann's charming, infectious enthusiasm with his keenly logical mind.

Elizabeth's looks were also an almost poetic blend of his and Meghann's best features. From infancy, Elizabeth had sported a full head of his bright chestnut hair; she even had the russet streaks Simon used to develop during the summer months. Judging by her suntan, she'd also inherited the ruddy complexion of Simon's mortal years instead of Meghann's porcelain skin that had to be protected from the sun even before she transformed.

But she had Meghann's almond-shaped, chameleon green eyes that went from apple green to darkest emerald depending on her mood, though the heavy fringe of dark brown lashes came from her father. And there was Meghann's full, bow-shaped lips and daintiness of form softening the chiseled, high-planed cheekbones and long, thin nose that bespoke Elizabeth's paternity.

All in all, a very attractive young woman, Simon thought and then realized he could hardly be the only man to form such an opinion. "Have you many beaux, Elizabeth?"

"Bows?" Elizabeth repeated, at first puzzled and then turning a charming shade of pink. "Oh, you mean beaux—boyfriends. Uh, nothing serious."

There was an outright falsehood, Simon decided swiftly. He did not need to intrude on his daughter's thoughts when that started flush (so very much like Meghann's!) and her averted eyes told Simon there must be at least one serious beau.

He was not surprised that his daughter was reluctant to discuss romance with him; matters of the heart she'd rightfully take to her mother. Simon's only concern in the matter was that his daughter not be like the lascivious young women of her age— distributing her favors freely and without thought to her reputation.

Like any father, Simon wouldn't even speculate that Elizabeth might not be . . . pure . . . but it was plain the girl had reached marriageable age. She must be married before some unsavory character came along and took advantage of her innocence.

Of course, times had changed. Simon wasn't going to force his daughter into an arranged marriage. The girl would pick her own spouse from the young men Simon had chosen among his mortal colleagues. All the bachelors on his list were well educated, handsome, impeccably mannered and heirs to vast fortunes. Obviously, Simon expected any young man marrying into the family to bring a suitable dowry in exchange for the extraordinary bride and immortality he'd receive.

"Dipshit!" Elizabeth shouted in annoyance at the radio and then colored profoundly at her father's censuring glare. "Sorry, Daddy. It's just this godda... I mean, idiot of a relief pitcher gave up a grand slam and the Mets lost the game."

Elizabeth might as well have been speaking in tongues for all the meaning Simon could derive from her explanation for the foul mouth she must have inherited from Meghann, who had no end to the sordid phrases she employed to express rage. Was it too much to hope for that Meghann would have curbed her tongue around their impressionable child? Elizabeth wasn't the only one Simon planned to reprimand this evening.

"Your language is not becoming to a young lady," Simon said sternly and saw the same irritated submission and stung dignity that always bloomed on Meghann's face when he rebuked her. "You are far too intelligent and I hope well-bred to employ the vocabulary of gutter people."

A brief, indecipherable darkening of Meghann's cat eyes was Elizabeth's only response before she shut the radio off and selected a CD that restored good humor to the car.

"You enjoy this music?" Simon questioned as Count Basie pounded out a frenetic swing tune, thankful Elizabeth didn't torture his eardrums with any of that ghastly rock music.

"Mom plays Big Band all the time," Ellie said. "She said that on your first date, you went to the Stork Club and danced to swing... and you were the best dancer she ever met in her life."

"Is that what caught her interest?" Simon laughed, remembering the girl who'd moved over the dance floor with the poise and tiny, perfectly molded body of a prima ballerina. "So this music has captivated you from childhood? Do young people still dance nowadays?"

"Not really," Ellie said, her tone expressing mild indignation at her own graceless generation. "But there are a few swing clubs I like to go to sometimes. Uncle Charles and Mom like to go sometimes and I tag along. You should see them together . . . they've won prizes for their dancing!"

As Uncle Charles was Meghann's beloved but homosexual friend Charles Tarleton, Simon shared Elizabeth's warm adulation for their combined skill. "And who do you dance with, Elizabeth?"

"Uncle Charles, of course," Elizabeth said. "Uncle Lee comes, too, but he hates dancing. And you know . . . some other boys there... Jimmy if he's staying with us..." Elizabeth broke off abruptly, giving her father an apprehensive glance at her unthinking, flippant mention of Meghann's former lover.

"Jimmy Delacroix?" Simon said in a carefully neutral tone, not wanting to alarm his daughter, particularly while she was driving. "He visits your mother?"

"Well, all of us," Elizabeth clarified, giving her father a beseeching glance. "You know, he and Mom are just friends. There's never been any..."

"Elizabeth," Simon broke in. "I have complete faith in your mother and her desire to honor our wedding vows." Simon meant what he said—he believed in Meghann's integrity, knew her interest in the annoying Delacroix creature was no more than pity for a fumbling, morose dolt that couldn't survive without some strong willed woman (Meghann, for instance) propping him up.

Besides, as long as Meghann held the man at arm's length, Simon would not only forgive but applaud her for keeping her former lover close by . . . even she probably did not realize how thoroughly she'd deflected any suspicion on their foes' part by her seeming alliance with Jimmy Delacroix.

"Daddy?"

"You must excuse me, Elizabeth," Simon said apologetically. "I was wool-gathering. What did you say?"

"I was asking if you think Mom was right," Elizabeth said, her tone of voice implying only a fool or a long-absent father not bent on remaining in his daughter's good graces would take Meghann's side against hers. "Surely once I'm earning my own living next fall, I should be allowed to have an apartment of my own and not live at home like some baby."

Simon smothered a laugh at the indignant little wrinkle in his daughter's nose and arched eyebrows meeting in a ferocious scowl—Meghann's classic expression in a temper. "Artistic achievement and superior intellect does not change the fact that you are far too young to live away from home. Your mother is quite right."

"Besides," he continued in a mollifying tone, "You told me Meghann and Dr. Winslow have given you a home of your own in the guest cottage. You can entertain, and set your own hours—within reason, of course. What more could you want?"

A sulky shrug was Elizabeth's response—plainly she'd wanted an ally in her quest for independence but Simon had no intention of contradicting Meghann's directives, particularly when he was in accord with them.

Soon, Elizabeth pulled off the Sunrise Highway and they became silent, breathing in the fresh salt air from the sea as they traveled down the sedate North Sea Road leading to Southampton Village. Simon wished they might have arrived during twilight, when the vast red sky striped with lavender streaks and the first stars of the evening offered an enchanting backdrop to the majestic dunes and endless vista of azure blue shore. But he took equal pleasure in the quarter moon peeking out from wispy stretches of clouds and poignant cries of seagulls all around them.

As Elizabeth guided the car onto their private sand road flanked on either side by well-trimmed hedges, Simon experienced an oddly painful gladness when he glimpsed the weathered gray shingle house with its turrets, secret porches and myriad windows looming ahead, a flag on top of the old-fashioned weather vane snapping smartly in the wind.

"We're home," Elizabeth said softly and Simon smiled in agreement. Yes, that's what he was experiencing... a feeling of homecoming. Whether it was his deep-seated love of the ocean or because this was the home he'd made with Meghann for the happy but brief months of her pregnancy, Simon felt attached to this land.

They climbed up to the main rotunda on the winding front steps made of wooden slats eroded by time and exposure from fresh pine to deep silver. Elizabeth put her key in the front door just as it flew open and an enraged Lee Winslow lit into Elizabeth, so intent on her he didn't even notice Simon standing to the side of the door.

"Elizabeth Baldevar Winslow, where in the hell have you been?!" Lee screamed and Elizabeth attempted to step back but Lee imprisoned her with a strong grip on her wrist. Simon's eyes narrowed at this treatment of his daughter, but he decided to first see what was so disturbing the mortal doctor. This fury, which Simon could immediately see was a response to a driving fear, was quite unlike the even-tempered, amiable man Simon remembered.

"Have you any idea what time it is?" Lee roared and answered his own question before Elizabeth could reply. "Ten o'clock... ten o'clock at night! Your interview was at two! I expected you home by six or seven at the latest, even with traffic. Wherever you were, you could have at least called me. I don't care how busy you were... it only takes five seconds to call and tell me you'll be late so I don't sit here tearing my hair out, wondering what the hell happened to you!"

"Lee..." Elizabeth began timidly.

"Don't you try and excuse yourself, young lady! You know the rules very well... the rules you, your mother and I worked out! Any time you're going to be late, you call! What are you going to tell me... you got caught in traffic? So what? What do you think Meghann got you that cell phone for? Have you forgotten there are reasons we have to know where you are? That there are... things... that might hurt or even kill you once the sun goes down? When you didn't turn up, when I couldn't reach you... I didn't know what to think. I was so worried. For all I know, some... some vampire could have had you, be doing God knows what to you!"

"You're quite right, Dr. Winslow," Simon said and moved in front of the mortal doctor who staggered back and took a sharp intake of breath at this unexpected visitor. "Some vampire did have Elizabeth and he hopes you'll accept his deepest apologies for any anxiety you've suffered through this evening."

"Simon?" Lee sputtered incredulously and Simon saw him grab the doorframe to support himself. "You... you're... you're back."

"That's what I was trying to tell you," Elizabeth said. "Daddy met me at school..." Elizabeth stopped cold, a deep blush suffusing her face when her shamed eyes met those of her mortal guardian, a man who had as much right if not more than Simon to consider himself her father.

"It's okay," Lee said to her and smiled reassuringly, though Simon saw a glimmer of pain in his eyes. "Your whole life we've told you I'm not your biological father."

"That doesn't mean I don't love you like one," Elizabeth said and hugged him fiercely. "It's just..."

"Hey," Lee said gently and returned Elizabeth's hug. "You don't owe me any apology. I owe you one—screaming like that. But you've always been so good about calling. Then your friend Meryl showed up and I thought to myself, 'Ellie would never blow off a friend. Something terrible must have happened if she didn't call.' I understand now. Once you saw your... um, Simon— it's only natural you got preoccupied."

"Meryl!" Elizabeth squeaked in guilty surprise. "I completely forgot. It's her birthday and we were supposed to go out tonight..."

"It's okay," Lee said comfortingly. "Meryl asked me to tell you to call her when you got home. Go call her and make your plans..."

"I can't go out with her tonight," Elizabeth protested and glanced at Simon.

"You think I expect you to entertain a dull, aged parent all night?" he said teasingly and kissed her forehead. "Go and meet your friend... as long as Dr. Winslow considers her a suitable companion."

"Meryl's a fine girl," Lee assured him and gestured for him to come into the house while Elizabeth dashed down the steps, heading for the guest house and a change of clothes after she kissed both men goodbye.

Lee led him into his former favorite room, a circular shaped atrium with walls made entirely of glass that faced the ocean. Settling down on a wrought-iron bench made comfortable with overstuffed cushions, Simon leaned back and accepted the straight bourbon Lee held out to him.

"I've got to apologize again," Lee said and sat opposite Simon on a white wicker chair decorated in a cheerful pastel fabric. "You must think you left your daughter with the male version of Mommy Dearest the way I carried on."

"It's my fault entirely. I startled Elizabeth so completely she forgot to call home. I'm glad you and Meghann take such stringent measures with her at night. And who is this?" Simon inquired, patting the head of a very friendly mixed-breed dog that came over to lick his hand.

"That's Patches," Lee smiled, gesturing to the dog's multi-colored brown, white, and tan coat. "You remember Meghann's setter, Max? He passed away of old age when Ellie was about eight... poor thing, she was so devastated. Meghann took her to North Shore and they wound up adopting Patches, along with a golden retriever named Sunshine because Ellie couldn't make up her mind which dog she wanted... and she said she felt one dog might be lonely without company. I think she'd have adopted the whole shelter if Meghann let her."

"Elizabeth likes animals?" Simon inquired, comparing this sweet daughter to the abominable disgrace of a son he'd disowned.

"Loves them," Lee answered. "Besides the dogs, we have three utterly useless cats lying somewhere around the house and five other part-timers Ellie leaves food out for each morning. She's amazing with animals... the wildest, most mistrustful animals will walk right up and lick her hand."

"She gets that from Meghann," Simon said, remembering her tender treatment of any stray she came across... be it a wounded cat or a pathetic drunk like that Delacroix creature she was so fond of.

"Now where is Meghann?" Simon inquired in a tone that hid how perturbed he'd been to enter the house and not have the slightest sense of his consort's presence.

"She's doing a summer seminar on Domestic Abuse over at Southampton College," Lee explained. "Eight to ten, once a week. She never went back to seeing patients after Ellie was born. She says she has more free time to devote to her daughter by teaching and writing articles. I expect her back any minute now."

"And where is Dr. Tarleton?" Simon inquired of the man's vampire lover and Meghann's dearest friend for more than fifty years. Before the children's birth, Simon could have cheerfully slaughtered the young vampire for it had been his meddling interference on behalf of Alcuin that led to Meghann leaving him for forty years. But the two enemies found themselves drawn together after the dreadful time Meghann had delivering the twins. Six weeks she'd hovered between life and death. Simon and Charles pushed all their petty grievances to the side in their efforts, along with those of Lee Winslow, to save her.

"Chicago," Lee said and gestured to a small flight bag on the floor. "He was presenting a paper on enzyme synthesis at Northwestern this week. I have a flight leaving at eleven-thirty to join him. We're uh... you see, he's going to transform me. We all discussed it together and decided Ellie's old enough to function on her own during the day.

"How wonderful!" Simon said sincerely. No one deserved transformation more than Lee Winslow. Simon studied the mortal critically, knowing the man was in his early sixties, and wondered if his elderly body could survive the rigors of transformation. But Lee didn't seem much different physically from the last time Simon had seen him seventeen years ago. True, the once ash-blond hair was now silver but he'd developed few wrinkles and his body appeared as firm through exercise and diet as it had been in his late forties. Simon focused his senses on the mortal's inner organs and found a firm heartbeat and no sign of any dark, foul disease running through his bloodstream.

"I'm ship-shape," Lee grinned at Simon's silent scrutiny. "Charles did a thorough examination about a month ago. I hate to rush out on you but it's past ten and I have to get out to the airport. Simon, is everything all right? I ask because you seem... sad. Is something bothering you?"

A great deal was disturbing Simon, but if he disclosed the truth, he knew there was no way Lee Winslow would board a plane and leave his foster daughter's side. It was a godsend that the mortal and his vampire lover were going away; now Simon could persuade Meghann with a minimum of argument to heed his wishes without her two friends around to encourage opposition to his plans.

"I merely find my hopes temporarily dashed by Meghann's absence," Simon replied with some sincerity, disturbed that his ill humor was so poorly concealed even a mere mortal could perceive it—he'd have to tread quite carefully around Meghann's far more acute senses. "After all, I come home to fulfill my promise to Meghann and return now that Mikal no longer needs to be hidden from the world and the wench isn't even here to greet me."

"Mikal!" Lee cried, his face filling with avid curiosity. "His face is no longer . . . deformed? Does he tolerate daylight?"

"Your plane, doctor," Simon reminded him. "As to my son, surely you understand that I wish to discuss him with Meghann before anyone else. That is her right as his mother."

"Damn!" Lee said, glancing at his wristwatch and hurriedly grabbing up his flight bag. "I've got to run. Of course I understand that you want to tell Meghann about Mikal first. I can get a full report when we come back on Friday. Charles thinks it will be... done... by then."

"Good luck, doctor," Simon said softly and clasped the mortal's hand firmly. Lee Winslow would need more than mere luck . . . transformation was a dangerous undertaking. Simon would decide after he'd spoken with Meghann if they should head to Chicago so Simon could assist with Lee's transformation. Charles Tarleton had never performed transformation and Simon was, even to his enemies, the acknowledged expert on the matter.

Sad, Simon thought reflectively as he left the atrium and headed for the living room with its deep bay windows and covered porch offering a view of the towering white sand dunes. Sad did not even begin to describe what he felt when he thought of the seventeen years he'd lost with Meghann and his wonderful daughter, sacrificed in the name of a despicable ingrate.

Simon shrugged off the troublesome thoughts. Only fools dwelled on that which could not be changed. It wasn't like he was some mortal father now limited to only a few brief years with Elizabeth, years in which he'd be a superfluous figure, competing for his daughter's attention with the husband and children she'd invariably have until he was eventually pensioned off to some home where he wouldn't be underfoot.

As a vampire, Simon had all the time in the world to make up for those unfortunately lost years. Soon he'd transform Elizabeth; guiding her through those first uncertain years of a vampire's existence would more than compensate for all he'd been forced to miss as she grew up.

Yes, he could make up for his absence in Elizabeth's life, as well as Meghann's. Ah, Meghann... his little firebrand that made life so much more diverting; Simon could hardly wait to see her. Anticipating a passionate reunion, Simon smiled at the living room with its parquet floors, simple tables of glass and chrome, and plush sofas and ottomans in various shades of sea green and the foamy gray color of the storm clouds that occasionally visited Southampton.

The room had changed little since Meghann first decorated it during those last happy months of her pregnancy when Simon presented her with the house as a bridal gift after they reconciled. The soft peach paint with green trim looked new but overall this room still reflected the elegant but comfortable taste he and Meghann had always had in common.

Even when they first met, when Meghann was merely the child of a working class background, she still had an instinctive flair for style that drew Simon to her.

Simon smiled at the one major change Meghann had made to the decor—photos of Elizabeth now decorated almost every inch of available wall space. Simon recognized many for Meghann had sent him and Adelaide duplicate prints. In his wallet was the twin to an enchanting composition of a gap-toothed Elizabeth, adorable chestnut curls pulled back with a pink ribbon, grinning over a vast chocolate cake lit with dozens of glowing little candles. He liked the picture very much, just as he enjoyed one of Elizabeth proudly showing off a menacing jack-o-lantern and various daytime shots Lee must have taken. But Simon's favorite picture had Meghann in the shot as well.

It was, Simon acknowledged, a masterful photograph, showing Meghann in profile, her face lit with the dazzling vitality he remembered so well. She held out her arms for Elizabeth, captured in midair by the camera, to leap into. Simon grinned at the achingly small ice skates on Elizabeth's feet, the steel blades reflecting the bright lights surrounding mother and daughter while the giant Christmas tree at Rockefeller Center provided a diverting background.

Fifty years ago, this portrait of Meghann couldn't be done but advances in darkroom technology and computer enhancement made it possible to take the blurry, ethereal image of a vampire and redefine it to resemble any photographed mortal.

The photo wasn't a masterpiece simply because it included Meghann. This black and white shot was no amateur work with its balanced composition, excellent lighting and deliberately underexposed print, giving the photo a surreal quality that made it seem more memory than picture.

Unfortunately, Simon knew all too well who'd preserved this slice of time for Meghann so she'd never forget what she felt in the moment her little daughter flew into her arms. Scowling, he slipped the photo out of its antique silver frame and glared at the inscription on the back: For the prettiest girls in New York. Merry Christmas, Maggie. Love, Jimmy.

Simon's lips thinned with anger when he reflected on the place that worthless Delacroix had carved in Elizabeth and Meghann's hearts while he was off raising Mikal. In her loneliness, could Meghann have weakened and given Jimmy Delacroix more than a roof over his head? Why else would the fool continue to sniff around her all this time?

With long, impatient strides, Simon crossed the living room and mounted the staircase, heading for the bedroom he used to share with Meghann. That one room above all others would tell Simon just how intimate Meghann's relationship with Jimmy Delacroix was.

Immediately, Simon saw his brief suspicions were unfounded for Meghann had all but turned these rooms into a shrine of their life together. In place of the photographs that graced the walls downstairs, here Meghann hung the paintings Simon gave her— her nursing Elizabeth, a portrait he'd done of Meghann in a floppy Edwardian hat decades before, and one of Meghann seated on the porch swing outside, her full, rosy cheeks and rounded figure just starting to hint at her burgeoning pregnancy.

Even more than the sentimental gesture of keeping his paintings in her most private sanctuary, Simon was reassured by the barren feeling he received when he stood over the large, wrought-iron bed, its dusky rose curtains pulled back to reveal the bed piled high with crimson pillows and gold silk sheets. The room, a sensual fantasy with cherry damask silk covering the walls, plush rugs of the same color, and myriad votive candles might as well be a nunnery for all the erotic impression Simon picked up.

Meghann had used this room for nothing but sleep in years, and she'd spent as little time here as possible. This room told Simon his consort had been faithful to him for nothing else could explain the sterile feeling that assaulted him as he looked around. Had Meghann a lover, even if she did not take him here, some hint of satisfaction would fill these walls where she slept instead of the bitter mix of sorrow and aching dissatisfaction that pervaded the room.

Simon's head snapped up like an animal sensing prey— Meghann was home. He knew it long before he heard the car motor purring along the sand road, knew it by the sudden electric presence growing stronger and closer to him.

Now Simon employed the astral plane to hurry down to the porch, arriving just as Meghann's 1958 Cadillac convertible pulled up in front of the house. Once it had been black with flames embossed on the rocket fins, now it was candy apple red with curling wisps of silver smoke gracing the fins. Simon grinned, remembering that Meghann had once told him she intended to make the classic automobile she'd owned for more than twenty years as immortal as she was.

Lounging against one of the Corinthian columns that graced the porch, Simon wrapped an impenetrable shield around his presence. He did not want his consort to see him just yet. First, he wanted a few moments to observe her while she was unaware of him, just as he'd done the first time they met.

Simon remembered every detail of their first meeting at a dreadfully boring party in 1944. He'd arrived in New York only a few days earlier and while the city pleased him immensely, Simon found no amusement in New York's high society, composed of dull nouveau riche and duller society people that had the laughable nerve to be proud of a lineage that was comprised of righteous prudes and low convicts that managed to carve fortunes out of the American wilderness. Simon could not even find diversion with the young women at the party for they thought to charm him by affecting a weary sophistication decades too old for them. Simon was prepared to leave and search the more sordid parts of the city for entertainment when he'd had his first glimpse of Meghann through the still strata of foul-smelling cigarette smoke pervading the rooms.

For one endless moment, it felt like time had stopped as Simon observed the young woman with her bone-white skin, vivid red hair and bright green eyes brimming over with a zestful, lusty quality that enthralled him. He knew immediately this was the woman destined to be his soul-mate for he'd never before felt such tempestuous passion in another living being and he meant to sample it—and her—immediately.

Now, almost eighty years later, Simon felt that same burning urge to possess the beautiful creature before him, take her and drown himself in the warm vitality she radiated so unknowingly. He looked at her, calmly turning off the car engine and yanking off her head a mousy brown wig Simon suspected she wore in an attempt to look older than the eighteen she'd been when he transformed her. Even performing those mundane tasks, Meghann exuded an unstudied sensuality that brought him to an almost painful hardness.

Simon crept stealthily closer to Meghann, leaning against her car while she glanced appreciatively at the ocean. What a delicious torture this was, standing near enough to breathe in the delightful, fresh scent of Meghann's skin, feel delicate wisps of red hair brush his face while she remained unaware of him—but to not touch her... not yet. He wanted to play with her a bit longer, draw out the pleasure he took in simply staring at her— maybe make her obey her master without even knowing of her compliance to his wishes.

Take your hair down, Simon thought, using his power to insinuate the suggestion deep in Meghann's consciousness and sound like no more than her own inner voice giving her a harmless, little impulse. Grinning broadly, he observed Meghann's small, shapely white hands reaching up to obey his command, grasping a few hairpins and shaking her hair free of the casual knot on top of her head.

Glorious, he thought, watching the lustrous curtain of waist-length red hair fall past her shoulders and automatically settle into perfect little waves down her back. How he'd missed that fiery hair, all paprika and cinnamon with small bits of pure copper highlights. Simon smiled broadly, remembering the first time his hands stroked Meghann's hair, how it almost looked like he'd caught a bit of fire in his hands but felt so soft and smooth against his skin.

In his preoccupation, some small bit of his aura escaped the tight sheath of invisibility, alerting Meghann to the presence a bare inch from her. Abruptly, she whirled around, green eyes wide with apprehension that turned to outright astonishment when she saw him smiling down at her. Meghann uttered a wordless little cry, bringing her hand to her mouth while her eyes blinked rapidly, as though she were trying to convince herself Simon wasn't a hallucination.

"Simon..." Meghann finally whispered in a parched, stunned voice when she lowered her shivering hand.

Uttering his name was all Simon would allow her to say before he drew her into his arms and molded his lips to hers. At first, the mouth beneath his was stiff with surprise and hesitation but when he moved the tip of his tongue against her tender, full lips Meghann began responding to him.

That's right, he thought when her arms went around his neck and her lips parted to accept him. Simon bent her body back and plunged into Meghann's well-remembered sweetness, breaking away from her only when he felt a dewy wetness against his face and hot, salty tears spilled onto his lips.

"No," he said gently and kissed away the crystalline tears spilling out of her bemused eyes. Meghann's tears still had the power to pull at a corner of his heart he'd almost forgotten existed, Simon reflected, remembering the minx who'd occasionally used those tears to wriggle out of a deserved punishment when he first transformed her. "Don't cry, sweet. There's no reason to weep now. We'll never be parted again."

Never be parted again, Meghann thought with savage happiness and impatiently blinked at the wretched tears that were blurring her vision of the man she'd waited so long for, the man she'd almost started to fear was never going to fulfill his promise and return to her.

Until she saw Simon's hawk eyes blazing down at her, Meghann hadn't realized how his absence had lacerated her heart. Long ago, she'd forced her mind and heart into a repressed state, feeling her sorrow for her missing husband and son would negatively affect her daughter. Instead, she'd immersed herself in raising Ellie and never allowed herself to acknowledge the burning need at her core that pulled at her even more viciously than blood lust for Meghann could feed her desire for blood but she could do nothing to assuage her body's violent longings. A few fumbled attempts at lovemaking with Jimmy Delacroix taught Meghann another lover would provide no succor. It wasn't Jimmy's fault but his hands on her body and caressing lips evoked no passion within her—she'd lain as if dead until Jimmy finally left her bedroom in a disgusted rage. There was no way Meghann could tell him she was utterly spoiled for other men after her passionate reunion with Simon.

Thoughts of the past seventeen arid, celibate years went through her mind fleetingly for there was no time to think now that Simon was real, solid flesh simultaneously soothing and invading her.

Meghann put aside her uncertainty and the simmering anger she felt at the long separation, lunging hungrily at Simon's crisp shirt, alligator belt, fine cotton trousers, and any other obstacle between her and the satisfaction that was finally within her grasp.

Simon smiled at her wild, impatient gestures and attacked her clothes with equal fervor, scowling darkly at the impediment of her blue jeans.

"Never wear this damned modern chastity belt again," Simon growled and wrenched her free of the denim with one swift tear that split her jeans in two. Then he brutally thrust his tongue inside her mouth while warm, roving hands explored flesh that screamed for his touch.

Wrenching away from his mouth, Meghann brought her lips to the tan nipples on his broad chest, favoring them with light, feathery little nips that transformed them into rigid peaks while she ran her long nails against the length of his hard-planed back. She'd almost forgotten the feel of a man's rough-hewn body and bulging muscles beneath her hands. To simply touch Simon excited her almost as much as the sharp teeth teasing her own nipples, the long fingers making swift work of the slippery cleft between her legs.

Simon hadn't forgotten any of her secrets. Rapidly, he found her center and an orgasm rushed through her. She collapsed against the shiny surface of the car, mewling her pleasure while Simon brought her legs around his waist and drove into her.

Meghann climaxed again when he penetrated her, emitting a short, sharp cry of delight when she felt her body throb around the hard, swollen flesh encased within her.

"My Meghann," Simon husked and put his mouth back on hers before she could reply, tell him yes, she was always and forever his Meghann, belonging only to him.

Meghann writhed eagerly beneath Simon, unmindful of the hard, aluminum surface she slammed against with each thrust. Nothing mattered but the pleasure consuming her, making the years of frustration fall from her like a bad habit. Each thrust, each burning imprint of Simon's hands and mouth renewed her, brought her back to eager, hot-blooded life.

An endless time later, when Simon was sure of her satisfaction, Meghann felt him move toward his own release and encouraged him with a clenching of her pelvic muscles. He gave her a quick grin and she watched his blood teeth emerge to slide deep within her neck.

Meghann squirmed in ecstasy as Simon fed from her and she brought her own fangs to his wrist, feeling another climax rock through her when his dark, delicious blood filled her mouth. How she'd missed this naughty game of being predator and prey, drinking and being drunk from while that greedy, iron-hard flesh rammed into her, bringing her to a final, cresting peak that made her scream in abandonment, scream so loud and long she was surprised she didn't blow out all the glass in the car.

Simon collapsed against her panting, slick form and then rose, pulling Meghann up with him. Lucky for Simon she'd saved some of his clothes, Meghann thought when she saw his shredded silk shirt lying beside one of the front tires.

"I've never made love on a car," Meghann said impishly and bit Simon's earlobe when he settled her on top of him. "Inside a car, yes, but never on a car."

Simon gave her a rakish grin and returned her playful bite with his own.

Meghann rested her head against his softly beating heart, luxuriating in the heat emanating from his body to warm her while the sharp ocean breeze blew her hair around and tickled her bare legs.

It seemed like forever since she'd felt this kind of wide-eyed exhilaration, since she looked up and felt awed by the beauty of the black velvet night and glowing white stars. How long since the night had performed these tricks for her?

Not since Simon left, Meghann realized, thinking not for the first time that the world had dimmed somehow when he left.

Not that she had any intention of feeding his immense ego and telling him that. Instead, Meghann let her fingers draw aimless little paths on his chest while she inquired, "Why didn't you write and tell me you were coming? Why didn't you or Adelaide write me at all in the past eight months?" Even their usual scant letters that never told Meghann all she longed to know about her son had been absent.

"I wanted to surprise you, little one," Simon told her and she felt his fingers entwine in her hair while his other hand reached out to pet and fondle in the soothing manner he'd always used after they made love.

"Why did you stay away so long?" Meghann raised her head, now ready to attack Simon with the angry barrage of questions she'd had almost two decades to form, an interminable length of years in which she'd waited night after night, year after year for Simon to materialize and then felt constant, bitter disappointment when he never did.

"Leaving you when I took Mikal was the hardest thing I've ever done. It took all the determination and will I possess to walk away from you and Elizabeth. But there are limits to my strength, Meghann. How many times could I come back only to tear myself away after some brief interlude? It was keep away or keep you forever, so until the time came when I'd never have to leave

55

you again, I had to stay far away and allow you to dwell only in my memory."

Meghann narrowed her eyes, thinking Simon's words sounded hollow to her ears, almost insincere. Not that Meghann thought he was lying for Simon, while amoral, sometimes cruel and occasionally verging on true evil in his behavior, was hardly ever dishonest. He'd hide things, omit important facts, but never did he out and out lie. So Meghann thought it more likely she'd just received a half-truth—yes, Simon might have found brief visits that had to end more painful than their protracted separation but that wasn't his only reason for staying away.

Meghann squared her shoulders, about to try and wrest from Simon whatever important and very likely unpleasant facts he was keeping from her, when his words and their meaning registered on her. "Never leave again—you mean you're back for good?"

"For good and ever," he promised, giving her a deep, lingering kiss that made her nerves tingle pleasantly.

Meghann threw her arms around him in a near chokehold and babbled in the happy, rushed way Simon always brought out in her. "That's wonderful... you and Mikal, home for good! Ellie's going to be thrilled—have you met her yet? Simon, you'll be so proud... oh, you did meet her? You introduced her to Mikal, didn't you? Have they gone out together? No? Well, why not? Isn't Mikal here? Simon, how could you come home without my son? Where is he? He isn't angry with me, is he? Simon, you did explain to him why we haven't met... that it wasn't because I didn't want to or didn't love him but you and I decided..."

Meghann trailed off, thinking whatever Simon wasn't telling her, it better tie in to why he'd shut her out of their son's life, or why that son still wasn't here to meet his mother. To her, Mikal was like a child she'd given up for adoption. Meghann had only seen the boy once when he was an infant and knew nothing about him save for the precious little Adelaide wrote—Mikal's well and safe, how's Elizabeth? Simon's letters rarely referred to Mikal; he only commented on things she'd written him regarding Ellie. Meghann knew nothing about her son, not his favorite book or color, what he looked like or even if he was able to tolerate sunlight, though the events of a month ago made Meghann and Charles strongly suspect Mikal had fulfilled Simon's theory that their vampire child would be able to walk in daylight once he matured to adulthood.

Meghann started to tell Simon what she and Charles had discovered in Ireland a month ago, ask him if Mikal was connected to the mysteriously slaughtered vampire colony, but Simon smiled into her uneasy, apprehensive eyes before she could speak and put a finger to her kiss-swollen lips.

"I don't wish to talk now," Simon said lightly and Meghann had a brief sensation of being in a dark, dank place with a keening wind howling all around her before she found herself sprawled on her bed.

"I don't care if you wish to talk or not—you better answer my questions," Meghann said and slapped his roving hands away, sitting up indignantly when she looked at the glowing candles she hadn't lit since Simon left. Sure of himself, wasn't he that he'd prepare the bedroom for a seduction he never thought she might resist. "You can't drag me along the astral plane and pin me to the bed without so much as a by your leave! You're going to tell me why my son isn't here and you're going to do it before... Simon!"

"Hush up, girl," Simon whispered before bending his head to continue tonguing the oversensitive red peaks of her nipples.

"Simon," Meghann protested weakly, feeling her will to resist fade as Simon divided his attention equally between both breasts, his hands and tongue waging a sensuous assault that filled her with a dull, heavy ache that made her moan in capitulation.

At her strangled whimper, Simon immediately withdrew his attention, capturing with one hand the hands that tried unsuccessfully to guide his head back into place.

"Lie still," Simon ordered and Meghann obeyed immediately, willing as always to do anything Simon ordered in bed, anything to receive the pleasure it was within his power to give or deny, depending on how much she pleased him.

Simon rewarded her submission by reopening the punctures in her neck, drinking from her until she lay weak and panting with desire beneath him, then securely tied her hands and feet to the four corners of the bed with black silk scarves. Drained of blood as she was, Meghann couldn't break the bonds. This was one of Simon's favorite games, for Meghann to lie open and helpless before her master.

Simon gave her a smirk of victory before rubbing the head of his long, thick penis against the blood still pouring from her neck.

'Please me," he ordered, putting the blood-covered organ to her mouth. Meghann suckled and licked with all the skill at her disposal, eager to prove herself worthy of satisfaction. A part of her, as always, was outraged by her compliance in this degrading game. Meghann had no idea why she gave in to Simon so easily for she'd never allowed any of her other lovers to dominate her mind and body as he did. Maybe she gave in to Simon because he'd never asked her permission, simply took and then gave back in such an abundance Meghann felt only a brief distress at her meek behavior.

You were made for this, Simon thought at her as he grew larger and harder within her mouth, one hand straying down to play with the over stimulated flesh between her legs.

Meghann felt the hidden bud of her sex grow dense and swollen beneath his knowing fingers and thrashed about as much as the restraints would allow, delighting in the pleasure Simon gave her while the small bit of blood on his penis restored some of her strength.

"No," Meghann cried when Simon withdrew completely, glaring down at her supine form as he stood by the bed. "Don't stop."

"Order me again, Meghann... tell me what I must do." Simon smiled cruelly at her dismay.

Meghann bit back a harsh retort and instead smiled invitingly, saying, "I want to do whatever you want to do... Master."

"You always were quick to understand," Simon said and plunged deep within her spread-eagled, waiting body.

That's right, Meghann thought, *take me.* She'd find a way to get even with Simon for his high-handed, controlling, but oh so pleasurable behavior later... much, much later. Later, she'd make him tell her why he became so upset whenever Mikal's name came up. For now, she only wanted to take from him all the satisfaction she could as they made love in the house by the sea where they'd spent some of their best times together.

Chapter Three

"Face it, Ellie. Mickey's a dud. Cut him loose and find someone who knows what he's doing."

Meryl Greenblaum, Ellie's girlfriend, spoke these words of wisdom as they chased their margaritas with shots of Cuervo Gold at Jet East. Though neither girl was twenty-one, getting into the trendy nightclub and buying drinks wasn't a problem—Meryl was going out with one of the bouncers.

"What if I'm the one that doesn't know what to do?" Maybe she shouldn't have done that shot—Ellie was starting to feel awfully lightheaded.

Meryl rolled her eyes and lit a cigarette. "Ellie, you can only go so far in technique when you've got a lousy teacher. It's time to try other guys. You weren't planning to marry Mickey, were you?"

"Of course not. But, I can't start sleeping around." Ellie hesitated, not wanting to offend Meryl, who was already on her seventh lover even though she and Ellie were the same age. But Ellie just couldn't see sleeping with men she hardly knew... not after her upbringing.

It wasn't like her mother raised her to be a prude or fed her any of that good girls wait till their wedding garbage the Christian Right was trying to push. No, Meghann had been honest with Ellie, telling her she'd been promiscuous and wanted Ellie to learn from her mistakes that sex without love was cheap and for the most part, unsatisfactory. Then there was Uncle Lee harping on diseases and unplanned pregnancy, reminding Ellie that even the best-made condoms had been known to break from time to time. With all that in her head, Ellie just couldn't see herself in a one-night stand.

"Who said anything about sleeping around?" Meryl protested. "But you need to get off this monogamy thing. You don't think Mickey sleeps with your pictures under his pillow when he leaves New York, do you? Come on, let's pick up some guys tonight."

"What about Carl?" Carl was Meryl's bouncer flame.

"He's not on tonight." Out of sight was apparently out of mind for Meryl.

"I can't tonight." Ellie had to touch base with her mother before sunrise and she certainly wanted to spend more time with her father. She'd only come out with Meryl to wish her a happy birthday, have a few drinks, and give her parents some time alone together. That reminded her—she had to swallow some coffee and buy gum before she went home. Ellie didn't know if the subterfuge would work against her parent's keen senses but it was worth a shot.

"Why not? How about the ones at the end of the bar?" Meryl sent a coy smile of thanks down to the two men at the other end of the bar who had sent over fresh margaritas.

"Boring," Ellie pronounced at the blond, bland, preppy clones flashing identical WASPy smiles. Nothing turned her off more than the drip-dry, permanent press monotony of the Ivy League with their button-downs, carefully pressed chinos and pastel sweaters worn over the shoulders. To Ellie, they all looked like they were conceived on the golf course, reared in prep schools and finished out their lives in one investment bank/law firm or another.

"God, Ellie, what is with you and those scruffy rejects you're so into?" Meryl complained. "If they don't have long hair and look like they need a bath, you're not interested."

"Tha's not true," Ellie heard herself slur and pushed her margarita away. Damn, she hadn't meant to get drunk—she couldn't go home like this! Mom didn't mind her having a drink or two, but coming home tipsy... Mom would kill her, wouldn't even trust her enough to leave the house to walk the dogs!

"It is true," Meryl replied, oblivious to her friend's predicament as she continued flirting with the WASPs. Pink Sweater and Green Sweater (the only differences Ellie could perceive in their appearances) caught her signals and started walking over. "Why don't you hit on that one over there—he looks like Peter Fonda in those old biker movies."

Ellie followed Meryl's finger and felt her heart do a minor flip-flop at the tall man with dark-brown hair styled in a wild duck's-ass that made him look like a deranged porcupine or Elvis Presley on speed. He had his back to Ellie so she couldn't make out his features but she was already deeply impressed with his lean, sinewy arms, sleeveless black leather vest and skintight jeans. This guy could definitely get her mind off Mickey if he was interested.

With an aggressive confidence borne of tequila, Ellie fished a twenty out of her purse and motioned to the bartender. "Buy that guy in the vest whatever he's drinking and tell him it's from me."

"Ellie!" Meryl hissed. She'd already claimed Pink Sweater and now Green Sweater watched uncertainly as his designated date tried to pick up another man.

"I was just kidding. You can't come on to that! He looks... sleazy!"

"Lighten up, Meryl." If anyone's a sleaze, it's you— playing musical beds. Did Meryl think her behavior was somehow elevated from the average bimbo because of the bank accounts and clothes of the guys she favored? Ellie had to make new friends.

Ellie watched the waitress bring the man a beer. He accepted the drink, and then turned around to thank his buyer, and in the next second all hell broke loose as his scandalized eyes met Ellie's panic-stricken ones.

"Oh, no!" Ellie moaned, burying her flaming face in her hands.

"What's wrong with you?" Meryl asked.

"I'm such an idiot," Ellie cried as Jimmy Delacroix stalked over to her. Only an idiot would attempt to pick up one of her mother's best friends in a bar she wasn't even supposed to be in. Jimmy wouldn't tell Mom, would he?

"What the hell are you doing here, Ellie?" Jimmy demanded.

"What are you doing here?" Ellie countered, though as an adult (albeit a vampire one) Jimmy had far more right to be here than she did. "Your last letter said you'd be home next week."

"Got done earlier than I expected. I'm here for exactly what this WASP asshole sniffing around you is here for . . . and he'd better back away before I kick his Chiclets teeth down his throat." Green Sweater tried to look unaffected by Jimmy's threat but a definite trepidation settled over his face.

Jimmy leaned in closer to Ellie, sniffing suspiciously, and then his gray-blue eyes glared down at her like the wrath of God. "Have you been drinking?"

"A little," Ellie said weakly, shocked into sobriety. "You, urn, cut your hair."

It was all the hair's fault, Ellie thought in an agony of humiliation. All her life Jimmy Delacroix had worn his hair in a ponytail. If he hadn't cut it, Ellie would have recognized him immediately and never felt that inexplicable rush of lust that was bothering her more than whatever consequences she might face at home if Jimmy told her mother about this.

"Come on," Jimmy said brusquely and dragged her off the barstool. "This is no place for you."

"Now, wait a minute..." Green Sweater put a restraining hand on Jimmy's shoulder and Jimmy grabbed the offending appendage in a grip that made the preppie blanch and clench the perfect teeth Jimmy had threatened to part him from.

"Can't you see she's jailbait, you asshole?" Jimmy snapped, not even looking at Meryl or her date. "Get this flick out of my way."

The preppie hastened to please, stepping well out of Jimmy's path.

Jimmy muttered not a word to Ellie as they cut through the thick crowd in the bar and stepped into the relative quiet of the parking lot

"Put this on," Jimmy barked when they reached his 1947 Indian Chief and handed her a helmet.

Ellie nodded meekly and buckled the riding helmet beneath her chin before climbing behind Jimmy.

Jimmy took off in a cloud of gravel and dust, shifting into first as they left the parking lot. Ellie felt some of her anxiety and mortification dissipate as the bike roared through Conscience Point and Shinnecock, leaving a trail of envious drivers stuck in the thick town traffic. Ellie had ridden on this bike since she was seven, clutching Jimmy's waist and laughing at the exhilarating speed. It felt like she was flying, that was the only way Ellie could describe the dull roar in her ears and scenery whizzing past her almost before it registered on her senses.

Unfortunately, the ride was over all too quickly as Jimmy pulled up at the guesthouse and cut the engine.

"What the hell are you wearing?"Jimmy snapped when she hopped off the bike and he took his first good look at her.

"Don't you like the color?" Ellie knew very well what Jimmy didn't like about her pink tank dress— she'd deliberately shrunk it two sizes too small.

"What I like about the dress isn't the problem," Jimmy growled and hauled her inside the house. "It's what those two creeps at the bar were going to like that's the problem. Ellie, if you wear a dress like that and accept free drinks, you're sending out a very clear message. Do I need to spell out what that is?"

"No," Ellie muttered, thankful that Jimmy at least wasn't saying anything about her attempt to pick him up. Ellie felt her cheeks flame and a curious tension rush through her body when she remembered the perfect line of his lean, rangy shoulders and arms as she stared unknowingly at one of her childhood uncles.

"Is that message what you want to send out?" Jimmy demanded. "That all a guy has to do to get under your too-tight skirt is buy you a drink?"

"It wasn't supposed to be like that," Ellie explained, though now that Jimmy had put it so baldly, Ellie wondered how she could have thought it would have been anything else. "Meryl and I were just going to have a few drinks..."

"You're only seventeen!"

"And I suppose at seventeen you were just drinking ice cream sodas?" Ellie questioned sarcastically, seizing the offensive. If Jimmy dared give her that what-I-did-isn't-the-issue-drivel...

'That's different," Jimmy said instead. "I'm a man."

"Don't get all huffy on me for saying the truth," Jimmy said at her narrow eyes and indignant glare. "Look, a guy can go to a bar and drink till he's shit-faced because he doesn't have to worry about some dirty sonofabitch trying to take advantage of him...

which is what would have happened to you tonight. Is that what you wanted, Ellie—to wind up in that asshole's Jag or Porsche with your dress around your face?"

"I just wanted to have fun. You know, a few drinks, dance maybe..."

"If you want fun, do it someplace else... and with someone else. I don't like that girl you were with... just another rich, spoiled nympho. She's a bad influence."

"Meryl's okay," Ellie asserted, though she had been tiring of her friend. Meryl did like to drink too much and lately she'd started snorting coke, something Ellie was definitely not into. All she'd have to do is come home with cocaine whirling around her bloodstream—Mom would have her head on a platter. "You know it's hard for me to make friends."

"Friends like that you don't need," Jimmy responded with finality. "Look, here's the deal—you promise me you won't hang out with that girl anymore and I won't tell Maggie what happened tonight. Agreed?"

Ellie nodded, trying to look put out but secretly relieved she had a valid reason to brush Meryl off. "So who am I supposed to hang out with?"

"Hang out with me," Jimmy said, giving Ellie a light-hearted grin that changed to concern when Ellie sagged against the couch. "Hey, are you okay?"

"I'm fine," Ellie managed to say though she felt anything but fine—more like deeply embarrassed and horrified because Jimmy's easy smile brought every pang of interest and desire she'd felt in the bar rushing back to the fore. What was the matter with her? How could she be lusting after Jimmy Delacroix—her mother's former lover?

In a daze, Ellie got up off the couch, not sure where she was going except she wanted to get away from Jimmy before he guessed the preposterous thoughts whirling through her mind that she thought couldn't be more obvious if she tattooed them on her forehead.

"Whoa," Jimmy said in concern when Ellie stumbled and tripped on a lamp wire, nearly bringing the lamp and herself down to the floor.

"Easy, kid," Jimmy said and put his arms around her waist to steady her. "How much did you have to drink?"

"Only one margarita and a shot of tequila," Ellie managed to say, feeling a strange tightening in her chest at Jimmy's warm hands on her. Thank God he was blaming her weird behavior on the tequila and not this sudden, bizarre attraction stronger than anything she'd felt for anyone—including Mickey. Even when they'd had sex, Ellie hadn't felt her bones turning to jelly the way they did when Jimmy simply smiled at her, let alone touched her.

"That's plenty," Jimmy sniffed disapprovingly and released Ellie. "When's the last time you ate?"

Ellie scrunched her face up, trying to remember. "I had a bran muffin around ten this morning..."

"Jesus," Jimmy muttered in amused disgust. "No wonder you're drunk, dopey. You can't go out drinking unless you have some food in your stomach. I'm gonna start cooking before you faint. While I russle up some food, why don't you change into something that doesn't look painted on?"

"Sure." Ellie made it to the bedroom without further incident, shutting the door behind her and examining the hectic flush in her face that could have been booze or sunburn instead of the rising passion Ellie knew it for.

What was the matter with her? She absolutely could not have a crush on Jimmy Delacroix. This was the stuff sleazy talk shows were made of. . . Men Passed From Generation to Generation... on the next Jerry Springer.

This wasn't simply depraved; it was impossible. No way would anything ever come of this. Even if Ellie was fool enough to tell Jimmy her feelings, he wouldn't go near her with a ten-foot pole. In his mind, she was Meghann's little girl; Ellie could tell that from his friendly palling around with her that had nothing in it of a man's attraction for a desirable woman. If Ellie tried to flirt with Jimmy, he'd simply laugh at her. No, that wasn't right— Jimmy would never be cruel like that. He wouldn't laugh but neither would he consider her as anything but sweet little Ellie, the child he'd known from infancy.

Unless she did something to make him see her in a different light—oh, God, what was she thinking? Ellie must be out of her mind to contemplate seducing Jimmy Delacroix. Ellie couldn't even imagine what her mother or Uncle Charles or Uncle Lee would think of her... or of Jimmy if he responded to her.

"Dinner's ready," Jimmy called.

"Coming," Ellie called back and frantically inspected her clothes. At first, her eyes strayed toward the leather mini's, stretch pants, and low-cut tops, but that was too obvious. And anyway, she wasn't trying to interest Jimmy, was she?

"Smells good," Ellie said, entering the kitchen in an ancient pair of jeans that showed off her long, slender legs and a red cotton shirt with scalloped sleeves and a scooped neck... an attractive look but nothing so over the top Jimmy would know in an instant what her intentions were.

But she wasn't going to have intentions, Ellie told herself firmly, miserably picking at Jimmy's sole culinary achievement, a Denver omelet.

"Something wrong with the food?" Jimmy inquired at her child-sized nibbles.

"No," Ellie said and forced herself to swallow a whole mouthful of eggs. "I'm just a little queasy."

Okay, Ellie thought and continued to shovel food into her mouth mechanically, I have a crush on Jimmy—it's not that surprising. After all, Jimmy was very attractive in his irreverent, wild way. He'd been around thirty when he transformed, young enough to retain all his dark brown hair, lean body, and the feature that most riveted Elli's attention—his wide-spaced, probing gray eyes lined in cobalt blue.

And it wasn't like Ellie had grown up with him as a surrogate father in the same way Charles and Lee were. Ellie had vague memories of Jimmy living with them when she was a little girl but he'd been traveling steady for more than ten years now. Jimmy still called the beach house home, but he only stayed for two or three weeks at a time before seeking out new locales. But Ellie knew his work wasn't the only reason Jimmy stayed away. She remembered those muffled, predawn arguments between him and Mom when they thought Ellie was asleep.

"Damn it, Maggie," Ellie remembered Jimmy pleading. "Why can't you get Baldevar out of your head? What is it with you and that piece of..."

At that point, Meghann would always furiously remind him Ellie was sleeping and the rest of the fight would take place outside, away from Ellie's ears. But Ellie could surmise the outcome by Jimmy's itchy feet—Mom refused him, so Jimmy took himself away from her and painful memories. Now, when Jimmy visited, he and Mom were friendly enough but there was always an underlying tension. Usually Jimmy spent most of his time with Ellie, taking her to movies and rock clubs when she got older, teaching her how to use a camera and letting her ride the Indian.

Sometimes Ellie had pretended Jimmy was her boyfriend on those excursions, not that he'd ever done anything remotely inappropriate, simply treating her with the same wry courtesy he used on everyone else. Those fantasies had been kid stuff, she knew. What she felt now was something different altogether— something dangerous that she had to suppress.

"How was your trip? Where did you go?" There, that wasn't bad at all. Her voice sounded interested and intelligent... not at all like some horny seventeen-year-old girl with depraved fantasies of seducing her mother's ex-boyfriend.

"L.A.," Jimmy said, wolfing down his omelet and home fries. "You were my inspiration this time, Ellie. I fell in love with those wonderful old houses in the Hollywood Hills."

Fall in love with me, Ellie wanted to shout and had to remind herself again that what she wanted simply wasn't going to happen. But she could at least be friends with Jimmy. "Can I see the pictures?"

After they ate and the dishes were stacked in the dishwasher, Jimmy and Ellie settled down on the couch. Ellie fidgeted impatiently while Jimmy rummaged around in his leather traveling bag; she could hardly wait to see his new shots. Over the past five years, Jimmy had established quite a reputation in the art world with his surreal, moody, compositions—a corsage, crumpled and abandoned beneath a harsh street light, a lonely little glow pouring from the window of an abandoned tenement, an electrical storm over an empty stadium. One of Ellie's favorite exhibits was his collection of Art Deco fringe work on buildings all but demolished by time, drugs, and crime. The brave, fanciful artwork of another time contrasting to the urban war zone surrounding it had created quite a stir when it appeared in the New Yorker a few years ago. Part of the sharp interest in Jimmy's photo essay was the way he'd used Meghann in the shot. Jimmy posed her leaning on the sagging windowsill, dressed to resemble the young girl she'd been in the forties. What made the photo so dramatic wasn't Meghann's clothes, but her blurred, half visible, vampiric image. As she stared down wistfully at the crime torn street, Meghann seemed a ghost from another time gazing unhappily at the devastation of the neighborhood she'd once known. Ellie was sure Jimmy would have won a Pulitzer for the powerful, evocative composition if he hadn't refused the nomination to avoid the publicity that was anathema for a vampire.

"Here," Jimmy said and gave Ellie a contact sheet, along with the magnifying loupe.

"This one," Ellie said and tapped the loupe against what she considered the best of the lot. "It's perfect. Call it *Cul-de-Sac.*" The picture was angled to show a twisting, winding road leading to a spectacular white house that reigned upon a high hill in lone splendor. The slant Jimmy shot on made the house seem to tower over the viewer, the black sky and silhouettes of trees on the edge of the composition serving to emphasize the graceful charm of the 1920s style European villa. The photo, like all of Jimmy's pictures, called up immediate, powerful emotions—a yearning to possess the beautiful house, to step into that photo that seemed to capture another, more glamorous way of life.

"*Cul-de-Sac?*" Jimmy said and ruffled Ellie's hair playfully, oblivious to the wave of feeling coursing through her that nearly made her feel ill. "What a coincidence—that's exactly the title I thought of when I saw the negative."

"Great minds think alike." Ellie tried to make the remark light but to her ears there was something almost bruised about her voice. Casting about for a new topic of conversation, she asked, "When did you get your hair cut?"

Jimmy smiled and patted the wild pompadour. "Like it? I was going through a vintage music store and I happened on an autographed copy of the Stray Cat's first album. I took one look at Brian Setzer and said to myself, 'Jimmy, you're getting stale. You've had long hair for almost thirty years. It's time for a change.' So I went to the nearest hair salon and showed the girl the album cover."

"A hair salon?" Ellie repeated, dumbfounded. "But Jimmy, what about the mirrors?" There were few mirrors in their house because Mom said she despised the partial image that greeted vampires—it was one of the only things that still had the power to make her feel freakish and unnatural.

Jimmy gave her a shy smile of pride and accomplishment. "Well, I remembered this trick Maggie and Charles taught me. The whole time the girl was washing and styling, I kept staring into the mirror and projecting the mirror image she expected to see. I had to look into her mind to see how her hands and scissors were moving over my head, the hair falling to the floor, and then I had to project her thoughts into the mirror. The haircut took about forty minutes and by the end I was exhausted. But I did a good job—no one there thought there was anything out of the ordinary about me."

"Jimmy, that's fantastic!" Ellie watched him beam at her compliment and thought here was something on her side... not that she intended to make a case for her wild desire but still. No way could Jimmy have just told that story to anyone in the world but her or another vampire. Ellie was one of the few people in the world Jimmy could be himself around—surely that gave her an edge over any mortal girl he might pick up for a night or two— and stop thinking such things, Elizabeth Winslow! "And it looks wonderful."

"You know what, though?" Ellie continued and dug into his bag. "I bet it looks even better when you put on sunglasses. Here." Ellie found his black aviator shades and slipped them over his eyes.

"You look great, Jimmy," Ellie said, no longer feeling quite in control of herself as her hands trailed lightly down his shoulders. What in the hell was she doing? Why did she remove her hands but keep her eyes glued to his mouth? Why was she sitting here imagining what it would be like to run her fingers over that generous mouth with its lower lip that always seemed ready to curve into a smile?

"Ellie..."Jimmy pulled off the sunglasses and Ellie saw his eyes were wide and uncertain as he stared at Ellie like she was someone he'd never seen before.

Ellie couldn't bring herself to say anything, but she moved her face an imperceptible inch closer to Jimmy's, close enough now that she picked up his scent—redolent of soap and something else, something ruggedly male that made her heart start pounding while her hands suddenly turned clammy and wet.

Ellie drew closer, entranced by Jimmy's alert, ready stare. The boys she'd dated never looked at her like this, solemn but filled with a restless, prowling energy. This was . . . this was the way a man looked when he wanted a woman!

Yes, Jimmy did want her! Ellie felt it, felt his desire as strong as her own. Her heart leapt up inside her and she felt exhilarated and nervous and giddily triumphant when she felt his hand wrap around the back of her neck and draw her so close Ellie felt her breasts brush the cool surface of his leather vest and instinctively she parted her lips...

Then in the next moment, Jimmy leaped off the couch and stuffed his contact sheet back into his bag with unseemly haste, staring at Ellie like she was a witch he feared might steal his soul.

"Look, Ellie, dinner was great but I've gotta go," Jimmy said, hurriedly grabbing up his tote and heading for the door. "I'm just gonna go up to the house, got a lot of film I want to develop..."

"The house?" Ellie had seen her mother's car when they came home. She knew Mom must have seen Daddy by now and Ellie didn't think anyone should interrupt them, especially Jimmy Delacroix.

"No, Jimmy!" Ellie said and made a wild grab at his hand but Jimmy seemed determined to keep distance between himself and Ellie.

"You can't go up to the house!" Ellie shouted as he walked through the front door and the near panic in her voice made him turn and stare in bafflement. "I mean, Mom's busy."

"Well, it's a big house, Ellie. Besides, I'll be in the dark room. She has no use for that."

"No, Jimmy, you don't understand. I mean, Mom's... well, you see she has... company."

Ellie watched Jimmy's expression intently; she wanted to see if he got jealous. But Jimmy merely looked taken aback for a moment, then his eyes cleared and he laughed.

"Well, good for Maggie," Jimmy said and shrugged. "It's about time she got her feet wet again. Don't worry about me. I won't get in the way of your mom and her 'company.' Now what's the matter?"

"You just shouldn't go up to the house," Ellie temporized and now Jimmy came back over to her, his expression darkening and a look of suspicion entering his eyes.

"Why not?"

"Mom's privacy?" Ellie suggested.

"What do you think—I'm going to barge in on her? Look, you know how sharp our hearing is. Wherever your mom and her boyfriend are, I'll stay well away from them."

"Jimmy, no, don't go to the house!" Ellie screamed when he headed for the door again.

"Ellie, what is the matter with you?" Jimmy demanded. "Give me one good reason I shouldn't go up there."

Ellie sighed. She hadn't wanted to be the one to tell Jimmy this, but she couldn't see any way short of a physical force she didn't have to keep Jimmy from going up to the house. "You shouldn't go up there because . . . because you won't like Mom's company."

"How would you know?" Jimmy asked and then his eyes narrowed with grim, nervous apprehension. "Ellie, who does Maggie have in the house?"

"My father," Ellie shrugged helplessly.

"Your father?!" Jimmy exploded and then uttered a vile obscenity under his breath. "Jesus Christ—Simon Baldevar is back?! Fuck! Did you see him? Has he tried to hurt you? You mean to tell me your mother's alone with that monster while you've had me here? What's the matter with you?"

"Don't you call my father a monster!" Ellie screamed back, insulted by the slur on Simon, as well as Jimmy's accusatory tone with her. "Mom's alone with him because she wants to be alone with him. She's waited all my life for him to come back."

"No, she hasn't," Jimmy argued, his expression one of disbelief battling with a kind of furious certainty. "How do you know Maggie's waited for him? Did she tell you that?"

"Of course she did." Ellie began but Jimmy, with a roar of fury that made her ears ring, stalked out of the house.

"Sonofabitch... that lying little..." Ellie heard Jimmy muttering to himself as she screamed at him to wait and struggled to catch up to him.

"Jimmy! Jimmy, wait! Please don't go up there. Let's talk about it..m."

Jimmy turned around and said in a low, hate-filled growl unlike anything Ellie had ever heard from him before, "This has nothing to do with you. Get back in your house and stay there until I come back. Don't try to follow me. I need to speak to your mother and I don't want you there when I do it. Understand?" Jimmy didn't even wait for a reply but turned on his heel and headed for the main house.

Ellie watched him go uncertainly. She wasn't going to try and stop him again but she didn't know if maybe she should call Mom and tell her about the storm front about to hit the house.

What was Jimmy going to do? Tell Mom off, get in a fight with Daddy? No, Mom would stop them before they came to blows.

Ellie shrugged and took Jimmy's advice, going into the guesthouse and shutting the door. By the time she reached Mom, Jimmy would be up there anyway. There was nothing Ellie could do now but wait for Jimmy to come back.

Besides, Jimmy was right—this did have nothing to do with her. Ellie might not know exactly what Jimmy's rage was about but she did know it concerned events that happened before she was born.

Not wanting to dwell on what might be going on at the main house, Ellie instead thought Jimmy had definitely tried to kiss her. Now all she had to do was think of a way to get him to try again, only this time she wouldn't let him pull away.

Chapter Four

As always, the name Simon Baldevar had a near magical effect on Jimmy, transforming him from a man into an unthinking lunatic who had only one objective—kill the sick sonofabitch that had ruined his life.

Transforming me was the biggest mistake you ever made, motherfucker, Jimmy thought at his unseen enemy as he cut through the dunes to reach the house quicker. *I'm not some puny mortal you can push around anymore. I'm a vampire and that means I'm finally strong enough to put you in the ground where you belong now that you've crawled out from whatever rock you've been hiding under for seventeen years.*

Why did he come back, Jimmy's still functioning part of his mind asked. Can't you see that none of this makes any sense? Maggie's supposed to hate him for abandoning her and Ellie. What brought him back?

Something was very wrong. First, Ellie didn't seem to hate him at all, like you'd expect someone to hate a deadbeat father. Instead, she defended the prick. And Maggie... what about Maggie, for Christ's sake? Why would she jump into bed with someone she's supposed to despise?

Well, Ellie had to be wrong about that, that's all there was to it. Jimmy absolutely refused to believe Maggie still had any interest in that monster. She must have lied to Ellie so the poor kid wouldn't grow up knowing what kind of evil degenerate her father was. Yes, that was it. Maggie didn't miss or love Simon Baldevar, no matter what she told Ellie. No doubt Maggie was fighting Baldevar right now, telling him to get lost. Jimmy had better hurry up so he could give Maggie whatever help she needed to get rid of him.

"What the hell?" Jimmy said aloud as the torn remains of a pair of blue jeans rolled past his feet. Jimmy picked them up and was immediately assaulted by an obscene psychic residue that proved beyond a shadow of a doubt Ellie was not wrong about Maggie and Simon Baldevar.

Jimmy balled up the torn jeans and strode toward Maggie's car, his expression that of an angry housewife clutching her husband's lipstick-smeared shirt. Here was the scene of the crime... for Maggie letting that dirty bastard touch her was nothing but a crime in Jimmy's mind. Jimmy focused his eyes on the hood of the car and saw a slight imprint that would have been invisible to mortal eyes... that of the very fine, very rounded ass his hands used to know well.

So after all these years of treating Jimmy like some sexless neuter, Simon Baldevar had only to show up at the door and Maggie got so hot she couldn't even wait to get in the house but did him right on her fucking car! Goddamn that lying, two-faced slut and her prim-mouthed rejections to hell!

This had nothing to do with jealousy, Jimmy told himself. He'd long ago put Maggie and her inexplicable denials behind him. What else could he do—spend eternity weeping and whining after her? No way! Fall off the horse, you get right back on and that's just what Jimmy had done. It was nothing short of amazing what the Nikon did for his sex life.

So Jimmy had made a new life for himself, though he never fell in love again, and was convinced he'd have no trouble with Maggie doing the same. As far as Jimmy was concerned, she could lay the New York Mets from the manager down to the batboy and he wouldn't blink an eye. But take up with Simon Baldevar?! Was Maggie out of her mind?

She must be, always had been when it came to Baldevar. Maggie O'Neill, the smart, sharp, ballsy woman he knew and loved got her brains turned to jelly by that asshole. It was nothing short of amazing the way the creep brainwashed her. Whatever mind-trip Baldevar did on Maggie, he made Jim Jones and Charles Manson look like bush leaguers.

Well, no more, Jimmy vowed and kicked open the front door, but he pulled back immediately in a combination of fright and confusion at how different the house felt. Usually the first thing Jimmy felt when he walked into the foyer was a cheerful openness embracing him, almost like a spiritual welcome mat. But that had been obliterated by a noxious, malevolent presence that made Jimmy feel insignificant and small, almost like he was standing in the presence of a god—a god that despised him and wanted to destroy him. Jimmy gulped nervously, wondering how he could have forgotten Simon Baldevar's aura—that dark, choking vibration he emitted and the way it always made Jimmy want to turn tail and run.

No! No, Goddammit . . . not this time! Jimmy meant to finish what that bastard had started with him eighteen years ago. Jimmy moved away from the stairs and that foul presence, but this was a strategic retreat; he had to get a weapon before he attacked Baldevar.

Jimmy hurried into the kitchen, gritting his teeth against the breathy little moans he could hear from upstairs. As he selected the longest, sharpest meat cleaver from the knife rack, Jimmy told himself Maggie's submission would work to his advantage. While Baldevar was busy screwing Maggie, Jimmy would sneak up on the couple and cut Baldevar's head off.

Jimmy brought the cleaver down on the marble countertop with all his strength, watching with grim satisfaction as it sliced through the solid block with one swift blow. Compared with marble, a little flesh and bone would present no challenge to this wickedly sharp blade.

Taking a deep breath, Jimmy ran up the stairs on tiptoes, trying to make as little noise as possible and reviewing Maggie's lessons on concealing your presence. Jimmy had little experience in camouflaging himself from another vampire but he figured his target was too engrossed in sex to notice him anyway.

Jimmy glanced at the double doors leading to Maggie's suite and called on his telekinetic power to make them swing open silently. Rushing through the sitting room, he saw that her bedroom door was open and ran past it soundlessly, the cleaver poised high over his head.

Jimmy stopped short, unable to take his eyes off Maggie sprawled in the center of the immense bed next to Simon

Baldevar, their naked bodies illuminated by a roomful of scented candles and moonlight filtering in from the large dormer windows.

I forgot how beautiful she is, was Jimmy's first thought at the sight of Maggie lying on her side, her red lips parted to reveal a darting pink tongue while her auburn eyelashes fluttered wildly against cloudy green eyes. It had been so long since Jimmy had seen Maggie like this, so dreamily relaxed and luscious, that his first reaction wasn't rage but a brief stab of desire until he got a clearer look at what the couple was doing.

Sickened but unable to look away, Jimmy watched Maggie grant Baldevar liberties he'd never even thought to ask for. Look at the way she let the depraved fiend tear into her neck while he rammed into her from behind. Was this why she'd rejected Jimmy? Good, clean sex didn't satisfy her—only sick shit like this turned her on?

Disgusted, Jimmy watched a thin scarlet line dribble down Maggie's neck, falling on the long, elegantly manicured hand fondling her left breast as Baldevar's other hand sank into the tight red curls between her legs. Jimmy couldn't be sure whether it was Baldevar's hand or fangs that made the masochistic bitch scream out, "Yes, yes... oh God, yes, Simon!"

At her ecstatic gasp, Jimmy screamed, "Whore!" at the top of his lungs and rushed toward the bed, brandishing the cleaver like a maniac but now it wasn't just Simon Baldevar he meant to kill.

Maggie's eyes flew open, revealing dismay and a surprised hurt that almost made Jimmy want to take back the vicious word reverberating around them.

Lord Baldevar raised his eyes a fraction though his fangs remained firmly lodged in Maggie's neck and glared at Jimmy, looking like a lion poised over the carcass of a felled zebra, his eyes sending an unmistakable message of deadly menace and cold desire to finish his meal.

Then the yellow eyes flashed and Jimmy felt something like an invisible hand seize the cleaver from his hand and make it calmly sail to a nightstand by the side of the bed.

Confused by the swift turn of events, Jimmy then felt that same unseen force slam into his gut like a monstrous sucker punch. He doubled over in pain and gasped for breath, the wind knocked out of him by the vicious attack.

I might allow you a painless death if you leave this room at once and cause no further delay to my pleasure, Baldevar's voice hissed in Jimmy's mind and on the heels of that unwelcome message came another, this one urgent but annoyed—*Just get out of here, Jimmy!*

With pleasure, you lying slut, Jimmy threw back meanly at Maggie and screamed at the blinding pain that filled his head. He clutched his temples and lurched out of the bedroom, breathing a sigh of relief when the pain vanished—obviously Baldevar was more interested in getting his rocks off than giving Jimmy an aneurysm or whatever he'd just done to him.

Careful not think anything else derogatory about Maggie while in Baldevar's immediate vicinity, Jimmy staggered down the stairs and threw open the front door, his only thought that he had to get as far away from that bedroom and its hideous secret as possible.

There was no need to ever go back inside that whore's house; he'd ask Lee to pack up his belongings and send them wherever. Jimmy had no idea where he was going, knew only that he intended to leave and never return. He didn't think he could ever look at Maggie again without remembering her moaning and thrashing while that bastard rutted behind her. Jesus Christ! Jimmy was no prude but what Maggie allowed Baldevar to do to her made S&M look as innocent and wholesome as a picnic in Central Park. Who in their right mind would want to feed and fuck at the same time? In Jimmy's mind, blood was blood and sex was sex and never, never the two should meet.

Jimmy kicked up the cold, dark sand, trying without success to reconcile the wanton creature that apparently craved the kind of sick, repulsive games Simon Baldevar liked to play in bed with the woman who had been his mainstay the past twenty-five years, his friend and teacher.

Fuck! Jimmy scooped up a few seashells and hurled them at the water. What was Maggie doing with that sonofabitch? Even putting aside all Baldevar had done to her, didn't Maggie have enough respect for her friendship with Jimmy to turn the despicable creep away and not jump into bed with him? Jimmy knew damned well if anyone ever hurt Charles or Lee like Simon had hurt Jimmy, Maggie would use every resource at her disposal to destroy them, not fuck them.

There was the explanation right there. Maggie could screw Simon Baldevar because she didn't value Jimmy's friendship. She'd let Jimmy live with her out of some sense of pity and obligation, just like that bastard Baldevar had told him.

Jimmy swallowed hard against the lump in his throat and brushed at his eyes impatiently. He had to be strong now and not cry when he thought of how alone he was now that he no longer had Maggie's friendship to rely on. Don't think of the lonely, miserable future playing itself out before him.

"Jimmy?"

Jimmy whirled around at the sweet, concerned voice and saw Ellie standing behind him, clutching a steaming mug she held outstretched toward him.

"I felt how upset you were," Ellie said and gestured to the mug. "I brought you some tea."

"Tea," Jimmy muttered and gave her a half-smile. Ellie's ability to ferret out his distress was hardly surprising, though he wondered if she took her extraordinary abilities for granted, growing up as she had in this house of vampires where such talent was the rule, not the exception. Ellie might not be a vampire, but Jimmy had never been convinced she was simply mortal either—not with that extrasensory power that seemed to grow stronger with each passing year. "You're Irish through and through, kid. Tea— the great cure-all to everything from a broken heart to a gunshot wound."

"Is your heart broken?" Ellie asked gravely and Jimmy saw some disturbing emotion flicker briefly in her eyes but it passed so quickly Jimmy wasn't certain of what he'd seen.

Jimmy shrugged. He'd never involve Ellie in his problems with Maggie, make her choose between him and the mother she loved so well—the mother that Jimmy, even in his hurt and fury, had to admit deserved her daughter's love.

Clucking over Jimmy like a mother hen with a hurt chick, Ellie led him the brief distance to her cottage and settled him in a comfortable deck chair facing the beach before she continued her interrogation. "What's the matter, Jimmy? Why did you get so mad when I told you Daddy was here and storm away? You didn't have a fight with him, did you?"

"Don't you ever call him that!"Jimmy snapped, almost spilling the scalding liquid all over himself. "That sick, lowlife dirtbag is not your father. Where the hell has he been for seventeen years? Lee's the one that hung your pictures on the refrigerator and helped you with your math and patched your knees up when you fell while the Earl of Assholes was off doing God knows what."

"Daddy had to take care of Mikal," Ellie said, sounding puzzled and a little uncertain of Jimmy's intelligence. "Otherwise, he would have raised me with Mom. Why are you making it sound like he went off gallivanting without a care in the world when you know the responsibility he had to Mikal?"

"Mikal?" Jimmy frowned, wondering if this new name explained Lord Baldevar's seventeen-year disappearance. "Who the hell is Mikal?"

It was Ellie's turn to look confused. "Didn't Mom tell you?"

"Tell me what?"Jimmy demanded, wondering with a sinking feeling just what Maggie had been keeping from him besides her apparently undiminished attraction to Simon Baldevar.

"That Mikal is my..." Ellie grabbed the cordless phone shrilling by her side. "Hello?"

"Mom!" Ellie glowed and Jimmy nearly chewed through the ceramic mug in an attempt to keep his mean-spirited thoughts on Maggie to himself. "What? Oh, yeah, sure. See you in a few minutes."

Ellie hung up and turned to Jimmy. "Mom wants me to come up to the house. She says she and Daddy have to talk to me."

"Oh, no!" Jimmy exclaimed and grabbed Ellie. "You're not going anywhere near that sonofabitch!"

What kind of self-pitying asshole was Jimmy, thinking he'd lost everyone that mattered to him? He still had this bright, beautiful girl he'd given his heart to the first time she'd put her chubby little arms around his neck. Hadn't Jimmy vowed that he'd never let anyone—especially Simon Baldevar—harm her?

No, Jimmy wouldn't leave after all. . . not by himself, at any rate. He'd stay right here, stick to Ellie's side like glue. If he left, the only things standing between whatever sick plans Baldevar had for his only child were a mortal doctor, Charles Tarleton, and her weak-willed mother.

"Stop it!" Ellie twisted out of his arms, her face a mask of indignant fury. "You stop running my father down! He's a good man... Mom told me so!"

"A good man?" Jimmy roared and let out a withering laugh. "Your mother's got one warped view of goodness if she thinks there's anything good about that piece of shit! Let me tell you about your good father, Ellie. Your mom ever tell you how he turned her into a vampire? He starved her for blood and then made her feed off her mortal fiancé . . . that's your good father! Here's another example of sainthood... when your mother first tried to leave him, Baldevar's reaction was to beat her to within an inch of her life, drain her of blood so she was defenseless and then nail her to a fucking roof so she'd be destroyed by the sunrise unless she begged his forgiveness. You want more goodness? Your mom lived forty years thinking that garbage was dead and out of her life so she found another man—me! And when Baldevar came back for her and saw us together, he put me on a rack to pay me back for touching his woman and ripped my fingernails out with a hot pincer! Does that sound like a good man to you?"

Ellie sank down into the deck chair, her face devoid of color and eyes so wide and blank Jimmy thought she might have gone into shock. Remorse stabbed at him... what the hell was he doing, all but clubbing the poor kid with his venomous words? Sure, Ellie couldn't go on with the sugarcoated view of Simon Baldevar Maggie had given her but Jimmy should never have blurted out the truth like that, hit Ellie with it so hard and fast.

"He changed," Ellie finally said and glared up at Jimmy, no longer a bemused child but an avenging angel. "I know my mother; she'd have nothing to do with someone like you described. She said Daddy changed after I was born."

Sure he changed, Jimmy snorted to himself. He changed so much he just tried to kill me—again—when I came on him and Maggie fucking.

"You don't like him," Ellie said and gave Jimmy a level stare that nearly made him suck in his breath with surprise. When the hell had Ellie grown up on him?

There was no way around it; the little girl he knew and loved was gone, replaced by a young woman with an exquisite, beautiful face that combined all her parents' best features.

But the change went deeper than her looks—though God knows Jimmy and just about every man in that bar had responded to her looks. What made Ellie an adult was the poise she carried herself with now, an assurance in herself that the awkward, gangling teenager Jimmy had seen a year ago lacked.

"I can accept that," Ellie continued, speaking with a calm determination that was also new. "I know Mom went out with you while she and Daddy were separated so its natural you and Daddy would never like each other. And she did tell me that she left Daddy because he was too dominating..."

"But then she and Daddy made up," Ellie's tactful but inaccurate version of the truth continued. "Now he's back and they want to see me and I'm going, Jimmy. You can't stop me anymore than I could stop you before. I don't care what you think of Daddy. All I know is he's been very good to me since I met him tonight. Lee likes him and Mom loves him. I'm going to see him now, Jimmy, and I plan to see a lot more of him and you can't stop me."

Jimmy stared into the clear green eyes filled with unwavering resolve and saw the only way to detain Ellie was to tie her down or keep her in check with his power and he'd never do that to her.

"Fine," Jimmy nodded and felt a small spurt of satisfaction at the surprise in Ellie's expression. "But I'm going with you."

"No arguing with Daddy," Ellie countered, her sweet looks clashing with the grim prison matron expression on her face as she glared up at him.

At hearing Ellie call that vicious cocksucker "Daddy," Jimmy had to silently count to ten before he could even trust himself to reply. "Look, Ellie, I'm not going up there to start anything with him. I just want to look out for you, okay?"

"Okay," Ellie smiled softly and shyly held out her hand for Jimmy to take as they started toward the main house.

Jimmy stared down at the long, slender hand, remembering that odd moment of contact between them after dinner. What the hell had that been about? One minute he and Ellie were talking and laughing like always and the next he was staring at her full pink lips and limpid green eyes beckoning him to come closer...

Jimmy mentally shook off the unwanted thoughts, telling himself he'd felt no more attraction to her than any man would feel at seeing a beautiful woman. He hadn't wanted to kiss Ellie before. No way he'd have such thoughts about a girl he'd known all her life, whose diapers he'd changed, for God's sake!

And Ellie hadn't felt anything toward him, Jimmy thought as he took her hand, ignoring the quivering tension in her grip. She was nervous about seeing Baldevar; she hadn't felt any kind of charge at the contact of her palm against his anymore than Jimmy had.

Mind out of the gutter, Delacroix, Jimmy told himself and firmly squelched the uncomfortable, downright wrong thoughts spinning around his brain. Jimmy was just upset about Maggie and he'd been without a woman for more than six months now. His reaction to Ellie was reflex, nothing more, and it would never happen again. What Jimmy had to concentrate on now was facing down Simon Baldevar for the second time in one night.

Jimmy inhaled and readied himself for battle though he didn't think even Baldevar was depraved enough to kill someone in front of his daughter. From what Ellie had told him, Baldevar obviously wanted her to have a good impression of him so he'd pretend to be whatever he thought Ellie wanted in a father. Decent, honest, loving . . . qualities as foreign to Baldevar as they'd be to Lucifer.

But Jimmy had no intention of letting him dupe Ellie. When they got up to the house, Jimmy was going to provoke Baldevar until the fiend ripped off his false mask of geniality and showed his daughter his true face. Once Ellie saw Simon Baldevar for what he really was, he'd lose whatever tenuous hold he had on

Ellie's heart. Then Simon Baldevar would be out of Ellie's—and Jimmy's—life for good.

"Simon, stop that," Jimmy heard Maggie giggle as he and Ellie approached the house. "Ellie will be here any minute now. What would she think if she saw us on top of each other?"

"She'd think her parents love each other very much," Baldevar replied in an infuriatingly self-satisfied tone. "And what is this Ellie business? I gave our daughter the fine queen's name of Elizabeth."

Baldevar had named Ellie? Why would someone who was disgusted with his mortal offspring name her? Face it, Jimmy, a voice told him contemptuously. Maggie lied to you. Baldevar loves Ellie, at least as much a sicko like that is capable of loving anyone. But if that were so, why had he disappeared after she was born?

"You know—at least you know if you read the letters I sent to Adelaide—that Ellie started talking at six months," Maggie was saying to Baldevar with her usual pride at Ellie's many accomplishments. "But no matter how hard she tried, she just couldn't say Elizabeth. Her name came out sounding like Ellie Bed—it was the cutest thing. So we started calling her Ellie Bed and then Ellie for short."

"You should be proud, Meghann. You've raised our daughter to be an extraordinary young woman."

"What kind of young man have you raised Mikal to be?" Maggie replied and Jimmy's ears prickled. There was that name again. Was Mikal some fledging vampire of Baldevar's? Even so, why should Maggie care about him and what did this Mikal have to do with Baldevar leaving Ellie and Maggie?

Ellie started for the French doors leading to the study but Jimmy pulled her back and made a shushing gesture—he wanted to find out who Mikal was.

Ellie scowled at the eavesdropping but Jimmy implored her with his eyes and she acquiesced, though she looked reluctant and uneasy. Now Jimmy guarded their auras as Maggie and Charles taught him, pretending a thick, black blanket covered him and Ellie from head to toe.

"Elizabeth's mind seems impenetrable," Baldevar said in reply, completely ignoring Maggie's question about the unknown Mikal, to Jimmy's disappointment.

"Simon Baldevar, how dare you pry into your own daughter's thoughts!" Maggie rebuked and Jimmy felt a slight measure of approval at her disapproving tone. So Maggie wasn't completely won over by Baldevar after all.

"I did not pry," the vampire replied, apparently unruffled by her criticism. "I am merely intrigued by that wall that seems to protect her mind. Has it always been that way?"

"I can see Ellie's thoughts to a certain degree," Maggie explained. "But it is difficult—nearly impossible if she makes attempts to block me like she did in the experiments Charles and I used to conduct."

"What kind of experiments?" Jimmy heard Baldevar ask with intense interest.

"Simple things, really. Ellie holding a playing card while we tried to identify it by reading her mind. But Charles and Jimmy never saw anything. I was able to identify the card roughly thirty percent of the time. And I always know Ellie's moods, but I've often thought that had more to do with a mother-daughter bond than vampirism. What Charles, Lee, and I always wanted to know is whether Mikal has the same gift for concealment."

"Meghann! What is this?" Baldevar asked in annoyance but something in his tone made Jimmy think his pique was just an attempt to change the subject. Whoever this Mikal was, Baldevar obviously didn't want to talk about him.

"*Nighttime World,*" Maggie said calmly. "It's one of Jimmy's collections. He's an excellent photographer—people are calling him another Ansel Adams."

Jimmy smiled at the praise, feeling much more benevolent toward Maggie, as Baldevar ripped into her.

"Indeed?" Baldevar queried acidly. "What people has that fool of a vampire exposed himself to? At the very least, any book involves a publisher, editor . . . perhaps an agent. Does the imbecile tour this book, promote himself so we must all stand on the precipice of discovery? And you! Have you forgotten everything I taught you of the discretion necessary to our existence? A coffee-table book accessible to millions is hardly discreet. How could you allow him to seek publication? Why didn't you guide him to a more circumspect diversion?"

Now Jimmy was ready to stamp into the study, but Ellie grabbed his forearm, her eyes sending an eloquent message to calm down before he went inside.

"I encouraged Jimmy because he has a brilliant talent," Maggie said heatedly. "And because he deserved something positive in his life after all you put him through. As for discretion, neither Jimmy nor I are the fools you think we are. Jimmy does no promotion whatsoever—no signings or speaking engagements, radio interviews, nothing. He won't even do gallery shows though people beg him to do them all the time. Even so, his books do well. Do you know he's rich now in his own right?"

"As opposed to leeching off your assets?" Baldevar replied sarcastically, appearing unimpressed by Jimmy's achievements. "Still, that you have developed Mr. Delacroix at all is a minor miracle. I truly did not think you would be able to make any kind of vampire out of such poor material."

"Do you have any idea how insecure you sound?" Maggie retorted before Jimmy could kick the glass out of the French doors and use a shard to impale Baldevar. "An intelligent, artistic, sensitive man is not poor material. But I must say, I'm surprised you're even taking it this well that Charles and I decided to mentor Jimmy or that I let him come back here after you left."

So was Jimmy—why wasn't the vampire lighting into Maggie for taking Jimmy back?

The answer came immediately. "I would have been angered had you broken our wedding vows and allowed the dolt back into your bed. But I knew I could trust your honor, Meghann. Taking Jimmy Delacroix under your wing was inspired. As long as our enemies saw you with that fool, it would be the final assurance they needed that our relationship was no more. All the time of my unfortunate absence, Mr. Delacroix has served quite ably in his role of decoy but now we may rid ourselves of him once and for all."

"Go straight to hell, you overbearing, arrogant motherfucker!" Jimmy screamed and stormed into the study, Ellie making a feeble effort to hold him back. "I'm not your fucking decoy and if you want to get rid of me, you'll have to kill me! Why don't you try, and show Ellie what you really are?"

"Whatever I am, I have never been called a snoop," Lord Baldevar said and gave Jimmy a cool, mocking grin. "I was wondering when you would decide to step inside and cease lurking at the door like a beggar appealing for alms."

Dismissing Jimmy with an arrogant turn of his back, Baldevar turned to Ellie and gave her a warm grin. "Good evening, again."

"Hi, Daddy," Ellie said uncertainly and ran to Maggie. "Mom!"

"Sweetie," Maggie breathed, letting her tall daughter grab her and spin her around before they sat down together on the couch.

Look at her, Jimmy thought sourly, glaring as Maggie pushed a strand of hair off Ellie's face. No longer was Maggie the stuff porn movies were made of; now she wore a demure brown sweater, floral silk skirt and her wet hair was neatly held back with a tortoiseshell hair comb. From wanton whore to wholesome schoolgirl looking younger than her daughter in the space of an hour—Maggie wasn't a vampire at all, she was a witch.

The witch fixed Jimmy with an icy green stare before her expression softened and she thought to him, *I'm sorry you had to see us like that, Jimmy. I meant to explain to you...*

How could you possibly explain spreading your legs for that... Jimmy groped in his mind for a suitable pejorative when a foul voice intruded into his consciousness.

Your jealousy will be the signature on your death warrant if you do not cease berating my consort.

Not even deigning to respond to Baldevar, Jimmy decided if he couldn't kill the bastard, it was time to see if there were other ways to cut him down.

"How was your class tonight, Maggie?" Jimmy asked in a pleasant tone, like there'd been no attempted double homicide earlier.

"Fine," Maggie replied with equal civility, though her wary eyes followed his movements like she would those of a rattlesnake.

"Let me give you a topic for your next class. Say one of your budding counselors sees a woman that was involved in a relationship with a sadistic creep that beat her regularly and raped her whenever the mood took him. For some bizarre reason, the ditz wants to get back together with the asshole—after he dumped her. How do you deal with a patient like that?"

Ellie shifted uncomfortably next to her mother, glancing between Maggie and Baldevar to see their reaction to Jimmy's thinly veiled gauntlet. Maggie's lips tightened slightly and Baldevar's only reaction was to turn to Maggie, waiting for her response with the passive interest of someone listening to a stimulating discussion at a cocktail party.

"First, I would advise them never to call a patient a ditz," Maggie said dryly. "Then I would remind them that if you pass judgment on a patient, there is a very good chance they'll abandon therapy out of a sense of shame and your role as counselor is hardly to bully your patient out of seeking help. Now, for the scenario you presented, background questions must be answered. Why did the parties separate? What does the patient feel she'd gain by resuming the relationship with her abuser? Has he sought therapy? If the patient has valid reasons for believing the abuse won't be continued and she feels she can forgive the past, I wouldn't automatically advise her to reject her partner."

"So someone should only reconcile with their partner because any sort of abuse is over?" Ellie questioned.

"Those are the only circumstances under which I'd agree to reconciliation," Maggie replied and Ellie sent Jimmy a triumphant glance that almost matched the smirk on her father's face.

Bullshit, Jimmy thought at Maggie, not wanting to yell at her in front of Ellie. *What I saw upstairs looked pretty goddamn painful and degrading. Would you want Ellie in that sort of relationship?*

What Simon and I do for pleasure is our business, Jimmy, Maggie scowled at him. *I've made my peace with Simon and I'd advise you to do the same.* Maggie glanced meaningfully at Ellie. *She's very dear to him... he'll leave you alive if for no other*

91

reason than just to please her. Please Jimmy, don't antagonize him any further. I have enough on my mind. . .

And between your legs, Jimmy thought rudely, and then glared at Baldevar. *You can't kill me for my thoughts unless you want to blow your Father of the Year carver.*

So you no longer seek protection from Meghann but now hide behind a child's skirts? I would not expect such cowardly actions even from one such as you, Mr. Delacroix.

Flummoxed, Jimmy could only gape helplessly while Baldevar crossed the room, sitting on an ottoman next to Meghann and Ellie.

"Daughter, I must speak with you and your mother on a matter of grave importance," Baldevar said, taking Ellie's hand in his.

"I want Jimmy to stay," Ellie said and even Jimmy couldn't see any shadow of disturbance or annoyance in Baldevar's inscrutable expression.

"Certainly," Lord Baldevar said calmly and turned to Jimmy. "Please take a seat, Mr. Delacroix. Perhaps you'd like a drink before we begin?"

Jimmy sat in a loveseat far from Baldevar, ignoring the subtle dig at his mortal drinking problem. "I'm fine."

I rather doubt that, the vampire said, continuing his clever game of only insulting Jimmy out of Ellie's mortal scope, before he spoke aloud again.

I'll be damned, Jimmy thought in wonder. The sonofabitch is beating me at my own game! Like Jimmy, Baldevar was trying to taunt Jimmy into attacking him in front of Ellie, so he'd lose her respect and love.

"Elizabeth," Lord Baldevar said to his daughter. "I have come home, not only because I've missed you and your mother, but because you must transform immediately."

"What?" Ellie stammered confusedly while Maggie leapt to her feet and Jimmy came over to Ellie, wrapping his arms around her protectively—Simon Baldevar would transform Ellie over his dead body.

"Who do you think you are," Maggie cried indignantly, "to just come back and demand Ellie transform without even consulting her as to whether she wants to! You didn't even have the basic respect for me, her mother, to ask my opinion. You don't make a decision like that and then expect the rest of us to follow you blindly. If Ellie ever transforms, it will be when she makes that choice as an informed adult, knowing the drawbacks as well as the advantages to being a vampire. But she will not transform now... she's only seventeen! Ellie has a full life ahead of her, a promising career that I will not allow you or anyone else to rip away from her by taking the sun from her like you did to me!"

Jimmy wanted to leap up and applaud. All right, Maggie slept with the asshole... so what? She was still willing to go the mat for her daughter that was far more important than anything she did in bed with Simon Baldevar.

"What do you mean, 'if' Elizabeth transforms?" Baldevar demanded incredulously. "Do you think I would sire a child and then allow mortality to steal her away? Of course Elizabeth will transform and take her rightful place in our world as my heir. Stop shouting, Meghann! There is no time for petty squabbling. Elizabeth must transform, not merely because it is her birthright, but because it is the only way to protect her from the threat Mikal presents to her life."

"Why would Mikal threaten Ellie?" Maggie cried just as Jimmy jumped up and demanded plaintively, "Who the hell is Mikal?"

Lord Baldevar's eyes cut between Maggie and Jimmy, finally settling on Maggie with pleased smugness. "I owe you an apology, Meghann. You have not forgotten discretion at all but behaved with admirable prudence. But the time for subterfuge draws to a close. Please feel free to tell Mr. Delacroix who Mikal is."

"Jimmy," Maggie said in a faltering, uncertain voice, her cheeks flaming red and her eyes filled with guilty discomfit. "I haven't been honest with you and for that, I've always been sorry. Whatever anger you feel, I deserve. All I ask is that you allow me to explain myself."

Jimmy nodded dumbly, wondering what secrets Maggie had kept from him.

"Ellie isn't my only child," Maggie said, the words tumbling out of her mouth as though they were something toxic she had to purge herself of before they poisoned her. "She's just my only daughter, my mortal child. When I was pregnant, I was carrying twins. One was Ellie and the other was my son, Mikal."

"You have a son?" Jimmy was too amazed to be angry. "What happened to him?"

"He was born a vampire," Maggie said, her green eyes tearing up and Jimmy thought he might finally have the answer to that inexplicable longing he'd sensed in her all these years—she'd missed her boy.

"You may remember that I once told you Simon believed the offspring of two vampires would have all our strengths and none of our flaws, that when the child grew up, it would be able to walk in daylight

"Our enemies were frightened of Simon ever having that power, obtaining it by drinking a small portion of his son's blood. We knew they'd try to kill Mikal if they found out about him. So Simon and I separated the children. Ellie remained with me while Simon took Mikal into hiding. In a way, having twins was a godsend because everyone expected a single birth from my pregnancy and assumed that was Ellie, a mere mortal. That's why Simon left... to make everyone believe he had no use for Ellie while he raised Mikal. He had to keep Mikal hidden until he was old enough to defend himself against anyone that would try to destroy him."

"And you thought I'd try to destroy your precious son?" Jimmy cried, the full impact of Maggie's confession and its betrayal of their friendship hitting him far harder than Baldevar's assault had in the bedroom. "Why the hell didn't you tell me all this when I came back?"

Numbly, Jimmy remembered that night when he came back after a year of floundering around by himself, trying to find a way to cope with the vampirism Baldevar had forced on him. He'd come to Maggie believing she was his friend and now he found out she'd taken him in so she could use him to carry on her ruse that Ellie was her only child and Baldevar had disappeared for God knows where.

"Jimmy, I couldn't tell you..."

"Why not?" Jimmy cried, ashamed of the tears he couldn't control, wanting to scream out his agony when he saw the pity in Maggie's eyes and the compassion shining in Ellie's. "How could you keep something like that from me? How could you lie to my face for seventeen years? My God, Maggie, you put me in the same category with the kind of sick piece of shit that would kill a baby because it might grow up to hurt them? How could you do that, how could you not tell me you have a son? Don't you trust me at all? Didn't I ever mean anything to you?"

"Jimmy..." Maggie said and tried to take his hands but Jimmy flung her off and ran out the French doors, not stopping until he reached the tide line on the shore.

"Damn you, damn you, damn you!"Jimmy screamed at the aloof moon staring down at him. Foamy black water lapped at his feet and ruined his shoes but Jimmy was oblivious to everything except a tiny voice whispering to him that the worst mistake he'd ever made in his life was the night he returned to this house and Maggie O'Neill.

Chapter Five

February 14, 2000

Jimmy Delacroix puffed uneasily on his cigarette, automatically hunching over to avoid the harsh, biting wind blowing in from the Atlantic Ocean. Cold didn't affect him much anymore but the awful low-pitched moan of the winter wind made him shiver anyway—a mental reaction instead of physical. The howling wind brought back all too plainly memories of the night he'd escaped the shuttered house a few yards in front of him. When Jimmy thought of that terrible night, his first memory was always the wind keening outside the tiny room where he'd regained awareness after spending almost a year in a stupor, brought on after he'd been transformed into a vampire by Simon Baldevar.

Baldevar! Jimmy spat on the sand—even thinking the name of the warped psycho who'd transformed him and deliberately botched the process so Jimmy would spend eternity as a mindless vegetable left a sour taste in his mouth. He stomped the butt of his cigarette beneath his boot and then cupped his hands around a silver Zippo lighter to light a fresh cigarette, reflecting on how thoroughly that bastard had ruined his life.

Before Lord Baldevar, life had finally been taking a turn for the better. It took time, but Jimmy was finally getting over the death of his young wife and infant son, killed by a demented vampire. Everybody thought Jimmy was crazy when he insisted he'd been a petrified witness while Amy and Jay were mauled by the thing... everybody but Maggie O'Neill, the enigmatic redhead he'd met eight years before.

She'd picked him up in one of the many bars he frequented, unable to face the night and the things he knew were out there unless he drank himself into insensibility. At first, Jimmy only thought he'd been lucky enough to find a pretty, funny, sexy-as-hell girl who could match him drink for drink. But it turned out Maggie had her own secret that she revealed when he told her what had happened to Amy and Jay. Maggie believed Jimmy's story because she was a vampire, transformed against her will by Simon Baldevar in 1944.

After getting over his shock, Jimmy moved in with Maggie, allowing her to teach him all about vampires and their vulnerabilities so he could avenge Amy and Jay by slaying the sick creatures that murdered their human prey during the day. Maggie did nothing of the sort, telling Jimmy any vampire could feed without resorting to murder, if they had the will to do so.

Those were good years, Jimmy remembered sadly, the six years they lived together and healed each other. With Maggie by his side, Jimmy could face the dark without getting blind drunk. As for Maggie, she told Jimmy she'd never expected to find a lover who could also be her friend; she never thought she'd trust a man again after suffering through the pain and humiliation that characterized her years with Simon Baldevar.

But then Baldevar resurfaced. It turned out he wasn't dead, as Maggie believed, killed the night she escaped him by putting a stake in his heart. No, the vampire had apparently bided his time and when he felt strong enough, he came back from the dead to reclaim Maggie and destroy anyone that tried to stop him.

Like me, Jimmy thought, a sick feeling building in the pit of his stomach when he remembered how the vampire tortured him and then, when he was on the edge of death, transformed him, leaning back and watching with immense satisfaction as Jimmy tried futilely to battle the chaos that overtook his sanity.

Goddamn him, Jimmy thought furiously and took several long strides toward the cobblestoned terrace, rage giving him the courage to face down his enemy. Goddamn that monstrous fiend to hell! Jimmy had become a catatonic simply because Simon Baldevar didn't want any competition for Maggie's affections, thinking she'd pity her mortal lover once he lost the ability to think or speak or do anything but drink blood and kill Jimmy herself to end his misery.

Jimmy snorted, thinking in that situation Maggie had gotten the better of Baldevar, telling the sonofabitch she'd abort the baby he'd impregnated her with by raping her if he didn't allow her to try to bring Jimmy back from the madness Baldevar had plunged him into.

And Maggie did fix Jimmy's mind through a combination of psychoactive drugs mixed in the blood she fed him and ceaselessly talking to him the way people did with coma victims. Awareness returned and brought with it the devastating news that he was now a vampire and had to call the creature he despised master. As if that wasn't bad enough, Jimmy had to sustain the blow of discovering Maggie and Baldevar had been lovers practically the whole time Jimmy lay mindless and unaware.

Why did she do it, Jimmy asked himself for the umpteenth time. Why would Maggie willingly embrace the monster who, according to her, ripped her away from her mortal life and thrust her into a life of sexual and spiritual bondage for thirteen years until she finally managed to get away from him? How many times had Maggie told him she hated Simon Baldevar and was fiercely glad she killed him, or thought she did?

If she was so happy to be free of Baldevar, then how the hell could she have stood before Jimmy a year ago, her body swollen with the bastard's child, tearfully confessing to Jimmy that she loved Simon Baldevar and Jimmy should just forget about her.

Jimmy, of course, had done nothing of the sort. He insisted Baldevar had used his power to warp Maggie's mind, bewitched her somehow. If Baldevar was dead, Jimmy knew Maggie would be free of his hold over her and start behaving like herself, instead of the simpering ditz Baldevar had reduced her to.

Baldevar had accepted Jimmy's challenge and they'd started to go at it but Maggie placed herself between them in an effort to stop the fight and wound up getting knocked to the floor.

Jimmy shuddered, remembering Maggie curled up on the floor, clutching her abdomen and sobbing in pain and fear as a monstrous crimson stain spread over her white nightgown. God, Jimmy had been so sure she was dying, sure that in trying to free Maggie from Baldevar he'd managed to kill her and her unborn baby.

He guessed Baldevar had been thinking along the same lines because the vampire forgot his battle with Jimmy and rushed Maggie out of the room, some mortal doctor trailing behind him as they took Maggie to an emergency surgery they'd set up within the house.

After Baldevar spirited Maggie away, Charles Tarleton, Maggie's best friend, had urged Jimmy to leave the house before Baldevar killed him, promising to contact Jimmy at his sister's house and let him know what had happened to Maggie.

Charles kept his promise, Jimmy thought and pulled a crumpled telegram from the coat pocket of his black duster, rereading the cryptic message—*Meghann is well.*

Jimmy surmised that meant she'd survived, though he had no idea what had happened to her baby. Even if Simon Baldevar was the father, Jimmy harbored no ill will toward the child and prayed Maggie hadn't lost it. Jimmy knew all too well what it was to grieve for a dead child.

Meghann is well. Jimmy scowled and returned the telegram to his pocket. Sure, she might be okay physically but as far as Jimmy was concerned, if Maggie thought she belonged with Simon Baldevar she was as far from well as you could get. Someone had to talk sense into her, get her away from the asshole. That's why Jimmy had returned to his enemy's lair, to free Maggie from Baldevar's clutches.

He'd tell Maggie he understood her reuniting with Baldevar— he'd brainwashed her, that's all. He'd explain that he wanted to start over now that they were both equal vampires and Jimmy wasn't just her boy-toy mortal.

Hey, hero, an inner voice spoke up sarcastically—the same pest that had needled Jimmy all the way to New York. *Do you think Baldevar's going to sit around twiddling his thumbs while you try to take his woman? You take another step closer to that house and pretty soon your head's gonna be on a spit.*

Jimmy swallowed nervously, knowing the voice was right— he was no match for Baldevar. No matter how much Jimmy despised Simon Baldevar, there was no denying his power and strength—he'd crushed Jimmy like a gnat every time Jimmy went up against him. That's why he'd been so cautious since he neared the estate; Jimmy's plan was to shield his presence as he'd learned to do over the past few months and only reveal himself when he caught Maggie alone.

Jimmy heard an odd whooshing sound, felt his long hair lifted by a sudden breeze and whirled around to face Charles Tarleton, clutching a wicked looking machete he held a bare centimeter from Jimmy's neck.

"Christ, Jimmy!" Charles snapped before he could say anything. He tucked the machete against his belt, reproach plain in his jet-black eyes. "What the hell are you doing, sneaking around the house and trying to camouflage your presence? My God, man, I was almost on top of you before I realized who you were... you were an inch from death!"

Despite the lecture, Jimmy felt some pride when he realized he'd been able to shield his identity from an older, more powerful vampire. But his shoulders slumped when he realized he'd had no inkling Charles was behind him, that his senses had given him no warning he was in danger.

"I wasn't hiding from you or Maggie. I just don't want Baldevar to know I'm here," Jimmy explained.

Charles gave him a disgusted look. "Simon would have felt your presence the moment you set foot in Southampton if he was here. Jimmy, you shouldn't have come here; it was a foolhardy and unnecessary risk."

"Baldevar's not here?" Jimmy perked up. "Is Maggie? I've got to see her."

"Jimmy," a light voice greeted behind him and he spun around again, this time seeing Maggie holding a baby girl dressed in a purple jumpsuit, chubby little arms encircled around her mother's neck.

Jimmy's first thought was that he could have seen this baby anywhere and known she was Maggie's child simply by looking at the spring green eyes that were the mirror image of her mother's. The baby was an adorable little thing with light brown ringlets curling under her ears, creamy skin and faint pink roses in her cheeks. He had a sudden impulse to pat one of those cheeks but held back, seeing in her expression the same wariness Jay had always displayed around strangers. Jimmy knew one sudden move toward her and the baby would probably burst into tears.

"Uh, she's scared of strangers?" Jimmy asked Maggie, seeing under her easy friendliness a certain caution—she wanted to know how he was going to react to this child she'd had with Simon. Jimmy knew Maggie well enough to know that if she thought for one minute he'd resent the baby because of its paternity, he'd lose any chance he had to reconcile with her.

"I don't know," Maggie replied after a slight pause, seeming satisfied that there was no hostility in his attitude toward her baby. "You're her first new person. Aside from the cleaning women, Ellie's only seen me, Charles and Lee since she was born. Oh, Jimmy, you never really met—this is Dr. Lee Winslow. He and Charles were . . . uh, they went out for a while and now they're together again. When we found out I was pregnant, Charles contacted him. He's an excellent obstetrician and he was more than willing to care for a vampire patient. If it weren't for Lee, Ellie and I might have died in that premature labor. Now he watches out for Ellie during the day."

Jimmy shook the outstretched hand of the middle-aged man standing next to Maggie and then turned to the baby. "Ellie? Is that your name . . . are you Ellie?"

"I'm Ellie," the baby replied solemnly and Jimmy laughed, eliciting a small smile from the baby.

"She talks already?"

"She started talking at six months," Maggie explained proudly. "Her development is far above average, Ellie already-"

"All right, Meghann," Charles said, smiling for the first time and turning to Jimmy. "Don't let her get started on Ellie's virtues—we'll stand here all night."

"I was only going to say she speaks on the level of a three year old," Maggie sniffed and turned to the little girl pressing her head shyly against her shoulder. "This is Jimmy Delacroix, honey. He's Mommy's friend."

Ellie braved a quick glance at Jimmy and quickly returned her eyes to the safety of her mother's shoulder.

"New," Ellie said to Maggie, her tone indicating new was synonymous with potentially dangerous in her mind.

"I know he's new to you, sweetie. But he really wants to make friends," Maggie said coaxingly. "Come on. Say 'Hi, Jimmy.'"

The baby shook her head negatively and put her small hands over her eyes, making Jimmy's heart lurch painfully. That had been Jay's trick, thinking if he couldn't see the person, they couldn't see him.

Jimmy swallowed hard and blinked back tears, trying not to think of his son, of the smile that lit up Jay's face when Jimmy returned from work and the toddler rushed at him on wobbling, clumsy little legs.

"Sad," a tiny voice said softly and Jimmy looked up, seeing Ellie staring at him with an expression of sympathy that was oddly adult. She pushed herself away from Maggie's shoulder and stretched her hands out to him. "Want a hug?"

"Ellie's psychic," Maggie explained at Jimmy's shock. "She feels intense emotions—knows when something's bothering someone."

"Come here," Jimmy said over the lump in his throat and smiled at the little girl that looked so concerned for him. "Jimmy definitely wants a hug."

Maggie handed him the baby and he took her carefully, one hand supporting her bottom while Ellie wrapped her arms around his neck.

He hadn't held a baby since Jay died and hadn't realized how much he missed it until his arms adjusted to Ellie's weight and he buried his nose in her sweet-smelling, baby-fine hair. Ellie returned his gaze steadily, moving one hand so it rested on his chin and in that moment Jimmy felt himself fall completely and hopelessly in love with Maggie's baby.

My baby, Jimmy decided, forcing himself not to see the chiseled features of high-bridged nose and slanting cheekbones that bespoke Ellie's paternity. From this night on, he'd never acknowledge that Simon Baldevar had fathered Ellie, from now on she belonged to him.

You're not Jay, Jimmy told Ellie and the little girl stared into his eyes with a focus that belied the attention span normal for a baby her age. *I know you're not my son and I'm not trying to replace him with you. But you're beautiful and sweet and innocent and I want you to stay that way. I'm not gonna let that sick sonofabitch Simon Baldevar hurt you or warp you the way he tried to do to your mother and me. God help him if he tries to take you from me. I'm going to keep you and Maggie safe; I promise.*

Jimmy heard a bitter laugh and looked up, seeing Maggie staring at him and Ellie with the oddest expression... deep sadness, frustration and something that almost looked like pity.
There's nothing to keep us safe from, Maggie said telepathically and even in the thought conversation Jimmy could hear her sorrow. *Simon's gone and he won't be coming back.*

What happened, Jimmy asked while he bounced Ellie in his arms, making her squeal with laughter. *Where did he go? Why did he leave his daughter?*

Because he has no use for her—I'll tell you everything later.

"Let's go inside," Maggie said aloud. "I don't want Ellie out in the cold."

Maggie led him to the study, a comfortable, homey room of overstuffed sofas, teeming bookcases, bright wood fixtures and various toys. Jimmy put Ellie down and she immediately scampered toward a large collection of matchbox cars in the corner of the room.

"Absinthe?" Maggie asked him while Ellie set up elaborate collisions, shouting exuberant vrooms and screeches at each crash.

"That's the only stuff that can get us loaded, right?" Jimmy asked, accepting the tumbler glass full of green, viscous-looking stuff.

"If you drink enough," Maggie replied and extended a bowl of sugar cubes to him. "Suck on these while you drink. You can't imagine how liberating it feels to take a drink. I couldn't have anything—cigarettes, absinthe, spicy food—while I was nursing Ellie."

"You smoke in front of the kid?"

"Outside," Maggie explained. "And in the solar where we keep the sound system; Ellie's not allowed in there. Don't eat the cars, honey." Ellie guiltily spat a miniature Camaro out and returned it to the racing course.

Jimmy took a large gulp of absinthe, choked at the unexpectedly strong, foul taste and shoved several sugar cubes into his mouth.

"You'll get used to it," Maggie laughed and licked her own cube. "Now tell me what you've done for the past year. I was so worried about you, a new vampire without anyone to counsel him. We called your sister but she told us you visited briefly around the New Year and then disappeared."

"Shit, Maggie, how long could I stay with my sister before she got suspicious? I mean, for a few days, she might accept that her whacko brother was just getting loaded and sleeping late but not getting up before sunset is weird even for me. Besides, she's living in a real remote area and there was no way I could get, um... well, get blood without arousing suspicion."

If Maggie noticed the way he blushed when he admitted to the blood lust and refused to meet her eyes, she said nothing, merely asking, "Where did you go when you left her house?"

"I bought a mobile home," Jimmy explained and Maggie's eyebrows shot up.

"You mean you've become white trash on wheels?"

"Not all vampires are fortunate enough to have a mansion in Southampton, Princess," Jimmy shot back and they both laughed. "It worked well enough for me. I'd park at some campground and then go to the nearest city for . . .you know."

"Jimmy," Maggie said softly and took his hand. "What's the matter? What makes you look at the floor instead of me when you speak of feeding? There's nothing to be ashamed of."

"Nothing to be ashamed of?" he cried, and Ellie looked up from her play at the loud noise. "How can you say that? We drink blood, for God's sake!"

"Only because we'd die if we didn't," Maggie replied. "To drink in the name of survival isn't wrong... as long as you don't kill or damage your hosts. I told you that a long time ago."

"And what if you do kill?" Jimmy whispered, his eyes on the Persian rug beneath his feet "You and Charles . . . don't you believe any vampire that kills his prey has to be destroyed?"

"Jimmy," Maggie said tenderly when the agonized shame he'd had to keep to himself for the past year overcame him and he started sobbing. She moved his head so it rested on her shoulder and started rocking him back and forth, much the same way she would have comforted Ellie if she started to cry. "Honey, I know; I know how hard it must have been. Jimmy, you don't have to tell me but if you do, I promise you've never done anything I haven't done..."

"But you didn't know! Baldevar told you had to kill—it wasn't till you met Alcuin that you learned better! And then you never killed anymore—what excuse do I have?" Jimmy howled, refusing any sort of absolution for the awful things he'd done. In his mind, he saw the young women he'd managed to lure from the seedy bars to his narrow bed in the trailer. He remembered the sex, the one time his crushing loneliness vanished, which was fine but then there was always that tantalizing smell of blood beneath their skin and soon his fangs would emerge, frightening his dates. They'd scream but Jimmy would order them to stop (he was still amazed by his power, the effortless way he could speak a command and it was immediately obeyed) and they'd become docile while he sank his fangs into their flesh. It was always so good and sweet, the blood pouring down his throat. So much better than booze was, the way it made his misery vanish and soothed him, made him feel so strong and untouchable. It was the best high he'd ever gotten in his life and once the blood was in his mouth, there was no way he could pull back or force moderation on himself. Despite all the promises he made before each feeding, he'd always find himself greedily lapping up every precious drop of the blood and soon he'd have to stare down in horror at the slack corpse he held in his arms. Then, like the monstrosity he'd become, he'd take his victims to some desolate field and incinerate the corpses to erase all evidence of what he'd done.

"Take Ellie," Jimmy heard Maggie say and he saw Charles scoop up the protesting child.

"No, no, no!" Ellie screeched, beating Charles's chest with her tiny fists. "Don't wanna go—I want Mommy! I don't wanna go, no!"

"Ellie," Maggie said and her stern tone cut through her daughter's tantrum. Ellie quieted but gave Charles and her mother a sulky look.

"Don't you want to play with me and Lee?" Charles wheedled. "I'll make you a peanut butter sandwich."

"Pea butter?" Ellie sniffled and gave Charles a haughty look that said she'd accept the bribe though she was still unhappy.

"Do you think it was that simple?" Maggie questioned when Charles and Ellie left. "Do you think Alcuin said 'Meghann, don't kill anymore' and that was it—I didn't need any other kind of help in resisting the blood lust?"

Jimmy wiped his face with the back of his hand, and shrugged.

"Jimmy," Maggie said and grasped his hands tightly, "our way... not killing... isn't learned easily. I can't tell you how I struggled... how I still struggle. It's like putting heroin in the hands of an addict and saying look but don't shoot. To drink blood and then have to force yourself to stop . . .Jimmy, I'd be shocked if you had been able to control the blood lust on your own. I know you've probably killed. I won't try to tell you not to feel guilty; taking life is a terrible thing. But what you should do is use your guilt to strengthen your resolve to resist the blood lust instead of taking the coward's way out and killing yourself by greeting the sunrise."

"How did you know?" Jimmy asked, disturbed by Maggie's picking up on that darkest notion of his. How many times in the past few months had he thrown open the circle window in the bedroom of his trailer near dawn, only to feel the first, agonizing pain of the sun rising—then came the scrambled frenzy to a closet or any darkened place so he wouldn't die?

"How do you think?" Maggie replied archly and gave him a bitter look. "You think I never thought of suicide? It was all I thought of before Charles found me and rescued me from Simon. I was so tired of killing, I hated myself for what I was doing but I didn't have the slightest idea of how to stop myself. . . anymore than you do right now. But Jimmy, I can help you; it's good that you came here. You can be at peace as a vampire, I promise."

"How?" Jimmy asked, feeling a stirring of hope. "How do I not kill?"

In response, Maggie stood up and beckoned him to follow her. She led him to a kitchen large enough for a restaurant and reached into the double-door refrigerator, handing him a transfusion pack of blood.

"Let it warm up for a few minutes," she instructed and sat down beside Ellie, perched in her high chair, tearing her peanut butter sandwich apart like a miniature scientist doing a dissection, instead of eating it. "Nothing tastes viler than cold blood."

"I thought of blood banks, "Jimmy said, not wanting to seem like a complete moron of a vampire. He joined Maggie, Charles, and the mortal Lee at the round oak table, the blood pack clutched in his hands. "I just didn't know how to get into them."

"Don't ever snatch blood from a blood bank," Charles admonished. "It's monitored too carefully because there's almost always a shortage. It's easy for us; Ballnamore was a licensed research lab so we had a right to draw blood. Now, Lee's a doctor, so what we do is pay healthy mortals for transfusions and solicit enough to last a year or so."

"So we never have to feed directly from people?"

Meghann sighed. "I wish, but vampires sicken if they go too long without fresh mortal blood."

"What's too long?" Jimmy demanded and opened the now warm transfusion pack, pouring the blood into an oversize coffee mug Charles gave him. He could taste the difference between fresh blood and a transfusion pack immediately—it was kind of like regular versus diet soda. But it wasn't bad and he did feel the familiar strength coursing through him as he drank.

"It varies," Charles shrugged. "I tend to need fresh feedings once a month whereas Meghann needs them bi-monthly. But packs are enormously helpful for new vampires. Through the packs, you can train yourself to make do with less and then when you feed from a mortal, it's easier to stop before you kill them. Also, Meghann or I will chaperone you when you feed for a while. Don't feel insulted—both of us had an escort when we were first learning to restrain the blood lust."

Far from feeling insulted, Jimmy was relieved that if he did get carried away, from now on he'd be pulled off mortals before he hurt them. "Uh, do you think it would be okay if just you went with me, Charles?" The last thing he wanted was for Maggie to see him reduced to a blood-hungry savage she had to pull away from his host like some ravenous dog being yanked away from raw meat.

Charles and Maggie exchanged a look before they both nodded, Maggie seeming to understand why Jimmy didn't want her with him when he fed.

"I'll just handle the other aspects of your training, Jimmy," she said.

"What other aspects? What are you talking about?"

"To begin with, simple tricks any vampire is capable of," Maggie said and started cleaning peanut butter off Ellie's face and hands. "Sit still, Miss... you don't want that sticky stuff in your hair. What do you need to learn? Telekinesis, flying the astral plane—that's very important, it can save your life if you need to escape or you're far away from shelter and dawn is coming. Also, we'll work on any dormant psychic ability vampirism has brought out in you. For example, transformation gave me the ability to summon spirits..."

"No," Jimmy said forcefully. "I don't want to mess with magic like all of you do. I'm no fucking sorcerer. Just teach me what I need to know to survive—that's all."

Maggie started to protest but Charles took her hand and something passed between the two of them that made her shrug. "Okay, Jimmy. If that's the way you want it. But flying the astral plane is something you'll need to learn for survival."

"Yeah," Jimmy muttered, not so much in agreement as acknowledgment of her words. He couldn't explain what made him so uneasy. It just seemed that once he became like Maggie and Charles, with their way of holding whole conversations without ever opening their mouths, appearing and disappearing as the spirit willed them that would be the end of Jimmy as a human. A cynical voice told him he'd stopped being human the moment Simon Baldevar forced his blood down Jimmy's throat but Jimmy shrugged it off just as he'd shrugged off Maggie. He'd learn to drink blood without killing and he'd adjust to never seeing the sunlight but as for the rest... Maybe it was stupid but Jimmy thought the more he behaved as a mortal, the easier it would be to pretend this whole awful nightmare had never happened.

Suddenly Jimmy remembered the terrible fights he used to have with Maggie, the way he'd beg her to transform him and she'd refuse, saying transformation was a curse. At the time, he'd refuted her words with bitter sarcasm—what the hell was so terrible about living forever and never getting sick or infirm? But now Jimmy understood. She'd been speaking of that awful feeling of being different, of standing to the side of humanity—observing but never belonging.

"No, Jimmy," Maggie said, not the least bit embarrassed that she'd eavesdropped on his thoughts. "We do belong... maybe not with humans... but we have each other. Some vampires, it's true, become cold and cynical. They live just to prey on victims, never allowing themselves to be touched by love. But Charles and I never feel alone; we have each other. Don't ever close your heart or feel you're an outcast. It's those feelings that can turn you into a monster, not the blood lust."

"Are those feelings what turned Baldevar into a monster?" Jimmy asked caustically, his tone full of all the anger and betrayal he'd felt when Maggie told him she loved the hateful bastard.

Maggie flushed but held his gaze and her voice betrayed no emotion when she spoke. "I don't want any false pretense between us, Jimmy. I did love Simon, in spite of what he is. But no matter how much I loved him, I still cared about you. I still did everything I could to help you."

"I wouldn't have needed any fucking help if your shithead boyfriend left me alone!" Jimmy snarled and Ellie whimpered. Immediately he lowered his voice, feeling ashamed of himself for yelling at Maggie when he'd still be a vegetable or dead if she hadn't helped him. "Look, Maggie, I just can't understand it. Why the hell would you love him after all he did to you, after the way he murdered poor Alcuin in front of you?"

Maggie and Charles both lowered their heads and Jimmy felt like even more of a heel. He probably shouldn't have brought Alcuin up—he knew they were both still grieving for the gentle priest-turned-vampire who had taken them both under his wing and taught them his way of living in peace with mortals.

"Simon does terrible things," Maggie said and just the way she said his name told Jimmy how much she still cared for him. He swallowed his rage and forced himself to listen to her. "But for all his monstrous behavior, he's also capable of great tenderness and love."

"Simon is a very different person when he's with her," Charles said quietly. "I was just as incredulous as you when they first reunited, Jimmy. But the way I saw him treat Meghann... so sensitive, so devoted to her and the baby... I really thought his love for her would change him. And of course, during Meghann's pregnancy, she really had no choice but to trust him—he was the only one that could keep her safe."

"Yeah," Jimmy agreed, remembering Maggie telling him that as soon as it became known that she was pregnant, all the vampires that used to fight on the side of Alcuin wanted to kill her. "I still don't understand that. I mean, I thought Alcuin taught you guys not to kill—going after a pregnant woman sounds more like something Baldevar would do."

Charles and Maggie exchanged another of their complicated, indecipherable glances.

"Before Simon transformed, he was an alchemist," Maggie told Jimmy, "He believed the secret to eternal life lay in transmutation of blood—purifying it of every flaw that left humans vulnerable to disease and old age. After he transformed, he worked on developing his theories, trying to discover why vampires could defeat death but be destroyed by sunlight. He finally decided that when you transform, your blood banishes many impurities from your system, but it's still not perfect. However, Simon thought there was one way to achieve a strain with all our strengths and none of our flaws—by mingling the blood of two vampires through conception. He thought a vampire baby would be immortal, walk in daylight and give its parents that same ability once they drank a small portion of the child's blood.

"Of course," Maggie finished with an ironic grin, "none of Simon's enemies wanted him to gain this ability. So they decided to kill me before I gave birth to a child that would free Lord

Baldevar from darkness and give him a deadly edge over other vampires during the day."

"You mean they thought he'd drink the kid's blood and then go around offing vampires during the day?" Chilled, Jimmy glanced at Ellie, noisily banging a plastic cup against the tray of her high chair. Was Baldevar planning to drink Ellie's blood and then murder every vampire in existence, with the possible exception of Maggie and Charles? It was hard to believe, looking at the giggling little girl with her just-washed face and innocent green eyes that she was a superhuman and utterly unique creature—a vampire unaffected by sunlight.

"Ellie's not a vampire at all," Maggie said shortly. "We discovered that shortly after she was born. She's mortal, with no signs of vampirism in her chromosomes or her behavior. She's only different from other babies in that she show signs of genius level intelligence and a highly developed extrasensory ability."

"So she's not a threat to those assholes that tried to kill you... they'll leave you and her alone?"

Maggie shrugged. "It certainly seems that way. At first, right after Ellie was born, a few came here to do battle. That's why Charles attacked you when we sensed a vampire's presence; we're still pretty edgy. But they haven't bothered us in a while... not since word got around that Ellie's just a mortal baby Lord Baldevar has no interest in raising."

There was a weird, rushed quality to the way Maggie said those last words that made Jimmy's eyes narrow. "What do you mean a baby Baldevar has no interest in raising?"

"He abandoned Meghann and Ellie," Charles said and Maggie shot him a grateful look. "He was so disgusted when all his plans and schemes gave him nothing more than a human child—a girl child at that—he wants nothing to do with mother or daughter."

"What an asshole," Jimmy proclaimed in disgust. "Blaming Maggie 'cause they had a mortal kid. And who gives a shit—it's still a baby to love." So smug did Jimmy feel in his superiority to his narrow-minded enemy that he never noticed the shuffling glances and tension of everyone else at the table. "So he just took off?"

Maggie nodded. "We have no idea where he is or if he has any intention of coming back. I don't think he hates me or Ellie; he left me the deed to this house and enough money to live comfortably for several centuries."

"So that makes everything alright?" Jimmy flared, angry because Maggie wasn't angry. "What the hell is the matter with you, Maggie? The asshole walked out on you both; you should fucking hate him—not give thanks cause he left you a beach house and a couple of dollars for his own twisted form of alimony. And when you combine that with what you tell me he used to do—how he beat you up and stuff—Christ, Maggie! What's it going to take to make you forget about him?"

"I'm never going to forget Simon," Maggie said and now her voice sounded ragged and squeaky, like she was trying to suppress tears. "I'm sorry, Jimmy, I know what you want. You want us to be like we were before and I won't lie to you. I don't think I'll ever be able to love another man, not after..."

"Mommy," Ellie cried in distress when Maggie put her head in her hands and started sobbing. "Mommy, no!"

"No, baby, don't cry," Maggie said, tears still streaming down her face though she tried to smile when Ellie started to cry at the sight of her mother so upset. Maggie shoved her chair aside and picked the little girl up before rushing out of the room.

"No, Jimmy," Charles said and grabbed Jimmy's wrist when he would have rushed after her. "Let her alone."

"She needs me! She needs someone to make her see."

"Jimmy." Lee spoke up for the first time and came over to take Jimmy by the arm and guide him back into his chair. "Can't you see how much it upsets her to talk about Simon? You're opening a very nasty wound and we can't have you doing that. Meghann needs time to heal."

"What the hell are you going to do to stop me?" Jimmy sneered and then stopped, appalled by the bullying tone of voice—he sounded just like Baldevar did whenever he'd threatened Jimmy.

To his credit, Lee neither cowered nor challenged him; he simply went on speaking calmly. "I won't have to stop you because I know you're just like Charles and me—you want only the best for Meghann. Isn't that right?"

At Jimmy's nod, Lee continued. "Now you seem to think the best is resuming your former relationship with her, becoming lovers again. But Meghann isn't ready for a lover, not yet."

"Are you trying to tell me we should let her spend eternity pining away for that creep?"

"Jimmy," Charles said and Jimmy's eyes narrowed at the slight amusement he thought he heard in the other vampire's tone. "It hasn't even been a year since Simon disappeared. I'd hardly say that counts as eternity. You must understand, no matter how much it hurts you, Meghann was very vulnerable during her pregnancy and she turned to Simon for comfort. And I must say, he treated her with extraordinary sensitivity and tenderness. I know you think he's nothing but a cold-hearted fiend and certainly you have every right to feel that way after the way he treated you. But just as Meghann understands your feelings, you must try and see things from her point of view. If you keep trying to ram your own hatred down her throat, you'll do nothing except drive a wedge between you. For now, give her time to grieve, time to heal."

Jimmy nodded his agreement. If anything proved Charles's point, it was the way Maggie had run out of the room when Jimmy kept needling her about Simon Baldevar. He should have remembered from all the years they'd been together that Maggie never liked to talk about Baldevar.

That bastard did some job with her head, Jimmy thought grimly and got up. "I'm just gonna make sure she's okay," he told Charles and this time the vampire made no protest when he left the kitchen in search of Maggie.

It took awhile of prowling the endless corridors of the house but Jimmy finally found Maggie when his sharp ears detected a low voice singing on the third floor.

Maggie and the baby were in a room that was plainly the nursery, with cheerful murals of fairy tales painted on the walls and expensive-looking baby furniture that consisted of a crib, toy trunk, a small bureau and a changing table.

Maggie was perched on a green-and-white striped window seat, her sleeping child lying against her breast. Maggie's chin rested on Ellie's head, the long cascade of her fiery red hair covering the baby like a blanket while she crooned a lullaby to her daughter.

Don't move, Jimmy silently implored and gave thanks when Maggie kept still while he squeezed off a few shots from the Nikon around his neck. What a perfect shot of mother and child reposing together; the sleeping little girl with her flushed cheeks and damp curls cuddled against the beautiful young woman who barely looked old enough to have a child.

Before transformation, Jimmy had considered himself a decent amateur photographer. Now what used to be a hobby was rapidly becoming one of the few times he felt at peace with himself. Behind the lens, Jimmy wasn't an outcast predator; he was a chronicler of life, seeing the night from an utterly unique angle.

When Jimmy gave her permission to move, Maggie turned to him and he was relieved to see her green eyes were clear and dry. "That's my first picture with Ellie. Of course, we have tons of pictures of her but we weren't able to get any of the two of us together. You're the only one who knows how to manipulate the negatives so vampires don't come out as the usual blur in a picture."

"It's no big deal," Jimmy shrugged.

"It is so," Maggie protested in a hushed voice so she wouldn't wake the baby and carried Ellie over to her crib. "How would you feel if you'd had no pictures of you and Jay together? I'm sorry, I shouldn't have said that."

"No," Jimmy told her. "I know what you mean and I'm glad I could take a picture of you and Ellie. I'll take plenty more if you want me to."

"I'd like that," Maggie smiled and pulled a pink blanket over the baby before tucking a golden-brown teddy bear into the crook of Ellie's arms.

"Goodnight, Princess," Maggie whispered and leaned down to kiss her daughter's forehead. Then, turning to Jimmy, she said,

"We have a suite with an extra walk-in closet. Maybe you could turn it into a darkroom."

Jimmy followed her to a room that, thank God, wasn't the same one Baldevar had imprisoned him in. This suite was on the north side of the house, overlooking the fir-lined private road instead of the beach. He could see that the extra closet in what Maggie called the day room would serve as a fine darkroom. Next, Maggie showed him a bedroom he immediately felt comfortable in with its polished wood floor and furniture decorated in solid earth tones.

"You'll be happy here?" Maggie asked a little anxiously and Jimmy almost laughed when he thought of the difference between this luxurious house and the cheap trailer he'd called home for the past couple of months. She might as well ask a wino if they'd prefer to keep their cardboard box rather than move in with her.

"I'll be happy as long as you want me here and you're not just asking me to stay out of pity."

"No, Jimmy," Maggie said, seeming surprised that he'd even think that. She came away from the window over to Jimmy's side and hugged him tightly. "Charles was right when he said you took a risk by coming here but I'm very happy that you did. I've missed you."

"I missed you too, Maggie," Jimmy whispered and tried to remember his resolve downstairs not to push a physical relationship on her but the hug was making it damned difficult. For one thing, her thick, long hair was tickling his hands as he grasped her waist and it didn't take a lot of imagination to remember making love with her on top of him, that brilliant red hair fanning out and teasing his chest.

No! He'd screw up his chances with Maggie for good if he kept panting at her, insisting she forget Baldevar and start up with him again. Maggie had been through a lot what with Alcuin dying, giving birth, and those other horrid vampires trying to kill her and Ellie. It was understandable that she'd turned to Baldevar and that the prick, with the centuries he had over her, all his Black Magic mumbo jumbo and most of all that damned blood link that connected any vampire with their master forever, was able to twist Maggie's thoughts until she thought she loved him. Jimmy knew Maggie had been brainwashed; all he had to do was make her see that.

But just try and tell all those good, rational thoughts to certain idiot parts of his body that were growing harder and more insistent by the second, tantalized by the tea-rose scent Maggie always wore and soft feminine curves of her body pressed against him.

Maggie stiffened in surprise and as she raised her head, Jimmy steeled himself for more recriminations.

But the jade eyes on his sparkled and her broad grin made Jimmy choke back his unspoken apology.

"For the past year, I've lived with two of the most wonderful men in the world," Maggie told him and made no attempt to pull away. "But they're homosexual and it's been a very long time since anyone made me feel like a woman instead of just Ellie's mother and a beloved but sexless friend."

"They'd have to be gay to see you as sexless," Jimmy grumbled and Maggie giggled, her old, full laugh that contained none of the hesitation Jimmy had sensed in her since he arrived. In that moment, all the tension between them melted and Jimmy finally felt himself in the presence of Maggie O'Neill, his sharp-tongued, reckless girlfriend instead of the sad, reserved woman who'd taken her place. "Maggie, I love you. But God help me, if you say 'I love you, too—as a friend', I might just wring your neck or grab the nearest stake."

"But you are my friend," Maggie laughed again. "Would you feel better if I said you're my enemy?"

"I'd feel better if you said Baldevar was your enemy," Jimmy said honestly, holding his breath until Maggie simply nodded instead of bursting into tears at Lord Baldevar's name again. "But I'm trying to understand, Maggie. You felt... something for him and that's why you won't do anything with me." The words nearly choked him coming out of his mouth, but it was worth it to feel Maggie sag against him in relief.

"I was so worried that you'd hate me for what I did with Simon—that you'd think I was nothing but a whore."

"I don't hate you, Maggie," Jimmy said into her hair. No, it was Baldevar he hated, for ruining what he and Maggie had had together, for impregnating her (though he already loved Ellie dearly) and making it so Maggie had to turn to him or die. The only thing Jimmy didn't understand was how Baldevar could win back Maggie's love and then throw it away just because their kid was mortal. . . that just didn't make any sense.

Jimmy felt Maggie tense up again and wondered if she was playing Thought Police with his mind again—poking through his thoughts was one habit she'd better break damned quick.

"What happened between me and Simon isn't the only reason I don't want things getting more... intense with us," Maggie said and pulled away from him. She sank down into the fat, feather-stuffed mattress of the bed and threw her arms over her head to stretch, prompting Jimmy's imagination into flights of erotic fantasies. "Jimmy, you must know by now how, um, possessive Simon is of me. He may have left but that doesn't mean he won't destroy anyone I try to replace him with."

"But that's not right!" Jimmy protested. "If he leaves, he can't expect you to stay faithful. It's not fair... it's not even sane."

"Fair and rational thought isn't always Simon's forte," Maggie said wryly. "Right or not, he despises you for what you mean to me and I don't want him to hurt you. I probably shouldn't even have you here but you mean so much to me. I hated the thought of you not being in my life anymore. It's selfish but I just can't let you go—I need you."

Jimmy sat down next to her and put his arms around her, emboldened by Maggie's words. "I need you too, Maggie. Look, I say in for a penny in for a pound. If Asshole comes back here and finds me, he'll try and kill me again anyway. At least let me be killed for being your lover instead of a platonic friend."

He'd hoped to make Maggie laugh but she only smiled sadly, though she didn't shrug off the arms that held her close to him. "Jimmy, it's a very tempting offer but it wouldn't be right. I'm just not capable of loving you the way you deserve to be loved. If I slept with you right now, I'd just be using you."

"I'm a man for God's sake—use me, please!" he rasped and this time Maggie did laugh.

"You deserve better," she said and kissed him lightly on the lips. "And until I can give you what you deserve—a woman who only wants you, only thinks of you—I think it's better if we're just friends."

"Okay," Jimmy finally said and gave her another hug, this time the kind of embrace one friend would give to another. "Just friends... for now." Maggie's words and the light, sweet kiss gave him hope that there would come a time when she got over Simon and they'd find their way back to each other. Besides, Jimmy knew Maggie was a highly passionate woman... he couldn't see her playing the celibate vampire for long. He'd just have to do as Charles and Lee suggested and give her time.

And he had nothing but time, Jimmy thought, smiling down at Maggie. Time was the one gift Lord Baldevar had given him so all he had to do was be patient and wait.

Chapter Six

Sixteen Years Later

Jimmy sat at the far end of a jetty and glared at the dark sea churning by his feet, indifferent to the water cresting over the rocks that was soaking his jeans and boots.

Either Maggie was a brilliant actress or he was the stupidest man ever to walk the earth, Jimmy thought furiously, feeling like a fool when he remembered all her tender sympathy and seeming love for him. To think all of that—the welcome home, the insistence she relied on Jimmy's friendship—was nothing but a calculated lie.

He should have seen through it, if not that night then any of the thousands of nights that followed when he'd plead with Maggie to love him the way he needed her to love him and always she'd hand him that simpering you-deserve-better-than-me bullshit.

Maggie was right he deserved better than her, a deceitful, conniving bitch that used him as her fucking beard for Simon Baldevar! That's what Jimmy had been for sixteen years—a beard, a convenient dupe she presented to the world as her lover (though he hadn't even gotten sex out of the miserable situation) while panting for the night Lord Baldevar would come back and Jimmy could be disposed of, no longer serving any purpose in her life.

"That's not true."

"You stay the hell out of my mind!" Jimmy yelled and glanced over his shoulder at Maggie, standing barefoot on the slimy rocks and daintily holding her skirt in one hand to keep it from getting wet.

Jimmy felt a turn of disgust for himself when he couldn't suppress a small part of his heart that saw nothing but beauty as

121

he glared at Maggie. A creature as base as she'd turned out to be had no right to look so bewitching, seeming like some faerie queen as she stared down at him, the moonlight outlining her dainty, china-doll features with silvery luminescence.

"Get lost," Jimmy snarled.

"I'm not going anywhere until you understand what happened," Maggie replied and crossed her arms over her chest, no longer a fey pixie but a creature as formidable as Morgan le Fay when she stared him down with her implacable green eyes.

"I understand just fine," Jimmy snapped and rose to his feet, feeling height might give him some advantage over the petite Maggie. "You needed me here to convince all your vampire enemies that you and shit-head were really through. So what if lying to me the way you did meant spitting on any friendship we'd had..."

"Stop it!" Maggie yelled and the shrill scream went through Jimmy like a knife, so for several moments he couldn't find the will to speak again while Maggie launched into her explanation.

"You're so fucking self-centered, Jimmy—everything's always me, me, me! How does this affect me? Why did Maggie lie to me?"

"Why did Maggie lie to me?" he roared rhetorically. "Because her lord and master told her to!"

"Shut up!" Maggie screamed and her fist flew at his solar plexus. So taken aback was Jimmy by the unexpected blow that he flew backward into the ocean. Had he been mortal, Jimmy might have been dragged into the deep sea by the brutal undertow, but as it was, he was able to climb back onto the jetty after getting a tenuous hold on the rocks.

"Are you going to keep your mouth shut and listen to me?" Maggie demanded, completely unapologetic as she glared at the dripping, shivering mess she'd turned Jimmy into.

"Will you feed me to a shark if I don't?" Jimmy replied sulkily, but sat down and removed his soggy boots, socks, and vest. He thought of taking off his wet jeans but decided the discomfort of wet denim was preferable to carrying on this argument in his underwear.

"Simon never told me to lie to you and if he had, I would've told him to go to hell—just like I should tell you for thinking such terrible things of me."

"But you did lie," Jimmy pointed out. "You never told me you had twins and you let me believe you and Baldevar were through."

"I didn't do it to hurt or exploit you. I did it for Mikal and I'd do it again if it meant my son's well-being." Maggie hunched down next to him and grabbed his hands with an inexorable grip he couldn't break. "I couldn't tell you about Mikal because you were too newborn to be able to keep the secret."

"What the hell is that supposed to mean?" Jimmy cried, deeply insulted. "Being a vampire made me stronger..."

"Stronger than mortals," Maggie broke in. "Not other vampires. Jimmy, I knew if you went anywhere and Charles or I weren't with you, any older vampire could pick up on your presence without you having the slightest awareness of them. They'd be able to spy on your thoughts and that would mean if I had told you about Mikal..."

"They'd see it," Jimmy finished. Christ, he hadn't thought of that at all, that some monster like the ones that tried to kill Maggie could spy on his mind and learn all about her son.

"All right," Jimmy nodded and watched Maggie's shoulders sag in relief. That gesture went to his heart more than anything else she'd done. Maggie had come running out here after him to explain herself; maybe she really did value his friendship in some way.

"I value you in every way," Maggie said, and then flushed. "Sorry, I shouldn't pry. But your thoughts are so intense they're coming at me whether I want them to or not. Don't you see, Jimmy? Suppose that happened on one of your trips?"

"I understand," Jimmy said and he did—part of the twisted truth, at any rate. "You were trying to keep Ellie and Mikal safe."

"Ellie!" Jimmy yelped and jumped to his feet. "Jesus, Maggie, what if he's transforming her while we're out here?"

"I'd know if something like that was being done to my daughter," Maggie replied. "But we should head back inside."

Feeling more amiable if not completely understanding of Maggie and her baffling attraction to Lord Baldevar, Jimmy took her arm and guided her over the slippery rocks as they made their way back to shore, his wet jeans squishing noisily as his thighs rubbed together.

"Maggie," Jimmy said, keeping his hand on her when they reached the relative stability of the sand. "I can understand that you needed to keep Mikal hidden but did you have to let Simon have him? What if we'd all gone to ground..."

"Ellie included?" Maggie demanded. "What kind of life would that have been for her?"

"What kind of life was it for Mikal?" Jimmy asked quietly and Maggie shrugged helplessly.

"I don't know," she replied and Jimmy saw the old frustrated helplessness that he finally understood shadow her eyes. "Simon never gave me any word of him."

"Holy shit, Maggie, you've got to be kidding me!" Jimmy exclaimed but one glance at her expression showed this was no joke. "Of all the fucking . . . how could he not tell his son's mother how the kid was? And how could you let this go on?"

"What could I do?" Maggie cried and Jimmy felt his throat tighten at how woebegone she looked. "You think I wanted to just wave goodbye to my son and leave him with Simon?"

"You didn't?"

"Of course not!" she yelled and Jimmy glanced uneasily at the house—surely Baldevar could hear her carrying on. "I'm not blind, Jimmy. I know Simon's faults... I bet I know them better than anyone in the world. I know what he's capable of and I knew what he could raise our son to be but I just couldn't see anything else to do but let him take Mikal. Besides, do you honestly believe I could have stopped him?"

God knows I couldn't have, Jimmy thought bitterly. "Don't beat yourself up, Maggie. You're right—you couldn't have kept him from Mikal."

"I don't think I would have tried," Maggie confessed and gave Jimmy a tired smile. "Does that shock you? Let me tell you about the night our vampire enemies found me alone. I fought them as best as I could but there were too many and I was weakened by pregnancy. Do you know what they did to me? They were going to kill me by scalping me and running a sword through my womb, then leave me wounded and bleeding for daylight to claim me. With the last of my strength, I called out to Simon and he came, Jimmy. He came to me and he destroyed every last one of those monsters and all he wanted for saving my babies and me was for me to love him. That night he saved me was when we became lovers again. After Mikal and Elizabeth were born and Simon proposed taking Mikal into hiding, I went along because I couldn't get that night he saved me out of my mind. I just kept thinking that whatever those sick sons-of-bitches had tried to do to me, imagine what they might do to Mikal. I knew I might not be able to protect my son from that, so I had to give him to Simon. I had to keep Mikal safe, Jimmy. Can't you see that? I had to keep him safe."

"Okay, Maggie," Jimmy said when she started to cry the miserable, rasping noises of a person that didn't want to cry, but couldn't stop. Jimmy gathered her up clumsily and held her tightly. "It's okay, Maggie. I understand." He understood that Maggie had had a choice that was no real choice to make—keep her son with her and know he'd grow up decent but might die if she couldn't defend him or give him to the one creature that could keep him safe, knowing all too well what Simon Baldevar might turn her son into.

"It's not okay," Maggie cried against his shoulder. "Every dark vision I've had of what Simon might do has come home to roost. Did you hear him? Ellie has to transform because her own brother wants to hurt her. My God, what kind of creature has my son turned into?"

"Like father, like son," Jimmy said, unable to keep his bitterness toward Baldevar inside. "Maggie, it's not your fault but if you give a kid to a psychopath, you have to expect..."

"Simon isn't a psychopath," Maggie argued. "A sadist, maybe... really more of a narcissist than anything else. Psychopaths lie constantly and can't maintain anything but surface relationships. Simon doesn't lie, he's capable of some empathy and maintaining relationships."

"Like the one he maintained with you while he went off with your boy?"

"Simon said he thought it would be easier on us all to maintain minimal contact," Maggie answered. "He wrote to me and Ellie all the time but we could never risk joining together until Mikal was strong enough to fight his own battles. And he never wanted the twins to have contact while they were children—he worried that Mikal would despise Ellie because she didn't have to be hidden away."

"It sounds like the sick bastard despises Ellie anyway," Jimmy said cuttingly. "No doubt dear old Dad taught him any mortal—including his sister—is just food."

"No! Simon loves Ellie. Jimmy, I know what he put you through and I'd never excuse it but there is a good side to Simon."

"Would that be the one that drained you dry while humping you?"

Maggie flushed and glared daggers at Jimmy. "What we do in bed is none of your business. We're not hurting anybody."

"Bullshit!"Jimmy replied. "You're my friend so I'm making it my business. Look, I know what we used to have is in the past—I can accept that. I want you to find a man who'll make you happy just as much as I want that happiness for myself. But you won't find it with Simon Baldevar. What he was doing in bed wasn't just some kinky sex and furthermore, someone is being hurt—you. Christ, how can you let him just... use you like that?"

"I know what it looks like," Maggie said and gave Jimmy the most complex look of pain, confusion, and reckless defiance he'd ever seen. "You think I'm Lord Baldevar's little sex toy . . . his blood whore, as so many of our kind have called me. And you want to know something? There are plenty of times I feel like a whore but I... I want him. When we're... alone... I want him anyway he wants to have me. It's like... nothing seems to matter anymore. I can't think when he touches me. My mind goes blank and all I know is his touch, the wonderful places he takes me while I sacrifice my pride and self-respect on the altar of his... uh, you know. Why do you think I left him, Jimmy? I hated the power he had over me, the way he controlled my mind through my body and the blood lust."

"Then why the hell did you go back with him, Maggie?" The question wasn't asked reproachfully but with genuine puzzlement. The things Maggie had just said to him—that she had been so open about her feelings toward Lord Baldevar astonished Jimmy. Jimmy wanted desperately to understand her and then help her. He wanted to help her the way she'd helped him so many times.

"I was once like you—before Simon transformed me," Maggie said and gave Jimmy a bleak little grin that made him want to weep for her, this complex woman he was only now beginning to understand. "I thought love was a safe, pleasant matter of finding a boy I had things in common with, who I thought was handsome, who made me laugh, and who'd be my friend... someone to raise a family with, grow old with."

"Then I met Simon," Maggie said and her voice was so low and far away sounding, Jimmy wondered if she was in a trance. "And I found out true love isn't about companionship . . . it's about desire and voracious need. It's about having that need take you over completely, dominate you with all its cravings and pulls so that nothing else matters. That's what I thought when Simon offered transformation—I want to be with him, above all else matters. And nothing did matter—not my scruples, my conscience or the mortal family I gave up without a second thought. He filled the world for me, Jimmy—he still does. And it wasn't just sex. It was the way he'd hold me when I woke up frightened, the way he was interested in my every thought, the way he filled my heart to bursting. I left him because I saw that love was turning me into a slave. A slave to my desires, to an insatiable need that rages and demands and won't rest until it's sated."

"Is that what you want to be now?"Jimmy asked and Maggie looked up at him with surprise, like she'd forgotten he was there, and then shrugged helplessly.

"Sometimes I don't think there's anything else I can be when it comes to Simon Baldevar," Maggie answered and Jimmy had an aching wave of pity for her. He couldn't even begin to imagine what this battle must be doing to her soul—her intelligent, forthright nature warring with the heart and body that craved Simon Baldevar.

"Don't look like that," Maggie smiled at him, and Jimmy wondered if Baldevar was any better at coping with her quicksilver mood swings than he was. "I'm not a lost soul. It really isn't like that with Simon and me anymore. I know it's difficult for you to believe, but he has changed in the seventy years I've known him. Yes, he's capable of brutality but he's also capable of deep love. You know I almost died when I had the twins. When I came out of my coma, Simon was crying over me... crying over my impending death. There is tenderness in him… haven't you seen it in the way he treats Ellie? I believe he could become a good man, one I could give my whole heart to without qualm."

"And I believe you need to take those anti-crazy pills you used to give me," Jimmy said.

Maggie's brows started to meet in an angry frown that became a perplexed question when a raw scream of panic and desolation shattered-the quiet around them.

"MOMMY!"

Jimmy and Maggie turned around to see Ellie flying down the beach, tears streaming down the face that leered at them ghost-pale from the darkness surrounding her.

"Ellie," Maggie whispered, her face as white as her daughter's. In an instant, she vanished, reappearing next to Ellie and reaching out to draw her into her arms. "Sweetheart, what's the matter?"

"Mommy..." was all Ellie could choke out and Jimmy, who'd chosen to run rather than fly the astral plane, exchanged a fearful glance with Maggie, all other matters forgotten in their concern for the shattered girl sobbing in Maggie's arms.

She hasn't called Maggie Mommy in ten years, Jimmy thought, not since she decided it was for babies. What the hell had happened to make her regress like this, to make her stare at them with glassy, unseeing eyes while she continued to cry?

"Ellie, baby, what is it?" Maggie asked soothingly and Jimmy could see she was fighting to keep her own terror out of her voice when she spoke. "Please tell me what's wrong."

"Did Baldevar do something... "Jimmy began and Maggie sent him a withering glance while she continued to rock her daughter.

At her father's name, Ellie came out of it a little and started speaking though her teeth chattered violently while she spoke. "Lee... Uncle Lee le... left your mail by your desk the way he always does. I thought I'd... I thought I'd sort it out for you while you and Jimmy were out here. Then I came to this box... I was going to open it up but Daddy snatched it away from me. He didn't have to look, he knew right away..."

"Knew what?" Maggie demanded when Ellie burst into fresh sobs. "Sweetheart, please try to calm down. Where's your father now?"

"Don't go in there!" Ellie screamed, though Maggie had made no move toward the house. "Don't go inside... I don't want you to see..."

"Ellie, please," Maggie cried. "You're scaring me. Please try and tell me what happened. What don't you want me to see?"

"Daddy knew what was inside the box," Ellie said dully as though she hadn't heard her mother's question. "I should have known, too, I should have felt how . . . how much evil and hurt surrounded it but I didn't, I had no idea. Oh God, why did he do this? Why? Daddy . . . oh, Mommy, Daddy's really sorry. Daddy's right, he's bad and he wants to hurt us but Daddy says he won't let him. But what if Daddy can't help us? He wasn't able to save . . ." Ellie wrenched away from her mother with a violent twist and vomited into the sand.

"Look what he's done," Jimmy cried furiously over Ellie's retching. "You let that sonofabitch back into our lives and he's already damaged her..."

"No!" Ellie screamed and raised her head. Hastily, she wiped the bile from her lips and shook her head at Jimmy. "Don't you be mad at Daddy! He didn't do anything . . . Mikal did. Mikal is the one who's going to try and get me and Mommy." Ellie threw her arms around her mother again, kneeling on the sand with her head on Maggie's stomach. "Mommy..."

"What, baby?" Maggie beseeched, stroking her daughter's hair. "What is it? Did Mikal send something to me?"

"Yes," Ellie said and her voice was hoarse and full of grief. "There was a note inside—'A belated Mother's Day present.' How could he do that to you?" Ellie started weeping again and wouldn't respond to any of her mother's increasingly frantic questions.

"She's hysterical," Maggie finally said to Jimmy. "Help me get her back in the house. I'm going to give her one of Lee's sedatives and put her to bed. Simon can tell us what's going on."

"Ellie," Maggie said gently, pulling her daughter to her feet. "Can you walk? I want to take you back to the house."

At the mention of the house, Ellie lost the last bit of color in her face and put her hands out as though trying to ward off something unseen by Maggie and Jimmy.

"No," she whimpered. "No, I can't go back... I can't... the box..."

Ellie swayed and Jimmy leaped forward to catch her and swing her into his arms.

"It's all right," he said helplessly when her arms went around him in a death grip and she buried her head on his shoulder, whimpering and crying. "Ellie, it's all right... I won't let anything there hurt you; I promise."

"No," Ellie moaned and raised pleading, frightened eyes to Jimmy. "Please don't make me go back inside."

Jesus Christ, what the hell had this Mikal done to put Ellie in a state like this?

"You want me to take you back to your cottage?" Jimmy suggested and he felt the wire-tight tension in Ellie's body ease slightly. But then she shook her head and said in a resigned tone, "I can't leave Mommy alone... she'll need me."

Maggie turned around at that and pushed wet curls off Ellie's clammy forehead. "Honey, I'm just going in to talk to your father..." she began but stopped when Lord Baldevar appeared at the French doors.

"Meghann," Baldevar said, gold eyes flat and lips drawn into a tight line. "Meghann, I am so sorry."

"For what?" Maggie screamed in a mixture of impatience and fear. "Would somebody please tell me what's going on?"

"Meghann, come with me," Baldevar said and held out his hand, tossing an order to Jimmy. "Put Elizabeth on the couch and pour her a brandy."

Jimmy wanted to snap back that he wasn't a servant but the brandy suggestion was a good one—it might be just what Ellie needed. Once inside, he pulled the stopper out of the crystal cognac decanter and rapidly poured three fingers of the amber liquid into a snifter and brought it to Ellie's lips, drawn into a grim line identical to her father's.

"C'mon," Jimmy coaxed, holding the glass while Ellie sipped at it sluggishly.

"Simon," Maggie said in a pleading voice and Jimmy saw the puzzled anxiety and building fear in her eyes. "Simon, what..."

Then her eyes cut to a cardboard box next to the table and she let out a low moan that made Ellie flinch and put her hands to her ears.

Maggie continued to stare at the box, her hair clutched in two fists on either side of her head with her eyes and lips clamped tightly like she was trying not to cry.

"No," Maggie said over and over, staring at the box with abject fear. "No, no, no..."

Baldevar put his hand on her shoulder and that broke Maggie's paralysis. She shrugged his hand off and ran to the box, pushing away layers of newspaper to find what lay underneath. Then she lifted something out and let out a scream unlike anything Jimmy had ever heard before. It was a primal howl, coming from the deepest part of her soul, a desperate keen filled with raw, uncontained sorrow that made Jimmy feel pain even before he knew what had happened, feel Maggie's pain cut through him and make him cry without knowing why he was crying.

Jimmy reached out blindly to draw Ellie against him, unmindful of the brandy that soaked them both when the snifter turned over.

"Maggie, what..." he started to say and then broke off when he saw what had made her scream like that—the box contained Charles Tarleton's decapitated head.

Jimmy heard himself breathing heavily and grabbed Ellie closer, unable to believe what he was seeing. No, was his first blind thought. He just couldn't be staring at Charles Tarleton's severed head. Jimmy swallowed hard and felt the nausea that had attacked Ellie start to work on his own system as his eyes took in the gruesome details of the long, stringy bits of gore hanging from the neck, the stretched, wrinkling skin and purple circles under Charles's cloudy, vacant eyes.

"Maggie," Jimmy said helplessly, not knowing what to say, not knowing if there was anything he could say. Jimmy could only guess at what Maggie was feeling. He knew how close Maggie and Charles were, knew that the special love she had for him that was, in a way, a stronger connection than she had with anyone else in the world—even Simon Baldevar.

Maggie didn't respond to Jimmy and he felt serious fear at the empty green eyes staring through the decapitated head.

"Maggie," Jimmy said again, but Baldevar shook his head negatively, then walked over and gently stroked Ellie's cheek.

"Go to your mother," Baldevar said and Jimmy heard something jagged in the vampire's voice, something he'd think was grief in another person. Could Baldevar be sharing in the palpable sense of loss that filled the room? "She'll hear you, Elizabeth."

Ellie nodded and left the protection of Jimmy's arms, kneeling down next to her mother. Jimmy saw that Ellie was careful to avoid looking at Charles's poor remains, focusing only on her mother's face.

"Mom," Ellie said hesitantly and Maggie looked up at her daughter with an expression of dumb, uncomprehending pain like a hurt animal or a small child.

"He didn't kill him right away," Maggie said and Jimmy's heart broke at how frail and utterly destroyed she sounded. Her hands trembled violently as she stroked Charles's lank black hair and her breath came out in odd, halting gasps as though she'd forgotten how to breathe. "I... I see what happened. He attacked my Charles in the day, like the coward he must be."

"Oh, God, why couldn't he have killed him then?" Maggie shrieked, tears pouring down her face and soaking the collar of her shirt. "Why did he do that to Charles? Why? He... he staked Charles during the day. He put a stake in his heart and then he sat there and he waited—just waited for sunset. He waited and thought of all the things he'd do to Charles when dark came and... oh, Charles. Charles, I'm sorry, I'm so sorry my son did this to you. To torture you like that when you were helpless and couldn't fight back before he finally let you go... why? Why? Why?" With each why, Maggie's voice scaled alarmingly and her eyes took on a harsh, disconnected gleam.

"Why?" she yelled again and Jimmy watched the glass panes in the French doors crack, the glass and chrome table shatter as Maggie screamed out her terrible rage and grief.

"Don't," Baldevar said softly and moved to take Maggie in his arms but she pushed him away with a strength borne of madness and despair. Whether unprepared for the attack or thinking a struggle would make Maggie lose whatever sanity she had left, Baldevar stepped away and moved Ellie back to the couch.

"Don't you touch me," Maggie hissed, barring her blood teeth and giving Baldevar a look of pure hatred. Jimmy heard Ellie gasp and immediately moved her head to his shoulder so she wouldn't have to see her mother like this.

"You've done this," Maggie snarled in a low, choked voice and Jimmy thought she'd spit venom if she could.

"You!" Maggie screamed as though he'd contradicted her though the vampire had done no more than stare impassively while she spoke. "You killed my best friend, you bastard!"

"Mommy, no..." Ellie started to say and Maggie whirled around.

"Stay out of this!" she cried in the harshest voice Jimmy had ever heard her use on Ellie. Ellie shivered and Jimmy clutched her tighter, praying she'd understand Maggie was simply hysterical.

"I'm sorry," Maggie said at the stunned hurt in Ellie's eyes but her voice was barely under control. "But you don't know what kind of monster he is... I should have told you. I shouldn't have tried to protect you by romanticizing him."

"This is all your fault!" Maggie screamed, turning back to Baldevar. "And mine too. I killed Charles because I put my trust in you. I believed you when you said you'd raise my son with kindness and sensitivity— that you wouldn't bring him up to be a coldhearted killer." Carefully, as though she was handling delicate china, Maggie wrapped Charles's head in a chenille throw rug she snatched off the sofa and then stored it back in the box before hurling herself at Baldevar.

"Bastard!" she howled and raked her nails down his cheeks. Jimmy blanched at the ragged, gouged holes that appeared on Baldevar's face only to disappear almost instantaneously. Maggie seemed even more enraged by the speedy vampiric healing process that wouldn't allow her to permanently scar Baldevar's skin and attacked harder, kicking, punching, and clawing while she screamed out her rage and grief in an incoherent, babbled torrent of obscenities and accusations. Jimmy was surprised that the vampire made no move to defend himself or even restrain Maggie, simply staring with soft compassion and pity at the howling woman doing her level best to kill him.

"Mom, please," Ellie pleaded in a soft whisper and Maggie stopped abruptly, only seeming to remember Ellie's presence and what she was witnessing when her daughter spoke.

"I want you out of here," Maggie spat at Baldevar and grabbed the box containing Charles's head, along with her car keys. "You caused this! You raised Mikal to hate, despite what you promised me. You forced your sick, twisted views on his innocent brain. You taught him to wallow in blood lust, to crave the kill! You nurtured his hate, encouraged it—but now the joke is on you because the thing he hates most in the world is you!" Maggie let out an appalling sound that might have been a laugh and continued to spit out the contemptuous, heated words that Jimmy thought probably hurt Baldevar more than her fists or claws had. "That's why you're here, isn't it? Mikal must have tried to kill you and I'm only sorry he failed! Now he's looking to kill anyone that might aid you—me or Charles or Jimmy or Ellie."

Maggie shoved the box at Baldevar, brandishing it like a weapon. "Look what you got from your hate, Simon! Look what your hate, what your failure to raise my son with any kind of decency, has cost an innocent man! Damn you, Simon Baldevar! Damn you for putting me in a position where I may have to kill my son to save my daughter. Get out of here! You're not welcome in my house... I won't have you being the lightning rod that brings death to Ellie! You be gone when I get back here... get out of our lives and make sure your sick, twisted son knows not to look for you here!"

Maggie started to turn on her heel then whirled around, fixing Baldevar with a look of steely contempt that contrasted oddly with the tears still running down her face. "You think I can't force you out of here, don't you? You think you can do whatever you want and I'll always go along because I'm helpless to act against you. Well, let me tell you if I ever see you again, I'll get a stake through your heart and this time I'll do it right! I'll cut off your worthless head like Mikal did to..." Maggie sank to the ground, weeping wildly while she rocked back and forth, cradling her best friend's remains.

"Stay away!" Maggie screamed through her sobs when Baldevar stepped nearer, his eyes still showing nothing but concern for her. "I mean it! I will kill you, I will! Jimmy, make him get out! You were right all along. Will you please look after my daughter? I have to do something for Charles."

Jimmy could only nod and Maggie came to the couch to kneel by her daughter, her voice gentler but still cracked and desolate. "Honey, I'd take you with me but I think you're safer here with Jimmy to look after you. I'll be back tomorrow night. Okay?"

Ellie nodded and kissed her mother's cheek. Maggie kissed her back then whirled out into the night. In a few seconds, they all heard the roar of a car engine and the squeal of tires as she took off.

"Maybe we should have stopped her, "Jimmy said uneasily, speaking only to Ellie. He was in complete accord with Maggie—out of her mind with grief or not, she was right to blame Simon Baldevar for this tragedy. Maybe now whatever hold that bastard had on her was obliterated for good. "I mean, she's so upset she's likely to drive that car off the road or into a tree..."

"She'll be fine," Lord Baldevar said briefly. "The drive will give her something to concentrate on." He went over to the sofa and knelt beside Ellie, picking up her slack, unresisting hands, ignoring Jimmy as though he didn't exist.

"It's a very frightening thing to see your mother lose control, isn't it?" he said tenderly and Ellie nodded through her tears.

"You mustn't worry or be angry with her," Baldevar went on in that same gentle tone. "Now I'm afraid I must leave you for a while. As Mr. Delacroix pointed out, it is dangerous for your mother to be alone."

"Daddy," Ellie said while he cleaned her face with a linen handkerchief. "Daddy, you won't hurt Mom, will you? You're not mad for what she said..."

"Your mother lashes out when she's hurt," Baldevar replied. "And this blow has hurt her very badly. Charles Tarleton was more than a friend to your mother; he was her anchor and support for many years. It will take a great deal for your mother... for any of us to recover from his loss. Dr. Tarleton was a very fine person and I shall always be grateful that he helped to raise you, Elizabeth. I am truly sorry that Mikal has brought this pain on all of us."

Baldevar's hurting, too, Jimmy realized numbly. Grief darkened his amber eyes to copper and he blinked constantly, as though holding back tears. Or maybe he was upset over Maggie's words, no matter what he said to Ellie. At any rate, it was the first time Jimmy saw his enemy without the cool, sardonic mask in place that tempered his emotions even when he was in a rage.

"I shall take care of your mother," Baldevar said and hugged Ellie close to him. "Now I must go to your mother but I cannot leave, Elizabeth, if I think you're in danger. Mikal presents a threat to all of us . . . I've already enchanted these grounds so he cannot enter. You must promise me that, until your mother and I return, you will not leave this estate and you will remain close to Jimmy Delacroix at all times."

Stunned at Lord Baldevar entrusting Ellie's care into his hands, Jimmy tried to catch Baldevar's eye but the vampire's attention was on Ellie. Not that he needed Ellie's promise, Jimmy had no intention of letting Ellie out of his sight.

At that thought, Lord Baldevar glanced over at him, an appraising, neutral stare while words flashed in Jimmy's mind with an almost painful intensity: *Protect my daughter with your life.*

Jimmy nodded automatically as Ellie said, "I promise," to Baldevar and the vampire got up, indicating to Jimmy that he wanted him to walk him to the door.

Jimmy followed docilely enough, not wanting to make a scene in front of Ellie, but once they were out of hearing range, Jimmy said in a low whisper, "You'd better keep your promise and not hurt Maggie."

"Meghann is already hurting," Baldevar said. "I'm merely ensuring her safety."

Jimmy nodded, resigned to the notion that their shared concern for Maggie and Ellie put him and Baldevar on the same side—at least until this crisis was over. This was the first time Simon Baldevar had ever talked to him instead of at him, the first time his words weren't some cutting remark or an attempt to intimidate.

"Where are you going to search for Maggie?"

"She's gone to Lee Winslow," Baldevar replied as though that were the most obvious thing in the world.

Of course, Jimmy thought. Where else would Maggie go but to break this awful news to Charles's mortal lover? Then Jimmy felt a pang of jealousy and grudging respect, realizing Simon Baldevar did know Maggie better than he did, for he'd been able to figure out where she'd go immediately.

"I can reach her in Chicago easily but I doubt we'll be back here before sunset tomorrow at the earliest," Baldevar said coolly. "Are there sedatives in this house?"

"Huh? Oh, yeah. Lee sometimes has trouble sleeping. His time clock is all screwed up because he tries to spend so many hours with Charles . . ."Jimmy broke off, feeling his own choking grief for the man that had done so much to help him adjust to immortality. Charles Tarleton had been Jimmy's friend, too, and his absence would leave a painful hole in his heart... as well as a desire to get his hands on the despicable creature that slaughtered him.

"My son is indeed despicable," Baldevar agreed, sounding both furious and resigned. "That is why you must protect

Elizabeth from him. Make sure she takes a sedative before you sleep for the day. I want her to sleep all day tomorrow until we are awake to protect her."

"Is that necessary?" Jimmy asked, not liking the thought of Ellie spending her daylight hours in a drugged-out stupor.

"Mikal's attack could come from any quarter," Baldevar responded. "Elizabeth says she will remain on this estate, but remember her youth, Mr. Delacroix. She might blunder unthinkingly into a trap; Mikal could lure her away from the house by having any of her friends contact her, say they are hurt or need her. I do not suggest they collaborate with him; they most likely would have no thought he was anything but another mortal for that is what he appears to be in daylight. I don't want Elizabeth responding to any temptation tomorrow. If she sleeps, Mikal cannot reach her for this house is barred to him."

"Okay," Jimmy nodded. "I'll make sure Ellie takes something." He thought she could use the Valium he planned to give her anyway, after all she'd been through tonight.

Baldevar nodded and with his hand on the doorknob to leave, he turned and gave Jimmy one last order, filled with a vehemence Jimmy couldn't have ignored even if he wanted to—*Keep my daughter safe, Mr. Delacroix.*

Chapter Seven

"You're very lucky, ma'am," the disembodied customer service voice told Meghann and she bit back an acid comment about brainless automatons putting their foot in their mouth when they didn't know the reason behind a last-minute flight. 'There's a seat available on Delta Airlines Flight 458 nonstop from New York to Chicago, first class. May I have your credit card, please?"

Meghann recited the information from memory, relieved that she'd gotten a flight on such short notice. She'd worried she wouldn't be able to leave New York tonight and then who would go to Lee? He must be wondering by now where Charles was ...

No! Ruthlessly, Meghann suppressed the dangerous thoughts. She couldn't think of Charles now; she'd go crazy if she did.

"Ma'am?" the operator said. "That flight starts boarding in forty-five minutes. Will you make it?"

Meghann glanced at the signposts on the Sunrise Highway; she was five exits from MacArthur Airport. "I'll be there."

She had to be there; the flight left at one AM and would touch down at O'Hare around four. A later flight and Meghann risked being exposed to daylight if there was the slightest delay. She put her foot down on the accelerator and pushed the Cadillac up to 120 mph, zooming past the thin night traffic.

Inevitably, Meghann heard the whirring siren and blinked at the flashing lights of a police cruiser behind her a few minutes later.

Go away, Meghann glared at the cop reflected in the rearview mirror and watched him cut the lights and siren, veer meekly into the right lane and pull off by the side of the road to wait for some mortal speedster he could ticket.

A dozen knives stabbed at Meghann's temples and she rubbed her head gingerly, wondering why she felt so ill at such a simple trick. Then she remembered how thoroughly Simon had drained her and realized she'd have to make a quick stop.

Meghann slowed the car to a normal speed as she drove through the ugly, blighted town of Ronkonkoma on her way to the airport, scanning its quiet streets and boarded-up strip malls until she found what she was looking for at a 7-Eleven. Pulling into the parking lot, she watched it detach from a circle of friends and wander over to her.

"Hi," Meghann greeted the young boy with a safety pin fastened through his nose, shocking pink hair, and vacuous eyes. She longed to tell him she could remember when the punk look was a sign of daring nonconformity and not the slick marketing gimmick MTV had warped it into.

"You're a Goth, right?" the boy said in greeting. "You've really got the vampire look down, especially those half-moon circles under your eyes they look so natural. How do you do it?"

I let the bastard who killed my dearest friend suck my blood while he screwed me. "Get in," Meghann said shortly and clenched her teeth at the nausea she felt from exerting that slight control over the boy's will. Just how much had Simon taken from her that her skin was pale enough to incite mortal comment and these baby tricks were making her sick?

The boy obeyed, either Meghann's command or his own libido, and vaulted over the car door onto the passenger seat

"I like your car," he announced and Meghann nodded her head in reply, her sharp eyes inspecting the area for a suitably deserted place to take her victim. "You're into the Goth scene? Me, too. You know, there's this club opening in Manhasset on Saturday. We could go together or something. It's gonna be really cool. They're saying there's gonna be this display like that hanging cop in Silence of the Lambs, some guy with his guts ripped out just stuffed over the front door. You pay the cover charge by putting the money in his abdominal cavity! I know it'll just be a dummy but that's still a great idea ... hey!"

Meghann pulled the car behind a Salvation Army dumpster next to a densely wooded area, cut the ignition and jumped on the hapless boy. She didn't even bother stripping him, just attacked the femoral artery in his left thigh through his pseudo-army fatigue pants.

The young man's blood, tinged with a pleasant overtone of marijuana, filled her mouth and Meghann drank greedily, feeling her grief abate in the dizzying high of the blood rush. With blood pouring down her throat and restoring her power, the crushing sadness faded and Meghann could almost forget Charles's poor, sorry remains lying in the trunk. Now Meghann's entire focus was on the strength coursing through her, strength and the sudden, irresistible desire to revel in the complete control she had over her prey. She could drain him to death if she wanted to and no one could stop her ...

But Charles wouldn't like that, Meghann thought and the blood in her mouth turned sour. She sat up abruptly, wiping her mouth and chin clean with a rag she took from the glove box. Charles wouldn't like it if she hurt someone. He was looking down on her now; she couldn't do anything to make him ashamed of her.

Meghann glanced at her victim, pale and shocked, but well enough. He was still conscious, fear making him look much younger as he stared in disbelieving terror at Meghann's fangs, his lips moving with no sound coming out.

"We had sex and then you got out of the car," Meghann said to the boy, relieved when she felt no drain on her energy as she reached into his mind. "You started walking back to your friends and a dog"—she glanced at his thoughts to see if there was any breed he particularly disliked—"a Doberman attacked you. You pushed him away before he could do more than bite your leg. That's all that happened tonight. Do you understand?"

The boy nodded and repeated Meghann's hypnotic suggestions when she asked him how he got the wounds on his leg. Satisfied, she dismissed the boy and tore through Ronkonkoma, reaching MacArthur Airport with ten minutes remaining to final boarding for her flight.

She checked in rapidly, enchanting everyone from the security guards at the metal detectors so they wouldn't see her when she walked past them to the flight attendant who believed the Queen of Spades card she handed her was a driver's license when she asked Meghann for identification before presenting her with her boarding pass.

Meghann sank into the plush first-class seat, indifferent to her surroundings. She could care less if she flew in the cargo hold as long as she reached Chicago tonight.

"Miss," a flight attendant said politely. "You'll have to store that in the overhead compartment."

You saw me stow it, Meghann smiled and the girl smiled back, going away thinking Meghann no longer held anything on her lap.

Meghann leaned back and shut her eyes, ignoring the instructions for emergency procedures and heaving a sigh of relief when the plane took off on schedule. Now she'd get to Lee tonight.

What if Mikal has killed him, too?

Meghann's eyes flew open and the fingers clutching Charles's remains tightened until the knuckles were white and strained with anxiety. Could Mikal have anticipated her agonized rush to Chicago? Was she blundering into a trap at Charles's house—Mikal waiting to kill his own mother?

Meghann shrugged off the disquieting thoughts. She wasn't going to change her plans. If Mikal had... done something to Lee, it would just be one more score she had to settle with this monstrous boy she could no longer think of as her son. Let Mikal try and get her. It wasn't daytime and he couldn't sneak up on her. If Mikal wanted a battle, he'd get one and hopefully Meghann would kill him before he got a chance to harm Ellie.

I can kill him, Meghann thought, ignoring the cries of her heart just as she had earlier when she screamed at Simon but wanted nothing more than to run into his outstretched arms and let him comfort her.

No! Simon was the cause of all this—to seek solace from him was like spitting on Charles's grave. This was all their fault, hers and Simon's. She'd killed her best friend because she allowed herself to trust Simon Baldevar when he swore he wouldn't raise Mikal to be a cold-blooded, remorseless killer.

No, Meghann thought wearily, *the whole mess went back further than that*. Her true blunder was the night she let Simon take her and impregnate her. Whatever darkness in her soul responded to Simon, it mingled with his own ruthless evil that night to create the monster that was their son. A child of vampires—how could they have expected anything but the curdled, bleak soul Mikal apparently had? Mikal should never have been born. If Meghann had just resisted Simon, none of this would be happening—Charles would still be alive.

But then Ellie wouldn't have been born either and Ellie was the whole world to Meghann. Ellie wasn't dark or warped, she was a sweet, good girl. Was Ellie so different from Mikal simply because she was mortal? Why couldn't Ellie be her only child? But such regrets were a stupid waste of time. Playing "if only" wouldn't give Meghann back her best friend. Nothing would bring Charles back now. Meghann could only try to protect Lee and Ellie.

Lee . . . how was she going to tell Lee that Charles was dead, taken away just as he and Lee were finally ready to be together forever? Lee had every right to hate her and Simon for producing the miserable offspring that slaughtered Charles. But no matter what Lee said, no matter how he tore into her, Meghann would keep him safe. It was the only thing left she could do for Charles, keep his mortal lover safe.

Charles, Meghann thought and saw him clearly in her mind's eye, reliving the night they became friends, the night he saved her from suicide. He'd found her huddled over a victim in some back alley, weeping and hating herself because she didn't want to kill anymore but didn't know how to stop. She'd never forget the kind, concerned face looming out of the darkness or the gentle, firm hand that pulled her off the cold street. Before he ever spoke a word, Meghann loved Charles, loved him for the way he'd seen past the worst in her to something good and decent that Simon Baldevar hadn't been able to warp.

What would have happened to her if Charles hadn't risked Simon Baldevar's wrath that night to take her away from him and helped her learn to tame the blood lust? And how many other times had Charles saved her from despair? No one, not her mortal father or even Alcuin had been there for Meghann as consistently as Charles. Not once in their sixty years of friendship had he let her down. Charles was always there to listen or offer advice or just be her friend. What was she supposed to do without him?

"Miss?"

Startled, Meghann opened her eyes and gazed at the middle-aged man seated next to her, the eyes beneath his black-framed glasses filled with concern.

"Are you all right?" he asked politely. "You were crying in your sleep."

"I wasn't sleeping," Meghann choked out and nodded her thanks at the cocktail napkin he gave her to wipe her face and blow her nose. "It's just. . . there was a death in my family."

"I'm sorry," he replied gravely and Meghann could see this nice, plain man really meant that. "May I ask who?"

"My brother," Meghann said truthfully, not able to stop crying now that she'd started. Crying was the only thing that mitigated the tight, clenching ache inside her. "He was murdered."

"That's just awful," her newfound friend said and Meghann saw several other first-class passengers around them nod their agreement. "Have the police caught the killer?"

"Not yet," Meghann said. The killer's my own son and he's still at large, he still presents a threat to my daughter and the only friends I have left—Jimmy and Lee.

"I'm really sorry," the mortal repeated and Meghann felt humbled by his simple desire to comfort and ask nothing in return. Charles had had that kind of unselfish nature, the kind Meghann had always aspired to—noble and giving, helping mortals instead of victimizing them like Meghann had almost done to that foolish boy tonight.

Well, Meghann could start improving herself right now, by doing something Charles would approve of. Clutching her comforter's hand, Meghann looked into his mind and then used the Sight to see what in his future would make him happy.

"Don't worry," she smiled at the thirty-nine-year-old man. "The new fertility treatment will work—your wife is going to conceive in three months."

"What the ..." the mortal started to stutter but Meghann shook her head gently and put a finger to her lips—*don't question how I know, just accept and be reassured.*

The mortal (*Bill,* Meghann saw) quieted and a few minutes later, the plane began its descent into O'Hare.

"Are you a psychic?" Bill asked as they walked off the plane together.

Meghann nodded, thinking she wasn't much of one if she'd had no premonition of Charles's death. What good was her much vaunted Sight if it didn't save Charles, if it might not give her any warning that Ellie was in danger? Meghann sighed and remembered Alcuin's many admonitions that vampirism did not make her a god and only the gods saw all the future might bring.

"Would you like a ride into the city?"

Meghann shook her head; it was now a quarter past four. Driving, Meghann wouldn't reach Charles's Hyde Park neighborhood for another hour at least. Thank God his home fell within the thirty-mile radius of the astral plane and she'd visited before so she could fly there now.

Meghann bid Bill goodbye and walked to the nearest ladies room, locking herself in a stall so no one would observe her disappearing when she used the astral plane.

Meghann shut her eyes and inhaled as Alcuin had taught her to, clutching Charles's remains tightly. Transporting objects across the astral plane was difficult, but not impossible; you just had to concentrate.

Meghann cleared her mind, shutting out all the grief and fear, willing herself to see and feel nothing, to try and float in a soothing nothingness. Soon her concentration was rewarded and she lost touch with the physical world. The harshness of the bathroom's fluorescent lights no longer burned against her closed eyelids; her nose wasn't offended by the overpowering scent of disinfectant and urine. All that was gone now and Meghann was ready to start her trip.

Charles, Meghann thought and envisioned her destination— the long, rectangular brick and limestone mansion on Kenwood Avenue where Charles had lived his mortal years.

Meghann remembered what Charles told her of his mortal life, that his father had been one of the robber barons of the late nineteenth century, making his fortune through steel factories and shipping. With wealth came a desire to climb and Charles's father attempted to ingratiate himself in high society through his children. Charles was sent to the best prep schools and then Harvard Medical School, only to be disowned when his disgusted father discovered his son's homosexuality.

Charles quietly vanished from his family's life, later becoming a vampire when one of his lovers transformed him, but he kept tabs on his mortal relations and felt only pity when the 1929 crash wiped out his family's fortune. Charles, who'd only been immortal a few years then and would not stir concern by his young appearance, diffidently offered his father money enough to keep him on his feet and allow the family to retain their home. But his father wanted nothing to do with "a dirty queer's filthy money" and refused the loan.

Charles bowed to his father's wishes for Alcuin insisted it wasn't a vampire's place to force his desires on humans and watched his family fade into obscurity, his father dying of tuberculosis in a charity ward ten years later.

But Charles still yearned for the house he'd grown up in and bought it when it came on the market in 1962. Meghann smiled, remembering Charles's glee and pride as he escorted her through the eye-catching house his father built in 1905.

Ellie was the one who'd pointed out that the house was a true example of Frank Lloyd Wright's style when they took her there for the first time at the age of ten. Already she had enough interest in architecture to point out to Meghann, Charles, and Lee the many modern innovations of Charles's home—the horizontal lines of the roof, limestone sills, art glass windows (pretty eggshell colored steel shutters were drawn over them during the day) and dramatic living space with its broad central hearth. How many times had she and Charles finished out a night by that cheerful redbrick fireplace with a few glasses of absinthe, not talking but simply enjoying each other's companionship?

"Meghann?"

Meghann opened her eyes and saw her thoughts had directed her over the astral plane very well; she was standing in front of the hearth now with Lee Winslow staring at her apathetically.

"Meghann," Lee said again and Meghann felt new remorse squeeze her heart when she saw the deep furrows around his eyes and mouth that had never been there before, the way his eyes had taken on a beaten, weary look like a tired old dog.

"I can't cry," Lee said dully and Meghann wanted to cry herself when she watched him shuffle over to the mahogany wet bar with the slow, fumbling walk of the very, very old. "I know I should, but somehow I can't seem to believe Charles isn't going to come walking through that door..."

"Who told you?" Meghann demanded, feeling a flush of anger. Why would Ellie or Jimmy decide to inform Lee of his lover's death over the phone and then hang up, thinking their job was done while Lee had to cope with his monstrous grief by himself in this lonely house? Such thoughtlessness wasn't like either of them.

"Simon," Lee said and Meghann started uneasily. She hadn't known he knew where Lee and Charles were supposed to meet tonight. Did that mean he was going to try and come here tonight, force his own selfish need for her attention on her? "Did Simon tell you how ... who did it?"

The tumbler glass of gin in Lee's hands dropped and shattered on the white Italian tile floor and Lee raised grief-stricken, enraged eyes to Meghann and she saw that, yes, Simon had told Lee everything. Seeing Lee's rage, Meghann prepared herself for the recriminations she deserved but Lee only held his arms out to her and said sadly, "Oh, Meghann. What are we going to do?"

Meghann dropped Charles's remains and held Lee tightly, knowing now he had no intention of blaming her. It would be selfish to cry of the guilt that drove her here and make Lee console her; she had to help him. "We're going to say goodbye to Charles. That's why I came here."

"A funeral," Lee said, soundly faintly surprised. "Of course." Then his gaze fell on the cardboard box by Meghann's feet. "Is that... Charles? I want to see."

"Please," Meghann said. "Don't look at that . . . Charles wouldn't want you to remember him that way." Bad enough the desecration Mikal had visited upon Charles was burned in her mind forever—let Lee hold something else in his heart when he thought of Charles. "Lee, you don't need to look at that to see Charles again. You know all vampires have at least one great gift. Mine is the ability to summon the spirits of my loved ones. Forget this empty shell and let me bring Charles's soul to you."

"Summon?" Lee asked and his voice took on a guarded optimism that made Meghann regret her words, for they'd given Lee a false hope in place of the comfort she meant to offer. "You mean you can bring Charles back, resurrect him?"

"Not exactly," Meghann said gently and her heart lurched when the hopeful light in Lee's eyes dimmed. "No one can bring the dead back to life. Death is ... death is the beginning of a different existence and usually, when someone passes on, their spirit can no longer communicate with those of us on the physical plane. No one knows why there's a barrier between the living and the dead or where the soul goes—not even vampires. But vampires . . . our souls seem to have a flexibility mortal spirits don't have, we can puncture the barrier temporarily. That's why I came here tonight. I want to give you and Charles some of the time Mikal cheated you of, time enough to say goodbye."

"What are you going to do, Meghann? Is this like a séance?"

"Something like that," Meghann said, almost smiling at Lee's naiveté. Like Jimmy Delacroix, he'd never wanted to know a great deal about the mysticism she and Charles dabbled in—those things that Lord Baldevar was a master of. Meghann shuddered, wondering if Mikal was not only able to survive daylight but also a sorcerer of his father's caliber. If so, what (if anything) would stop him?

Enough of that, Meghann scolded herself. Concentrate on the task before you. Besides, she knew Simon's guarded ways well enough to know he'd never show anyone all his tricks ... not even his flesh and blood.

"Get me some hot water," Meghann said to Lee, whose eyes widened with surprise at her banal instruction but hurried off to carry out her bidding.

With Lee out of the room, Meghann removed Charles's head from its chenille wrapping, kissing the forehead reverently. She made the Sign of the Cross in the center of Charles's forehead and over that drew a seal of protection with her fingertip.

"I love you," Meghann said and carefully placed Charles's head in the large, black cauldron hanging in the fireplace.

Lee came back to the center room, and handed her a steaming pail of water. She poured the water into the cauldron and built up a fire with some kindling Charles kept by the fireplace, no matter what the season.

Soon there was a glowing fire though it raised the already muggy temperature in the room to something unbearable. When Meghann went to switch on the air conditioning, Lee explained the central air system was malfunctioning and the repairman was due to arrive tomorrow afternoon. There was a fine sheen of perspiration on Lee's face and Meghann's clothes felt plastered against her body, her long hair stuck to her back in wet, stringy clumps.

Meghann waved her hand and the lights went out, the flames from the fire casting eerie, elongated shadows along the wall. She didn't really need the darkness but used it to distract Lee—she didn't want him to concentrate on the odor of roasting flesh when the cauldron started to boil.

Walking clockwise, Meghann cast a circle to protect her and Lee from any mischievous spirits attracted to her ceremony that would try to mimic Charles, using the cauldron as the northernmost point of the circle.

"My God," she heard Lee breathe in awe when a thin band of golden light appeared around them.

"It's all right," Meghann whispered and took his hand, looking deep into his heart to find his love for Charles and combine it with her own. She took that love and imagined its essence as a windstorm, a small speck at first but gathering more and more momentum as she concentrated and fed it all their love for Charles, their need for him and grief at his passing. When Meghann felt the essence as a living, breathing thing, she pulled back from Lee and grabbed the whirlwind force she'd erected in her hands, throwing it up and away from her with all the force she could muster while she screamed, "Charles!"

"Excellent, Banrion." Meghann heard a dearly familiar voice congratulate her and she turned to see Alcuin standing by her side.

No matter how heavy her heart was, Meghann could always feel some calm settle over her spirit at Alcuin's sporadic visitations.

"How well you choose to employ your gifts, Banrion,"Alcuin said, smiling proudly as he stared at the hearth.

Meghann turned to the fireplace and her breath caught at the handsome young man standing there with black hair and cheerful black eyes, wearing a Panama white hat and a cream-colored linen suit reminiscent of the early twentieth century. It made sense for Charles to appear as he'd been in his youth, for Meghann had summoned him to the place where he spent that youth.

Meghann smiled tearfully at her friend's fetch, watching him and Lee speaking earnestly, their eyes happy but resigned to their inevitable separation. Strange that she couldn't make out what they were saying to each other, stranger that they didn't seem aware of her at all.

"Charles," Meghann started to say and Alcuin clamped his hand on her shoulder.

"No, Banrion. This time is for them alone," he whispered, pointing to the male couple embracing. "Now you must come with me."

"Come with you? But..." Then Meghann saw her body slumped by Lee's feet and understood Alcuin had extracted her soul so she could walk in his dimension.

Soon the physical world became blurred and indistinct, only Alcuin having any substance as they wandered through something like a thick fog.

"You spoke very bravely to Charles's lover, Banrion, telling him Charles's death is not as crushing or final as it could be," Alcuin said and Meghann had an impression of something like a warm hand settling over her. It wasn't a physical sensation, more like she received the emotions such a touch would evoke—

caring, love, and pride. "But do your words bring comfort to your own heart?"

Meghann couldn't answer; she only stared up and beseeched Alcuin with a deep, stinging pain that came out of her soul as soundless, phantom tears.

"My poor young queen," Alcuin said and Meghann felt his touch on her the way it would have been in life—his thin, skinny arms that were so strong and comforting despite their wasted appearance, the feel of his woolen monks robe brushing against her skin in a way that reminded her of her treasured childhood blanket. "Cry here where no one sees; purge your heart of this bitterness so you may regain the strength you'll need to keep your loved ones safe."

"Charles didn't deserve what happened to him!" she cried against Alcuin's chest. "He didn't, he didn't!"

"No more than you deserve the hair shirt of guilt and reproach you're whipping yourself with now. Look at me, Banrion." Alcuin took her by the shoulders and she tilted her chin to meet his eyes. "This tragedy is not your fault. Had you any inkling Charles was in danger, would you not have done all you could to save him— even given up your own life to save his, just as you'd do if someone threatened Elizabeth?"

"But Mikal is my son," Meghann protested.

"You are not to blame for Mikal's actions," Alcuin said firmly. "He has made his own choice to use all his talents and abilities for destruction and you did not affect that choice—nor did Simon Baldevar. You must not hold him responsible for Mikal."

"What?" Meghann said dumbly, certain she misunderstood for she'd never expected to hear Alcuin defend the vampire he'd spent four hundred years attempting to kill for his sadistic, depraved behavior toward mortals and vampires alike.

"Simon Baldevar was an altogether different being before he met you," Alcuin said quietly. "He was an unfeeling, cold monster that gloried in the pain he brought to others. When he took a consort, I thought you would be one of his victims and I did not see how wrong I was in that assumption until your children were born. He loves you, *Banrion*, and that love has tempered the darkness in his soul. Not completely, it's true, but you gave him something he never had before you—a heart, and the ability to care deeply for someone besides himself.

"You cannot rip that heart away from him now when he needs you so badly." Alcuin's specter hands clutched hers with a grip that crushed the bones together and made her cry out. "Simon needs you, Banrion, and this is no time to selfishly indulge your grief for Charles by pushing him away to soothe your guilt."

"Selfish?" Meghann cried and tried to wrench away from Alcuin but this was his world and her resistance to his power weak. "I want Simon out of our lives to save Ellie, to..."

"To punish him, to make him pay for the pain that's tearing you apart. Banrion, you cannot begin to know the hell Simon has already gone through over Mikal. If you withdraw from him now, when he most needs your love and support, he will have nothing to sustain him when he battles Mikal to save you and Elizabeth. Look carefully, Banrion, and tell me if this is what you want for it is what you will bring to pass if you allow Simon to fight Mikal alone."

"Alcuin?" Meghann called, suddenly alone and in a dark, cold place she thought might be familiar though she couldn't be sure she'd ever been here before.

Silence greeted her repeated calls and Meghann inched forward, determined to find her body and leave this bleak netherworld. Her foot hit a solid barrier and Meghann looked down, screaming at what she saw.

"No," she moaned. "No, no." Lying at her feet was Simon Baldevar, a broad sword lodged in the center of his heart and a large pool of blood rapidly forming around his body. His eyes were shut, his face ashen and still with his bright chestnut hair standing out in ghastly relief against the pallor of his skin.

"Is this what you want, Banrion?"

"No!" Meghann screamed at the invisible voice and its unspeakable portents. "No, no!"

Meghann fell on her knees by Simon and the hideous vision was so real she not only heard the dull splat as her knees hit the crimson puddle of blood surrounding her lover's body but also smelled the thick odor of iron and copper permeating the darkness around them. Frantically, Meghann pulled at his death sword with all her strength, even though she knew the weapon had already done its work and removing it from his heart would not bring Simon back.

"Please don't die," Meghann pleaded with the unresponsive body, her tears mixing with the dark, stagnant blood that soaked her clothes and stained the stone floor. "Please don't be dead. I couldn't stand it if you leave me, too. Oh, please come back. I'm sorry, I'm so sorry. I didn't mean any of those horrible things I said. Come back, Simon. You can't leave me ... no, not you, too! No!"

"Meghann," she thought someone called out from the thick darkness and peered hopefully into the shadows but there was no one here except the corpse of a man she'd realized too late she loved and needed.

"I don't know what happened," Lee Winslow's fretful voice said, his voice sounding weak and thin as though it was coming to her from a great distance. "She ... she brought Charles here and we were ... we were saying goodbye. Then the lights came back on and she's screaming and carrying on and she can't hear me ..."

Meghann screamed again when the mists surrounding her became so thick she could no longer see Simon's body at her feet. Frantically, she crawled around in the thick fog, crying from fear at the mist she couldn't penetrate and desolation at no longer even having the poor comfort of claiming her dead lover's body.

A stinging pain spread over her cheek and Meghann raised her hand, bewildered by the attacker she couldn't see. She spun around in the fog while more blows rained down on her face.

"Stop it!" she screamed at the harsh, open palm slaps that were snapping her head backward. "Stop hitting me, stop it!"

"Open your eyes, girl," a voice she knew as well as her own ordered her curtly. "Open your eyes and come back to me."

"Simon!" Meghann gasped and found herself back where she belonged, in her body with the mundane comfort of the physical world surrounding her and the horror she'd just witnessed banished by the bright amber eyes fixed unwaveringly on hers.

"Simon," Meghann said again, glancing up at him and thinking he seemed ten feet tall as he towered over her. Then she saw her outstretched feet, felt the leather cushion pillowing her head and realized she was lying on the sofa while he stood over her.

Wordlessly, Meghann held out her hands and she felt fresh tears form when his warm, blessedly alive hands reached out to take hers.

"I thought you were dead," Meghann sobbed as he gathered her up, cradling her close to him. "It was so real... I saw you there ... dead. Simon, I don't want you to die, you can't leave me."

"Hush," Simon said and smiled at the restless hands roving over the planes of his cheek and jaw to reassure herself of his presence. "I will never leave you, little one—neither by choice nor by death. We shall be together always, I promise you."

"But Alcuin ... my vision. Simon, my visions always come true—"

"If nothing is done to alter the future," Simon broke in and pulled her closer, smoothing her hair. "Did Alcuin never teach you what a premonition is?"

"A warning," Meghann said and Simon smiled at her response. The grin turned to a puzzled frown when Meghann started crying again.

"What is it, sweet? Don't grieve so. I will avenge your fine friend."

"No," Meghann sniffled and glanced up from the shirt she'd soaked. "I just don't understand . . . how can you come in here and hold me like this, love me after all those horrible things I said?"

"Do you think me a fool, Meghann," Simon questioned tenderly, "that I would hate you for words spoken in utter grief and misery? I know you so well, too well to take offense when you behave like always—going off to lick your wounds in privacy instead of allowing someone else to pluck the thorn from your paw."

Simon smiled wryly at Meghann's wide-eyed astonishment, firmly tucking her head against his shoulder as she ruminated that Simon did know her, far better than she'd ever imagined. Meghann had friends, but Simon was right. . . she did prefer to deal with grief on her own, never allowing anyone to see her pain if she could help it.

For as long as she could remember, Meghann had resented Simon's way of shutting her out, never making her privy to his innermost thoughts. Now she discovered the same secretiveness in her own soul. She too kept a certain distance from others and that reserved quality made her and Simon more alike than she'd ever guessed.

Meghann leaned her head against Simon's chest, feeling the old peace and security wash over her. Nowhere else did she feel as safe and comforted as she did in Simon's arms. Here she felt the bitterness and choking fear start to ease, here was her place to catch her breath, to heal. Even Alcuin couldn't shelter her like this, Meghann thought, snuggling against the heat of his skin.

Had a part of her known all along Simon was nearby as she rushed to Lee, felt him shadow her steps and only come close when she needed him? And had that knowing given her the strength to rise above her grief and perform for Lee the magic that reunited him with Charles? Meghann felt guilt and shame nip at her when she thought of how easily she'd discarded this love, preferring to lash Simon with her misery and grief as Alcuin had accused her of doing.

"I'm sorry," Meghann said, the harrowing events of the night leaving her limp and weak as Simon cradled her and rubbed his lips against her hair. "I had no right to hurt you like that."

Simon buried his hands deep in her hair and leaned down to graze her lips. There was nothing sexual in his touch; it was just Simon's way of telling her he'd forgiven her, that there was no need for apologies.

"Did you have to hit her so hard?" Lee questioned reproachfully and Meghann broke off the kiss, feeling it was rude, as well as shameful, to flaunt her lover before Lee in his grief. "I can see your hand prints all over her face."

"She's lucid again, isn't she?" Simon didn't set her down on one of the leather cushions but kept her on his lap. Though Meghann was glad for the contact, she worried that their closeness could only remind Lee of his terrible loss.

Now is no time to worry over propriety and I have no intention of letting you move so much as a centimeter from me ever again.

"How did this happen?" she demanded and saw Simon needed no clarification of what she meant.

"Dawn will start soon and I need time to explain our son to you, Meghann. We'll retire now and discuss him tomorrow night on our journey home."

"We will not!" Meghann protested heatedly. "We'll discuss it right now, there's nearly an hour ..."

"Meghann!" The low timbered sharpness in Simon's voice and narrow gold eyes made her subside immediately, reflexively shrinking away before his arm clamped around her waist to keep her in place. "I planned to talk to you and Elizabeth of Mikal this evening. But between you wasting time soothing that imbecile Delacroix's hysterics and then ... this .. .there simply wasn't time. Now you will wait until tomorrow evening when we have the time and cool heads to discuss this situation properly. Do you understand?"

If she lived to be a thousand, she'd never completely understand Simon Baldevar. She could all but flagellate him with her words, maul his face, and he'd forgive her immediately, but let her disagree with the creature or contradict him and he sat there glaring icy disapproval. Meghann shook her head and sighed, thinking it would take a far more adept psychologist than she to crack Simon Baldevar and his baffling psyche.

Simon was just lucky she felt bad enough about the way she'd behaved earlier to give in to his highhanded orders gracefully. On any other night, she'd spend any time remaining until dawn telling him exactly what she thought of his behavior.

If you want to give in gracefully, wipe that sulky frown off your face, Simon smirked at the red-gold eyebrows drawn together over her nose.

Meghann started to scowl even more fiercely when he spoke again: *I knew temper would lighten your grief.*

Meghann leaned back, almost smiling when she thought how well Simon knew her, to trick her into an anger that had done more to heal her than any soothing words.

"Shall we retire?" Simon asked, giving her a lazy grin and Meghann nodded but Lee spoke up before they could rise.

"Not yet. There's something I have to discuss with you both." Lee cleared his throat and stood up, his eyes steady and full of resolve as he addressed them. "I want you to transform me. Now, tonight."

"What?" Stunned, Meghann turned to Simon, fully willing to allow him to handle this bombshell development. What had bought this on? Meghann hadn't thought Lee would want to transform now that Charles was gone.

"I'm tired of being useless," Lee said and Meghann saw fury and determination light up his normally tranquil eyes. "Mikal killed Charles but I can surmise that Charles is far from his last victim. Simon, he's going to go after Ellie and Meghann, isn't he? That's why you were so sad this evening. You have to protect your wife and daughter from your own son."

Simon merely nodded, grasping Meghann's wrist to warn her to keep quiet until Lee was done speaking.

"I wasn't able to help Charles." Lee swallowed and Meghann saw his fists clenched tightly in his trouser pockets. "But I'll be damned if I stand on the sidelines while Mikal goes after Ellie. She's my daughter as much as yours and I'm going to do everything I can to protect her. That means being a vampire, for once having the strength to fight for the people I love instead of being shunted into the background, a useless mortal everyone has to protect. No more! From now on I fight back."

"It will be as you wish," Simon said and the vise on Meghann's wrist tightened. "But I cannot stand by and let you demean all you've done to protect Elizabeth, who you rightfully point out is your child, as well as ours."

"I want to do more than be your mortal babysitter," Lee insisted and Meghann sprang at him, twisting out of Simon's grip.

"Ellie would never have been born if it wasn't for your skill and I would have died with her," Meghann said, taking his hands. "You saved me from hemorrhaging, from bleeding my baby away. You gave up your career to raise and shape Ellie, not merely babysit her, as you put it. You didn't need to be a vampire to do all those things, Lee. Are you so sure you have to become one now?" What she didn't say was she wasn't sure how much a novice vampire could help against the apparently formidable creature Mikal was.

"As a vampire, I can whack the head off anyone that tries to hurt her," Lee said firmly and Meghann floundered, not sure how or even if she should pursue the argument.

Simon made the decision for her. "Dr. Winslow is right, Meghann. As an immortal, he can protect Elizabeth and avenge his lover, which is his right. And you are right to respect Mikal's power, Doctor. He is a powerful adversary and that is why I do not want anyone left at his mercy simply because they are mortal. Do you understand now why I insisted Elizabeth transform, Meghann?"

Meghann did understand, though it broke her heart to think of her daughter giving up the sun and taking on the burdens of immortality at such a young age. To see Ellie struggle with the blood lust.

"Better than seeing her dead," Simon said harshly and then addressed Lee. "We can start tonight. You will be bled to the point of death to trigger transformation. Tomorrow, you will feel weak and listless. Remain in bed and attempt to digest nothing but cool water. You may notice a certain transparency to your reflection—that happened to Meghann before I completed her transformation. Tomorrow night, you drink our blood to complete the process."

Meghann shuddered, knowing full well how many complications could arise after Lee drank their blood—transformation induced psychosis like Jimmy had suffered, severe physical deformities. Even death in the worst case scenario. Then she relaxed, remembering Simon's incomparable skill in the art/science of transformation. If anyone could guide Lee safely into immortality, it was he.

"Which of us do you want to bleed you?" Simon asked Lee and Meghann saw the mortal doctor's startled gaze shift from her to Simon and back again to her.

"Let's go to your sleeping quarters," Simon said after Lee made his choice.

In a masculine bedroom of leather and dark wood, Lee dressed for bed and lay on his back against the taupe bed sheets, suddenly looking uncertain and scared.

"It's all right," Meghann said into his ear and sat beside him, holding his hand. "It doesn't hurt that much. Did Charles ever bite you?"

"Sometimes," Lee whispered, his face flaming as Meghann uncomfortably shifted, wishing she hadn't had to ask for this detail of their private life together.

"Then you know what it feels like," she said shortly to cover up her embarrassment. She leaned down and kissed Lee on the lips, her emotions maternal and caring as she brought his wrist to her mouth and gently punctured the skin with her blood teeth.

As Meghann drank, she focused less on the blood filling her and more on the images of Charles she received from Lee's thoughts. With Lee supine and dreaming beneath her, Meghann saw her best friend and the impressions were so crisp and sharp she almost thought them reality.

This feeding was giving Charles back to her! Meghann drank thirstily, her heart aching as Charles rose up before her, smiling and laughing in Lee's memories. She saw Charles bouncing the baby Ellie in his arms, holding his arms out as she took shaky steps toward him. She saw Charles and Lee hand in hand in some dark park, stopping by a bench to sit and breathe in a balmy summer night. She saw them having a snowball fight outside the Southampton house, her best friend's cheeks red with cold and his black hair falling sloppily into his eyes as he laughed and fired the harmless snowballs at Lee.

Charles! Meghann's soul screamed out and she plunged into Lee recklessly, wanting him to give her more of his memories, not able to let her dear friend go away from her again.

A violent tug on her hair yanked her off Lee and when Meghann spun around to hiss at the interruption, Simon pinioned her arms by her side to keep her still and said mildly, "No more. You'll kill him."

"Charles ..." she began helplessly and fell into Simon's arms, weeping and crying out, "It doesn't stop hurting."

"The pain won't always be so strong, little one. Someday it will subside and you'll be able to experience happiness again, even while you mourn your friend."

"Is Lee okay?" she asked a few minutes later and wiped her mouth clean with the silk handkerchief Simon gave her.

"As well as his current state will allow," Simon said and gestured to the shivering, fever-stricken mortal tossing in and out of an uneasy sleep.

Meghann tucked Lee under the sheets and planted another kiss on his clammy, perspiring brow. She knew there was nothing she could do to stop his fever—he must suffer through this misery to transform. But what would it be like to see Ellie lie like this, hurting and weak, knowing she could do nothing to ease her daughter's distress?

"Call Elizabeth," Simon said, either sharing her concern or nosing around her mind with his usual intrusiveness. "She'll worry if she doesn't hear from you."

"Did I scare her?" Meghann was ashamed of herself, falling apart and carrying on like that when Ellie needed her to be calm, to support her through this first tragedy of her life.

"Meghann." Simon knelt by the edge of the bed and ran his fingers along her jaw, smiling up at her with love and admiration. "You do not have to be perfect to be a good mother to your daughter. Do you think Elizabeth considers you some emotionless mannequin, incapable of experiencing sorrow and pain? Elizabeth isn't frightened or disappointed in you because you had a strong reaction to Charles Tarleton's death. But she is concerned and you should call her."

"I don't need a phone to talk to Ellie."

"Show-off," Simon teased and tickled under her chin, like she was the cat he sometimes compared her with. "Don't sap your strength or our daughter's when there is a perfectly good phone available."

Nodding her compliance, Meghann led Simon to the guest bedroom and used the phone on the nightstand, yawning hugely as she waited for Ellie to pick up. Dawn was approaching; she could feel it in her bones now. What was taking so long, Meghann wondered when the phone rang for the sixth time. It was five o'clock in Chicago, close to six in New York. Even if Ellie was asleep, Jimmy might still be awake to answer the phone but it was just ringing and ringing. Anxiety clutched her heart— had something happened to Ellie and Jimmy?

Then Ellie picked up the phone, her breathing labored and voice rushed, and Meghann felt the nasty spurt of panic subside. "Sweetheart, where were you? Were you sleeping? Then why didn't you pick up right away? And where's Jimmy, he should have gotten the phone—you were on the terrace and didn't think to bring the cordless with you? Yes, honey, I'm . . . well, I'm better. Lee's okay, considering. We'll talk about Lee tomorrow, when your father and I. . . yes, Ellie, he found me and I'm thoroughly sorry for everything I said to him and I'm sorrier you saw me like that." Meghann's eyes misted and she clutched the phone tighter before she spoke again. "Thank you, sweetheart. Anyway, we should be back around eleven tomorrow. I know that's late but your father doesn't want anyone handling our bodies during the day. Promise me you'll do like your father asked and stay at the house all day tomorrow. Don't pick up the phone. Don't leave the estate for any reason. No, I'm not nagging ... okay, maybe a little. Just stay put... I love you, too. Yes, I'll tell him. Good night."

Frowning, Meghann hung up the phone and turned to Simon. "Something's wrong with Ellie."

"She's not harmed?" Simon demanded, his face pale and lips set in a narrow line.

"No, nothing like that. But I get the feeling she's hiding something from me . . . maybe she doesn't want me to know how frightened she is." Meghann decided not to tell Simon that her hackles had been raised because Ellie didn't sound frightened or even all that sad. Instead, her voice was remarkably light and happy... the furtive, sneaky happiness that came from doing something your mother didn't know about and likely wouldn't approve of. The last time Meghann caught that tone, Ellie tried to sneak off to Fort Lauderdale for spring break with friends from school after Meghann and Lee vetoed the trip on the grounds that Ellie was too young at fifteen to travel alone and they worried about her being unprotected at night. Meghann intercepted Ellie because of that furtive tone when she insisted she was merely going to the library instead of leaving for Florida. Naturally, Meghann put a stop to Ellie's plans and grounded her for the first and only time in her life.

But what kind of mischief could Ellie have gotten up to in the five hours since Meghann had last seen her? Meghann shrugged and decided her imagination was running away with her. Most likely, Jimmy had somehow managed to get Ellie's mind off the trouble and she felt guilty for being diverted.

"Ellie sends her love," Meghann smiled at Simon, watching him strip off his oxford-cloth shirt with a stray pang of desire she was too heart sore and tired to do anything about.

"There's always tomorrow night," Simon smiled back, reading the implicit message in her hungry eyes. "And every other night for the rest of our lives."

"Will there be a rest of our lives?" Meghann asked, removing her own clothes and climbing into bed beside him. Soon, she found her favorite sleeping position, sprawled on top of Simon with his chin resting comfortably on her head.

"I want an eternity with you, Meghann, and I will not settle for anything less. I won't be cheated out of all the time I lost with you and Elizabeth. We'll deal with this adversity and then there will be all the time in the world to love and play." Absently, Simon kissed the top of her head. "Sometimes, little one, I think I missed this—knowing you lie beside me through the day—more than anything else."

She'd missed this too, going to sleep with her arms locked firmly around Simon instead of confronting the seemingly endless expanse of a bed no one shared with her. She hated going to sleep on cold sheets, her arms empty and heart filled with a hollow feeling of loneliness. How she'd missed Simon's presence making her feel protected as she slept through the day.

"Simon!" Meghann's head popped up and she scanned his eyes anxiously. "Mikal might know we're here. He could try to do to us what he did to Charles."

"No, Meghann," Simon said and returned her head to the hollow in his throat. "Even if Mikal knows where we are, he would never attack my resting place."

"Why?" Meghann asked and felt the coming dawn, impervious to her fear, force her mind and body into the vampires' daylight stupor.

"Because he's already tried and failed," was the last thing she heard Simon say as his arms tightened around her.

She didn't hear Simon sigh, "My poor little love," as he gazed down at her or know he thought her pale, tired face with its tear streaks made her resemble a battered rag doll, used and tossed away by a careless child.

And Meghann never felt the quick brush to his lips or heard Simon vow, "I'll keep you safe, Meghann ... you and our daughter. I swear I will."

Chapter Eight

After Baldevar left, Jimmy put Ellie to bed in her old room and took a shower. He scrubbed his legs, which had turned blue from the wet denim bleeding onto his skin, and wished he could rinse the leaden sadness and worry from his mind as easily as he attacked the indigo stain on his thighs.

Showering quickly so Ellie wouldn't be left alone too long, Jimmy toweled off and emerged from the steamy bathroom ten minutes later, wrapped in a terry cloth robe.

He knocked softly on Ellie's door, not wanting to wake her if she'd fallen asleep but at the same time warning her of his entry.

"Ellie?" His heart in his throat, Jimmy stared at the empty sleigh bed in dread. Where was she? Jimmy didn't care that Baldevar insisted he'd enchanted the beach house against immortal trespassers. Jimmy couldn't shake off the irrational feeling something awful had happened to Ellie while he showered. "Ellie, where the hell are you?"

"Over here, Jimmy," her voice floated out from Charles and Lee's suite and he sagged against the walnut bedpost in relief. If he weren't so distracted, his senses would have detected the whisper of her heartbeat coming from the other end of the house even before he stepped into the empty bedroom.

"What are you doing in here?" Jimmy asked, running into the room. "I thought you were going to sleep."

"I wasn't tired," Ellie shrugged and her dull, grieving eyes flicked over him.

"What are you doing?" Jimmy repeated gently, noticing the shambles the room was in and the large black trash bags at Ellie's feet. Why was she taking Charles and Lee's room apart?

"Someone has to do this," Ellie said and gestured to the clothes. "I... I thought Uncle Lee shouldn't have to come home and confront Charles's clothes, all neat and hung up, like . . . like they were waiting for Uncle Charles to come home and wear them again."

"Honey, no," Jimmy said and hugged her tightly, pushing aside some heavy wool sweaters so he could sit down on the bed with Ellie, sobbing against his shoulder. "You don't have to do this. I'll take care of it. Don't cry. Come on, let me help you back to your room."

"No," Ellie protested even while he walked her into the hallway. "This has to be done before Mom and Uncle Lee get back."

"Look, your mother's in Chicago and you know the astral plane only works for thirty miles," Jimmy reasoned. "She has to wait for sunset tomorrow before she can go anywhere. That means she's not getting back here until ten at the earliest. We'll have plenty of time tomorrow to do this... together. Don't you dare try and do this during the day by yourself. It's not a job for one person." Carefully, Jimmy tucked Ellie back into bed, pulling the cotton sheets and comforter up to her chin. "Now get some rest, would you? You must be exhausted."

"Don't go," Ellie pleaded as Jimmy stood up. "Stay with me."

"Sure," Jimmy said and perched on the edge of the bed. "Scoot over a little, would you?"

Obligingly, Ellie moved toward the center of the huge bed and Jimmy leaned against the headboard, thinking he'd remain here until Ellie finally fell asleep.

But Ellie had other ideas. "Jimmy, do you think you could sleep here? My room has shutters to protect you during the day. I don't want to wake up by myself."

Jimmy wondered how Maggie would feel about him sharing a room with her seventeen-year-old daughter. Naturally Jimmy would rest on the floor and give Ellie the bed. Still, Ellie wasn't a child anymore, and Jimmy didn't know if they should sleep in the same room.

Get a grip, Jimmy told himself disgustedly. He was being a prude of the worst sort, putting some kind of half-assed morality ahead of Ellie's obvious distress. She just wanted someone to watch over her—was that so bad? Jimmy had no doubt if Maggie were here, Ellie would probably stay with her tonight.

"Okay," Jimmy said and something loosened in his chest at Ellie's sudden, grateful smile. He thought he should tell Ellie it was her doing him a favor, relieving his loneliness. He hadn't fallen asleep with someone else in the room for decades, not since he met Maggie. When he'd been mortal, she absolutely refused to let him spend the day in her bed . . . Maggie didn't want anyone to see her in her resting state. Actually, Jimmy wasn't that crazy about Ellie seeing him in his waxen, embalmed-looking daytime slumber but he figured she had to be used to it by now. Jimmy knew Maggie had let Ellie sleep in her room when she was little though she continued to bar the door to Jimmy even after he was immortal—no doubt thinking scumbag Lord Baldevar wouldn't approve.

"You want some of that Valium?" Jimmy asked but Ellie shook her head, curling up into such a ball of misery. The only thing Jimmy could do was reach over and pull her against him, stroking her bright caramel hair like he'd done when she was a little girl. Poor kid, it wasn't enough a man she looked up to like a father was murdered—he'd been murdered by her own twin and now that twisted sibling was looking to hurt Ellie as well. Jimmy couldn't even guess what she was going through. No wonder she didn't want to sleep alone.

"I know," Jimmy murmured while Ellie wept. "I know, honey. It's terrible what happened . . . you go right ahead and cry. Try and get it all out."

"I'm scared," Ellie cried and looked up at him beseechingly. "Jimmy, I'm so scared for Mom. What if Mikal gets her?"

Gritting his teeth, Jimmy forced himself to say words that only a day before he'd have sworn on his life would never come out of his mouth. "Maggie will be fine. Your . . . father will protect her. He's very strong, Ellie. He's managed to destroy everyone that ever went up against him. He won't let anyone harm your mom."

As he spoke, Jimmy knew he was telling Ellie the truth. Much as he despised Lord Baldevar, the fiend did have a great deal of power and Jimmy knew he'd use every bit of it to ensure

Maggie's safety. Still, it galled Jimmy to have to say anything even vaguely complimentary about Simon Baldevar, to have to invoke his name to soothe Ellie. How did the rotten sonofabitch do it? Even when he wasn't here, Baldevar managed to move Jimmy into untenable positions.

"Why is Mikal doing this?" Ellie asked, her big green eyes fastened on Jimmy's like he had all the answers, making him feel absurdly smart and protective. "Why?"

"I don't know, baby," Jimmy answered and continued petting her hair. "I don't know." Of course Jimmy knew. They were suffering through this nightmare because Simon Baldevar had spawned a son as eager to revel in the pain of others as he was. That Ellie had turned out as sweet and perfect as she was, was a testament to the good in the mother that raised her and the absence of her loathsome father while she was growing up.

But Jimmy couldn't run Simon Baldevar down in front of Ellie. Right now, she needed to believe he was invincible, that he'd keep her and her mother safe. Soon enough Ellie would have to face what Simon Baldevar truly was, but tonight wasn't the time for that.

"Shhh," Jimmy soothed and felt the wire-tight tension in Ellie start to ease as she slumped against him. He used the sleeve of his robe to dry her eyes, silently marveling at how right it felt to hold Ellie, how her long, slender body was the perfect complement to his own rangy form. Funny that he couldn't seem to remember any other woman ever fitting into him so well.

It didn't take long for other parts of Jimmy to agree with his assessment of the situation, parts that to his utter mortification were starting to lengthen and swell against the cool curve of Ellie's thigh.

Embarrassed by his erection, Jimmy started to push Ellie away, stammer out an apology but, to his amazement, she pressed herself against the hard flesh and looked up at him with the same eager expectation she'd had when they ate dinner together and he almost kissed her.

She wants me, Jimmy thought and that knowledge only made him grow harder as he fell into a delicious trap of flushed cheeks, long-lidded, sleepy looking eyes and full, pouting pink lips pursed together as Ellie stared up at him in mute entreaty.

"Kiss me, Jimmy," she whispered.

Jimmy needed no more persuasion than that breathy little plea. Desire blotted out all other thoughts until it seemed there was no past or future but only a present where Jimmy couldn't battle the gnawing ache inside him that screamed for him to take her. He forgot Ellie's youth, forgot she was Maggie O'Neill's daughter, forgot everything but the ripe, eager body arching beneath him impatiently.

With no thought but seduction, Jimmy gently pushed her down onto the bed and settled his weight on top of her, feeling a dizzying throb at the way she melted beneath him. He caressed her breasts through the thin cotton T-shirt she wore and kissed her, actually moaning at the unexpected heat of her moist mouth and cool little tongue boldly darting out to meet his own.

He'd never enjoyed kissing anyone this much. Ellie molded her mouth to his like she'd been made for him and her earnest attempts to copy his movements excited him to a fever pitch of desire utterly new to him.

Then she started to arch her pelvis against his heaving, twitching cock and Jimmy almost buried himself at that moment but reminded himself he wasn't some college boy or animal to just ram it in. Using the never-fail trick of recalling batting averages to calm down, Jimmy wrested free of her lips and stripped Ellie free of her T-shirt while he threw off his robe to enjoy the sensation of his naked skin against hers.

He smiled at the golden honey color of her tanned skin contrasting against the marble white of his own. Jimmy wanted to know every inch of that sun-kissed skin, rubbing his lips against the warmth of her was nearly as good as feeling the sun warm his own skin again.

Ellie trembled as Jimmy breathed in her unique scent, tart and fresh, unmarred by artificial perfumes. Ellie undressed was a surprise to him. Despite her queenly height, she had a small bone structure that made her seem fragile and delicate as his hands explored her.

Jimmy's lips moved past her flat stomach and waspy waist to take in her breasts, wonderfully high and conical shaped with tempting strawberry colored nipples that beckoned him to come closer.

Jimmy fastened his mouth to the aureole of her right breast while his hand swirled around the bounty of her left breast. Ellie came to life beneath him immediately, her body buckling while the nipple puckered and tightened beneath his eager tongue and teeth.

"Jimmy," he heard her moan and he felt the passion start to rush through her bloodstream. Jimmy forced back his blood teeth, roused by the heady fragrance he detected beneath her golden skin, back by sheer force of will. Damned if he'd let blood lust destroy the good, simple pleasure of sex.

When he had the trenchant need for blood firmly under control, Jimmy grabbed the thick, pulsating organ between his legs, ready to drive it between Ellie's exquisitely curved thighs.

But then he made the mistake of looking into Ellie's eyes, cloudy green eyes that reminded him of another emerald-eyed lover he'd once had—one that would kill him if she knew what he was doing with her daughter.

With a sharp cry, Jimmy threw himself off the bed and grabbed his robe, fleeing the bed before he did something even worse than what had already transpired between him and Ellie. Walking was difficult since his cock had not gone down one centimeter, impervious to guilt and demanding that he go back to Ellie or use his hand at once.

Limping to the hallway, Jimmy sagged against the wall, asking himself when he'd turned into some kind of child molesting, low-riding, Woody Allen motherfucker that attacked the daughter of his former lover.

What was the matter with him? All Jimmy knew was he'd been waylaid since that foamy mug of beer appeared in his hand and he turned around to scope out a possible lay and found himself seriously interested in the willowy brunette it actually took him a few seconds to recognize as Ellie. What the hell had happened to the long-legged, coltish teenager she'd been only a year ago? When had Ellie turned into a woman, a very desirable one at that?

Desirable or not, Ellie Winslow was one woman Jimmy could never have. It wasn't right to lust after a young girl you'd known since she was a toddler scampering around the house. It made no difference that Ellie hadn't seemed reluctant, indeed had encouraged his advances. That would cut no ice with Maggie if she found out what had happened. She'd put all the blame on Jimmy and rightfully so.

Ellie couldn't be held responsible; she was just indulging in some teenaged fantasy about an older man she'd known all her life. Her grief for Charles and worry for Maggie had put Ellie in a vulnerable state and Jimmy was a lowlife snake for taking advantage of it. The one thing he'd done right was leaving the room before things went further.

If Ellie hadn't needed his protection so badly, Jimmy would have slunk out of the house right then, never to return. What he was feeling for Ellie was wrong and he knew it. But Jimmy didn't know if he could turn it off, so he thought it best to just avoid being alone with Ellie until Maggie got back to look after her.

His sharp ears picked up a pair of feet rushing along plush carpet and Jimmy briefly thought of taking off but told himself to stop being such a coward. Was he not only a pervert but also a wimp that he couldn't face Ellie and tell her they had to forget tonight?

So Jimmy remained slumped by the wall and waited for Ellie to emerge from her bedroom, wearing nothing but the skimpy little shirt that barely covered her long, exquisitely molded thighs.

"Why do you keep running away from me, Jimmy?" Ellie demanded, crossing her arms beneath her breasts so the hemline of her shirt was raised perilously high on her thighs. "You have some nerve, not finishing what you started."

"Huh?" Had she come out of the room with a stake in her hand, Jimmy couldn't be more flummoxed. Ellie wasn't like Maggie, blurting out whatever came to mind in anger. Ellie usually hid her feelings behind a wall of nonchalance, a quality

Jimmy privately thought she must have inherited from Lord Baldevar.

"How dare you just walk out on me like that," Ellie steamed, her face mottled red with anger and scorned pride. "There were two of us in that bed, you don't call all the shots. You could at least have the common decency to talk to me."

"Talk to you about what?" Jimmy demanded, determined to nip this in the bud. Ellie was talking as though there was no history between them but a possible sexual encounter. She'd conveniently forgotten he was her mother's ex-boyfriend, that Ellie could very well have been his daughter instead of Simon Baldevar's. "There's nothing to discuss. What happened in there was a mistake."

Ellie's eyes narrowed into tiny green slits and her fists lashed out to attack his chest, not with the dainty outrage of a petulant movie heroine but solid jabs and punches any prize fighter would envy.

"Mistake?" Ellie screamed while Jimmy grabbed her hands and pushed her against the wall to keep her still. "Fuck you, Jimmy! How dare you call me a mistake."

"Not you," Jimmy broke in, thankful for the vampiric strength that enabled him to hold Ellie still without exerting too much force on her wrists. "What we almost did. For Christ's sake, Ellie, you're only seventeen. I had no business touching you."

"I'll be eighteen in December," Ellie replied, as though that solved everything. "And I want you. Don't you want me?"

Jimmy almost laughed. Lucky Ellie couldn't see how much he wanted her, wanted nothing more than to throw her over his shoulder and take her back into the bedroom. "Ellie, it's not just a question of want."

"Oh, yes it is," she cried, trying to wrench out of his grip. "Answer my question, Jimmy. Do you want me?"

"So what if I do?" he yelled into her stubborn, angry face. "I'm not gonna have you, you can be sure of that! I'm not some sleazy asshole that hits on children!"

"I am not a child!" Ellie screamed back and Jimmy felt like even more of an asshole when he saw her stung expression. "I haven't been a child for a long time... you can't be a child and keep the secrets I've had to keep. Did you have a degree by the time you were seventeen? Child! How dare you minimize me like that!"

"Okay," Jimmy said and held up his hands for silence. "I'm sorry. I shouldn't have called you a child. But there's one fact you can't argue with—you're Maggie's child. Ellie, can't you see how wrong that makes all this?"

"Only if you still want my mother," Ellie said, her eyes not moving an inch from his. "If you... if you still want my mother and I'm just some substitute, then I... I don't want to do this. I don't want you comparing me with her, thinking of her when..."

"No!" Jimmy cried before Ellie could finish. "No, Ellie, I wasn't thinking of Maggie at all. I only thought of you."

Ellie's smile, a swift bloom across her face that melted her haughty features, made Jimmy smile back almost as a reflex. Before he knew what was happening, the body pressed against his lost its taut, strained feeling and a limpid softness took its place.

"Ellie." Jimmy pleaded weakly and she laughed, the confident, self-assured laugh of a woman, not a teenaged girl.

"Give me one good reason why not," she said.

"How about a thousand?" Jimmy sighed, petting her silky, bright hair he couldn't seem to keep his hands off. "I don't want to hurt you. You deserve better than some cheap one-night stand."

"Is that all you want from me, Jimmy?"

How could he tell her that was all he'd had for the past eighteen years? That was the impenetrable barrier between him and Ellie. Jimmy couldn't tell her he had plenty of sex, but the last time he made love was with her mother.

"Talk to me, Jimmy," Ellie said and reached up to brush heavy locks of hair off his forehead.

Jimmy didn't know if it was that lover-like gesture or her eyes shining with such empathy and concern but Jimmy found himself confessing everything to Ellie.

"She broke my heart," Jimmy began and knew Ellie needed no explanation of which she he meant. "After Jay died, I was a wreck... a drunk, half-crazed wreck. She plucked me up out of the gutter and turned my life around. She taught me to fight back, made me strong and good in a way I'd never imagined I could be. I would have laid down my life for her; I loved her so damn much. I'd never met anyone like her... so full of life and fire. She took me in and made me her friend and lover but she never said she loved me. Do you know what that's like, to love someone with all your heart and know they don't feel the same? I tried so hard to make her love me but she wouldn't."

"That's because she loved someone else," Ellie said softly and Jimmy nodded.

"Yeah," he said on a shaky breath. "That was the hell of it... she was in love with someone else. I never wanted to admit that, even to myself. But finally I had to face it and after that, I... I shut down. I was empty inside. I couldn't imagine loving someone else. I didn't ever want to feel that kind of pain again. So that's why I don't want to start anything with you, Ellie. You deserve better than me. You deserve a guy who'll love you with all his heart."

"I know about love," Ellie said and put her hand over Jimmy's heart. "Once I thought I might be in love but then I knew I wasn't."

"How did you know?" Jimmy asked, bemused by the sudden rush of jealousy he felt toward this unknown man Ellie thought she loved.

"I couldn't tell him what I am," Ellie answered and pressed down hard on his chest with her hand. "Don't you see, Jimmy? I can be myself with you. You know all my secrets and I know yours. You don't have to pretend with me and I'm not interested in anyone but you. Isn't that more than you have with any other woman?"

"Ellie..."

Ellie reached up and put a finger over his lips. "Let me finish. You say I deserve a man who'll love me. I know you love me, Jimmy. You've told me so plenty of times. I know what you're going to say—that isn't the same as being in love with me. Well, I don't expect you to be in love with me, yet... even though I'm in love with you. I realized that tonight, that I've loved you for a long time without being aware of it. Any time I got interested in a boy, it was because he had long hair or he was funny or he liked rock and roll. Every boy I've ever dated reminded me of you in some way. I love you, Jimmy. I want to be with you."

Ellie took a breath but Jimmy didn't interrupt. Had she any idea she was offering him exactly what he'd always wanted? For someone to make him their center the same way he longed to give all that scorned, rejected love he'd had for Maggie to the right woman? Was it possible that woman was Ellie?

"You say I deserve better than you," she continued in that level voice that bespoke maturity far beyond her seventeen years. "First, I don't agree with that. I think you're one of the finest men I've ever known but you just don't know it. But let's say you're not as good as you could be. I know some of what you told me about my father—the awful things he's done—is true. But he's better now and that's all because of Mom. She made him a better man." Ellie ignored Jimmy's rolled eyes, disbelieving huff, and went on. "Who's to say I can't do the same for you? Let me make you love again, Jimmy."

Did Ellie have any idea what she was asking of him . . . that he let go of his hurt and make himself vulnerable by putting his heart in her hands? What if Ellie grew bored with him in a few years and dropped him? Jimmy didn't think he could survive another rejection, didn't know what he'd do if he didn't have Ellie in his life.

Wasn't that his answer right there? Jimmy loved Ellie, loved her so much he couldn't bear the thought of life without her. It wasn't Maggie that brought him back to Southampton all these years; it was Ellie. Not that Jimmy didn't care for Maggie, but it was Ellie that kept drawing him back here. Ellie with her slanting smile, bubbling over with enthusiasm about her latest design. Jimmy looked over the vista of years gone by and saw himself showing Ellie his contact sheets, respecting her insightful analysis of his pictures, her sharp eye that knew what worked and what didn't. He saw the moonlight swims and long talks... all of that done under the guise of their unusual friendship. Now there was something different, a chance for something more enduring between them. Jimmy thought he'd be a fool if he didn't at least try and pursue it.

Jimmy put his hand over Ellie's and probed her eyes, trying to see any last-minute trepidation. "You're sure?"

Ellie's response was to stand on tiptoe, kiss him square on the lips, and wrap her strong legs around his waist.

He put one hand beneath her to hold her steady and thought about nothing but his need to satisfy this wonderful girl who was offering him so much, so unhindered.

Jimmy felt ready to burst and knew he couldn't wait much longer. But first he had to assure himself Ellie was ready for him. He wanted this to be as good as possible for her. He slipped his fingers inside her, groaning at the warm, dark wetness he encountered.

Suddenly Ellie's eyes widened and a strangled whimper escaped her, one of shock and need.

"Do it," Jimmy told her as she thrashed around in his arms. Jimmy started moving his fingers in a slow-motion tickle, his sure-fire technique. "Come on, honey."

Ellie needed no further encouragement. Throwing her head back and digging her nails into his back, Ellie came screaming her pleasure, throbbing wildly around his fingers. His last rational thought was if that were what Ellie felt like around his hand, what would it be like when she throbbed around...?

Jimmy had no idea how they wound up back on the bed with him lodged firmly inside her while his hands dug into the firm expanse of her ass to move Ellie's hips in the rhythm he craved. Now it was his turn to scream and howl as he felt Ellie climax again and followed her blindly.

"I'm thirsty," Ellie announced a few minutes later and Jimmy wearily raised his head from her breasts.

"I'll go down to the kitchen," he volunteered, reluctant to leave the comfort of the cool sheets and Ellie sprawled in contented languor, a smile of almost feline satisfaction on her face.

"Thanks, Jimmy," Ellie beamed and held out her arms. Leaning down, he kissed her as thoroughly as though he expected to be gone for days and not the ten minutes it would take him to get some drinks.

Jimmy stopped in his bedroom and threw a packet of cigarettes and a lighter in the pocket of his robe. On impulse, he went to his chest of dresser drawers and withdrew an item buried deep in the top drawer.

"Lemonade okay with you?" Jimmy asked, returning to Ellie's room with a pitcher and two tall glasses.

Ellie nodded and drank deeply, startling Jimmy when she held out her hand for the cigarette he'd just lit. "When did you start smoking?"

"A few months ago," she shrugged and impatiently gestured for a cigarette. Jimmy lit one for her, thinking he'd certainly introduced her to far darker vices than smoking this evening.

"What's going through your mind?" Jimmy inquired after they smoked in silence for a few minutes. Ellie looked happy, but she could be experiencing some compunction now that their love making was reality and not fantasy.

"I'm relieved," she said immediately and Jimmy laughed at the unexpected word.

"Why relieved, honey?"

"I thought I was frigid," Ellie told him which caused Jimmy wondered what kind of ass she might have been with to form that opinion. No doubt some young kid that didn't know any more about sex than she did.

Not that Ellie hadn't been wonderful . . . she'd been everything Jimmy could hope for. But he could tell by the way she moved, with unsure but instinctive passion, she wasn't that experienced. Not that Jimmy would mind teaching her... he was just thankful she hadn't been a virgin. Maggie was going to go ballistic when she found out what happened—imagine how she'd react if Jimmy had not only slept with Ellie but had deflowered her.

He might not have taken her virginity but he had given Ellie her first climax. Jimmy wouldn't embarrass Ellie by telling her he'd known, by her astonished eyes and thousand volt smile, that the rush of feeling pulsating through her was a new and wonderful experience. Jimmy leaned back, not aware that his own pleasure at his prowess was making his mouth stretch into a foolish grin that matched the one on Ellie's face.

"What's with that dopey smile?" Ellie asked and Jimmy snuffed out his cigarette in reply, pulling a willing Ellie beneath him.

"I was just thinking there's at least three hours before sunrise and I don't want to waste them smoking."

"Me either," Ellie smiled and arched hungrily beneath him.

And they took full advantage of the time left with Ellie growing more relaxed and curious. She wanted to experiment, and Jimmy gladly took on the role of teacher, thinking her education would be one long, delightful course in sensuality.

The phone rang just as Jimmy had initiated Ellie into one of his favorite pursuits—sixty-nine. He'd just tasted her musky, bittersweet juices while he felt that velvet tongue explore his cock when the phone on Ellie's nightstand shrilled at them. At the first ring, a cold, leaden ball settled in Jimmy's stomach and he felt himself shrivel up instantaneously.

He was rolling off Ellie even before he felt a hand reach up to push him away. Jimmy threw a pillow over his face as he heard Ellie pick up the phone with a shaky hello. All the warm desire in him turned to ash. Jimmy listened as Ellie fed her mother some cock-and-bull story about why she'd taken so long to pick up the phone.

Though Jimmy was relieved at this evidence Maggie had survived her trip to Chicago, he had a fervent and futile hope he'd never have to set eyes on her again.

Not only would this be the death knell of his friendship with Maggie, Jimmy knew she was going to do her damndest to destroy him. Knowing Maggie as well as he did, Jimmy thought, her mildest reaction to his sleeping with Ellie would be to crush his balls in the blender and feed them to the cats while he watched. From there, she'd work her way up to more sadistic tortures before she finally cut off his head and let him die.

'That was Mom," Ellie said unnecessarily after she hung up, her face as taut and worried as Jimmy imagined his was. "She and Daddy and Lee are coming home tomorrow night. Jimmy, I don't think we should tell everybody right away. I mean, with Charles and Mikal... It just isn't the right time."

"Hon," Jimmy said and ran his hand over her petal-soft cheek, "Maggie won't need to be told . . . she's going to know what happened thirty seconds after she steps through the door tomorrow. I wouldn't be surprised if you already got her antenna up by how jumpy you sounded. Either we tell your mother or wait for her to guess. And it won't look good if we don't have the guts to tell her we're together." Lee Winslow wouldn't exactly be jumping for joy and Jimmy refused to even speculate on Simon Baldevar's reaction. Somehow Jimmy did not think he was what that psychopathic asshole had in mind for a son-in-law.

Ellie bit her lower lip pensively. "I guess you're right. I mean, sometimes it seems like Mom knows things about me before I know them myself. But I don't want to bother her when I know she's got so much on her mind. Jimmy, what are we going to do?"

Even in his queasy apprehension, Jimmy had to smile at that "we." Pushing long, sloppy locks of his hair off his face, Jimmy turned to Ellie and took her hands. "I've been thinking about it ever since the phone rang. The way I see it, we have one chance to make this whole crazy thing work out. One.

"The problem," Jimmy continued, "is that your mother will never believe I love you. She's going to think I used you or worse, she might think this whole thing is a grudge fuck against her—my sick way of getting even with her for choosing Simon Baldevar over me. The first thing I want you to know is that's absolutely untrue. Your mother had nothing to do with what happened tonight. And I'd never have touched you if I didn't want a relationship. But Maggie will never buy that unless we do something to show her we're serious about each other."

"How do we do that?" Ellie asked.

In reply, Jimmy reached for the terry cloth robe he'd dropped on the floor and scooped out a small gray jeweler's box.

"Marry me, Ellie," he said and popped open the box to show her his mother's wedding ring, a small marquise cut diamond ring in a yellow-gold setting. Jimmy didn't find it necessary to tell Ellie he'd once presented her mother with this ring and received a firm rebuff.

"Jimmy," Ellie said, her face blank and unreadable as she stared at the ring.

Please, Jimmy prayed. Don't let her give me any of Maggie's wishy-washy I-don't-know-if-this-is-the-right-thing-to-do bullshit that amounted to No. Jimmy didn't want to get shot down again, hear that while he was perfectly acceptable as a bed partner, Ellie had no need for him otherwise.

"We can't get married now," she finally said and Jimmy's heart sank. "Not with Charles barely cold... it wouldn't be right. We'll have to put it off, get engaged first. An engagement would show Mom we're serious about each other. But we have to let some time pass... out of respect."

"Engaged?" Jimmy repeated stupidly, feeling there might be some reason to continue living after all. "You mean you want to marry me?"

"Of course I do," Ellie said and held out her left hand expectantly. Shaking like he was in the midst of the DT tremors he used to get, Jimmy finally managed to slide the ring on her ring finger.

Ellie held her hand up to the light, dazzling red and blue prisms reflecting from the diamond. "Oh, Jimmy, it's beautiful."

"You're beautiful," he said and grabbed her roughly, crushing her to him so she wouldn't see his tears, tears of gratefulness mingled with fear. Charles's decapitated head floated before him, reminding Jimmy of the threat they were all living under now.

He wouldn't let anything happen to Ellie, Jimmy vowed. He wouldn't let that sick, twisted vampire brother of hers take her from him.

"Why did you sound so surprised when I said yes?" Ellie asked, still admiring her ring.

"Ellie, look at me," Jimmy commanded and Ellie turned her eyes to him. "Do you understand what a commitment this is?"

"I thought we were past you talking to me like I'm five," she complained and rolled her eyes. "Love, fidelity, for better or worse, in sickness and in health, till death do we part . . . yes, I understand what a commitment marriage is. What do you think— I'm going to run around on you, ask for a divorce in six months?"

"If you do I'll drown you," he said half-seriously. "It's just you're very young to get married... or engaged."

"Mom was eighteen when she and Daddy got together," Ellie shrugged. "You were my age when you got married."

"That was a shotgun wedding," Jimmy reminded her. "I couldn't keep it in my pants and nine months later I had a son to prove that. And I don't think Amy and I would have stayed together. I would have met my responsibility to Jay but sooner or later we would have gotten divorced. We were both too young and too different to make it work. The only thing we had in common was an ignorance of birth control."

"Well, I think you and I have a lot more in common than that," Ellie countered. "We're both smart, artistic, have the same interests. We're sexually compatible... that's a lot more than most couples have to go on. About my being young... so what? What am I supposed to do, waste my twenties dating jerks I know don't interest me? I've already figured out what I want... you. I'm not going to change my mind in five years or ten or a hundred."

"That brings us to the next problem," Jimmy said. "If we get married, you have to transform."

"Of course," Ellie said calmly. "Daddy already said I have to transform."

"Don't talk about him," Jimmy snapped with automatic antipathy. "Look, putting his high-handed orders aside and even what we feel for each other— are you absolutely sure you want to transform? Do you know what it means to be a vampire?"

"After seventeen years of living with them, how could I not?" Ellie asked with mild exasperation. "Jimmy, I have to say you and Mom have been a little unrealistic about this whole thing. It never occurred to me that at some point I wasn't going to transform. Maybe this is a little earlier than I expected but that's okay. I'm going into business for myself anyway... I'll just meet my clients and design at night. I know about the rest, the blood lust and stuff. I figured you and Mom would help me cope with that. But Jimmy, think about it. What else is there for me but transformation? Did you think I was just going to finish out my mortal life and die while you all continued on? What would that make me? Some brief interlude in your lives? Don't you want me around forever? Jimmy?"

181

"Tired," he managed to whisper and sagged against the pillows. It was practically six o'clock—that he was awake this late into the night surprised him. Blearily, Jimmy opened one eye and saw Ellie had closed the shutters—he was safe from daylight.

"Course I want you around," he slurred and felt Ellie relax next to him. "Want you forever but... just didn't want you... want you unhappy..."

"I'll be happy as long as we're together," Ellie whispered into his ear and Jimmy, with a last burst of energy, wrapped his arms around her as they drifted off together.

"We'll be together," he promised, not sure if he spoke the words aloud or he was already dreaming. "Forever."

Chapter Nine

Meghann eyes snapped open, wide and filled with terror at the excruciating pain that felt like her skin was being stretched then peeled off her body. Whimpering, she glanced down at her arms and saw they were an appalling reddish purple, liberally covered in fever blisters that burst into oozing little rivulets of pus before her eyes.

"It's all right, little one," she heard Simon say and looked up from her wounded skin to see him driving a car unknown to her, while she was huddled on the passenger seat.

"Where are we? What's wrong with me?" Meghann cried in fear at the roiling nausea ripping through her and deep chills that made her shiver uncontrollably and wrap her arms around her body even though she burned with fever. What had happened to her? Why was she so sick?

"Exposure," Simon explained and her eyes registered on him long enough to observe that his white skin was burned to the bright pink of a negligent sun-bather. "It's early for us, only six-thirty."

"Six-thirty!" Meghann exclaimed in disbelief but the digital clock on the car stereo confirmed his lunatic statement. "But it's sunnier, Simon! We shouldn't be outdoors for another hour, at least. Have you gone crazy? You'll kill us both! And how in the world did you wake up so early?"

"Don't upset yourself," Simon said curtly when Meghann hunched over, retching out a thin, sour stream of blood and bile on the car's tan upholstered bottom. "You'll make it worse. I know you're in a great deal of discomfort. I'd hoped you'd sleep through our journey."

"Journey?" Meghann frowned and glanced behind her to see Lee sprawled and unconscious on the backseat. "Where are we going?"

"Midway Airport. . . my jet awaits us. You know I rise earlier than you because of my advanced age and I thought we should get back to New York as soon as possible. As to my decision to chance the sun, look outside, sweetheart."

Meghann looked up at the sky and saw nothing but heavy, black clouds pregnant with rain that beat down on the car windows in fierce, torrential gusts.

"Any doctor will tell you ultraviolet rays can filter through clouds and leave you with an even worse burn than you'd get on a sunny day," Meghann pointed out through her chattering teeth. Why did Simon look so well while the weak light of the hidden sun seemed to slip under her bones and eat her alive from the inside? Had Simon perhaps already drunk enough of Mikal's blood to be immune to the pre-twilight sun?

"Relax," Simon told her and she felt the car come to a stop. "We're here . . . you're safe now. All you need is to get indoors and feed."

Simon was right—no sooner had he lifted her from the car (Meghann was so weak she could not even wrap her arms around him as he carried her) and taken her into the haven of the Learjet's windowless private cabin than Meghann felt the pain drift away and a fathoms deep drowsiness take its place.

"Not yet, darling." Meghann felt Simon shake her awake and thrust a bottle of blood into her hands.

Meghann sniffed and came to a sluggish awareness at the copper scent emanating from the pint bottle. Blearily, she put the bottle to her lips and drank in great, thirsty gulps while Simon toweled her dry. She felt the bottle fall from her hands but she fell asleep even before the bottle's dull thud sounded as it landed on the plush carpeting.

Mommy, Mommy, help me! I need you . . .

"Ellie!" Meghann shouted, wild eyed with fear as her arms stretched out in automatic protectiveness to grab the child that called out for her.

In an instant, Simon was at her side, clutching her trembling hands. "It's all right, little one. Just a bad dream..."

"No!" Meghann insisted. "Its Ellie... she needs me!"

"Of course she does. And we're only an hour away from Southampton now." Simon smiled at Meghann's bewildered expression. "You do not remember getting on my plane?"

Meghann frowned, puzzling over a vaguely remembered discomfort and brief vision of sun-reddened, blistered skin. "Not really, no. Where's Lee? Is he... did he make it through the day?"

In response, Simon took her hand and guided her to the jet's bedroom where Lee Winslow reclined on a king-sized bed decorated in plain bed sheets that he'd drenched through with perspiration.

"Lee," Meghann sighed and pushed wet, sticky hair off his brow, relieved that he was still alive and knowing there was little else she could do to ease his suffering. She poured ice water from the carafe Simon gave her over a linen cloth and ran it across Lee's face, gently bringing him into a sitting position while she coaxed him into taking a few sips of water.

"Charles," Lee moaned and Meghann's heart contracted with fresh grief. She couldn't know if Lee, in his fever, mourned for his lover or maybe he was lucky enough to be in some hallucinatory world where he and Charles still walked together.

"Come along, Meghann," Simon said and pulled her off the bed. "Lee will pull through this and we'll finish his transformation tonight. I must speak to you now."

"Mikal," Meghann said, almost glad to have something divert her from her worry over Ellie and Lee, even if it was her son's unsavory tale. Ellie . . . something was the matter with Ellie, more than the brief concern Meghann felt last night. That had been a conviction her daughter was hiding something from her, now Meghann felt her little girl was in some kind of trouble—she needed her mother.

I'm coming home, baby, Meghann thought to her and felt the anxious sensation hanging over her dissipate slightly—as though Ellie had heard her and was soothed by her mother's promise.

"Here," Simon said and shoved a thick manila file into her hands. "Read this and then we will discuss Mikal."

Meghann opened the folder and inhaled sharply at the contents. "This is an MRI scan of Mikal's brain."

"It is," Simon said and Meghann's heart sank though she felt no real surprise—not after what Mikal had done to Charles. That action was enough to convince Meghann her son was a predator without capacity for empathy or love but here was scientific evidence of Mikal's deformities.

In recent years, neurologists had proven there was an organic basis for psychopathy. The report Meghann held in her hands indicated Mikal was brain damaged, not in the sense of mental retardation but in his emotional development. Most significant were abnormalities in the structure of Mikal's amygdala. The amygdala, part of the limbic system, was central in feeling emotion. A malfunctioning amygdala could, among other things, prevent an individual from feeling fear—one of the chief characteristics of psychopaths.

"You couldn't discipline Mikal," Meghann said. It wasn't a question. "He didn't learn from punishment—no matter how severe you were or what you deprived him of." Even if Simon used physical force to discipline him, as Meghann didn't doubt for a minute he had when his attempts to mold his son were frustrated by Mikal's seeming defiance, psychopaths had extremely low electrical skin conductivity, thus reducing the capacity to experience physical sensation, be it pleasure or pain.

"That would be true in a psychopathic mortal," Simon said. "But there was one thing I could deprive Mikal of to force him into some semblance of behavior—blood."

Meghann hadn't thought of that. "So whenever he misbehaved you starved him?" No wonder Mikal hated his father. "When did you conduct these tests?" Of course Simon couldn't trust any mortal neurobiologist to conduct these tests—he'd do it himself. Simon had money and connections enough to gain access to the equipment, as well as the sharp mind of a vampire that would allow him to master any mortal science.

"When Mikal was nine. There'd been a disturbing incident and I wanted to see whether the boy was suffering from a physical malady to produce his atrocious behavior."

"What did Mikal do to disturb you?" Meghann knew Simon well enough to know a son with an astonishing capacity for evil and a disregard for conventional morality wouldn't distress him the way it did her. A psychopathic child would only become a problem when he disregarded his father's ethical standards, libertine though they might be in anyone's eyes but Lord Baldevar's.

"You know me well, little one," Simon said and leaned negligently against the arm of the couch she sat on. "That Mikal indulged his blood lust avidly and in rather creative ways did not concern me overmuch. I knew early on Mikal had little use for affection but I did not fault him for that, did not try to stubbornly press a heart on the boy as you might have done. It was plain Mikal could not feel love, but unlike you, Meghann, I can empathize with our son. Four hundred years I lived without love and my life was not some bleak hell; it was quite interesting and entertaining.

"Not," Simon said, taking Meghann's hand at her indignant glare, "as interesting or beautiful as it's become since you entered my life, but amusing all the same. I knew Mikal, detached and cold though he might be, could have everything he needed—a first-rate education, dominion over the mortals and some of our kind as well, wealth, superb strength, and the ability to walk in daylight. That was more than enough to fulfill anyone."

How could it be, Simon, Meghann thought sadly, that in all this time I haven't so much as dented your offhand assurance that there was nothing wrong with feeling you were above others and their lives were yours to do with what you wished.

"Enough," Simon snapped at Meghann's disapproving thought. "I will not have you condescending to me simply because I refused to suppress Mikal's natural instincts where his prey was concerned. As far as I am concerned, I have honored the vow I made to you at our son's birth. I did not merely train his blood lust; I also provided him with an excellent education, an appreciation for the arts, and certainly instilled in him love and respect for you, our extended family, and any beings mortal or otherwise that he might eventually befriend."

"So my son spent his childhood as a miniature serial killer," Meghann said caustically. "With you cramming in little bits of schooling and culture between kills. You're right Simon—how could I ever think you hadn't done the very best for him?"

"Don't be sarcastic, Meghann. It does not suit you. Our son was no low serial killer like those penny-dreadful dregs that titillate modern society and its penchant for violence. Mikal killed when he needed to feed and that was all—like any proper vampire that does not make itself miserable through adherence to quaint mortal laws regarding the so-called sanctity of human life."

Meghann dismissed the insult to her own decision to leave her prey alive and continued her interrogation. "So what did Mikal do at the age of nine that was so atrocious only brain damage would excuse it in your eyes?"

"Many things disturbed me before that final incident. First, he's lazy," Simon said, and Meghann knew anyone with Simon's ambition and drive to succeed would indeed be disgusted by idle offspring. "No interest whatsoever in making his own way—he once had the nerve to demand a trust fund of me!"

Simon Baldevar was no miser, Meghann thought, recalling all the jewels and luxuries he'd bestowed on her over the years, but she knew he'd never hand out a lump sum of money unless he thought there'd be some gain in the long run. Mikal would have had better luck asking his father to part with his immortality instead of his gold. "Maybe Mikal had other interests beside monetary ones."

Simon made a sound that could have been a snort in someone less elegant. "Oh, he had other interests. Millions of them, all so fleeting and varied I can hardly recall most of them. One night he would be consumed by astronomy and the next night the subject would bore him unendurably and he'd make no effort to continue his studies. But as he got older, I will say this much for him—in the brief space of his infatuations, he could educate himself to a post-doctorate level on any subject. So he picked up fragments of knowledge here and there but never were there long-term interests, any need to devote himself to a subject."

"A short attention span drove you to conduct an MRI?" Meghann asked incredulously.

"Of course not... I merely attempted to discipline that. No, I decided to test him because of what he did to his pet."

"His pet? What kind of animal did you give him? Why hurt an animal when he had humans to kill?" Meghann cried.

"You are quite right," Simon said. "Mikal never did bother harming animals because humans provided more entertainment in their suffering. The boy is utterly indifferent to animals. When I said, 'pet,' Meghann, I meant a human child I procured when he was five. I thought he could learn social interaction from it."

Meghann thought and made a mighty effort to keep her face impassive. *Simon, Simon . . . if you talked this way in front of Mikal, is it any wonder what he became?*

Simon gave her a look she chose to ignore and went on. "The whole purpose of the pet was to teach him the friendship and respect for mortals I knew you wanted him to feel . . . that I myself wanted him to feel, since his own twin was born mortal. So I brought him a bright, mortal child orphaned when its mother went to jail. I chose a nine-year-old boy."

"Why did you choose a child so much older than him? Was a nine year old on Mikal's intellectual level when he was five?"

"Intellectual and physical level," Simon clarified. "Our son's metabolism was nothing short of fantastic in his early years. By the age of ten, he was as developed as a fourteen-year-old boy."

"Is his metabolism still accelerated? What's to stop him from continuing on into old age and dying by the age of thirty?"

"Pity he will not," Simon said bitterly. "His metabolism tapered off when he reached the age of fifteen... resembling a full-grown man in his twenties. Now Mikal is like us, Meghann—he does not age or change at all."

Interesting, Meghann thought. "So what Mikal do to his, er, pet?"

"I thought Mikal could form an alliance with the child, that they would entertain each other. At first, that was exactly what happened. Suddenly there was a playmate, someone to socialize with beside Adelaide and myself. The boys studied together and developed normal male interests. I taught them both the art of fencing and they enjoyed hunting game around the island I reared Mikal on. I was greatly encouraged because though you could not say Mikal was affectionate toward his pet, he certainly seemed to enjoy his company."

"Then what happened?" Meghann asked, having some idea of the grim answer from Simon's narrowed gold eyes. She thought Mikal might have killed his "pet" because psychopaths formed only the shallowest attachments and if Mikal had been bored one night, he could as easily kill his companion for stimulation as a normal person could decide to watch television to alleviate their boredom.

"I would not believe so young a child capable of such savagery," Simon said with a distant look in his eyes, like he was reliving the incident. "It wasn't so much that he killed the boy as the motive behind the killing."

"What was his motive?" she asked, chilled by Simon's hollow tone and bleak eyes.

"Mikal is a most unnatural boy," Simon said, his mouth curling down in derision of his own child. "By the time he was nine, I did not find it necessary to constantly supervise his activities—he and his companion roamed free over the island. But it was growing close to dawn and Mikal was still unable to tolerate direct sunlight so I began to look for the boys. I found them—Mikal and what was left of the other boy—on the most remote corner of the isle. Mikal may be brilliant but he still thought like a child, that if he just hid the evidence of his crime, there would be no repercussions.

"Mikal was so engrossed with the body that he was unaware of my approach. I smelled death miles away but cloaked my presence because I wished to know why Mikal would slaughter this creature that was the closest thing to a friend he had. I soon had my answer and it was in that moment that I first wished I'd never had a son. Mikal destroyed the other boy because certain overtures Mikal made were rightfully spurned."

"Overtures," Meghann felt her face color when she realized just what overtures Mikal must have made to put that appalled, seething look on Simon's face.

"Mikal is a base sodomite," Simon said, almost spitting out the words. "The other young man . . . his pants were down around his ankles and his legs covered in blood. After the boy refused him, Mikal apparently attacked his femoral artery and then raped the hapless boy when he was too weakened by blood loss to run away. But... if that were not enough... when I discovered Mikal, the mortal boy was long since dead but that disgusting boy was still riding his corpse."

Though Meghann did not have Simon's aversion to homosexuals, she was sickened to hear a child of hers indulged in necrophilia.

"I yanked him off his victim and bled him almost dry," Simon said, his hawkish eyes hard and remote. "Then I threw him into the cellar for a fortnight... finally I gave in to Adelaide's pleas and ended his punishment before he could starve to death. By then, I'd had time enough to calm myself and look at the situation rationally. Perhaps the fault lay with me, bringing Mikal a male child as companion. I should have recognized that he'd need a woman nearby when his sexual nature was awakened but he did not have to attack the boy—there were plenty of mortal females on the island he could have used for his urges."

It would take someone as crazy as Mikal might be to tell Simon it did not matter that he'd bought his son a male companion—homosexuals were born, not made. Nor did Meghann think now was the right time to antagonize Simon by telling him an attraction toward men was the least of Mikal's problems.

"I decided the boy might be sick," Simon continued, oblivious of or ignoring Meghann's thoughts. "And the tests you hold bore out my theory. Since this . . . deviancy . . . wasn't entirely Mikal's fault (again Meghann kept her silence, not bothering to correct Simon to tell him nothing on Mikal's brain scan would account for his homosexuality) I forgave him. I also acknowledged that perhaps the situation grew out of his isolation so from then on I took him on trips when I had to leave the island for business."

Where exactly had Simon taken their son in his misguided attempt to change Mikal's sexual orientation—a whorehouse? Actually, Meghann thought it quite possible Mikal would have slept with women as easily as men; psychopaths usually weren't all that choosy in their many partners.

"Tell me more about him," Meghann said, changing the subject before she goaded Simon into an argument they didn't have time for. "You say he matured at a dramatic pace? Is he tall and muscular . . . like you?"

"No," Simon answered. "He is tall, but quite thin and gawky in appearance. You see, he has never been able to digest any substances but blood and water so he never gained much weight. But he's strong all the same... stronger in some ways than us."

No wonder he doesn't empathize with us, Meghann thought. Mikal can't even enjoy our basic pleasures like fine food... he has no idea of what it is to be human.

"I knew about Mikal's strength before you came back," Meghann said and Simon gave her a surprised look. "He was responsible for the Ballnamore massacre, wasn't he?" Ballnamore had been Alcuin's sanctuary in Ireland, the place he invited all the others that shared his desire to leave mankind in peace. After his death, Alcuin had left the place to Meghann and Charles, but to reside in the Georgian fortress meant battling every self-righteous vampire that wished to destroy Meghann for no better reason than her bearing of Simon Baldevar's children. Deciding the game wasn't worth the candle, Meghann and Charles simply allowed their enemies to keep Ballnamore and an uneasy compromise developed, the same one Alcuin and Simon had observed for centuries—Meghann, Charles, and Ellie would keep to their corner of the world while their enemies enjoyed free reign at Ballnamore.

But eight months ago Charles was overcome with a terrible certainty that there had been some sort of catastrophe at Ballnamore. Unlike Meghann, Charles had shared a bloodline with some of the Ballnamore vampires and he'd know if they were hurt or killed.

Meghann and Charles's best attempts to clarify his premonition were thwarted by cloudy, obscure visions that explained nothing. In the end, they had no choice but to chance a confrontation and go to Ballnamore. But when they arrived there was nothing there. Ballnamore was deserted, an Irish ghost town.

From the wide-open windows and French doors, Meghann and Charles deduced someone had invaded the sanctuary and the corpses had been reduced to ash by exposure to the morning sun. But who had the power to invade a vampire stronghold and slaughter over thirty immortals?

"A vampire with the ability to walk in daylight," Simon said, cutting into Meghann's thoughts.

Startled from her deep rumination, aching again for the departed Charles, Meghann asked, "Was Mikal acting on your orders?" At the time, Meghann and Charles believed this might be Mikal's introduction to vampiric society, carefully orchestrated by his father. Once other vampires had a taste of Mikal's power, they would make no attempt to cross him or Lord Baldevar.

With a twisted grimace, Simon shook his head. "The boy ran away a year ago... I have no control over his actions."

Meghann absorbed that statement and all its disturbing implications. If Simon couldn't control the destructive force their son apparently was, then who would stop him?

"When did Mikal become immune to sunlight?" she ·asked, remembering the infant whose strange, fragile eyes could not even handle artificial light.

"It was a gradual change, as I expected," Simon answered. "As an infant, he built up a resistance to lamps and I was able to keep him in lighted rooms. He remained as we are . . . defenseless against the sun... until he was in his early adolescence. Then he reported to me that he was gradually waking up earlier and earlier, finally feeling nothing at sunrise."

"Does he sleep at all?" Meghann questioned.

"A few hours each day, never at night. Usually, if what he told me is the truth, he takes a brief nap between eight and ten in the morning. For some reason, he always feels drained at that time. But even then he does not need a dark place to rest . . . merely pulling the shades provides enough darkness for him to rest. Daylight cannot destroy him. Our son can only be slaughtered, I believe, by decapitating him or removing his heart."

"He has all his power during the day?"

"No," Simon replied and Meghann felt her anxiety lessen at this evidence Mikal wasn't completely invincible. "During the day, his strength is hardly more than that of a fit mortal boy his age."

"What about his occult powers?"

"He has few to begin with," Simon said and explained further at Meghann's surprised look. "Mikal is in some ways like Elizabeth, a puzzling mix of vampire and mortal characteristics. But whereas Elizabeth is mortal dominant with some vampiric features, Mikal is the opposite. He has a vampire's superior physical strength; his telekinetic talent is quite impressive. And certainly Mikal can mold mortals to his will. His best advantage over other immortals is that he can conceal his own thoughts completely, just as Elizabeth does. But other than that, Mikal has no vampiric abilities. He cannot summon, nor perform the simplest sorcery... he cannot even travel the astral plane."

"Even in his soul?" Meghann asked disbelievingly for Ellie was able to meditate and then separate her soul from her body to wander the astral plane. Meghann had taught Ellie that trick when her daughter began to menstruate and could not tolerate the severe cramping. With her soul free of the chains of her pain-wracked body, Ellie felt no pain and stayed out of her body for hours at a time.

"Sometimes I wonder if our son has a soul," Simon said cryptically. "I told you the boy ran away a year ago?" At Meghann's nod, she saw Simon's jaw clench and pain darken his golden eyes before he continued. "It is because Mikal fears for his life should I catch up with him. He ran, like the coward he is under all his bullying and pathetic posturing, after I discovered Adelaide's corpse."

"Adelaide!" Meghann felt quick tears sting her eyelids, not from her own grief but at the thought of what Simon must have gone through when he discovered the woman who'd been like a mother to him for nearly five centuries had been murdered by his own son.

Knowing no words of hers would mitigate Simon's grief, Meghann embraced him, bringing her lips to his in a slow, careful caress. This was how she and Simon communicated best; it was her touch that might bring him some peace.

Simon's response was immediate: grasping her tightly and kissing her with a sweeping thoroughness that left her dizzy and breathless. It seemed Simon wanted to take everything within her, take over her soul completely, and Meghann willingly gave herself to him, thinking Alcuin was right—Simon did need her. By letting Simon take her with fast, driving hunger, drink the blood he'd infused her with so long ago, Meghann was telling him she'd shoulder some of this unspeakable burden they faced— destroying their son to keep everyone else they loved safe.

For a long while, they held each other silently, the only sounds in the cabin coming from the bedroom where Lee moaned and thrashed in his delirium. Then Simon's grip eased and he tilted Meghann's chin up. "There isn't much time left, little one. I need to tell you all you must know of our son before we land."

One Year Earlier

Looking for all the world like a slumbering vampire, Simon was well aware of the intruder creeping into his room. He knew this confrontation had been a long-time coming and almost looked forward to its bitter climax. Not for the first time, Simon appreciated the quarters he'd chosen in this dank pile of stone. The castle had been constructed during the early Middle Ages, when such monuments were meant for defense first and beauty second, if at all. There were no windows in the grim, stone chamber—that meant his assassin could not simply throw open draperies or shutters to destroy the vampire he mistakenly thought was sleeping.

Simon gave no indication he was awake, keeping still as he heard the whispery sound of the silken curtains surrounding his bed being pushed back. It was only when the would-be killer's sword came whooshing down to separate Simon's head from his torso that Simon's hand lashed up and he grabbed the sword, easily disarming his stunned son.

"Shall I say good morning or good afternoon, Mikal?" Simon inquired casually of the young boy who stared at him with an uneasy mix of simmering resentment and cautious apprehension. "I know you are not foolish enough to try and slay me in the evening hours, are you?"

"I do not worry, Father," the thing that dared to call itself his blood replied with equal calmness. "The sun is at its zenith . . . soon you shall tire and then I will dispose of you."

In response, Simon smashed the sword hilt against Mikal's nose. Screaming from the pain, for Mikal's body had no restorative powers during the day, the boy clutched his bleeding nose, hissing and screaming when his father grabbed him and forced him facedown into the bed.

"If my blood teeth functioned during the day, I could feed now and end your sorry existence," Simon whispered, fighting the weariness that attempted to overtake him. Mikal was right— Simon had but a few moments to disable him. "But I shall have to content myself with merely breaking the snake's back."

Simon took the sword and drove it through the small of Mikal's back, slicing neatly through the boy's left kidney. He would not decapitate Mikal for that would mean giving up forever on his chance to experience daylight.

Flopping down next to the squirming, agonized boy. Simon managed to whisper in Mikal's ear, "By the time you get that sword out and your body recovers, it will be sunset and I shall finally correct the mistake of your birth, young fool."

In a way, Simon was thankful for the vampiric slumber that descended upon him. There would be no restless tossing and turning, no tense apprehension as he waited for dusk. Instead, Simon fell into a deep, unclouded rest, waking up refreshed and ready to do battle.

When he awoke, the battle was every bit as ferocious and vicious as Simon expected it to be. He awoke and Mikal recovered at very nearly the same moment and they attacked each other, each grasping for possession of the sword that would decapitate the other vampire.

Simon had never thought his son would be easily dispatched. Belying his fragile appearance, Mikal had the power of ten vampires and a psychotic rage empowering him

Not that Simon was any weakling, easily he sidestepped every killing blow with an agility borne from centuries of practice but he could not seem to strike any offensive thrusts to force Mikal off him and grab the sword. Soon Simon realized that he was expending himself on a futile cause. Physical might would not aid him, so Simon turned to his most formidable weapon—the demons he'd spent centuries paying homage to so they might assist in just such a predicament as this.

"Ahriman," Simon thundered and felt Mikal's grip on his neck tighten, making a pathetic attempt to try and strangle his father before he finished the incantation that would destroy Mikal.

"Dies mies yes-chetbene done fet Donmina Metemauz," Simon whispered and thought he finally saw terror in his son's inhuman silver eyes. "I order all ye that are bound to do my bidding to appear hither and without delay. Come forth, all ye that abide in Darkness and hold in your unnatural thrall this wretched boy that attempts to do evil against his sire. Come to me at once and do as I command!"

The screaming wind that yanked Mikal off him to throw him against the hard stone wall and mad keening of a thousand unholy souls was even more than Simon could have hoped for. Momentarily bewildered, he watched his son scream helplessly at the invisible presence that pinned him to the wall and could not be moved no matter how Mikal howled and thrashed.

Simon took his time rising from the bed, choosing to shower and dress for the evening before he attended to Mikal. The demons would not lose control of their prisoner, nor would they dare disobey Simon and attempt to take possession of Mikal for Simon had not given them permission to do that. They were only allowed to hold Mikal. After the boy was dead, Simon would give his infernal aides a few of his mortal prisoners as tribute. The demons could possess their already lost souls, luxuriate in the feel of a human body until the frail human form collapsed under its evil burden and died.

As Simon wrapped himself in a black silk wrapper (there was no purpose to donning a suit that might be soiled by Mikal's blood), he wondered why Adelaide had not interrupted the fight she must have heard. Even assuming she'd accept Simon's decision to put Mikal down, this silence was uncharacteristic of her.

In fact, as Simon allowed his senses to travel over the castle, the only presences he could detect were his own, Mikal's, and the mortals he'd stored downstairs. Where was Adelaide?

Worried now, Simon rushed to his former nurse's chambers and felt an unfamiliar lump form in his throat as he beheld the corpse on the bed. Mikal showed no mercy or compassion, even for one who'd reared him so tenderly. Judging by her splayed open legs, Mikal raped Adelaide after he staked her. Swallowing his distaste, Simon gently turned her around and scowled at the small deposit of semen dripping from her anus. It was not enough Mikal practiced this unnatural perversion on men; he had to debauch a woman who'd done her best to mother him?

With great reverence, Simon removed the wooden stake from Adelaide's heart, ignoring Mikal's insane screams reverberating through the castle. Then he cleaned her body and prepared it to lie in state, dressing Adelaide in her best red silk gown and brushing her hair so it spread across her chest as a raven and white veil. Finally, Simon placed her decapitated head as it lay at a proper angle with her body.

"Rest in peace, my good nurse," Simon whispered and tenderly kissed her cold lips. "Know that I shall avenge your death immediately."

Later, Simon would carry Adelaide's body to the solar and leave the windows open so the sun might cremate her and then he would gather up her ashes, preserving them forever. But now wasn't the time to dwell on the sadness he felt at Adelaide's untimely death—he must deal with Mikal.

Grabbing the sword from his bed, Simon advanced on his prey, the only way he would allow himself to think of Mikal now. This screeching boy was no son to him, never had been. He was only one of Simon's few failures, an abominable creature that should never have been born.

But before Simon sent Mikal into the abyss he so richly deserved, he would finally drink of the Philosophers' Stone. Grabbing a thick chunk of Mikal's lank black hair, Simon forced his head back and buried his blood teeth in the exposed vein of Mikal's forcibly arched neck.

At the first swallow of his son's blood, Simon fell back, choking and sputtering before his body forced the unwanted presence out and Simon began to vomit in great, rasping heaves.

At the sickness, Simon's concentration wavered and the demons lost their hold over Mikal. Wasting no time, Mikal hurried at his father but Simon managed to snarl, "Attack!"in Latin and the monsters rushed at Mikal.

Simon heard his son scream "No!" and he raised himself to his knees just in time to watch Mikal take a running leap through the stone wall of the castle and fall screaming the three stories to the jagged, rocky ground below. Soon enough Mikal's body healed and he pulled himself off the ground, staring up at his father with the same cool detachment in Simon's amber gaze.

"Soon, Father," Mikal finally shouted and Simon knew Mikal acknowledged the standoff between the master vampire and his preternatural offspring. Weakened by the poison blood, Simon could not attack Mikal again and Mikal was too frightened of his father's sorcery to chance another confrontation.

"Soon indeed," Simon said, not bothering to shout, as he knew Mikal could hear his quiet but emphatic utterance.

"I was too merciful tonight," Mikal yelled with all the fury of rebellious, subdued youth as he climbed aboard a speedboat he'd beached on the isle's shore, not taking his eyes off his father for one second as he made his escape. "Next time it won't be some useless old bitch I slaughter. Before I take your life, Father, it shall be Meghann and that bitch daughter of yours I tend to."

Present Evening

"And that was the last time I saw Mikal," Simon concluded. "Though I have followed his foolish, bloody trail around the world."

199

Why did he kill the Ballnamore vampires after he ran away?" Meghann asked. "Why not make allies of them to help destroy you?"

"My guess is that Mikal may have approached them only to be rebuffed. After all, Mikal stands for everything those pious fools averred—complete domination of prey, indulgence of the blood lust in any manner one desires. So Mikal did as he does with every annoyance. Obliterate it."

"Why does he want to kill you?" Meghann asked, wondering if Mikal's antipathy for his father stemmed from something more than unresolved childhood hostility. "Does he consider you an annoyance?

"Of the worst sort," Simon said with a brief, ironic grin. "His chief reason for desiring my death, Meghann, is that he believes I am all that stands between him and complete, unquestioned rule over the entire world."

"What?" Meghann would have laughed if not for the deadly earnestness on Simon's face.

"Lunacy, isn't it? Only the youngest and least intelligent of us entertain such mad fantasies. I told you Mikal's aims are ill conceived. He does not consider that, one, he has limited power in the day so an assassination attempt by any mortal means would kill him, and two, there is not a government in this world who would hesitate to destroy a vampire that attempts to rule the world."

"So Mikal thinks he'll kill you and set up some sort of *coup d'etat* to topple every government and reign as a vampire tyrant?"

"Precisely," Simon and Meghann saw the corners of his mouth lift in derisive amusement. "Like I said, the goal is preposterous and he has laid no real ground work to make it come true. All he does is reveal himself to some mortal misfits."

"Has he made them vampires?" Meghann cried out, terrified of an entire army of sun-resistant vampires like Mikal.

"Did you not hear what I said about Mikal's blood sickening me?" Simon said in response. "Mikal's blood is toxic, Meghann."

"But you drank it when he was a boy—you told me you drained him when you found him with that..."

"Mikal's powers hadn't fully evolved then. Drinking his blood gave me no extra power because Mikal had no resistance to sunlight then. It was only when he was full-grown that his blood became a repellant."

"So Mikal's blood is useless to us? We can't drink it?"

"I have pondered that often and this is my conclusion: Mikal is a new species of vampire, no? I confess, I feel rather foolish not to have thought of this before but apparently to receive Mikal's gifts we would have to retransform, in a sense. Vampire blood is toxic to the system unless the recipient is first drained of all their blood. Obviously, since Mikal is not a vampire the way we are, anyone that wishes to drink of him would have to first be drained and then drink his blood... transformation all over again. However, given Mikal's unusual strength, I would hardly recommend approaching him in a blood-starved state. The only way we can obtain his blood is to kill him, save his blood, and then one of us shall drain the other before we drink his blood."

"You haven't answered my original question, Simon. What's to stop Mikal from draining his 'mortal misfits' and suffusing them with his blood?"

"Do you become ill when you drink from me or any other vampire, Meghann? Of course not... that Mikal's blood is strong enough to poison us is proof positive it would kill a mortal outright.

"Besides." Simon continued with a wolfish grin, "I happen to know he attempted transformation with miserable results—I saw the corpses and drew a small portion of their blood to prove conclusively Mikal's blood was the toxin in their veins that killed them. But you interrupted me... Mikal does not attempt to recruit only mortals; he has also scouted out some of my own spawn."

"Vampires you transformed? Did they accept?"

"Why would they?" Simon said with a lift of his eyebrows. "Would you prefer the iron fist of a mad despot over my relatively lax rule?"

Meghann considered that and decided Simon had a valid point. By and large, Simon Baldevar dealt fairly with his fledglings. His requirements for transformation were simple and non-negotiable... he demanded one hundred percent of their mortal wealth and any attempt to cheat him was dealt with in harshest manner. In exchange, Simon offered his incomparable skill at transformation and a brief training period before sending the new immortals out into the world—Meghann was the only vampire Simon chose to keep by his side.

"So all your fledglings rejected Mikal's offer? Did he kill them out of spite?"

"Those he could find," Simon shrugged. "Most of them have lived for centuries and were able to avoid Mikal. Of course, one or two were mad enough to join my son but I shall attend to them once this sordid business with Mikal is finished."

Meghann nodded, resisting the urge to shudder when she thought of how Simon would "attend" to those vampires that betrayed him to join Mikal. "Why didn't you come to me earlier... when Mikal first killed Adelaide? Maybe we could have saved Charles."

"I hoped to deal with Mikal myself and spare you," Simon said simply and Meghann nodded, knowing Simon had tried to protect her from what their son was. It was pointless to point her finger and blame Simon for Mikal's flaws. She knew pragmatic Simon Baldevar would never have instilled Mikal with this fevered mania to take over the world. That was the usual grandiose, idiotic aim of a psychopath—complete control over their environment, sublimating everyone around them to their whims.

"Did you tell Mikal anything about us?"

"Very little," Simon replied. "I imagine he learned of your whereabouts when he went to Ballnamore. No doubt he tortured the information from one of those fools and then made his first victim Charles Tarleton to taunt me twice—once to say he could slay those I've given my protection to and once to attack on the periphery of my heart, his victims gradually becoming those closest to me."

"Why did you finally come to me?" Meghann asked. "Did you... is Mikal somewhere near Ellie now? Do you have some kind of evidence he's in New York?"

"No, little one," Simon assured her. "I arrived simply because I could no longer bear to be separated from my wife and child. I had no idea I would arrive in time for Mikal's despicable slaughter of your dear friend. But don't worry, sweet—he won't harm anyone else. I will protect you, Elizabeth, and Lee." It came as no surprise to Meghann that Simon omitted Jimmy Delacroix from the list of those he'd watch over.

"You do understand what needs to be done?" Simon asked her softly, his eyes almost looking regretful as they held hers.

"How will we stop him?" she asked, unable to say aloud that she knew Mikal had to be killed.

"What was Alcuin's plan to destroy me when I first emerged from obscurity to reclaim you?"

"I was bait," Meghann remembered. "He didn't take me back to Ballnamore because he wanted to flush you out by leaving me in the open. Alcuin knew you'd come for me and then he planned to kill you... and that's what you're going to do with Mikal! You know he's found out where we live because he sent... because he sent that awful thing to me. You're going to lift the barrier from the house and let him enter and then you're going to attack! But what if he strikes during the day?"

"We will sleep elsewhere during the day," Simon explained. "And return to Southampton at night. We will not have to wait long, Meghann. Mikal is impulsive and impatient. He will not be able to resist his chance to hurt you and Elizabeth."

Meghann nodded her consent to Simon's plan and they were silent when the plane descended into Gabreski Airport, the private airstrip that serviced the helicopters and private planes of the rich residents of the Hamptons.

From Gabreski, it was only a ten-minute drive to the beach house. Meghann and Simon made no attempt at conversation—he was busy driving while she attended to Lee, wrapping a blanket around him to minimize his shock while she put a cold compress against his forehead.

Grimly, Meghann stared out the tinted window of Simon's Bentley, thinking the grim rainstorm that had followed them from Chicago matched her mood. She watched the rain pour down on the world in a thick, heavy sheet that cleared the roads of all but the most foolhardy mortal drivers and wondered if the clouds that had settled over her own mind would ever lift. For even if Mikal was destroyed before he hurt anyone else, Meghann had already lost Charles, all ready felt in her heart a galling pain at the abhorrent task ahead of her.

When they pulled up in front of the house, Simon helped Lee shuffle up the steps to the rotunda while Meghann rushed ahead of them, hands over her head in a feeble effort to avoid the rain.

Meghann shook her waterlogged hair and kicked off her dripping sandals on the porch, frowning because she couldn't feel her daughter's presence anywhere within the house. Where was Ellie? Why wasn't she greeting her parents?

Both those questions were answered when Jimmy Delacroix threw open the front door, disheveled and panicked as he grabbed Meghann and screamed "Maggie, Maggie, thank God you're back... Ellie has disappeared!"

Chapter Ten

The words were barely out of Jimmy's mouth when Simon launched himself at Jimmy with a rumbling, wolf-like snarl, the force of his attack hurling Jimmy off his feet while Meghann stumbled backward, falling away from Jimmy's grasping hands.

"You failed to protect my daughter, you miserable swine?" Simon roared and wrapped his hands around Jimmy's neck, seeming determined to decapitate him by sheer brute force. "I'll have your life for this!"

"Simon, no," Meghann pleaded, snapping out of the miserable daze Jimmy's words threw her into. "Don't hurt him."

Simon ignored her, his entire attention focused on strangling Jimmy. Meghann stared in alarm at Jimmy's bulging, unfocused eyes and blue skin. Was it possible to suffocate a vampire?

"No!" Meghann said, putting more strength in her voice. "If you kill him, we'll never find Ellie."

"What the devil are you talking about?" Simon snapped, not letting up one bit on the pressure he applied to Jimmy's neck. "It is his fault entirely that she's vanished. I ordered him to watch over her all last night and then sedate her so she'd spend the day asleep and unmolested. Somehow, he failed. Unsurprising, considering what he is."

"But he was the last one to see her alive," Meghann said and her voice broke on that last word. What if Ellie was no longer alive? No, no!

I'd know if she were dead, Meghann thought desperately. I'd feel it. Hadn't she heard her daughter call out to her barely an hour ago, telling Meghann she needed her? But what if Ellie had been killed since then?

"Meghann." Simon rushed over when she began crying frightened, miserable tears. Jimmy fell to the floor, gasping for breath, while Simon embraced Meghann, crooning. "Don't weep, we'll find Elizabeth and bring her home safe."

"But we need Jimmy for that," Meghann sobbed, blowing her nose loudly in the silk handkerchief Simon gave her. "Don't you see? We have to piece together when she disappeared and we can't do that if you kill off the last person to see her."

"You are correct, Meghann," Simon said and glared over at Jimmy, now making an effort to stand while he gingerly rubbed his neck. "I shall attend to you after we find Elizabeth."

"Fuck you," Jimmy muttered and it was hard to say who looked more surprised, him or Simon, when Meghann screamed, "Stop it!" in a voice that shattered the beveled glass sunburst panel in the front door.

"Stop it!" she yelled again, shrill and furious. "I'm so tired of you, both of you... behaving like such goddamned children! What the hell is wrong with the two of you? Stop it, or... or get out. I mean it. You can both just get the hell out of here and I'll... I'll find Ellie myself."

Simon and Jimmy both stared at her in sullen silence for several moments before Simon turned to Lee and took his arm, escorting the weak mortal inside the house. As he passed Jimmy, Simon's mouth curled but all he said was, "We'll be in the study," in the same crisply authoritative voice he'd use to address a servant.

Jimmy seemed about to retort but glanced over at Meghann and nodded curtly.

"What's the matter with Lee?" he asked Meghann as they walked into the house together.

"He's transforming," Meghann replied.

"Jesus!" Jimmy exclaimed. "Why the hell would he want to do that with Charles gone?"

"To defend his daughter," Meghann said and her voice trembled.

"We'll find her, Maggie," Jimmy sad and pressed her hand tightly. Meghann felt the tension and fear in grip but instead of intensifying her feelings of dread, they calmed her somehow, as though she could find succor with someone as concerned for her daughter as she was. "I feel that Ellie's okay, that nothing... bad...

has happened to her. Come on, reach out with that famous Sight of yours and feel if Ellie's all right."

"That's what I plan to do," Meghann said, pleased that Jimmy was starting to think like a vampire and implored her to call upon her occult powers. "Did Ellie sleep in her old room last night?"

"Huh! Uh, yeah."

Meghann glanced at him quizzically, and then decided that brief hesitation she heard in his voice was merely anxiety. "Then that's the first place I'll go, after I ask you a few questions. I know I'll be able to pick something up on Ellie if I stand in her bedroom."

"Yeah," Jimmy muttered, looking rather ashen to Meghann. He must still be off-balance from Simon's attack, she thought.

In the study, Simon didn't even wait for Jimmy to seat himself but immediately demand, "When did you last see my daughter?"

"Right before I went to sleep," Jimmy said, looking at Meghann instead of Simon. "A few minutes after Maggie called."

"Did you sedate her as I requested?"

"That's not fair," Meghann answered before Jimmy could speak. "Even if Jimmy did force something on her, the strongest sedative we have in this house would knock her out for twelve hours at the most. She could have woken by six and left the house before Jimmy rose for the evening."

Simon neither disputed nor conceded Meghann's point, simply saying thoughtfully. "I do not believe she was abducted from the estate. I have no impression of a struggle. It is my belief that someone lured Elizabeth away... she left here of her own free will."

Meghann nodded agreement, wondering who the hell could have been so persuasive after she and Simon had both pleaded with Ellie not to leave the house for any reason.

"A friend probably wouldn't have such influence," Simon ruminated, his thoughts running parallel to Meghann's. That leaves only one option. Has Elizabeth any serious beaux, Meghann?"

"Mickey Hollingsworth," she answered immediately.

"Who the hell is Mickey?" Jimmy demanded sharply and Meghann turned to him, her eyes narrowed speculatively. Why in the world should Jimmy care who Ellie dated?

"Ellie's boyfriend," Meghann answered, deciding the unpleasant note in Jimmy's voice was probably some proprietary, fathering instinct. He'd helped her raise Ellie almost as much as Charles and Lee had.

"You say his name is Mickey? What does he look like?" Simon demanded, with a hard, driving edge that was the closest thing to panic she'd ever heard in his voice.

"Tall," Meghann said, cudgeling her memory for details of a boy she'd only met once. "Very tall and thin. Long black hair, wears it in a ponytail..."

"When did Elizabeth meet him?"

"Six months ago," Meghann answered promptly and then the full impact of her response hit her. Six months ago was when Mikal had gone to Ballnamore and possibly tortured those vampires for information on where his mother and twin sister lived.

"No!" Meghann screamed, horrified and sickened to think Ellie's first boyfriend might be...

"No!" she repeated and jabbered nervously at Simon, "I'd have recognized Mikal. His eyes, they're still that strange silvery color, aren't they? Mickey has blue eyes, plain old blue eyes."

"Have you ever heard of contact lenses?" Simon questioned tonelessly, looking as disturbed as Meghann felt.

"How could I not recognize my own son?" she cried.

"Meghann," Lee interrupted, his voice barely above a whisper. "I think I hear the computer in the den."

Meghann cocked her ear and heard the chimes Ellie had chosen to herald the announcement of an e-mail. She rushed into the den, Simon and Jimmy following fast on her heels. The e-mail could be from Ellie.

Please, Meghann prayed as she fumbled with the mouse to open the message. Let Ellie be safe. Let her have just been thoughtless and left the house for some silly reason. I won't even yell at her for making me worry; I just want her to be all right.

The e-mail had a video clip Meghan downloaded and then she found herself staring into the leering face of a boy known to her and Ellie as Mickey Hollingsworth but Simon immediately called Mikal.

"Maggie," her son said affably, the camera focused entirely on his face... his face!

"How is he doing that?" Meghann said through numb, cold lips. "Vampires don't show up on film."

"One of his mortal characteristics," Simon said tersely. "He has a mirror image. I've often wondered if the ability to cast a reflection is related to his inability to fly the astral plane."

Meghann stared dumbly at the computer, trying and failing to find and resemblance between the sepulcher image on the screen and he endearingly awkward boy those nondescript contact lenses that his Mikal's true nature? Certainly, he could not allow his eyes to be seen in public. People would run from him screaming in horror if they saw those flat, silver eyes that looked like two nickels welded into an unearthly pale face with a fine tracery of reddish veins marring the white surface. Meghann suspected Mikal had deliberately starved himself before making this video to appear as grotesque as possible before his mother.

The video image of Mikal spoke with malevolent cheeriness, all his comments directed to Meghan. "I hope you do not mind my informality but I simply cannot address you as 'Mother' or think of you as Meghann, the exalted angel perching on Father's pedestal."

The camera panned back to expose the room behind Mikal. Meghann screamed at the image behind him: Ellie nude, shackled hand and foot with thick steel cuffs to a dark wall, her legs spread while her head lolled on her shoulders.

"Ellie," Meghann moaned at the sight of her daughter's body, a hideous mass of deep purple bruises and shocking welts. Shakily, Meghann's hands touched the computer screen, caressing it as though she could reach Ellie and provide some comfort to her child's tortured body.

Mikal strolled over to Ellie and lewdly placed his hand between her legs but Ellie didn't stir. Thank God, Meghann thought. Thank God her daughter had outwitted this monster by retreating to a state where nothing he did could disturb her.

But Meghann could be disturbed, especially when Mikal first flicked his tongue between his sister's legs and then attacked her left thigh, consuming Ellie's blood save for the slight crimson trickle that poured down her leg and gathered in an unsightly pool by her feet.

"Ellie," Meghann cried again, and the ghastly sight of her daughter being tortured by the twisted beast that set out to lure his unsuspecting twin into incest started to fade as Meghann's mind spun out of control. Her last thought before chaos enveloped her was that the despicable monster taunting her from the computer screen couldn't possibly be...

"Mickey," Ellie said, holding the hand of a pleasant but not overly handsome young man. "This is my... sister, Maggie."

Meghann smiled ruefully at that hesitancy no one else would catch as Ellie introduced her daughter to call her sister as it was for Meghann to hear it. But the ruse was a necessity.

"Hello, Mickey," Meghann said and shook the boy's hand "I've heard so much about you. Please come inside for a few minutes."

Did she sound too stuffy, Meghann fretted as Ellie and Mickey accompanied her into the atrium where Charles and Lee waited. God, she'd sounded so starched and pressed with that 'I've heard so much about you' business. In her own defense, she didn't entirely have the hang of this yet, meeting and greeting her daughter's boyfriends.

Can I really have a daughter old enough to date? Meghann reflected with some incredulity. In theory, of course, Meghann was old enough to have a great great granddaughter going on dates but Meghann couldn't reconcile the plump bundle she's cuddled and cooed as to the whip-slim young lady smiling at her boyfriend.

"What are your plans for tonight?" Lee questioned and Meghann smiled archly, thinking he sounded even more stilted than her.

Well, no wonder... poor Lee was the one who'd written out a prescription for birth control after Ellie's stammered request.

This entire meeting had come about because Meghann, Lee, and Charles insisted on meeting the boy Ellie said she might not be in love with, but was serious enough about to want to pursue a sexual relationship.

"You don't have to be in love to enjoy sex," Meghann said during the heart-to-heart that followed Ellie's request. She was determined not to lie or fill Ellie's head with ideals she'd never lived up to. Meghann hadn't loved any of the men she took to her bed after she left Simon. "But at the very least, you ought to like and respect them... and make damn sure they respect you."

Mickey certainly seemed respectful, Meghann thought, to Ellie and the rest of them. He complimented the house and exhibited polite interest in all of them.

He smiled when Ellie spoke of Lee's many contributions to infertility treatments and asked insightful questions of him and Charles, currently engaged in enzyme synthesis work that might provide cures to people stricken with diseases like MS, but he showed the most interest in Meghann's psychoanalytic research.

"In another century, you'd be called a witch," Mickey said with a trace of upper-class British accent. "Seeing into men's souls the way you do."

"One generation's sorcery is another's science," Charles said, smiling at Meghann as he filled her wine glass.

Mickey nodded and then spoke in a voice Meghann found charming. It seemed like he was always on the verge of laughter, listening to some delicious joke only he could hear. "I hope you will not think less of me, but I must confess I have a penchant for the true-crime novels written by so many of your contemporaries, Maggie. I love the way they allow you to glimpse of a dark mind."

"I don't think less of you at all, Mickey," Meghann smiled. "But you must be careful with those books. There are a few gems but most of them are unspeakable trash, written quickly and with little thought at all."

"Is there any book you'd recommend?" Mickey asked "I'm done with my courses at Oxford now and I'm finding it difficult to nourish my mind without aid of my schoolmasters."

"Helter Skelter," *Meghann said after a moment's thought.* "Marvelously insightful, well-written, a brilliant account of Charles Manson and his 'family.'"

"Wasn't Manson somewhat unusual?" Ellie put in. "I thought psychos preferred to work alone."

"They usually do," Meghann said, thinking not only of mortal psychopaths but vampires. For the most part, they were lone-wolf predators. Her friendship with Charles and marriage to Simon Baldevar were most unusual in their world... vampires tended to remain unattached, not wishing to share their prey with any fellow immortals nearby.

"But Manson managed to gather a nest of misfits together," Mickey said, looking boyish in his avid interest. "How do you think he did that, Maggie? Put the instability of his family members to work for him?"

"He was intensely charismatic," Meghann replied "Not unusual in sociopaths. They have a tendency to blend in with their surroundings, to be able to identify a person's strengths and weakness, and then prey on them to suit their own warped needs."

"So the cult leader must charm his devotees by exploiting their weaknesses and becoming sort of a father figure?"

"Something like that," Meghann said, and then the conversation shifted, focusing on Mickey's early graduation from Oxford.

"What are your plans now that you've finished school?" Lee asked and Meghann gave Charles an impish look, both of them smothering a laugh at how adult and staid Lee sounded when he grilled their daughter's boyfriend.

Mickey grinned sheepishly and shrugged "At the moment, I'm weighing my options, which is a tactful way of saying I don't have the foggiest notion of what to do with myself. I've thought of pursuing law, starting my own business... everything and nothing. Me and my Oxford degree will probably wind up inquiring earnestly whether the customers would like fries with their order."

Everyone laughed and Meghann saw what had charmed Ellie, Mickey's deprecating sense of humor. Meghann had to *admit she liked the boy herself. He wasn't what she'd look for in a man and she thought it unlikely he and Ellie would remain involved long, given how young they were, but he was a fine choice for her first boyfriend. Meghann grinned at Ellie and Ellie smiled back, basking in her mother's silent approval.*

"Would you like to stay for dinner?" Charles asked the young couple. "We're making your favorite, Ellie: fettuccine alfredo."

Ellie shook her head and explained, "We're going to the movies and the show starts in about twenty minutes. Then we're meeting some friends after."

"No time for old folks," Charles whispered to Meghann, who punched him playfully in the arm.

The three of them walked Ellie and Mickey to the front door where Mickey grasped Meghann's hand, all his twinkling humor gone, replaced by grave earnestness.

"You have a good house," he said, meeting Meghann's eyes squarely. "Full of love and happiness. My own parents... well, they've been on the outs for years and I never felt such warmth and love... no matter if you are somewhat unconventional." Mickey was referring to the careful lie the Lee had adopted Ellie and her 'sister' from a biological mother that died years before and raised them with his lover. "I hope you'll welcome me back, Maggie. I like it here."

"Of course, Mickey," Meghann said warmly, liking this earnest boy more and more. "You'll always be welcome here."

"Maggie!"

Meghann's eyes fluttered open and she stared up at Jimmy, pulling her into a sitting position and holding a glass to her lips.

"Thank God," Jimmy muttered as she became more alert. "I thought I'd lost you. You were out cold."

"He tricked me," Meghann said, sipping the absinthe to put some warmth in her ice-cold body. "I can't believe I didn't see it."

"See what? Who Mikal was?"

"More than that," Meghann said, though she was appalled that in that entire meeting neither she nor Charles had any idea they were conversing with another vampire. Mikal was so young. What would he be capable of as he matured? "I made Simon's spell worthless. Mikal was able to get in here today and abduct Ellie."

"What are you talking about?" Jimmy said and helped her over to an overstuffed easy chair. "I thought the house was barred to all vampires..."

"...that weren't invited," Meghann finished. "He made it all seem so innocuous, standing on the threshold to the house and grasping my hand while he asked me to make him welcome. Perfect location, perfect timing to repel any later spell. Mikal could come in here today because I, the mistress of the house, held his hand and told him he was always welcome in my home. Fuck!" Meghann screamed in frustrated self-reproach. "How could I not have the slightest idea what Mikal was? How he was manipulating me?"

"It's done," Jimmy said, unable to offer any kind of comfort. "What we have to concentrate on now is getting Ellie back from him, before he kills her."

"He's not going to kill her." Meghann said. "Mikal is keeping her alive as bait. He wants me and Simon, all of us, to come charging after her. Then, if he succeeds in destroying us, no one stands in his way."

Turning away from Jimmy, Meghann glanced at the blank computer screen. "Jimmy, turn the computer back on. Much as I hate it, I have to see if there's any clue as to where Mikal is keeping Ellie. And Simon... where's Simon? We have to start planning..."

"He's gone... took Lee with him and vanished."

"Gone?" Meghann asked incredulously. "What do you mean, gone? How could he leave and why would he take Lee?"

"Gone," Jimmy snapped and Meghann saw his anger was directed at Simon, not her. "And don't ask me where he went because I don't have the slightest fucking idea. All I know is you started to scream and passed out and then he... I went over to you, to try and revive you, and when I looked up, he and Lee were gone."

"How long ago did he disappear?" Meghann demanded, suddenly knowing exactly what had happened. Her brief unconscious spell hadn't been a result of overworked nerves—

Simon had reached into her mind and forced her to sleep while he went to deal with Mikal on his own.

"Three hours ago," Jimmy said, confirming Meghann's suspicions.

"We have to hurry," Meghann said and rushed over to the computer, cursing when she saw the mangled hard drive, a hopeless tangle of wires and metal.

"Damn it!" She banged her hand down on the leather-paneled desk. "There was a clue in that e-mail...Simon knows where Mikal and Ellie are. He's gone to battle Mikal but he wants me out of it. Damn him! I won't sit here and pace helplessly while my husband and daughter are in danger. And Lee! Why did Simon take Lee with him? He's so sick, not even transformed. How can Lee help him against Mikal?"

Jimmy shrugged and said, "Is there some other way you can find Ellie? I mean, you're her mother, I know there's a link between the two of you."

"Yes," Meghann said, her mind buzzing furiously. "Come on."

"Where?" Jimmy asked, sounding strangely apprehensive to Meghann.

"Ellie's bedroom," Meghann said, taking the oak stairs three at a time. "It has the most recent psychic impression. That's where I'll connect to her. Just pray we're not too late. Simon has a three-hour head start on us. We need to hurry, Jimmy."

Meghann paused at the door to Ellie's room and gave Jimmy a rushed list of commands. "I need every weapon we have: the magnum and the .44, at least two bowie knives for each of us, and two axes. You get everything together so we're ready to leave as soon as I find out where Ellie is. Go on, hurry!"

Meghann watched Jimmy's retreating back for a moment, wondering why he suddenly looked so uncertain, and then shrugged the thoughts away as unimportant. She needed to concentrate on finding Ellie.

Meghann entered her daughter's room, took in its musty odor, unmade sheets, and for one horrible moment thought Mikal had raped Ellie before he abducted her. But as Meghann concentrated on the room and its psychic residue, she discovered to her appalled, outraged dismay that Mikal wasn't Ellie's only lover.

Jimmy skulked around the house uneasily, gathering the weapons Maggie requested into an all-purpose black canvas duffle bag. He kept waiting for some kind of shriek when Maggie's senses informed her of what had happened in Ellie's room last night. It was too much to hope that Maggie, in her grief and worry, might not discover he and Ellie were lovers.

But minutes crept by with excruciating slowness and there was no furious scream, just an ominous silence. Finally Jimmy had everything they needed and no reason except cowardice to avoid going back up to Ellie's room and confronting Maggie.

It wasn't that he was ashamed of what he'd done, though he knew he should be. Jimmy loved Ellie, and fully intended to marry her. But he didn't want to face Maggie now, with Ellie missing.

Ellie should be here. Only she could convince Maggie that Jimmy had not taken advantage of her, like that bastard Mikal had. Jimmy felt no disgust at discovering Ellie's first lover was her twin brother. No, that was wrong. Jimmy felt marrow deep, instinctual horror, but it was all directed at Mikal. Ellie was just his helpless victim. Jimmy wouldn't turn Ellie away, he just wanted to find her and hold her, tell her they'd get over what her brother had done to her together.

Quit stalling, Jimmy told himself and headed for the stairs. What kind of knight-in-shining-armor was he going to be for Ellie if he couldn't even face her mother and make her accept that he and Ellie were in love, wanted to get married?

At the base of the stairs, his eyes firmly cast on the floor; Jimmy noticed a small slip of paper lying by the front door, right underneath the mail slot. There was always a chance he was wrong but Jimmy would swear that red square with Gothic black lettering hadn't been there when Maggie and Lee came home.

Jimmy snatched the heavy paper up and opened the front door, screaming, "Why didn't you put it in my hand, you chicken shit motherfucker? Even your old man doesn't sneak around like this! And Ellie told me you're a lousy fucking lay, too!"

Jimmy's challenge went unheeded, no psychotic young vampire popped out of the dunes to attack him. Then Jimmy glanced at the flyer in his hands and wondered if he were mistaken, if some hapless mortal solicitor that would think a crazy man lived in this house had just left this.

He'd show Maggie, Jimmy decided, get her take on it.

"Maggie," Jimmy called as he poked his head around the half-open door leading to Ellie's room, forgetting his apprehension in his eagerness to show her his discovery. "You've got to..."

That was all Jimmy got out before a hand yanked his hair and used it to fling him halfway across the room.

"What the..." Jimmy stammered before a foot connected solidly with his ribs, breaking at least two of them.

Jimmy grunted, having no time to absorb that irritating blow before a flat palm smashed into his nose, pulverizing it.

Jimmy made an effort to get up and Maggie sent him back down by kicking him in the neck, all the while screaming some inarticulate diatribe of rage. Jimmy caught only a few phases— "perverted piece of shit" and "child-chasing asshole" among them.

Shit, Maggie knew what had happened and her reaction was exactly what Jimmy had predicted to Ellie, right down focusing the brunt of her assault on his testicles.

"Listen to me," Jimmy grunted, making a grab for her hair to pull Maggie off him.

"Listen to you?" she spat and he felt real fear at the white-hot fury blazing in her eyes, turning them to green glass. "Listen to some...some sneaky, sleazy, lowlife that hits on an innocent child? I'll kill you, you sonofabitch, I'll kill you!

"No," she suddenly contradicted herself and hopped off him, though not before giving him two stinging slaps, back and front handed, across the face.

"I won't kill you at all," she said in a nasty purr that chilled Jimmy. "I'll tell Simon what you've done and let him decide the best way to destroy you."

Now Jimmy knew how betrayed and angry Maggie was. She would willingly hand him over to Lord Baldevar.

"You don't understand," Jimmy said, knowing he was pleading for his life.

"You're right," Maggie snapped, looking at him like he was a loathsome crust she'd found on the heel of her shoe. "I don't understand and I don't want to understand. I never want to understand the workings of your sick, twisted mind—you're as bad as Mikal. Worse, because I trusted you. I thought you were my friend, and Ellie's as well. I never thought you'd...you'd use my child, an innocent girl that's loved you all her life, to settle whatever score you think you've got with me and Simon."

"I didn't use her!" Jimmy screamed, insulted and hurting more from Maggie's dismissal of him than any of her physical blows. "I love Ellie. I love her and we're going to be married."

If he thought that statement would win him any points that hope was brutally dashed when Maggie burst into cutting, sardonic laughter that made her sound exactly like her Simon Baldevar.

"You think I'd let Ellie marry you?" Maggie asked, sounding like she'd bless the union of Ellie and an open sewer before she gave her daughter to Jimmy. "I will find her, Jimmy, and save her and when I do, believe me she's going to do better than you. I won't let Ellie ruin her life and devote herself to some pathetic, emotional cripple. What is it, Jimmy? Instead of me, now you want Ellie to hold your hand through eternity because you're too weak to make it on your own? Booze or a girl, Jimmy always needs some crutch to get him through the night."

"You fucking poisonous bitch," Jimmy said, past shame and well into fury that matched that of the woman glaring down at him.

With that comment, Maggie lunged at him but this time Jimmy threw her off and then held out the bowie knife he had at the small of his back before she could attack him again. "You're going to listen to me, Maggie."

"Or what?" she laughed humorlessly. "Think you'll win Ellie over by killing her mother?"

"I don't want to kill you, Maggie," Jimmy said, not entirely truthfully. "I just want you to listen to me and I'm holding this knife out to keep you off me while I speak my piece."

"I have no interest in anything you have to say." Purposefully, Maggie turned her back on him. "You're dead to me, Jimmy Delacroix. Now get the hell out of my house and don't ever come back."

Jimmy didn't move one step toward the door. "What the hell would you know about love? How dare you condemn me and Ellie after hooking up with Simon Baldevar?"

"There is no you and Ellie, you fucking child-molesting creep," Maggie snarled, whirling around. "I don't want my daughter having anything to do with you."

"Well, she wants to have something to do with me just like I want her," Jimmy said and brandished his knife again when Maggie's hands curled into claws.

"We love each other in a good, positive way. Not that you'd understand anything like... I don't have to drink her blood to get it up."

"Get it up?" Maggie retorted, now looking sickened, as well as outraged. "You think I want to hear about you getting your dick hard for Ellie? You sick, twisted fuck. When she was a baby, you wanted to be her daddy and now you want to be her... Jesus, I don't know what!"

"Her husband," Jimmy said firmly, trying to meet Maggie's eyes but she wouldn't even look at him. "And not because I need someone to hold my hand. What a cheap shot that was. Like you don't need Simon Baldevar to chase after you when you lose your mind and take off without a thought for anyone but yourself. If you'd stayed put last night, Ellie might be here now!"

Maggie's face crumpled and Jimmy saw all the fight go out of her. She slumped against the picture window and when Jimmy saw her mouth and eyes fractionally scrunching up and down, he knew she was trying not to cry.

"Jesus, Maggie," Jimmy said and tossed his knife to the floor. He didn't go over to her, not because he feared more fighting but because he thought he wasn't worthy to comfort her. Talk about cheap shots. How could he say something so vile to Maggie when

219

she was so worried about Ellie? "I'm sorry. I never should have said that. You're a vampire, too. None of us could have done anything to protect Ellie during the day, it doesn't matter where you were."

Maggie said nothing and Jimmy plowed on, determined to make her understand what happened. "It's not what you think, Maggie. Ellie... I never would have touched her if I didn't love her, if I didn't think we could have a relationship."

"She's so young," Maggie said but her words lacked the heat of a few minutes ago.

"Aren't you three hundred years younger than Baldevar?"

Maggie shrugged. "More or less. But Simon wasn't around when I was growing up. My mother didn't count him as an honorary father."

"Lee is Ellie's father," Jimmy said, discounting Lord Baldevar completely. "You know that. After I knew it was over between us, I didn't spend that much time here. Certainly not enough to be a father."

"But how can you see Ellie that way?" Maggie asked, looking genuinely perplexed.

"I don't know," Jimmy shrugged. "I have no answer except that it started last night when I came back. Ellie was an adult, no longer your baby. What can I say, Maggie? She's everything I want... smart and tough and talented... like you.

"Not that I want her to replace you," Jimmy said quickly. "Sure, Ellie's a little like you ... you're her mother. But she's different. We're different. I always depended on you, Maggie. But with Ellie... it's like we depend on each other. We complement each other. I can see us together years from now, helping and supporting each other. I don't need her to hold my hand, Maggie. I want to hold hers, I want to find her and comfort her and help her get over Mikal. She and I...we have something between us, something magical I can't explain."

Maggie looked up at that, seeming surprised and no longer angry. She gave Jimmy a sad smile. "That's what love is, Jimmy. A special bond only the two of you understand, something that can't be presented to or analyzed by anyone else. Maybe now you'll understand my feelings toward Simon a little better."

Jimmy would always think Maggie was selling herself short as far as Baldevar was concerned, but she was right, he did understand. He understood what it was to care about someone so much you'd defy every convention, kick over every obstacle just to be with them.

"So it's okay?" Jimmy asked.

Maggie gave him a wary glance and shook her head. "I don't know, Jimmy. I need time to think about this and I certainly need to talk to Ellie. I want to hear from her that she feels the same way and ready for the kind of commitment you want. But I...I don't think you're using her or that this is something cheap and tawdry. Just give me time, Jimmy."

Jimmy nodded. "Will you let me help you find her?"

Maggie laughed bitterly and gestured to the empty room. "I don't exactly have an army at my side. I need all the help I can get."

"Then look at this." Jimmy took the red-and-black card out of his back pocket and handed it to Maggie.

Maggie glanced at it only a minute before her eyes widened and she whispered, "The address."

"What about it?" Jimmy frowned and glanced over her shoulder.

"Don't you remember?" Maggie whirled around to face him. "16 Shelter Rock Road; it's the house where Simon took me after he killed Alcuin! The house where we conceived the twins."

"The house where he tortured me," Jimmy whispered, his legs suddenly wobbly. He sat down on the bed, remembering Simon Baldevar's trap as though he'd fallen into it yesterday. The sadistic, jealous vampire had no use for Maggie's mortal lover so he lured Jimmy to the house and then put him through hell to pay Jimmy back for laying his hands on who he thought of as his woman.

"You said you'd gotten rid of the house!" Jimmy cried, shuddering when he thought that Ellie might be wearing the same shackles that had imprisoned Jimmy, that Mikal might be tormenting her in the same spot where his father had once tried to kill Jimmy. "You said you sold it out from under Baldevar when he kidnapped me!"

"I did," Maggie said and explained. "Last night, when I ran off, I needed to feed. I found some kid and he told me all about this cool Goth club opening in Manhasset. This must be it." Maggie contemptuously flicked the invitation to a place unimaginatively called Immortal Light. "Rather Freudian title, that. Would you care to guess what Mikal's planning to do there, what sick fantasies he's going to enact? According to my little friend, the main charm of this sick, decadent place is that you pay the admission by stuffing it into the body cavity of a disemboweled corpse. Naturally the kid thinks the body is going to be wax, but we know better than that. Don't we, Jimmy?"

"Baldevar," Jimmy said, seeing his own horrorstruck certainly reflected in Maggie's eyes. "Mikal thinks he's going to kill his father and then stuff him over the front door of his club."

Maggie nodded grimly. "We have to stop them. I just pray Simon had his own preparations to make before he set off for the house. We have to get there before Simon confronts Mikal."

"Why?" Jimmy asked, sensing that though he and Maggie were united as long as Ellie was missing, she might feel differently toward him after this was resolved. "I hate to say it but Baldevar can handle anyone. No one wins against him, not even Alcuin, who you told me had four centuries on him."

"Alcuin visited me last night," Maggie said. "He told me I couldn't let Simon confront Mikal on his own. That he'd die, him, Ellie, and Lee!"

Jimmy could care less if Simon Baldevar died but with him gone, there'd be nothing standing in the way of Mikal killing Ellie and Lee if he and Maggie arrived too late to save them.

Jimmy had no idea why Lee Winslow was involved in this anyway. Why Simon had spirited him away? Why would Simon Baldevar confront this son with no one to help him but a sickly, transforming mortal? It just didn't make any sense, Jimmy thought, as he and Maggie set off for the house where Lord Baldevar had set everything happening tonight in motion eighteen years ago.

Chapter Eleven

Simon guided the car off of the Sunrise Highway and drove into the Pine Barrens, a vast area near Southampton comprised of marshes and swamps surrounded by skeletal, burnt stumps of trees that leered out from the darkness like gnarled sentinels when lightning illuminated the car's path.

Simon was glad of the fierce storm raging outside. No mortal hikers or park rangers would brave the steady downpour and hurricane-like gusts of wind to interrupt Simon's ritual at any crucial point.

Simon cut the engine and turned to Lee Winslow, semi-conscious and shivering uncontrollably. Simon put his hand on the mortal's wrist, registering the clammy skin and weak, thready pulse with some alarm. It was just as he'd thought—Lee's older body was having grave difficulty withstanding the shock of transformation.

"Dr. Winslow," Simon said, grasping the mortal's wrist tightly and infusing him with some of his own strength. Simon imagined his power as a circuit rushing through Lee's bloodstream, healing all in its path, and soon Lee sat up, looking around in a dazed manner as his fever abated for the first time that night.

"Ellie," Lee muttered, sitting up in alarm and then slumping back down from dizziness. "I heard Meghann screaming. What has Mikal done to Ellie?"

"Try to remain calm," Simon said. "Panic will weaken you. Mikal has abducted Elizabeth to force a confrontation with me. He thinks I'm going to foolishly blunder into whatever trap he's set."

"Oh, God," Lee sighed, his waxen, pale skin turning whiter with fear. "Simon, what's he going to do to her?"

"He won't kill her," Simon said shortly, leaving the rest unsaid. Mikal had no choice but to keep his sister alive because he knew Simon wouldn't chase after a corpse but that did not mean the twisted, venal boy would not spend every drop of jealous, resentful energy on his helpless twin, visiting frightful tortures upon her. Simon could not only hope that no matter how mutilated Elizabeth was when they found her, she still had life enough within her to undergo transformation. Simon knew immortality was likely the only way to heal his daughter after Mikal was through with her. "Not if we find him soon."

"We?" Lee said. "Where are Meghann and Jimmy?"

"Meghann is at home where she belongs," Simon answered, ignoring the reference to Jimmy Delacroix. Pity he'd already been transformed or Simon would have used him for the ritual. Then Delacroix would serve a purpose for once. "It is bad enough Elizabeth's been hurt. I will not endanger Meghann by exposing her to battle. I enchanted her so she would sleep until this is over."

"You want to attack Mikal with me at your side?" Lee Winslow was intelligent enough to know he, as an utter novice, would not be of great aid to Simon.

"I want your immortal body," Simon said, choosing his words carefully. "But to use you means putting you at great risk."

"I've known all along there's a risk of death with transformation," Lee said. "I still want to try. I have to help Ellie."

"I plan to do a great deal more than transform you this evening, Doctor," Simon said, determined to make full disclosure before starting the ceremony. "I will use your new, invincible body in ways you cannot imagine. You will not be aware of what I am doing because you, the mind and soul behind your physical body, will not be here."

"Simon, you're speaking in riddles. Tell me what you mean. If my soul isn't in my body, where will it be?"

"I do not know," Simon said candidly. "No occultist has ever figured out where the soul of a possessed body vanishes to."

"Possessed," Lee said and Simon saw real fear enter the mortal's eyes, though he didn't appear ready to cry off Simon's proposal. "Simon, are you planning to put some... daemon in me?"

"That would be foolhardy, not to say dangerous in the extreme, for no daemon with a body all its own would heed my wishes. An immortal body is all those creatures want—why should it obey me when I have no more to offer? You shall be possessed but not by such a terrible entity as that... merely a force with the power to assist me when I face down Mikal."

"Will this force take me over forever?" Lee asked quietly and Simon saw the trepidation behind the seemingly calm tone.

"No possession lasts forever," Simon explained. "The force I plan to invoke would not try and force you from your body as a daemon would. But it is possible you could die when I perform the ceremony or your body could be mortally wounded when I confront Mikal. Finally, it is possible that when I release the entity from your form, your soul will simply not be able to find its way back. You may remain wherever you are."

Lee nodded and said steadily, "Do whatever you need to save Ellie, Simon."

Simon nodded and helped Lee out of the car, feeling almost humbled by the other man's quiet courage. There'd been no turmoil in his mind. Lee Winslow handed over his life with no thought but for saving Elizabeth. How fortunate his daughter was to have this man for her foster father. If Lee didn't survive tonight, Simon would make certain his sacrifice was not unheralded—he would tell Meghann and Elizabeth that Lee Winslow had died a hero's death.

He would also make certain Mikal paid for all he'd put his family through. Meghann would never fully recover from Charles Tarleton's death or those ghastly images of Elizabeth so hurt and mutilated—they were branded into her heart and mind forever. Mikal would pay dearly for the hurt he'd caused Meghann, taking the life of so good a man as Charles Tarleton, and putting into jeopardy this equally good man, Lee Winslow.

Simon took Lee's hand again, grasping it in a firm handshake that was as much salute as possible farewell. "You are a fine man, Lee."

"So are you, Simon," Lee said softly. "I was so scared of you at first. You seemed so... cold, but you were a different person altogether with Meghann. I'll never forget the way you stroked her hair and held her close to you while you fed her your blood. And I've seen the way you do your best to protect Meghan and Ellie. I know if something happens to me tonight, you'll keep them safe."

"You have my word," Simon told him, reflecting that this was the first true friend he'd had since John Dee, Elizabeth I's renowned astrologist, died. Strange that Lee Winslow's homosexuality had never bothered Simon when he usually despised sodomites—his own son included. But there was so much to admire about Lee that it had never been difficult to overlook his one character flaw.

Simon pushed dripping strands of hair off his face and wiped his eyes clear of the pouring rain—there was no more time to speak. In tonight's ceremony, time was of paramount importance. Lee Winslow's transformation must take place between midnight and one am. The first hour of the new day was the only suitable time for the conjuration Simon planned.

It was now eleven o'clock. Simon used his blood teeth to open the vein in his wrist and held out his bleeding hand to Lee. Understanding Simon's intention, Lee raised Simon's wounded wrist and drank the vampire's blood to complete his transformation.

The first swallow affected Lee like a jolt of electricity. His entire body shuddered and his eyes rolled into the back of his head before he crumpled to the muddy, water logged earth. Simon pulled a sheet from the trunk and laid Lee on it, securely tying his hands to one of the pine stumps behind him. Any transforming mortal had to be restrained lest they hurt themselves.

Simon knelt beside Lee and examined him. He was now in the second stage of transformation, characterized by convulsions, fever, and vomiting. As the vampire blood coursed through his system, Lee's body underwent a radical and extremely painful change. Skin, muscles, bone, organs, blood... not one part of the body was unaffected.

From experience, Simon knew this stage of transformation could take anywhere from several hours to a fortnight. His own transformation took more than two weeks but Simon suspected that was because no vampire watched over the process: he'd transformed by stealing a vampire's blood and then John Dee did what he could to assist Simon. Tonight Simon planned to rush the process along so Lee's transformation would be completed at the same moment Simon was ready to invoke.

The crucial moment in transformation came when the physical metamorphosis began to taper off and the semi-transformed mortal regained awareness. Many could not handle the shocking process and lost their minds. The vampire guiding them had to keep a firm hold over his fledgling's psyche, guide them through the pain and terror to complete transformation.

I am here, Lee. Simon spoke into the mortal's delirium-laden mind. *I am your master now. Come to me and the pain will lose its grip. Find me, reach out to me.*

He felt a tremulous, hesitant touch in his mind and knew Lee was hanging on. Simon didn't worry that this strong-willed man would lose his mind, but he did worry his frail, mortal heart might give out if transformation wasn't accomplished quickly.

Simon pulled a large suitcase from the trunk, filled with objects he'd packed in anticipation of finding Mikal. First, he removed a small packet of sulfur and used it to cast a counter-clockwise circle that included himself, Lee, and the tree he was tied to. A few inches beneath that circle, he made another sulfuric circle the exact diameter of the outer circle. The rain poured down and melted the sulfur until it almost blended into the soil but that did not bother Simon—a thunderstorm provided powerful energy that would aid him tonight.

But it did mean he had to work quickly to activate the circle. Simon burned a red candle, guarding the flame from the rain with his hands. When the wax began to run, Simon used the wax to write the names Agla and El between the outer and inner rim of the two circles.

The red candle and names corresponded to the Fourth Pentacle of Mars, which provided power in war and Simon considered himself at war with his son.

Next, Simon drew the Fourth Pentacle a few inches from Lee with dirt he'd taken from the North End graveyard, the oldest cemetery on Long Island. Simon laid Lee Winslow on the pentacle, making sure his head faced east, in the direction of the rising sun. Lee's limbs were arranged with the arms and legs in cruciform position to later invite the spirit Simon needed to rise from the dead.

Now the magic could begin. First, Simon consecrated the circle, speaking in the Latin tongue as he'd done since he was a mortal magus. "By the holy, terrible, and ineffable name IAH, at which the whole world doth tremble, I beseech thy confidence and grace, that all discord and strife fly from this circle and you bless and sanctify my humble assembly this evening. Amen."

At the close of his prayer, the sulfuric outline burst into flames no earthly rain could douse. The blue-white fire burned bright, impervious to the rain that drenched Simon's clothes and poured down his face. The fire almost seemed a holographic image, emitting warmth but layered with a transparency that reminded Simon of his own image when he looked into a mirror.

Pleased that his circle was activated and no unwelcome infernal visitors could enter and try to force themselves upon Lee's body, Simon went to the tree Lee was tied to and tore off a limb, consecrating it as his magic rod for the evening by attaching steel caps to each end and magnetizing it with a lodestone. Next, he used his blood teeth to bite off a circle of bark in the center of the stump and place a small, perfect ruby in the hole.

Now a small offering had to be made. Simon withdrew several stone philters and a gold plate from the suitcase. Onto the plate, he poured a small bit of wine, resin, sweet oil, and virgin's blood from one of the captives he'd used to feed Mikal. Placing the offering at Lee's right hand, Simon said, "O high and powerful beings, may this sacrifice be pleasing and acceptable to thee that you may bestow your favor upon my work this night."

Simon glanced at Lee and saw the moment of transformation was at hand. Awareness was creeping back into his expression and sharp, ivory blood teeth emerged from his gum to cut open his lower lip—Lee Winslow now had a vampire's body. Holding the rod up to the thundering sky, Simon roared, "By virtue of He who created all things and reigns eternal, I conjure and command that ye bring the spirit of the slain vampire, Alcuin, Bishop of Kent, to answer my demands and come unto me. I, Lord Simon Baldevar, as thy killer, order ye, Alcuin, into this new immortal form I have provided. In the great name of God, Tetragrammaton, I say arise, arise from your sleep and come do my bidding else suffer everlasting torment. I charge and command thee, Alcuin, to awaken. Awake, awake, awake!"

Simon's deep voice rumbled through the desolate area as he held the pine rod up to the heavens and then touched Lee's heart with the magnetized tip.

Lee's eyes widened, as if with great surprise, and then clouded over, becoming utterly vacant for a moment before they darkened and changed. Now the eyes staring up at Simon were those of a much older soul than Lee Winslow, reflecting wisdom it had taken centuries to obtain and the same self-righteous piety that always annoyed Simon unendurably on the few occasions he'd confronted Alcuin.

How Simon wished he could have called upon any soul but this pompous prelate he despised. Charles Tarleton would be a fine ally by his side but his soul, dead so short a time, was in a state of transition now and it would be near impossible to bring him into a new body so soon after his death. There were other dead immortals Simon could have called upon but none of them had Alcuin's powers. Prejudiced though he was, Simon was forced to admit his enemy was one of the most formidable sorcerers he'd ever encountered. Simon had no idea how many vampires had joined Mikal's futile quest but none of them would be able to stand against his and Alcuin's combined power. Now he had to see if Alcuin would assist him, if the love he had for Meghann were stronger than the enmity he felt toward Simon.

Alcuin sat up, blinking eyes that were not his and marveling on what it was to hear sound again, to feel sensations like cold rain landing on skin to make it pucker up into gooseflesh.

"Uncle." Alcuin heard an icy voice and saw Simon Baldevar glaring down at him, holding a hunting dagger with the sharp point poised to attack the throat of the body he inhabited. "I have summoned you to do my bidding. I do hope you will not force my hand to strike Lee Winslow's body in defense against any attack from you. Think how it would hurt Meghann to lose her friend."

"You do not need that weapon, Nephew," Alcuin said, surprised that the voice he spoke with had his own earthly timber, his queer accent that stemmed from the old English. He'd thought he'd sound like Lee Winslow. How very strange all this was, to use another's vocal cords and yet sound like yourself!

"Of course I don't," Simon said and hard gold eyes appraised Alcuin thoroughly before he resheathed the dagger. "You will provide assistance this evening, not only because I have summoned you, but out of love for Meghann."

That last sentence was spat out and Alcuin flinched when he felt the rage that lurked beneath his nephew's customary, imperturbable expression. "I do love Meghann. She is the daughter I never had. Why does that anger you so?"

Simon laughed humorlessly and gave him a dark glare. "I did not transform Meghann to provide you with a child, my dearest uncle. You cost us forty years with your meddling ways."

"You cost yourself forty years with Meghann," Alcuin said pointedly, "with your brutalizing, cruel ways." Alcuin would never forget his first meeting with Meghann, how the poor, hurting child had wrung his heart dry with the way she held her head high despite her misery and begged him to teach her to resist the blood lust Simon inflicted on her.

At the time, Alcuin could not begin to comprehend why Simon chose this wholesome girl for his consort, unless he was satisfying some perverse need to twist that indomitable core of goodness in her. It was decades before Alcuin learned, to his great shock, that Simon Baldevar loved Meghann for the same reasons he did—that he too cherished her bright spirit and had no desire to break it.

So why did Simon treat her so abominably that she ran from him and sought sanctuary with Alcuin? Alcuin snapped the bonds holding Lee's hands to the pine stump and continued to gaze quietly at the fierce gold eyes glowering down at him.

"Here," Simon said and tossed a dark bottle at him. "I knew you would balk at taking prey so drink this before you starve the body I've provided."

Alcuin drank the blood without savoring it as other vampires did, for he'd mortified his sense of taste when he was a mortal priest so he would not overly enjoy food and drink.

Alcuin fed with quick, economic motions, feeling great pity and some admiration for Simon Baldevar. Had he known from the beginning that Meghann was the end of his cold, callous existence? How it must have frightened Simon to love her and know that love made him vulnerable, made him need someone for the first time in four hundred years. How he'd fought against his love for Meghann, hurting her before she could hurt him because he didn't know how to trust her, how to let her into his heart completely.

"What a maudlin, insipid fool you are," Simon said contemptuously and Alcuin started, realizing he could not conceal his thoughts while he occupied this newly transformed body. "In Meghann's words, Uncle, please do not waste time 'psychoanalyzing' me. There is a great deal we must do and I do not know how long you'll remain in Lee's body."

A slight lift in Simon's voice made his last statement a question and Alcuin smothered a smile when he thought how difficult it was for Lord Baldevar to admit ignorance on any subject.

"I cannot be certain either, Nephew," Alcuin replied, not wanting to antagonize Simon. If he'd never known before, tonight would have proven to Alcuin just how much Simon loved Meghann and Elizabeth. He had called upon his deadly enemy to help him keep them safe. "My guess is your spell cannot possibly last beyond sunrise. The body feels strong now but I think it will weaken the longer I remain in it."

Simon nodded and handed Alcuin a broadsword from the trunk, eyeing him suspiciously for a few minutes before something in Alcuin's expression convinced him he would not attempt an attack against him.

"You know Mikal abducted Elizabeth?" Simon asked as he closed the circle, giving proper obeisance to the spirits that aided him before the sulphuric fire extinguished.

"I felt Meghann's pain," Alcuin answered, a hint of reproach in his tone. "She should be by your side."

"Women have no place in battle," Simon said curtly and gathered up his rain-soaked supplies, tossing them back into the trunk. The storm was letting up, the rain no longer pelting the two vampires but falling down on them as a gentle mist. "Meghann is safe."

"She'd be safer with you, Nephew. Now she'll blunder into this melee on her own. I feel she's awakened from your spell. You couldn't enchant her, transform Lee, and invoke me simultaneously—something had to give and it was your hold on Meghann."

Simon's gaze turned inward and Alcuin knew he was meditating on the link between him and Meghann, master vampire and fledgling, husband and wife. Simon must have felt her alertness for his hawk eyes narrowed and he muttered a smothered oath before he hurried to the driver's side of the car and put the keys in the ignition.

"Hurry," Simon ordered and gestured to the passenger seat. "We can still dispose of Mikal before Meghann arrives."

"There is business between us first, Simon," Alcuin said quietly, making no move to enter the car.

Simon heaved an exasperated sigh and left the car out of gear. "What business could that be, Priest? We are enemies, it is true, but I thought surely one as holy as you could put aside his hostilities to rescue an innocent like my daughter."

"Your daughter is an innocent that is true. But have you forgotten the thousands of innocents you killed and debauched over the centuries? If you can love Elizabeth, can you not feel compassion and pity enough for mortals that you will finally leave them in peace?"

Simon's lips curled in a frightful grimace and for a moment Alcuin thought Simon would spring at him. But he only snarled, "You opportunistic, self-serving mealy-mouthed fool! Do you think to hold my daughter as the ransom to finally convert your great enemy to your insipid ways? Go to hell, Priest!"

Alcuin saw Simon was moments away from exorcising him from Lee Winslow's body and spoke quickly. "I would never refuse to help someone is such dire circumstances as your daughter. I make no demands of you, Simon Baldevar. I am only asking that you consider a different way, a way that would end the last bit of strife between you and Meghann, for you know very well the guilt that tears at her when she takes mortal lives to satisfy the blood lust. Think how happy you would make Meghann if together you both taught Elizabeth to drink without slaughtering her prey. Simon, you have reveled in the agony of your prey for more than four hundred years and taught your son to take pleasure in pain. Isn't it enough now? Can't you even consider letting go of your hate?"

"I can consider ripping out your tongue before I must endure another word of this sentimental homily," Simon snapped and Alcuin knew he hadn't reached him. Perhaps Meghann and Elizabeth might someday pierce the cold armor around Simon's heart so that he'd put aside his sadistic, vicious ways once and for all. "Now if you plan to help me rescue my daughter, get in the car and stop wasting precious time or I shall take my chances with Lee Winslow at my side."

Alcuin entered the car quietly, not wanting to antagonize Simon any further for it would be nothing short of disastrous if Simon had to face his son alone.

Chapter Twelve

Mikal Baldevar sat in his office, gazing moodily into a round mirror on his smoked, opalescent glass desk. Normally, he felt very happy and smug in this haven he'd designed for himself but tonight his mood was so low the sleek, ultra-modern room with its chrome-plated steel and aluminum furniture, glass walls and curving mirrored panels went unnoticed as he focused all his unhappy attention on his reflection.

It just wasn't fair to be so plain, Mikal thought glumly, especially considering his genes. What he wouldn't give for his father's striking handsomeness, with those haunting gold eyes and sharp cheekbones. Then there was Meghann with her flaming hair and mermaid eyes, accentuated by dramatically fair skin. With parents like that, it was a cruel twist of fate for nothing better to be staring back at Mikal from the mirror than blade-thin features, an uninspired line of colorless lips, a beaky nose and too high forehead crowned by lusterless black hair.

It was as though his twin, Elizabeth, had stolen his share of beauty while they occupied Meghann's womb, leaving Mikal with nothing while she took all the best their parents had to offer. Surely Elizabeth, with her jade eyes, long, curving body, and fluffy brown curls was exactly what Father expected beautiful swans like himself and Meghann to produce, while he reacted with disdain to his ugly duckling son.

Mikal's lower lip jutted out in a childish pout and he glared at the mirror until the glass shattered. Then he picked up a shard and idly started carving up his bare arms in pentagrams and geometric designs, watching his mutilated flesh and lacerated tendons heal instantaneously.

It had never failed to disgust Father when he came upon Mikal carving up his own flesh... earning him yet another visit to the cellar and blood deprivation. Then again, so many things that Mikal enjoyed appalled Father. He was not supposed to take men for sex, scar his own skin or reveal himself to the mortals.

That last codicil annoyed Mikal more than all the others. It was bad enough to confine himself to women when Father was around and leave his skin alone but why did he have to hide from the weak mortals? Why did he have to wear the specially made contacts that hid his snake eyes instead of launching himself into a thick crowd of humans, laughing at their shock, glorying in their mass terror as he flaunted his superior strength? But no, Father said such thoughts were the province of the mad. Father's argument was that the mortals outnumbered them and had the daylight edge—even over Mikal, who had little strength to defend himself during the day. That was why vampires must skulk about in secrecy.

Well, Mikal was working hard (grinding his teeth when he remembered Father's many lectures about his supposed laziness) on eliminating that daylight advantage and soon he'd be ready to let the world know of his existence.

Mikal's glass shard reached an unyielding hardness and he looked down at his forearm, seeing he'd cut himself down to the bone. He pulled the glass away and watched the ghastly wound close up, feeling no pain as usual.

As a boy, Mikal had been very curious about pain. The pain he caused the animals he caught on the island, the pain of his prey as his fangs ripped into their flesh. He wanted to know why the mortals cried so when their flesh bruised and the blood ran from grisly wounds. After all, Mikal watched blood flow from his own body with no feeling but indifference. What did pain feel like? Mikal never knew any pain—even on the occasions he deliberately broke his bones, there was naught but a mild irritation before the bone knotted up and healed. Sometimes he felt an uncomfortable sort of pulling and dreadful nausea when Father saw fit to deprive him of the blood, but Mikal had no idea what pain was . . . his skin seemed immune to any kind of feeling but that of sexual stimuli. It wasn't until Father rammed that sword into the small of his back and left him to suffer the long, dreary hours until sunset that Mikal finally understood pain and loathed it almost as much as he loathed the creature that inflicted it.

Mikal's lips curled into a vicious snarl that would have cracked the mirror had he not already done so and he let out a low growl of rage when he thought of Father besting him so easily, even in the sunlight. The old vampire hadn't even looked surprised to see Mikal leaning over him, much less scared. To the contrary, Father seemed to welcome the intrusion to his resting place and the opportunity to humiliate his son before killing him.

Roaring his displeasure now, Mikal stood up and flung the heavy bronze and glass desk across the room, red faced and trembling as renewed hate for his father washed over him. He hated Father... hated him, hated him, hated him! He hated him for his cool poise and the ironic distance at which he kept his disappointing offspring, for never once displaying the uneasy fear Mikal inspired in all others—even other vampires.

Well, Mikal had a way to break Father's cool spirit once and for all now. Grabbing a fresh shard from the mirror, Mikal turned to the black glass wall on his left and the occupant that hadn't stirred at all during his fit. . . his badly beaten, much raped, shackled sister, Elizabeth.

Elizabeth was barely recognizable as the wildcat that screamed vicious curses at Mikal and his human assistants hours before, desperately trying to appear angry instead of frightened while they beat her. Mikal had systematically drained the fight from his twin sister until she appeared as she did now, unconscious and beaten almost to pulp. In some areas where he'd broken her bones, like her fingers, the skin was taking on a puffy, blackish-purple hue that Mikal thought could turn into gangrene if she lived long enough to develop blood poisoning from her untreated wounds. But she couldn't die just yet; she must be a living presence when Father arrived so Mikal forced himself to break off the torture lest it become too much for her puny, mortal body.

Mikal admired the contrast of Elizabeth's colorful injuries against the dark backdrop of the wall. He'd inherited some of Father's drawing ability; perhaps he'd paint his dying sister's last moments. After all, her corpse would soon grow too fetid to hang in his office forever. He'd use bright acrylics to capture the vivid grotesquery of Elizabeth's green and yellow bruises, the brilliant crimson splashes of blood and he'd accentuate the model's shocking condition against a black canvas for maximum contrast.

"Sister," Mikal said and walked over to tickle her slumping chin. "What I should really attempt to capture is your expression when I unmasked myself." How satisfying it had been, after nearly a year of laboring to be the fawning boyfriend little Ellie Winslow wanted, to watch Elizabeth open the door for him at the beach house and scream when she saw his true silver eyes instead of the tame blue contacts he wore in the mortal world.

He had to give his sister credit, though. She did not faint or plead when she realized who he was—rather she aimed her knee directly at his genitals and attempted to run up the stairs behind her. It had been easy to catch her, even with an aching crotch that didn't heal immediately in daylight. But Elizabeth did put up enough fight for Mikal to wind up chloroforming her to subdue her and bring her to his lair, where he immediately began her torture, wanting her to wake up to pain and humiliation.

Mikal started to harden when he thought of Elizabeth's body thrashing from side to side, making a futile effort to dodge his blows and blink back the tears of pain and embarrassment when he and his apprentices took her in any manner they desired. Father and Meghann would die, absolutely die when they saw what Mikal had done to their precious, sheltered daughter. Speaking of which . . .

"We must make you more presentable, dear Sister," Mikal purred at her, his anger forgotten as he began designing an elaborate vigil from the Legementon on her flat stomach. How very ironic, to desecrate his sister's body with symbols from Father's treasured text of black magic.

Mikal sliced through Elizabeth's skin, smiling at the blood path that followed the jagged edge of glass, forever damaging his sister's flawless—but mortal, and therefore vulnerable—white skin. He licked at the scarlet river flowing down her legs, reflecting that his twin's blood had a potency other mortals lacked. There was a tinge of the dark, heady taste of a vampire in her, a legacy from their parents.

"What exactly are you, lover?" Mikal inquired of the mute girl. "Not a vampire and not a human... a misfit, then, just like your brother. If you were merely human, you couldn't continue to dodge my tender ministrations or those of my drones."

Mikal felt his good mood begin to crumble, as Elizabeth remained unresponsive. The sly bitch had escaped him a mere hour after her torture began. One minute her green eyes were glazed over with pain and terror, the next they were cloudy and lifeless. For one anxious moment, Mikal thought he'd killed her but he found her pulse easily enough. Elizabeth, mere mortal though she was, had managed to escape, in her soul, at any rate. Now Mikal had the equivalent of a waxen dummy in his clutches—no fun at all.

"She is still on the astral plane?"

Annoyed, Mikal turned from his sister and stared at the intruder—a vampire with a delicate, almost ethereal beauty of long, silver-blond tresses that flowed past her hips, deep-set eyes of a rare turquoise color and full, pouting red lips.

"Do you think Father will appreciate my handiwork, Gabrielle?" Mikal said in greeting, gesturing with the bloodied shard to the wound on Elizabeth's abdomen. "He always was a patron of the arts, no?"

Gabrielle gave Elizabeth's mutilated body a disinterested glance before she grasped Mikal's wrist and licked the dripping red shard in his hand clean. "Simon will consider the wounds a fleeting nuisance—something that transformation can heal easily."

"But she is not transformed now," Mikal argued, thinking his sister would never transform—he planned to murder the entire family before dawn. "Any scars she has now she'll carry for eternity."

Gabrielle shook her head at him and sprawled her voluptuous body on a Corbusier chaise of black leather mounted on a contoured tubular frame, making it look like a long, lazy S. With her bright eyes, Gabrielle was the only touch of color within the chrome and glass room. Mikal had little use for the bright wood fixtures and vivid colors Father so enjoyed.

Giving him a seductive pout, Gabrielle pulled her navy silk dress down to reveal a satiny, flawless white breast, pursing her lips at Mikal's indifference. "When I was young and mortal, some brute of a marquise branded me with his family's crest. The mark obscured my nipple but it vanished after Simon transformed me. Also, a tooth I had pulled grew back a month after transformation."

Mikal could hardly miss the way Gabrielle's voice caressed his father's name, informing him that she was still enamored of the charismatic vampire despite the fact that she'd chosen to betray him by aligning herself with Mikal. He knew the reason for the defection, but bored with torture of his catatonic victim, decided to work on Gabrielle instead.

"Why did Father transform you?" Mikal asked to begin the diatribe.

As he expected, the gem-bright blue eyes darkened and the luscious red mouth flattened into an unattractive grimace. "We met in 1789. I was a courtesan servicing only the highest caste of the French court. Your father was a wealthy foreigner some duke entertained by bringing him to me.

"Simon didn't make himself known to me immediately. At first, he was simply another debauched patron though his tastes were a bit... darker... than any I'd encountered before."

Mikal grinned, thinking of his father's quaint, old-fashioned ideals toward women. It was perfectly all right to amuse yourself with bad girls, but you must cherish the good girl, the one you made your wife. What a conservative creature Father was at heart. . . playing at romantic love by abandoning a life rich with perverted fantasy and orgasmic excess to embrace monogamy with a naive virgin! Mikal was certain that Meghann was never asked to allow other women to take her or exposed to the sadistic bacchanals that Gabrielle claimed Father used to adore. How Father could not be bored out of his mind with Meghann, Mikal wondered as he listened to Gabrielle.

"I noticed that I always awakened tired and drawn after a night with him but I blamed that on your father's demanding ways. Then one night he allowed me to see his blood teeth and explained he'd drunk from me for months but mesmerized me so

I'd forget the experience. Now, though, he was willing to initiate me into his life, make me the immortal hunter of mortals he was."

"Why?" Mikal asked, thinking he might have respected the man his father used to be before he ruined himself by falling in love with prim little Meghann who would ultimately be his ruination. Gabrielle's stories painted a picture of a warlord, a creature that grabbed every opportunity and used it to expand his power—Mikal wanted to know how he'd done that throughout the centuries. Once Mikal knew Father's secrets, he could use them for his own advantage.

Gabrielle gave him a wanton smile, her breast still exposed for his viewing . . . once a whore, always a whore, Mikal supposed. "Simon explained that he'd read my thoughts—knew I'd been quite helpful to the crown in disposing of several wealthy nobles, receiving a high fee for my services, as well as my discretion. Simon said he expected me to perform the same duties for him, only now my quarry would be vampires.

"He told me all about that sanctimonious fool, Alcuin. How he kept trying to destroy Simon because he enjoyed killing his prey," Gabrielle continued, telling her story with obvious relish. "The old bishop kept about him a company of men as celibate as he was, at least before he made your mother and Charles Tarleton his apprentices. Simon intended for me to seduce Alcuin's guards. He said once he taught me the arts of mesmerism, those wizened creatures would become helpless clay in my hands. How right your father was. Without exception, every one of them fell into my bed, at least until Alcuin got wise to my plan and revealed my identity to the rest of his followers."

Mikal shook his head in admiration for Father. Using a vampire whore to lure his enemies and then cut their heads off while they sported themselves with her was brilliant. The beauty of the plan was his father's decision to use a vampire as bait—a mortal woman could not deceive immortals and Gabrielle had the strength to help Father subdue their victims. "Why didn't Father use this trick on the great Alcuin instead of waiting until the close of the twentieth century to dispose of his nemesis?"

Gabrielle's smile thinned until it almost vanished entirely. "The vampire priest had no interest in sex . . . Simon said it would be futile to even try to destroy Alcuin by using a woman."

"But Father did destroy Alcuin by using a woman," Mikal said, deliberately antagonizing Gabrielle. "Meghann."

"Meghann!" Gabrielle spat, her reaction to his mother's name was all Mikal could have hoped for. Her delicate nostrils quivered with outrage and her angelic face took on a mottled red, jealous cast. "Do you know your father never asked one thing of that. . . that creature? Everyone else served him in some way. I had to prostitute myself before all his foes to deserve immortality, others served Simon for decades before he transformed them, and still others had to give him all their earthly holdings. But Meghann... your father gave her his blood, his wealth, his protection... his love, all in exchange for her staying by his side."

In other words, Mikal thought as Gabrielle continued ranting, *Father bestowed upon Meghann all the things he denied you.*

"And he did not use Meghann to slaughter Alcuin. He simply had to slay the priest to get his hands on Meghann. Though why he wanted her, I have no idea. Simon should have killed the bitch when he killed Alcuin!" Gabrielle finished and Mikal noticed her long nails digging into the chair's expensive leather cushion.

"If Father killed Meghann, I would not have been born," Mikal reminded her. "And stop destroying my furniture. Father paid good money for it." Mikal grinned smugly, remembering how he'd raided one of Father's safety deposit boxes in London and absconded with more than five million dollars to start his new life.

"Simon could have used Meghann for his brood mare and then disposed of her after she gave birth," Gabrielle replied, looking sulky and petulant as she removed her offending claws from the leather seat. "Bearing children... that is all that plain, simpering bitch was good for. I never understood what Simon saw in her."

"Meghann is hardly plain," Mikal pointed out, enjoying Gabrielle's poisonous glare. "She may not be as beautiful as you, but. . . perhaps Father has a penchant for redheads." Yes, indeed,

Father had a penchant for luscious redheads with voluptuous bodies and a simmering passion that lurked beneath that moralistic, goody-goody exterior. Having met Meghann, Mikal appreciated Father's taste. "I plan to sample her charms myself."

Mikal complimented himself on managing to startle as jaded a creature as this centuries old whore that looked at him askance. "She is your mother!"

"So?" Mikal raised his eyebrows. "You cannot tell me you would give a damn what I do with Meghann."

"You promised I could kill her!"

"Yes, yes," Mikal said impatiently, sure Father would kill his double-dealing vampire mistress long before Meghann arrived at the estate. Mikal only kept her around because he hoped fighting another vampire would weaken Father before Mikal attacked him. Pity he'd only been able to recruit Gabrielle, that all those other sniveling, cowardly creatures were too frightened of Father to take him on. Well, Mikal had plans for all those that refused him. Oh, did he have plans for them!—once Father was dead.

"Think about it, Gabrielle. First, I cripple Father when he sees that." Mikal pointed carelessly at Elizabeth, pale and bleeding behind him. "Then Meghann arrives and sees Father about to die... I want that bastard alive when she comes here. I want him to watch her beg me not to kill him. I want him to writhe on the floor, helpless to stop me when I order her to strip, when Meghann begs me to spare her husband and daughter. I want him to scream for mercy when she lets me mount her to keep them alive, when I take her, my precious mother, in front of Father."

Gabrielle came forward and dropped to her knees before the vast bulge in Mikal's jeans. She tore his pants off and brought him to a rapid climax. Normally, Mikal preferred men for fellatio, enjoying their instinctive knowledge for pleasuring a cock, but Gabrielle's mouth and tongue was by far the most expert Mikal had ever encountered in a female. Perhaps some of her consummate skill was learned in Father's bed. If that was the case, Mikal could barely wait to have Meghann before him.

One thing Mikal was certain of... Meghann's chief charm for Father lay in her purity, a wholesomeness of spirit that even blood lust could not dim. What a pleasure it would be to turn

Father's Madonna into his disowned son's whore before Father's dying eyes. With that gratifying thought, Mikal climaxed into Gabrielle's eager, waiting mouth.

"Raping Meghann when Simon is helpless to stop you... how diabolical. You are indeed your father's boy," Gabrielle praised him, stepping behind him to gaze at the unconscious Elizabeth thoughtfully. "Why don't you find her soul and force her back here? I'm sure her cries would do a great deal to unnerve him if he loves this girl as much as you claim he does."

"Travel the astral plane so Father's devils can claim me?" Mikal said, hoping the withering scorn in his voice hid his uncertainty. He didn't want Gabrielle or any of his army knowing he could not travel the astral plane, or that he was weaker than Father in some ways, despite his ability to walk in daylight.

Of course, Gabrielle couldn't read Mikal's superior mind but she too must have been thinking of his unique talent for she asked, "When do I drink your blood and defeat the sun?"

"Did you not say I am my father's son?" Mikal questioned. "You must earn my blood, as you earned his.

"First, you help me kill him and Meghann. Then we'll greet the new day—together."

Gabrielle nodded and then cocked her head at the same moment Mikal looked toward the door with interest. A few minutes later, there was a deferential knock and Mikal called out, "Enter."

A young boy came into the room, fussily groomed and painted to resemble his conception of a vampire, all graveyard chic obviously influenced by the movies and comic books of the fifties and sixties; a style that was quite different from the silver-studded, leather-bedecked, black trench coat style of some of Mikal's other acolytes. As Mikal inspected the white pancake that smothered the mortal's natural skin tone, black stained lips, frilly lace cravat and sweeping red velvet cape, he praised himself once more for choosing these "Goth" mortals to carry out his plans.

At first, Mikal had wavered between the mentally unbalanced outcasts that yearned to be "children of the night" and the Aryans, those seething, vicious mortals of Caucasian descent that lived only to hate those they considered to be lesser races.

The Aryans attracted Mikal because many of them already belonged to militias where they'd already been trained in warfare, thus providing Mikal with a well-trained, psychotic army when he revealed himself and made his demands on the mortal world. Too, the white supremacists were so well-versed in hatred, so abused and despised for most of their lives that Mikal knew they would rush to embrace a creature such as himself that promised them the chance to make all those they considered inferior bow down in fear of them. Also, it did not hurt that Mikal, thanks to his British father, was the embodiment of their Aryan ideal with his Anglo-Saxon heritage. He would feed their hate, inveigle them to his side through transformation. As vampires, they could conduct tortures they'd never dreamed of on the "mongrel" mortals that currently treated them with withering contempt.

Unfortunately, the Aryans (American ones at any rate) proved disappointing when Mikal finally encountered them. Much of his approval stemmed from the venomous rhetoric posted on the Internet, that miraculous tool that kept Mikal from complete boredom during his isolated upbringing on the Scots island where Father imprisoned him.

Finally escaping Father's rigid control, Mikal headed to the States with the highest expectations and infiltrated a small white-power militia in the Midwest, but he only needed a few days in the commune to see these slow-wits wouldn't serve his purpose at all. The Aryans, like loyal but not overly intelligent bulldogs, committed great acts of violence only at the behest of their firmly established superiors and Mikal could see it would be an uphill struggle to redirect their slavish devotion toward him.

Too, he soon discovered the neo-Nazi (why anyone would choose to revere a government that lost face before the entire world was beyond Mikal) values the white supremacists embraced clashed with his own debauched path. The mortals that beat their women regularly and overwhelmingly preferred the company of their racist male friends reacted to Mikal's propositions as though he'd suggested they drink rat poison! In many ways, their furrowed brows, hoarsely croaked obscenities and swinging fists reminded Mikal of the appalled disgust Father displayed when he discovered his son's bisexuality.

Of course, Father had been able to bully Mikal into abandoning the diverting pastime but his Aryan victims lacked Father's strength and were unable to repel him. Then again, by the end none of his strapping companions seemed to want to repel him. In an amazingly short time, their squeals of outrage turned into grunts of desire as Mikal forced himself on them. He probably could have kept them as lovers for an indefinite period but preferred to drain them of their blood while they squirmed beneath him.

But most shocking of all, Mikal couldn't use the Aryans because his very existence was an affront to their simple, Christian ideology. They actually thought him some monster like the amusing creatures on their televisions and movie screens! It was nothing short of amazing that in this day and age humans actually thought to defeat a vampire by thrusting into his face that annoying stick of wood with the suffering Christ on it. The whole experience only proved mortals were as stupid as Father always claimed they were. Piqued beyond measure, Mikal slaughtered the entire camp of Aryans and set fire to their miserable compound before setting off to find mortals eager to carry out his bidding.

He soon encountered the Goths, young mortals that for the most part longed to escape their monotonous lives by becoming vampires—or their concept of a vampire. Granted, the vast majority of Goths were simply indulging in a harmless fantasy but others were obsessed to the point of madness . . . these were the mortals Mikal revealed himself to. How they rejoiced when he displayed his blood teeth and fed before them, making a special production of snarling and growling while he tore into his prey with theatrical savagery. All Mikal had to do was let these special mortals witness his feedings, perform a few simple telekinetic tricks, tell them the story of his battle for supremacy with Father that sounded just like one of their beloved role-playing games, and they fell at his feet, devoting their entire lives to Mikal in exchange for the blood that would make them vampires.

Mikal was not making empty promises to his mortal clique; he fully intended to transform them and all the other chosen that would be drawn into his club. He'd patiently weed through the thrill seekers and merely curious, selecting those that wanted the power behind the makeup and extravagant clothing, mortals that recognized the great strength that came with the ability to defy death and knew how to wield it against the rest of the world.

The whole process would take time; Mikal recognized that he'd have to be patient. Contrary to Father's belief that Mikal had no more thought behind his plans than the poor lunatic mortals that waved imaginary swords in asylums and called themselves Napoleon, Mikal had planned his strategy meticulously. He knew he could not take over the world in the course of one mortal lifetime. True dominance would not be achieved for centuries—it would be a slow, gradual elevation of power. Mikal would start with his club, select and train his army. Then, when there were vampires enough that shared Mikal's resistance to sunlight, they would make their first bid for power . . . take over New York City, perhaps. If Mikal had wealth, the weapons arsenal he planned to obtain from poverty stricken nations, and an immortal force with superhuman strength, mortal governments would have no choice but to give in to his demands. Mikal would start small, taking only a minor territory and expanding his empire over centuries until finally, he and only he, ruled this world he'd been born into.

"Master," the boy said and his slightly raised tone informed Mikal the mortal must have been trying to gain his attention for long moments now. Shaking away the last remnants of his pleasant daydream, Mikal turned to the kneeling mortal.

"You may reward yourself," Mikal said with the grand loftiness of a medieval liege lord and gestured to Elizabeth. The ghoulishly costumed mortal arose from his knees and hurried over to Elizabeth, sucking with great gusto at the still bleeding wound on her torso. Idly, Mikal wondered what possible pleasure mortals drew from drinking blood but what did he care as long as it kept his minions docile?

Finally, the mortal boy (Mikal never bothered to remember their names) raised his bloodstained mouth from Elizabeth and turned to Mikal, kneeling as all mortals were bade to do when they spoke to him. "I have done your bidding, my lord."

How these vampiric mortals loved to use arcane language! They'd be so disappointed to encounter a being like Father, who far preferred the language of high finance to the Renaissance English he'd spoken in his mortal youth or Meghann, with her distinctly New York accent discussing pennant races and psychology instead of clans and coffins. "My mother received the invitation?"

"Your mother did not pick it up, Master," the boy said. "There was another vampire there... at least, I think he was a vampire."

"Another vampire?" Mikal frowned. Who could this immortal be—Mikal had killed her best friend, Charles. Could Meghann have transformed Lee, Elizabeth's surrogate parent?

"What did he look like?" Gabrielle questioned and the sharp light flashing in her eyes told Mikal she knew exactly who this friend of Meghann's was.

"He had brown hair and blue eyes," the mortal reported and Mikal saw the pulse in his throat quicken when he stared at Gabrielle's half-naked form. "I think he was in his early thirties and he was . . . loud."

"Loud mouthed?" Gabrielle said with amusement. "Crude, perhaps?"

"Yes," the boy nodded, eager to please.

"It is Jimmy Delacroix," Gabrielle informed Mikal.

"Who is Jimmy Delacroix?"

Gabrielle's turquoise eyes widened with astonishment. "Simon never told you of Meghann's lover?"

"Meghann had a lover?" Mikal echoed disbelievingly. Adelaide had told him of some separation between Meghann and Father but she'd never said anything about Meghann taking other men while she was away from Father. Frankly, Mikal was surprised that Father still desired her after she allowed others to despoil her.

"A mortal she trained to kill off your father's allies during the day," Gabrielle clarified and Mikal gave her his full, fascinated attention—perhaps Meghann wasn't his father's simpering plaything after all. "Simon allowed her... and the rest of us... to think he was dead for forty years. You know Meghann escaped your father by putting a stake in his heart—no? Well, that is a tale for another time. Suffice it to say the ungrateful bitch attacked your father thirteen years after he transformed her and sought sanctuary with his great enemy, Alcuin. When Simon challenged Alcuin to regain Meghann and his power, he took care of Jimmy at the same time."

"Tried to kill him?"

"That would have been too merciful," Gabrielle smirked. "No, Simon transformed the fool; turned him into a mindless, bloodthirsty savage. Obviously, Simon meant to present Meghann with the ruined creature and have her kill her own lover out of pity. But she healed the man instead and made him a true immortal... no one knows how."

Meghann had talents Mikal had never guessed at . . . and a nerve to defy Father he found electrifying. It was a shame he had to kill her. Before he did though, he'd have to ask her why she went from being Father's enemy to his willing consort once more and subsequent mother to his children.

"Is this Delacroix still her lover?" If he was, Mikal's plans were ruined. Father wouldn't run to save an unfaithful whore or the daughter she bore him.

"Delacroix isn't involved with Meghann." It was the mortal that said this and Gabrielle and Mikal both turned speculative eyes toward him at the unsolicited comment

The boy reddened and gulped nervously. "It's just... he, uh... Jimmy. He, um, seemed... attached to... to her." The mortal pointed hesitantly at Elizabeth.

Mikal's eyes narrowed into silver slits. "What did this Jimmy Delacroix say to make you think he has some attachment to my sister?"

"Master, please!" The boy's lips trembled and he looked at Mikal with great apprehension.

Mikal put a comradely arm around the mortal's shoulders, pulling him close and speaking benevolently. "Don't worry... I won't harm you if this Delacroix said something abusive toward me. Just speak and don't make me waste time looking into your mind or I'll have to put you on the wall with my sister."

The boy whimpered and then said hurriedly, "He... he called you a 'chickenshit motherfucker' and then said that... that your sister... called you, a... lousy lay."

Even Gabrielle backed away at the livid, pulsating rage that overtook Mikal. With a bellow that shattered the mirrored panels and glass walls, Mikal launched himself on his unconscious sister, wrapping his hands around her throat as if to force the insulting words out of her.

"What the hell would you know about sex, you whey-faced, passive bitch?!" he screamed while Elizabeth's vacant eyes started to bulge from their sockets. "All you ever did was lie there with your legs spread while I did all the work!"

"Mikal..." Gabrielle said nervously and he turned on her furiously.

"Shut up, shut up, shut up!" Now the marble ceiling was showing cracks and the floor beneath them trembled. Still, Mikal carried on, not sure why he was so angry—whether it was Elizabeth's derisive comments about his prowess or that she'd cheated him again, taking a lover before he killed her. Of course Jimmy Delacroix was Elizabeth's lover—with who else but her lover would she have a frank, sexual discussion? The little whore . . . Elizabeth was supposed to die as a receptacle for her brother's lust but she'd offered herself to someone else—another vampire at that.

Mikal would never be sure how much time went by as he beat Elizabeth, fists smashing through her teeth, destroying her fine nose, slamming through her jaw. By God, she'd wake up before he was through with her . . . Mikal would make Elizabeth wake up, make her see all he'd done to make her the ugly child, the hideous thing no one wanted to look at or acknowledge as their own.

"No!" Mikal yelled when he felt her heartbeat weaken. Spitefully, he kicked Elizabeth, shattering her rib cage. "You won't die on me... not yet." He couldn't lose control like this. It would make him the reckless fool Father always accused him of being.

Mikal glared at his toppled desk, and soon the top drawer shot open, displaying a cattle prod that shot into his waiting hand.

"I bet you don't just lie there for Jimmy Delacroix," Mikal snarled at Elizabeth. The other mortal huddled by Gabrielle, no longer needing makeup to look bloodless and horrified. Gabrielle, on the other hand, did not appear scared, but uneasy and exasperated.

"What do you think you're doing?"

"I want Elizabeth to jump for me like she did for Delacroix." Mikal slid the cattle prod into his sister's vagina and turned it on to full strength, watching her body convulse so strongly her manacles came off the wall and she slid to the floor.

"Enough," Gabrielle said when Mikal stooped down to recharge the prod dangling at an obscene angle from his sister's body. "Where are your wits? Your father is here!"

All the senseless rage drained from him as Mikal felt the presence he should have been alerted to long before Gabrielle told him of it. Father was here and making no effort to conceal his presence as he stormed into the house.

"Not alone," Mikal said and demanded of Gabrielle, "Is it Delacroix with him? I know it isn't Meghann. I've been around her; I'd recognize her aura."

Gabrielle frowned, blue eyes darkening to almost black as she concentrated. "I don't understand... it's an old soul but I sense a newly transformed being. What trick is your father up to?"

"Who cares?" Mikal said mournfully, grieving not for the mortals downstairs that Father and his unknown friend were dispatching so easily but for the destruction of his meticulously decorated quarters. The sleek glass furniture, elegant mirrors, and steel trappings... all parts of a style Father abhorred... all that splendor was to surround Mikal when Father was lured into this room. Now he'd destroyed the room in a temper—the same temper that was Father's excuse for never giving him nice things and insisted on Spartan quarters for his son.

"Look at this," Mikal said in a voice suspiciously close to a whine and extended his arms to encompass the cork insulation behind his ruined glass walls, the debris surrounding them. "Now he'll laugh at me."

For a moment Gabrielle looked startled but then her expression cleared and she smiled reassuringly. Her hand reached out to stroke his shoulder but then she remembered Mikal hated being touched unless he was copulating and even then only on his cock.

"Your father will have no chance to laugh if you attack quickly and forcefully. First, we must figure out the identity of his companion . . . whether he is a threat. Your father's reputation precedes him. There are many who would jump at this chance to gain his favor."

That wasn't the impression Mikal had. As far as he knew, Father put his trust only in Adelaide, Meghann, Charles Tarleton and the mortal Lee . . . that must be it! He'd transformed Lee Winslow. Mikal almost laughed, thinking he had indeed depleted his father's forces if he must rely on a brand-new immortal to help him fight Mikal and Gabrielle, a vampire with centuries of power behind her.

"He is no one important," Mikal said and rapidly began making plans. So what if Father murdered the mortals . . . Mikal could always get more to replace them. Killing off the humans didn't get Father any closer to Elizabeth . . . for that prize, he must go through his son and ex-mistress.

"Take my sister into the anteroom," Mikal said to the mortal and gestured to a secret passage through one of the destroyed mirrored panels. "Do nothing further to harm her and don't drink her blood. Guard her well and you, fortunate human, shall be my first transformed general. Now go!"

The mortal obeyed immediately, struggling with the burden of Elizabeth's dead weight as he lugged her through the dark passage and disappeared from sight.

Mikal turned to Gabrielle and tossed her a broad sword he scooped up off the floor. He'd had his weapons in an attractive display over the wall behind his desk but they'd fallen to the floor when his anger destroyed the room. "You go and engage Father. Don't kill him... simply wound him or lead him into this room with your fighting."

Gabrielle nodded and vanished into thin air, never suspecting she was employing a power Mikal did not have.

Mikal shrugged at the condition of his room and took his own sword from the untidy pile on the floor, waiting for his father to appear so he could finally destroy him.

Chapter Thirteen

When they were a few miles away from Manhasset, Simon took his eyes off the quiet highway and glanced at Alcuin. While he was certain the priest would kill Mikal to save the innocent Elizabeth, there was another issue that had to be resolved before they reached Mikal's lair.

"I'm certain Mikal doesn't have much immortal support against me," Simon said and Alcuin listened with a grave courtesy quite different from the unyielding condemnation he'd displayed in life toward Lord Baldevar. "When Mikal approached the others and did not offer his blood immediately to seal the bargain, I'm sure they were wise enough to see he was enticing them with false promises and had no intention of parting with his special gifts. Knowing Mikal to be a liar, they would of course refuse to join any battle against me."

Lee Winslow's brow furrowed as the mind possessing his body considered Simon's words. "Mikal can't be the only vampire on the grounds. Why would he confront you alone?"

"He won't be alone," Simon said and there was dear disdain in his tone. "I said he doesn't have immortal support because most of our kind are too smart for him. Unfortunately, even vampires have fools among them that will flock to my son... as well as those grudging souls that wish to avenge whatever slights they think I've committed against them."

Simon waited to see if Alcuin would make any snide remarks about his long list of enemies, the adversaries that plagued any powerful creature, but the dead priest said nothing, merely staring at Simon with the old watchful calmness that was one of the few things in the world with the power to disturb him.

"I'm sure between us we can subdue any vampires that side with Mikal," Alcuin finally said quietly.

"It is not the vampires that concern me," Simon said and fixed his penetrating gold stare on Alcuin. "My son is a fool in more ways than one—he thinks to build himself a power base by forming a guard of misfit mortals that follow him with the lunatic zeal of crusaders charging against the infidel. They will fight to the death for Mikal and the transformation he promises. Like Mikal and any other vampires there, we must kill those mortals to save Elizabeth."

Simon waited for Alcuin's response with some tension. Would this vampire pacifist balk at Simon's directive and refuse to kill any mortals in Mikal's employ? If he did, Simon would exorcise the priest from Lee Winslow's body immediately and face Mikal alone for Alcuin would be of no use to him unless he agreed to slaughter anyone, mortal or vampire, who had a hand in abducting Elizabeth.

Alcuin used Lee's thin lips to form a sad smile. "Nephew, you know very little of me, of the path I urge vampires to follow. It is not necessary for me to explain myself to you tonight. Just understand this: I will help you vanquish anyone, mortal or otherwise, who attempts to foil our efforts tonight."

Simon nodded his approval and they continued along the empty road in silence.

"What in the world has he done to my home?"

Simon exclaimed when they pulled up to an elegant whitewashed brick wall that was utterly ruined by a gaudy red, neon sign welded into the middle of it; the sprawling, bright script flashing the words, IMMORTAL LIGHT—A REFUGE FOR CHILDREN OF THE NIGHT.

In disgust, Simon got out of the car and hopped the ten-foot wall, hearing Alcuin jump behind him. Once they got on the grounds, Simon searched in vain for the estate he used to own.

Half the lush Edwardian garden that used to grace the estate was paved over to make an appalling cement parking lot while the other half was a nightmare garden of creeping ivy, fake trees sporting miserable, drooping leaves and wrought-iron tables with spindly matching chairs.

Idly, Simon wondered about the presence of the five black and purple hearses lounging in the parking lot. Was his son considerate enough to ferry his victims to funeral parlors when he was through with them? More likely, they were part of some gimmick to lure customers into this vampiric watering hole. Simon's respect for mortals, always scant, now plummeted entirely when he considered that there were mortals depraved enough to pay to enter this monument to bad taste.

The external changes were bad enough but Simon was most offended by what had happened to his house or rather, the destruction of his house. The red-brick central structure flanked by two stately wings no longer existed, its place preempted by an abominable black-shingled, windowless sprawl of a house that looked a demented child's block creation with ungainly, jutting wings.

Idly, Simon wondered what Meghann, with her penchant for the false science of psychology, would make of the windowless residence. Would she think as he did, that the odd dwelling was a reflection of Mikal's grudging, closed-off soul—not allowing anyone to see the emptiness inside him?

"The fool," Simon said contemptuously and Alcuin turned to him, curiosity reflected in Lee's pale blue eyes.

"You call him a fool because he thought to upset you by leveling the house where Meghann conceived?"

"Mikal does not have emotion enough for such motives," Simon laughed unpleasantly. "My misguided offspring did not bulldoze the house to hurt my feelings. Rather, he thinks to obliterate my ability to travel the astral plane by building a house I've never been in. The fool does not realize it is not the house that matters but the ground it is on. I've been here before and I can certainly use the plane at will."

"But I cannot," Alcuin reminded him. "How do you wish to plan our offensive?"

Simon almost smiled at his enemy leaving the planning in his hands. Politics certainly did make the strangest of bedfellows; a vampiric sorcerer working side by side with the creature he'd slain long ago.

I shall appear inside, Simon said, speaking telepathically with full confidence Mikal would not hear him. Already Simon had intuited his son's presence and knew the boy's attention was elsewhere; he had no idea his father was on the estate. There are naught but mortals guarding the downstairs.

Alcuin nodded. *If there are immortals with Mikal, they are not near us now.*

No matter Simon's dislike for this centuries old enemy, he had complete respect for Alcuin's ability to ferret out any immortal threat. Simon used the plane, feeling a dank blackness surrounding him before he opened his eyes, staring up at a gray stone gothic archway more suited for a medieval cloister than a modern nightclub in his estimation.

A bullet grazed his neck and Simon whipped around, seeing a young mortal woman clutching some automatic brand of gun.

"Priest!" Simon bellowed and spread his hands, lifting his body up and out of harm's way as he sailed at the girl.

Simon focused his power on the girl's hands and she lost control of her weapon, screeching her terror when the gun flew into Simon's hand. He crushed the weapon to pulp within his strong grip, then glared at the girl and wrapped that same inexorable power around her heart. Dispassionately, he watched her face contort in agony before she crumpled to the floor, clutching her heart.

Two other mortals, both boys, rushed into the room and abruptly skidded to a halt, watching the deadly tableau of the vampire killing one of their own by simply staring at her. So transfixed were they by Simon's power that they never even thought to use the automatic weapons trembling in their hands.

When the girl took one last, strangled breath, Simon raised his eyes and glared at the boys, his lips curling into a derisive smirk when they simply dropped their guns and ran for the front door.

They threw open the heavy, silver-studded door only to encounter Alcuin, looking on them with profound sadness even as he caused the aneurysms that killed them instantaneously and without the pain Simon made the girl suffer.

From a dark western wing, five more mortals rushed at them, brandishing wooden stakes and making snarling vows to destroy Mikal's enemies.

Simon allowed Alcuin to deal with them while he investigated a low, drumming vibration that reached his keen ears.

Stalking over to a set of closed double doors made of brass and decorated with elaborate wrought-iron handles carved in the form of gargoyles, Simon threw open the doors and took in an immense, too-posh room that was apparently the dance hall of Mikal's club. Simon took in each over decorated, macabre detail from the red-and-white tiled floor cunningly designed to form a montage of thorny stems and crosses to the crimson upholstered walls with fussy, fake sconces serving as lights and thick black velvet portieres concealing some sort of stage.

In the center of the room, there was a large, circular bar that looked like it had been constructed from tombstones. Simon vaulted over the bar and found a mortal crouching by the mirrored liquor display.

She was a plain child, the little beauty she had marred by the angry puncture wounds dotting her neck and chest. . . was Mikal finally displaying some interest in women?

"Master," she called in a voice that shook almost as much as the hands clutching a switchblade she thrust menacingly at Simon.

Simon glanced at her thoughts and nearly jumped on the shivering mortal, intent on tearing her limb from limb, when he thought of a better punishment. This venal bitch would look upon death as paradise when he was through with her.

"You enjoy disfigurement?" he inquired with deadly softness before he reached into the girl's mind and made her drag the switchblade across her forehead.

"No!" she cried and made a desperate attempt to stop her hands but she was now a puppet in the hands of a creature far more powerful than she. With malicious humor, Simon wondered if the girl still considered it such a dream to encounter vampires as the switchblade she no longer controlled gouged her cheek.

"You will do to yourself everything you did to my daughter," Simon commanded with implacable menace. His jaw clenched violently when he watched the sharp knife cut the girl's pale lips, stab violently through spots all over her face and finally cut out great, clumsy chunks of her mousy brown hair. While she destroyed her face, the girl sobbed helplessly... sobbed as his precious daughter sobbed this afternoon when Mikal stepped back and allowed this ugly, loathsome girl to take her twisted anger and sick jealousy out on Elizabeth.

"Now the punishment begins." Simon leaned down and concentrated the entire weight of his power on the girl's mind. "You will get up and walk out of this house, forgetting everything that has happened to you for the past year. Your last memory is running away from your parent's home in Illinois. After that, there is nothing. Now leave!"

Simon watched the bleeding, injured girl walk out of the room, destined to live the rest of her miserable life as a grotesque freak, suffering the punishment she'd tried to inflict on Elizabeth. Even with their immense talent and dazzling tools of skin grafts and plastic, no modern physician would be able to stitch that broken face back together.

Simon swallowed hard, finding it almost unbearable to dwell on the images he'd received from the mortal... lovely, sweet Elizabeth crying in pain and terror, completely unable to understand how a boy she'd come to trust could turn into this monster that tortured her.

Simon's one consolation was that Meghann was not here, would never know the extent of their daughter's suffering, the pain and humiliation Elizabeth endured at her brother's hands. The knowledge of Elizabeth's pain was something Simon would carry to his grave.

He could spare Elizabeth, as well as Meghann, once he found her. Before transformation, Simon would hypnotize Elizabeth, remove every element of the terrifying afternoon from her mind so she remembered nothing. It would be like it never happened, no shameful memories would cast their shadow over his daughter's life.

"There is a nobility in you I never guessed at, Simon Baldevar," Alcuin said with something in his voice Simon had never expected to hear—respect. "Why not concentrate all your ability on finding Elizabeth and healing her instead of lowering yourself to the level of these savages by feasting on their pain? It is not your place to punish them."

"And whose place it?" Simon demanded. "That of your omniscient god? He moves too slowly for my taste, Priest. Enough debate—I must find Elizabeth."

Elizabeth, Simon called, reaching out into the void surrounding him. It did not surprise him when there was no answer to his repeated calls. Elizabeth had retreated to a place where no pain would reach her and would not leave it easily, even to answer the signal of a worried father. Meghann, no doubt, could have connected with her daughter easily. Simon, lacking the bond Meghann had formed with their child, would have no choice but to explore this house until he found some sign of Elizabeth.

"Simon!" Alcuin shouted and Simon moved quickly but not quickly enough to evade the cold touch of steel to his throat. His attacker must have appeared behind him or Alcuin would have disabled the vampire before it reached Simon.

The body pressed against his, despite the rigidity bought on by tension, had the supple softness of a woman. A very shapely woman whose body Simon had used many times at his leisure.

"Gabrielle," Simon greeted his unseen captor neutrally. "Who else would join my feckless son but the whore I scorned so thoroughly?"

"Bastard!" she shrieked just as Simon expected her to and he used her lapse of concentration to wrap his foot about her ankle and trip her. Gabrielle fell to the floor in a graceless heap and her sword slipped off his neck with naught but a slight nick.

Gabrielle spun away from him, dashing out of the room at breakneck speed with Simon at her heels, Alcuin fast behind him. Simon did not have to tell the priest that Gabrielle was leading them to Mikal, as he'd no doubt ordered her to do. Mikal thought he was leading his father into a trap but he did not know of the formidable magus Simon brought with him.

The house was a bizarre, mazelike structure of confusing doorways and spiraling staircases that Simon sensed led to dead ends. There were signs pointing to various amusements until

Gabrielle took a sharp left turn and the look of the house became more businesslike with storage rooms and darkened offices.

Now Gabrielle was running toward an open door. Simon let her nearly pass through it before he removed a sharp dirk from the small of his back and flung it through the air, watching the weapon find its target with deadly accuracy as it settled between her shoulder blades.

Simon heard a gargled moan and knew the knife had found some portion of her heart, enough to render Gabrielle immobile and helpless unless someone removed the dirk. He watched the doorway for a few moments to see if Mikal would come to her aid but Gabrielle remained on the floor, moaning and making a vain effort to crawl into the room.

He waits for you, Alcuin said. *We must get past him to find Elizabeth.*

Simon nodded, knowing his daughter was nearby; the entryway to her prison was within the room where Mikal lurked. Simon felt his son now, felt the familiar aura of unpleasantness that enshrouded Mikal's soul.

Simon could have tried flying the plane to evade Mikal, but he had not come here merely to find Elizabeth... he must also kill this thing he'd spawned so it would never present a threat to Meghann or Elizabeth again.

I shall go in now, Simon said. *Mikal will lunge at me immediately. When he does so, enter the room and restrain him.*

Not waiting for a reply, Simon stalked to the open door, his sword drawn and ready. He looked past the prone Gabrielle and shook his head at the wrecked room. What had disturbed the volatile creature now? Mikal was so prone to senseless rages; it was part of the sickness Simon had sensed in him since he was a child. He should have killed the boy when he first sensed the jarring wrongness within him, but for once Simon disdained logic and made a decision based on nothing but a futile hope the child would change as he grew older.

Simon was not so simple minded that he'd step through the open door and allow Mikal to leap on him. Rather than use the astral plane, as Mikal probably expected him to do, Simon glared at the walls on either side of the doorway and focused on crumbling them. Surprisingly, it took more energy than Simon expected and his head throbbed uncomfortably by the time large cracks appeared in the walls, bringing down sections of the wall so Simon could leap through a jagged hole on the left side of the doorway.

His feet had barely touched the ground when he saw movement out of the corner of his eye and a heavy desk came rocketing toward him. Simon ducked the object and then glared at it, making the thing crash against a wall and shatter into a thousand harmless pieces.

With a high-pitched screech, Mikal rushed out of the darkness, attacking his father with a sword Simon had given him for his tenth birthday. Father and son battled for a few moments before Simon roared, "Alcuin!" and heard the wounded Gabrielle gasp behind him.

The thin black strips Mikal called pupils dilated at the sight of a man he knew as Lee Winslow, sword in hand, advancing on him with the expertise of a medieval knight.

At first it appeared this battle would proceed as Simon expected it to. He and Alcuin were able to corner Mikal, Simon knocking his son's sword out of his hand and Alcuin raising his blade to cut the boy's head off. He'd been right to invoke Alcuin... now Simon would not need to drain his energy by summoning daemons to restrain Mikal while he killed him.

Then Simon noticed the sword Alcuin held trembled violently and the priest looked dismayed, almost ill as he turned frightened eyes to Simon.

Alcuin opened Lee Winslow's mouth to speak and in that moment, all the priest's age old wisdom faded from Lee's eyes and Simon knew Alcuin's spirit no longer occupied Lee's body. Something had forcibly driven him from Lee's body and now Simon's only aid against his son was a novice vampire blinking confusedly, not knowing where he was or why he held a sword.

Bewildered by this turn of events, Simon could only gape as Lee mumbled, "Simon," in a disoriented manner.

Saying Simon's name were the last words Lee Winslow ever spoke. Recovering his wits quicker than his father, Mikal grabbed his sword off the floor and managed to behead the perplexed new vampire.

As Mikal's sword reached Lee's neck, Simon got his own sword up to try and block the move but Mikal drove his foot into Simon's shin.

Simon muttered a swift oath when his shin bone broke under Mikal's daunting strength and he spun away before Mikal could use the sword on him.

Lee Winslow's body had not even hit the floor before Mikal launched himself at his father who limped because his leg would take another minute or so to heal. But even wounded Simon could handle himself in a duel and deflected each deadly blow Mikal attempted to land.

"Foolish, Father," Mikal growled, looking more snakelike than ever as his strange eyes contracted and narrowed. "You think I didn't learn from our last loving encounter? I knew you'd resort to your wizardry but I expected more daemon soldiers. I didn't think you'd bring some necromantic slave to my home! Who occupied Lee's body?"

"Your father called him Alcuin," Gabrielle moaned from the floor while Simon blocked a thrust to his heart and then used his sword to push Mikal away from him.

"Alcuin?" Mikal said and laughed nastily, spinning near Gabrielle and yanking the knife from her back. "Well, Father, I must applaud your ingenuity, using your old foe to kill me. But Father, I am so much smarter and more resourceful than you. Use your so-called sharp senses and feel the strong material supporting these walls. It is steel, Sire. Did you not tell me spirits cannot stand steel. That your way of controlling your precious daemons was to threaten their essence with imprisonment in a steel box? I knew if I reinforced one room in this house with steel, you could not invoke those damnable imps of yours! To think I unwittingly saved myself because your puppet man could not sustain possession in my steel embrace!"

Inwardly, Simon cursed his own stupidity. He'd been so focused on slaughtering Mikal and rescuing Elizabeth that he completely failed to perceive the presence of steel in this house. Now Mikal and Gabrielle, hurt but able to clutch a sword, were advancing on him, attempting to corner him as he and Alcuin had done to Mikal.

But Simon had one more weapon up his sleeve: the truth.

Simon gave Gabrielle an inviting smile that widened at her suspicious glare. "My dear strumpet, you are hurt. Don't you need blood to regain your full strength? Why not drink from my son... that is, if he'll let you."

"I said after he's dead," Mikal said swiftly and flinched at his father's cutting laughter.

"You lying little fraud," Simon mocked his son and turned again to Gabrielle. "Don't you see this young whelp will never offer you his blood, not now when you are wounded or ever? He cannot let you drink it even if he wanted to. Mikal's blood is poisonous."

"No!" Mikal yelled and ran at Simon, only to be blocked by Gabrielle who planted her body between father and son.

"You know I am right," Simon whispered, thinking how easy it was to manipulate women as he wrapped his arms about her hand-span waist. Smothering a quick grin when he thought Meghann might not approve of this strategy at all, Simon kissed the exposed, petal soft skin of Gabrielle's shoulder and spoke in the low, honeyed tones of a lover while Mikal looked on in frustration. Mikal knew if he raised his sword to Gabrielle, he'd be giving his father the perfect opportunity to cut off his own head while he was occupied with the female vampire.

"Think, Gabrielle," Simon purred in the silvery whisper he'd used shamelessly on women his whole life to get whatever he needed from them. "Have you seen Mikal transform anyone, immortal or human? The boy's blood is toxic. I know because I've attempted to drink it. How do you think he got away from me? I swallowed his blood and could not chase after him due to the sickness that followed. Mikal's blood only makes us ill; we cannot absorb his power by drinking of him. So why not kill the idiot boy before he exposes us to mortal scrutiny with his moronic plans to take over the world?"

To Simon's complete amazement, he saw Mikal grow pale and his lips curled into a distressed pucker of a child who is told something he desperately wanted is out of his grasp. So Mikal thought he could transform, still harbored fantasies of creating his own loyal, immortal army.

"Halfwit," Simon thundered at the boy and saw Mikal's hands tremble with impotent rage as his father smiled coldly. "The dead mortals, did you think them an accident? What of my illness when I drank from you? Your blood is worthless. Just like you."

Mikal's face went nearly purple with fury and Simon heard several flat, loud cracks resound through the room and glanced at the walls, expecting them to crumble under whatever assaults Mikal inflicted, but it soon became apparent it wasn't the room Mikal was trying to destroy.

Gabrielle stiffened abruptly, emitting a shrill, startled cry of pain and fear as every bone in her body simultaneously broke.

"Worthless, am I?" Mikal screamed and launched himself at his father again. "Can you break a skeleton with the mere power of your thoughts, Father, or are you confined to damaging inanimate objects?"

No, he could not use telekinesis to crumble the bones of an immortal opponent—before tonight Simon had never known a vampire who could. Mortals, yes, their hearts and bones were pulp to a vampire, but breaking down a vampire's defenses to destroy their body with mere force of mind was unheard of. What was more unsettling was that Mikal could use this power with such little effort he was able to engage in swordplay at the same time Gabrielle slid to the floor, rendered by Mikal to a gelatinous, shapeless puddle of skin, muscle, and hair.

Simon focused his mind on Gabrielle briefly and was astonished to find she was still alive, though with no more awareness than that of a severely hurt animal. Given a vampire's restorative powers, it was possible her bones might knit back together, but she would certainly need blood to accomplish such a trick. Even if Simon was inclined to save the life of a trollop that had a hand in abducting his daughter, there was no way he could have broken off his battle with Mikal to assist Gabrielle.

Then Simon felt something icy enter his own body, attacking his wrist with the force of a sledgehammer, and knew Mikal was trying this same trick on his father.

"No!" Simon screamed and concentrated every ounce of power he had on the invasive power, immersing himself in it and then expelling the intrusive force from his body, making it rebound on the one that attacked him.

It was Mikal's turn to scream in outraged surprise when his own left wrist cracked, unfortunately not the hand clutching his sword or Simon would have had the perfect opportunity to decapitate him.

With a drastic change of emotion typical of all madmen, the rage vanished from Mikal's bright silver eyes and they became calculating as he smiled at his father.

"Shall we sing truce, Father?" Mikal questioned as they circled each other warily, neither opponent ready to launch a new offensive strike.

"Truce?" Simon laughed to cover the sense of relief he felt when he finally detected some sign of Elizabeth. She was somewhere behind one of these walls, guarded by a frightened mortal. His daughter was badly hurt, barely alive, but the more Simon concentrated on her presence, the more he was certain transformation could save her. "What do I stand to gain by settling with you?"

"Your daughter," Mikal smiled. "Come, Father, lay down your sword and I shall allow you to remove Elizabeth from my home."

"Your home?" Simon questioned sarcastically. "Useless whelp, what industry have you ever worked at to earn the funds to purchase this land? This estate was bought with the monies you stole from me like a common thief. That makes this my home and I fully intend to destroy you like any unwelcome trespasser."

For once, stinging words didn't drive Mikal into one of his howling tantrums. Instead, he mimicked his father's mocking grin and said calmly, "Gabrielle served some useful purpose before she died." Contemptuously, Mikal kicked the boneless lump of flesh at his feet. "You and Meghann have a history I knew nothing about."

"And was none of your business." Simon moved a bit closer to his son, trying to get within striking range but the boy slithered a few feet away, careful to stay in the center of the room and not blunder into any corners.

"It is none of my business that my own mother attempted to kill you and you were such a soft-hearted fool you forgave her? Father, I know now why you brought that vampire zombie with you, why you tried to turn Gabrielle against me. You cannot kill me anymore than you could kill Meghann. You're utterly incapable of destroying those you love, no matter what they do to you!"

"You think I love you?" Simon's tone was so low there was something almost gende about the withering condescension in his voice. "Love a misguided brute that uses his own sister to satisfy his twisted needs? It's quite true that I love Meghann. But that love is precisely what makes your own life forfeit, idiot boy. Do you think I will allow anyone to live that threatens her safety?"

"You do not fool me, Father." Mikal tried to sound as detached and scornful as his father, but his silver eyes blazing with injured vanity and tightly pursed lips told another story. "How many opportunities have you had to destroy me? You squandered every last one of them. I know you cannot bring yourself to kill me but, be warned, I have the power to slay you. You are powerless in this room, Father. Your magic is of no use to you and you do not have even a tenth of my strength. Prostrate yourself before me and I shall allow you to save your daughter... and the mother I have no doubt is hurrying here."

"I prostrate myself before no one," Simon said coldly, surprising Mikal with a sudden kick at his breastplate. Moving with the swift reflexes Simon had taught the miscreant, Mikal put up his sword to block the attack and Simon pulled back.

"Why won't you even consider my offer, foolish Father?" Several shards of glass flew at Simon but he easily evaded them by leaping high in the air as he directed a large chunk of plaster at his son's head. Mikal ducked out of harm's way, the assault and counterassault resulting in another stalemate between father and son.

"You offer peace because you know you're defeated." Simon came at Mikal, forcing his son back with a series of harsh, swift blows. Mikal managed to hold onto his sword but Simon saw his eyes narrow with concentration, knew his son could not duel him and focus his attention on another telekinetic attack. "You did not know you cannot transform others. I know how your mind works, megalomaniac boy. You thought you could build up some army of vampires with your power, didn't you? Now you know you'll not have a single ally. That means no one to defend you during the day and nothing but enemies at night. If one of us does not kill you, the mortals may be able to accomplish your assassination during the day. You have no one at your back, Mikal. You're finished."

"Never!" Mikal yowled as he met his father's assault with, if not equal skill, equal intent to fight to the death. In all the deathly quiet house, the only sounds were steel clanging against steel as the two vampires launched into each other with renewed hatred, each filled with the same malevolent determination to destroy the other.

Chapter Fourteen

"Maggie, look... they're towing the cars away. Traffic is moving again!"

Meghann put the car in drive for the first time in twenty minutes and viciously hoped the drunken mortal that caused the accident that trapped her and Jimmy on the Long Island Expressway would spend the rest of his miserable life trapped in a wheelchair. It was incomprehensible that she might lose everyone she loved because a traffic accident prevented her from reaching them in time.

Meghann!

"Jesus Christ!" Jimmy grabbed the wheel when Meghann bolted upright, her face devoid of color but for the emerald eyes bright with pain. Narrowly they missed a collision when the block-long Cadillac swerved into the left lane. "Maggie?!"

"My chest! My chest!" she gasped, hands fluttering up to her heart. "Oh God, it hurts... can't breathe... feels like someone stabbed me."

"Hang on," Jimmy said and guided the Caddy into the breakdown lane while Meghann panted miserably, trying to force air past the monstrous pain radiating from the center of her heart.

Jimmy turned the engine off and helped Meghann stretch out on the long, cream leather seat. He pulled her T-shirt up and then said uncertainly, "Maggie, there's nothing the matter with you."

"Huh?" Meghann got her hands up and inspected the skin around her heart, stunned when she felt no wound or blood, just a slightly elevated heartbeat.

"Thank God," Jimmy said when she sat up slowly, still feeling a nasty ache in her chest. "I thought you were having a heart attack or something. Maggie, is it possible that this was a psychic attack . . . that Mikal hurt you the same way Baldevar hurt me last night?"

Meghann started to say yes, that was entirely possible, and then she remembered the scream she'd heard just before she felt the pain—how the masculine voice calling out to her was filled with raw despair and panic.

"Simon!" she yelled. "Simon, no . . ."

"Maggie!"Jimmy gave her a rough shake, speaking in a firm, no-nonsense voice that cut through some of her blind fear. "Talk to me... we don't have time for you to faint or throw a fit. What is it? Was Baldevar hurt?"

"I think Mikal impaled him or stabbed him or something. I felt it," Meghann said and ran her hand over her undamaged heart. "Jimmy..."

"Is Baldevar dead?" Jimmy demanded and Meghann knew what he was thinking. If Mikal had killed Simon, there was no one left to protect Ellie with the possible exception of Lee.

"I don't think Simon's dead," Meghann replied, but she couldn't be sure if that conviction was based on the psychic link she thought was still unbroken by death or was she merely deluding herself with desperate hope? "Come on, dammit! We have to get to Mikal's . . . there isn't a second to waste.

"Simon . . . he's dying, I know he is! And who knows what Mikal's done to Ellie? Jimmy, I can't feel her anymore. It's been hours since she called out to me! I don't know if she's unconscious or... oh, God, we have to hurry!"

"Shove over," Jimmy said and gently moved her to the passenger seat. "Keep calm, Maggie. We're about twenty minutes from Manhasset now. Five, the way I'm planning to drive."

Jimmy roared through the night while Meghann huddled miserably, straining to establish a telepathic link with her husband or daughter. Ellie and Simon, she couldn't lose them both! Meghann couldn't conceive of living in a world where her child no longer existed.

And Simon... Simon! This was supposed to be our time, Meghann thought, feeling bitter, salty tears run down her face and land on her lips. Simon was supposed to come back to me, to

Ellie and me... once Mikal was a grown man. We were supposed to be at peace; I was ready to welcome Simon back.

God, please hear me, she prayed. *Maybe Simon Baldevar has committed terrible sins and you might not care if he lives or dies but I care! Please, God. I know there's good in him. Look how he charged after Ellie. He can be good. I'll make him good, God, if you just help me save him. And Ellie, you see what a wonderful girl she is. You can't take her away when she's barely had a chance to live. Spare them both, God. You've already taken Charles, my dearest friend. Isn't that enough?*

Meghann knew her prayers were superstitious ramblings, childlike in their simple desire for some all powerful deity to fix her problems, but she couldn't help herself. What else could she do but pray when she was stuck in this car?

As promised, Jimmy pulled up to the house in minutes, looking up in surprise at the garish structure in front of him. He'd dreaded going back to the place where he'd been tortured, only his love for Ellie could have dragged him back to this horrible place. But the elegant home he'd remembered was long gone and the gaudy substitute in its place had no power to scare him, save his anxiety for Ellie.

"We'll have to split up," Maggie said and turned to Jimmy, clutching his hands. "I'll search for Simon and you go to Ellie. It's safer to travel the astral plane than go wandering around the house."

"But, Maggie, I've never..."

"You've been in the house," she interrupted. "Changed as it, you've still been on the land. You can travel the plane to get to Ellie."

"No," Jimmy said. "I meant, I've never travelled the astral plane." He cursed his stubborn refusal to learn vampiric ways when they could have helped him save Ellie.

"You can do it, Jimmy. It's not hard. Just concentrate on my voice and think of Ellie. Think of Ellie and..." Maggie's voice faltered and she seemed to choke on her words. "Think of how much you love her. Feel your way to her."

Jimmy shut his eyes, listening to the hypnotic lilt in Maggie's voice. He did think of Ellie, how beautiful she'd looked last night when she agreed to marry him. Jimmy kept his eyes shut and Ellie's face became a sharp contrast to the darkness all around him. He saw her chestnut hair spread against the light-blue pillow cover, her flushed cheeks and gleeful eyes as he put the diamond on her finger. *Ellie,* he thought. *Ellie...*

Then he felt something like the cutting wind that blew off the Atlantic Ocean in winter months and, remembering Maggie's edict, he kept his eyes firmly shut as he focused on finding Ellie.

The wind died and Jimmy opened his eyes a slit, bemused when he found himself in a dark room instead of standing by the brick wall outside with Maggie. So he'd finally traveled the astral plane. It was no big deal, Jimmy thought, over so quick you hardly knew what was happening. Aside from the cold wind, Jimmy had had no sense of going into another dimension, of his body breaking down into the incorporeal spirit that traveled the astral plane.

As Jimmy's eyes adjusted to the oppressive darkness, he began to make out details of the cramped room with steel walls that was no larger than a broom closet but so heavily shadowed he couldn't be certain of his hand in front of his face.

Jimmy inched forward and his foot brushed a soft lump that felt like human flesh. Jimmy bent down and pulled a Zippo lighter out of his jean pocket—this was the first time since he transformed that he encountered darkness so thick his vampire eyes couldn't pierce it entirely.

The blaze of light from the cigarette lighter revealed a short, pudgy mortal boy—couldn't be any older than fifteen judging by the peach fuzz on his face. Jimmy put two fingers on the boy's neck, surprised when he noted the kid was still alive but unconscious. Inspecting his body for injury, Jimmy felt a massive lump at the back of his skull. Someone, maybe Baldevar or Lee, hit this kid with force enough to incapacitate him but keep him alive.

But why not kill him? Jimmy frowned when he noticed a long wooden stake clutched in the boy's slack hand. None of this made any sense . . . keeping the kid alive or that he was here in the first place.

Maybe this Mikal wasn't such a threat after all. What kind of vampire was dumb enough to use mortals for defense? Sure, Maggie had trained Jimmy to slay vampires but that was only during the day, when they were insensate and vulnerable. It had been understood from the beginning that Jimmy wouldn't go near a vampire at night—he'd never have a chance. So why was Baldevar's kid keeping a mortal around, arming him with a wooden stake that would do as much good as a swizzle stick? An entire platoon armed with Uzis could come at a vampire and they'd all be dead within five minutes flat. Didn't Mikal know that?

Jimmy shrugged off his bafflement—what did it matter what Mikal knew or didn't know? Jimmy should be grateful the kid was an idiot; it would make saving Ellie and Lee that much easier.

Then Jimmy looked to the right of the mortal's head and decided Mikal wasn't an idiot at all, more like a rotten, cruel, sonofabitch that he'd kill at the first opportunity.

"Ellie!" he cried and crawled over to a corner of the room, yanking on the stark white foot he'd noticed out of the corner of his eye.

"Ellie, my God, who did this to you? I'll kill him with my bare fucking hands . . . oh, God, Ellie." Jimmy wasn't aware of the tears streaming down his face as he took Ellie's battered, naked body into his arms.

His hands shaking, Jimmy took her pulse and had a moment of serious terror when he felt nothing—but then there was a weak sort of blip... Ellie was hanging on by a thread. Helplessly, Jimmy took in the beautiful chestnut hair hacked off to her skull and irregular bald patches all around her head. Her hair wasn't the worst of it, though. Turning Ellie around, Jimmy discovered she'd been flogged. There wasn't an inch of flesh on her that wasn't bruised or cut, blood still trickling out of some of the worst wounds like the obscene graffiti on her stomach. Opening her mouth, Jimmy was appalled to discover her front teeth had been knocked out.

"Baby," Jimmy cried and took off his shirt, not wanting Ellie to be humiliated by her injured nudity any longer. His first thought was that he should get Ellie to a hospital but another glance at her body made him discard that idea. Jimmy wasn't a doctor but he knew Ellie had lost a great deal of blood and the weakening heartbeat told him she might not survive long enough for him to get her to a hospital and some of her wounds, especially the deep cuts on her face, looked like they'd create permanent scars. There was only one thing Jimmy could think of that would restore Ellie's strength and heal her completely— transformation.

But Jimmy didn't know shit about transformation... except that his own had led to a psychosis he'd never have recovered from if not for Maggie. What if Jimmy fed Ellie his blood and she went crazy? Worse, what if her wrecked body couldn't handle the shock of transformation and she died? But she was going to die anyway; he had to at least try and heal her. But maybe he should pick Ellie up and try to find Maggie... or Baldevar. Yes, Baldevar! Jimmy might despise him but he knew Simon Baldevar was an expert at transformation; he'd apply all his skill and guide Ellie through the process safely.

Jimmy gathered Ellie up, intent on carrying her out of the room and setting off in search of Lord Baldevar, when he noticed a thick, black patch on the floor next to her. At first, Jimmy thought it was Ellie's blood but then he sniffed harder and inhaled the thick copper potency only a vampire could produce.

Gently lowering Ellie back to the floor, Jimmy swirled a finger in the blood and brought it to his tongue, almost gagging when he tasted the same blood that had turned him into a vampire nearly twenty years ago.

This was Simon Baldevar's blood! So where the hell was he? Jimmy knew nothing short of death would have taken him away from his injured daughter. Reswabbing his finger, Jimmy drank more of the blood, trying to receive some psychic impression of what had happened in this room before he arrived.

As he drank, fuzzy, dreamlike images swirled through Jimmy's mind. He saw Baldevar clutching a sword and using the hilt to strike the mortal standing guard over Ellie—of course! Now Jimmy knew why the kid was still alive. Simon Baldevar had every intention of transforming his daughter; the first thing a new vampire needed was a huge quantity of fresh mortal blood. This lowlife kid helping Mikal was intended for Ellie's first feeding.

So what happened? Why hadn't Baldevar been able to transform Ellie? Jimmy drank more of Baldevar's blood but received nothing but a hazy feeling of great pain . . . that must be the pain that made Maggie scream out in the car and clutch her heart.

Now Jimmy understood everything. Baldevar had gotten into this room and plowed through the mortal watching over Ellie. But then Mikal got the better of his father somehow, injuring him before he could transform Ellie. Jimmy had no idea if Lord Baldevar was dead or not... he only knew that he was Ellie's last chance for transformation.

Jimmy's mind raced, frantically trying to recall everything Maggie or Charles ever told him about transformation, remembering the miserable circumstances of his own transformation. First, a mortal had to be drained of their own blood to the point of death or they'd reject the vampiric transfusion. A glance at Ellie's white, bloodless face and the vicious puncture wounds dotting her neck, breasts, and thighs told Jimmy that phase had already been accomplished.

Jimmy knew transformation had a better chance for success if the candidate was in peak physical condition. Poor Ellie was about to die but Jimmy hadn't been in much better condition when Baldevar transformed him so there was proof an injured person could survive the process.

The last step was to make the drained mortal drink the blood of a vampire host. Taking a deep breath, Jimmy tried to will his blood teeth out and cursed when nothing happened. Jimmy's fangs had only ever descended when he was in the grip of blood lust and now, with nothing to entice him, the blood teeth remained firmly lodged in his gums.

Frustrated by this unexpected obstacle, Jimmy pulled a switchblade from his leather hip holster and used it to cut his wrist open. An angry fountain of dark, thick blood spouted out and Jimmy forced Ellie's jaws apart, putting her open mouth to his bleeding wrist. He propped her unconscious body up into a sitting position so she wouldn't choke on the blood pouring down her threat.

Ellie's body spasmed violently, as though he'd just applied jumper cables to her heart. Her eyes flew open, only the whites showing as they rolled into the back of her head, and the awful convulsing grew so bad Jimmy could barely keep her still.

"Ellie!" he shouted, struggling to hold her down with one hand while the other hand remained at her mouth. He wasn't sure how much blood she needed to drink to transform, so he decided to let her feed until the wound closed up on its own.

Ellie gave no indication she was aware of him, merely shaking like she was in the grip of a grand mal seizure while deep, animal-like grunts issued from her throat.

"Ellie!"Jimmy shouted again and then felt something take him over, something he'd never be able to describe to anyone else or understand fully as long as he lived.

Whenever he fed, Jimmy felt some connection with his prey, their thoughts and feelings. Maggie and Charles had taught him to focus on those emotions, saying he'd have a much greater resistance to the blood lust if he remained aware of his prey as a person with a life he had no business ending.

So Jimmy was used to experiencing a psychic link when he fed but it was nothing compared with what he felt when he allowed someone to drink his blood. Now Jimmy understood the dark intimacy behind bloodletting, why Maggie and Simon Baldevar were so eager to drink from each other while they made love.

Sex was wonderful but it didn't plunge Jimmy into Ellie's soul, make him feel almost welded to her as she devoured his blood. It seemed there'd never been anything in the world but Ellie, her mind and soul opening up to Jimmy just as his opened to her. No thought was secret between the two of them. Jimmy's shared blood mingling with Ellie's, irrevocably changing her from mortal to vampire, bonded them together forever, made them think as one, feel as one.

Jimmy felt like he was inside Ellie, almost felt like he was Ellie just as in some weird way she was him. He felt her sickness as he fed her his strength, felt her fear and forced her to drink of his confidence, felt her great pain and wrenched it away from her, taking it into his own strong, healthy body where it was broken down and banished forever.

There weren't exactly words between him and Ellie—what they shared now went far beyond that. But as Ellie continued to drink, Jimmy felt himself plunged into a gray kind of nothingness, a world of gauze and confusion . . . the world Maggie had rescued him from when she restored his mind.

No, Ellie! Jimmy thought he shouted, desperately trying to hold onto her. *You can't stay here. It's dangerous! Come back to me, come back.*

I'm scared, Ellie answered back in the eerie, soundless way that was the way of this world. *I don't want to hurt anymore; it hurts so much... let me go, let me go!*

No! Swallowing his fear, Jimmy plunged into the chaos that had claimed him after he drank Simon Baldevar's blood. Better than anyone else, Jimmy understood this place of living death where shadows trapped you as tightly as straitjackets, using fear as their restraints. Jimmy knew what it was to be held prisoner by your fear, that the seductive appeal of this half-there world was the promise that you'd never have to be afraid again.

But you'll never feel again either, Ellie, if you stay here. You'll never love, you'll never be. Your life will be over; you'll just be an empty shell marking time until you die. Jimmy didn't actually say those words but they were the sentiment behind the emotion he tried to convey to his poor, hurting lover. *Ellie, please come away from here. Come back to me. I'll love you and heal you and so will your mother. Ellie, please, you have to come back to us. You'll be a vampire now—no one will ever hurt you again like Mikal did.*

Jimmy, I want to come back, I do! But I can't find my way— I'm lost.

Come to me, Ellie, Jimmy said and strained with all his might to clutch the shivering little bit of Ellie's essence. *I love you, baby. Come to me, give me your hand, I'll get you out of here. I promise.*

Suddenly Jimmy felt something rush at him, almost strangle him as it wrapped around his soul and clung to him. For a moment, Jimmy thought it would pull him down and he and Ellie would both drown in this horrible place but Jimmy forced himself to concentrate on the real world, cutting through the layers of fright and panic like a swimmer attempting to break through the water and reach the blessed surface.

"Jimmy?"

Blearily, Jimmy managed to get one eye open, feeling as lethargic and weak as a mortal with a serious flu. "Ellie? Ellie!"

Shock propelled Jimmy out of his lassitude, making him sit up with his eyes bulging out as he took in the transformed Ellie. Already she'd healed so much that her face was clear of wounds, save for a few pink scratches that looked like the remnants of faded scars. Her chestnut hair completely covered her scalp again and she had a third set of front teeth to replace the ones Mikal had punched out... along with two new, sharp pointy ones that cut into the tender flesh of her lower lip.

"Jimmy, what's wrong with me?" she cried and he noticed the goose bumps covering her skin, the way she wrapped her arms around herself while she shivered uncontrollably.

Jimmy felt her sickness, her need, and a surprising pang of regret when he realized he'd have to initiate Ellie into her new life.

"Its blood lust," he said as gently as he could and wrapped his arms around her, guiding Ellie to the unconscious mortal. "Honey, drink from him..."

Ellie needed no further encouragement. Bemused, Jimmy fell back when Ellie threw off his grip and fell on the unconscious boy, ripping into his flesh with all the frenzy of a starved vampire. Greedily, Ellie tore into his neck and drank the blood in great, thirsty gulps.

Mentally snooping for the first time in his life, Jimmy read Ellie's thoughts, knowing she felt nothing but relief as the tremors eased, the icy chills fled her body, and warm, invincible strength began to flow through her veins. Ellie was too consumed with need to feel any guilt or distaste for what she did. He knew that feeling well. But he didn't condemn Ellie. There was time enough to teach her to resist the blood lust as he'd been taught to. For now, Ellie should drink as much as she needed to regain her strength. Besides, this mortal was no more deserving of life than her scumbag brother.

Finally, Ellie raised her lips and Jimmy felt a brief, disturbing thrill at her full lips doused in inviting, warm blood. "You, too, Jimmy."

"Huh?" he said, unable to get over how sexy Ellie looked, with newly grown hair falling past her shoulders and creamy white skin that showed no hint of the abuse she'd suffered through.

"You, too," Ellie said impatiently and gestured to the near dead boy at her side. "I feel you're weak. You have to feed, too."

Ellie was right, Jimmy felt limp and sluggish. Stretching out, he sank his teeth into the puncture holes Ellie had already made and drank what little blood she'd left for him. Scant though it was, Jimmy drank enough to restore his strength so he could leap up and catch Ellie in a bear hug.

"Thank God you're all right!" Jimmy started to bend his head and kiss her but Ellie pushed him away, looking frightened and confused.

"What happened, Jimmy? Where am I? Why did you transform me?"

"You don't remember anything?" Jimmy said, thinking what a blessing her amnesia was. Ellie had been put through hell. . . there was no need for her to remember the ugliness she'd suffered through.

Ellie frowned, deep in thought. "The last thing I remember is going to sleep last night. You proposed to me and we fell asleep. What happened? Is it nighttime already? Are Mom and Daddy and Lee back?"

"Oh, honey." Jimmy sighed, wishing like hell he didn't have to be the one to tell her about Mikal. How did you tell a sweet, innocent girl she'd just been vilely used by her own twin brother?

Jimmy took her hands, kissing each in turn before he met Ellie's worried eyes. "Baby, listen carefully. Nothing I'm about to tell you was your fault. You did nothing to deserve what happened to you. Understood?"

"What happened to me?" Ellie demanded, now looking apprehensive, as well as worried.

Grimly, Jimmy explained the true identity of the boy she thought of as Mickey. At first, Ellie refused to even listen until Jimmy explained it had been Maggie who had identified Mikal when she saw him on the video clip he sent. Jimmy underplayed the graphic contents of the video, merely saying Mikal kidnapped Ellie and then sent the video as a cyber ransom note. "Do you remember him coming to the house? Obviously, you'd have welcomed him inside as your friend . . . that's why he was able to abduct you."

Ellie shook her head, the pretty flush of blood leaving her cheeks as deep mortification and repulsion took its place, making her look gray and sick. "I told you, I don't remember anything that happened since last night. You're telling me my first boyfriend turned out to be my twin brother, that I've been having sex with . . . oh, God!"

"Ellie." Jimmy kissed her deeply, not so much out of passion as to show Ellie he still loved her, that the awful ruse Mikal had played on her didn't disgust Jimmy or make him want to break off with her. With his kiss, Jimmy tried to convey understanding but not pity—Ellie would hate thinking she was someone to be sorry for now. "Sweetheart, it wasn't your fault. You didn't know."

"I should have known," Ellie cried, refusing to accept Jimmy's comforting words. "I'm psychic; you know that. I should have felt a connection to Mikal . . . my God, he's my own twin! I shared a womb with him."

"Mikal's stronger than you," Jimmy said bluntly.

"Hell, he was able to fool your mother and Charles... vampires couldn't even see through him! Don't blame yourself for any of this. Mikal is the one that used you."

"So what happened today?" Ellie asked. "What did he do to me that was so bad you had to transform me? And where's Mom? Or Daddy? Or Lee?"

Again, Jimmy didn't tell Ellie the whole, unsavory truth. He merely said Mikal and the band of mortals he had with him hurt Ellie to provoke Lord Baldevar into rushing onto the estate. "He knew your dad would come running if he thought you were in danger. Baldevar came here the minute he knew where you were and tried to keep your mom at home by hypnotizing her. But Maggie woke up and then we came here to help rescue you."

"What happened to Daddy?" Ellie said, her voice scaling up with alarm. "Did Mikal hurt him? What about Mom and Lee?"

"I don't know," Jimmy admitted. "Your mom . . . when we got closer to the house, she said she had a feeling your dad was hurt. I don't know about Lee. For some reason your father took Lee with him. When Maggie and I got here, we split up. She went after your dad and Mikal, and I came to you."

"You mean Mom and Daddy and Lee are still fighting him . . . alone?" Aghast, Ellie stood up, ready to charge through a black opening but for Jimmy's restraining arm. "Jimmy, don't you dare try and stop me! I won't let Mikal hurt my mom! I'm a vampire now; I've got to help Mom! I feel her somewhere in this house... she needs me, Jimmy. Come on, come on!"

"Hold it," Jimmy said, ignoring the nails clawing into his skin as Ellie struggled toward the door. "We'll go but we're going to do this right. Don't you see Mikal wants everyone to blindly charge after him? We have to set up some ground rules."

Jimmy grabbed the wooden stake on the floor and thrust it into Ellie's hands while he removed a .357 Magnum from an arm holster. The Magnum wouldn't kill Mikal but it would throw him on his ass. Then Maggie, Simon, or Lee could cut off his head.

"It's not much but it'll do," Jimmy said, gesturing to Ellie's stake. "If you get a chance, drive it into his heart. Now, stay behind me at all times. Understand?"

Ellie nodded and they went off together to search for Maggie, Lord Baldevar, and Lee in the ominously silent house.

Chapter Fifteen

Meghann watched Jimmy disappear, and then slumped against one of the iron spikes, exhausted. It was a good thing Jimmy couldn't see her now; he'd never have agreed to let her transport him along the astral plane if he knew she'd pushed herself to the point of depletion to propel him to Ellie's side. Now Meghann's own ability to fly the plane was severely impaired so she had to face down Mikal without the safety hatch of being able to fly away from danger.

Well, so be it... nothing was keeping her from Simon. Meghann reached into her backpack and withdrew a naginata, the infamous sword of the medieval Japanese warrior monks. Alcuin had given her the weapon nearly fifty years ago, because he believed the naginata with its slim wooden tang and short but lethal, edge-tempered blade was the perfect weapon for a petite woman with small hands. Hopefully, her skill with the weapon would give her a swift victory over Mikal.

Simon, where are you? Help me, Meghann pleaded as she cut through the nightmare garden of false ivy and weeping willows to reach the house. *Simon, if you're alive, please reach out. It's Meghann. Answer me, answer me! Tell me where to find you.*

Meghann couldn't be sure but she thought she felt something urging her toward the front door, assuring her no obstacle would bar her way. Meghann glared at the thick black doors studded with silver bolts and they swung open, revealing a long, dark corridor with doors leading to various wings. There was also a spiral staircase balanced so precariously it looked like it would fall any minute. There was something deeply familiar about that staircase. Meghann's eyes narrowed in concentration when she tried to remember where she'd seen it before.

Of course—Ellie created that staircase! Meghann's eyes widened, remembering the blueprints her daughter had shown her, full of shy pride when she told her mother a boy she'd met at school was so impressed with her talent he asked her to design a rambling, fun-house interior for a club he wanted to establish. Meghann cringed to think how badly the shocks of the past two nights had numbed her mind that she didn't immediately connect Immortal Light with the designs "Mickey" solicited from Ellie.

Meghann looked at the dark mansion with new, informed eyes. If Mikal followed Ellie's sketches, then the double doors in front of her led to the dance floor. From that main room, there were several offshoots. One could play out elaborate vampire fantasies in the gaming rooms that came complete with computers and software while other rooms were quiet parlors for guests that found the frenetic noise of the bar too much. If Meghann remembered correctly, there were even two mini-theatres where one could watch horror films and a small dining room in case any of the Goth guests should get hungry.

Meghann was tempted to head for the dance floor but there were the other wings to be considered, as well as that careening staircase that replaced the elegant mahogany one she remembered. Upstairs there were hotel rooms for guests spending the night, several large halls for people who wished to use the club for conventions, and finally a business annex for planning day-to-day operations. So where was Simon in this confusing maze?

Which door, Meghann asked and this time the unseen presence was stronger. It felt like someone took her hand and guided her to the imposing set of doors with gargoyle handles glaring at her in stony silence.

Be prepared, a voice said as Meghann used telekinesis to open the doors and this time there was no mistaking the voice. It was definitely Simon!

Prepared for what? Meghann asked, so overjoyed at this indication Simon was still alive she almost missed narrow trail of blood artfully camouflaged amidst the thorn and crucifix floor.

Meghann leaned down, one hand clutching her sword while she used the other to taste the blood on the floor, praying it didn't belong to Simon.

Lee, Meghann realized with a sinking feeling in the pit of her stomach when she tasted blood she'd drunk last night. But Lee's taste, though immediately recognizable, was different now, containing the heady iron aroma only vampires produced. So Simon had completed Lee's transformation! But why? It didn't make any sense for Simon to charge after Mikal with no one to aid him but a newborn vampire.

Meghann frowned at the blood trail, knowing she was missing some piece of this puzzle but having no time to ponder the mystery. She had to find out what the blood trail led to, where Mikal had dragged her bleeding friend and if he was still alive.

The ragged red line ended abruptly by a raised dais concealed by thick black curtains. As Meghann walked toward the dais, the curtains parted to reveal a sight that made her scream in paralyzed horror, not caring who she alerted to her presence.

The dais led to a small stage with the inscription *Unity in Darkness* written over it in black, Gothic script. About an inch beneath the sign, Lee Winslow's body hung ten feet off the floor, thick cables attached to his arms and legs to keep him suspended in midair, welcome, mother was written in blood on his bare torso, and his head was missing.

"Lee," Meghann cried, ready to rush forward and drag her friend down to the floor. But as she ran to him, she felt an invisible, iron-strong hand grab her shoulder to keep her off the stage.

Meghann, no!

She couldn't be sure who warned her away, whether it was Simon or whatever remained of Lee, but she knew to disregard it would be the signature on her own death warrant. If she dropped her sword and kept her back turned to the rest of the room while she worked on freeing Lee, she'd be a ludicrously easy target for Mikal. But that didn't mean she'd allow the desecration Mikal had visited on Lee's helpless body to continue.

Meghann glared at the cables wrapped around his arms and legs. Within seconds, the thick black cords snapped and Lee

Winslow's body fell to the stage floor. Now Meghann leapt onto the stage and turned her attention to the black curtains. When they fell of their rungs, she grabbed one to decently wrap Lee's remains.

"Lee," Meghann cried again as she made the makeshift shroud, weeping soundlessly. This was too much. She'd lost Charles and Lee in the space of two nights. How could they both be dead, two of the finest men she'd ever known? Meghann stared at the black bundle, not seeing the shocking sight Mikal had reduced her friend to but the kind, competent doctor who'd guided her through her pregnancy, applying all his skill to keep her and Ellie alive when she went into premature labor. She saw Lee cuddling Ellie, walking the floor endlessly while the baby howled in teething misery, never showing the slightest strain or irritation at the screaming infant. And she saw him as he must have been tonight, allowing Simon to transform him and trying desperately to save Ellie, never caring that he was risking his life.

Meghann wiped her eyes and caressed Lee's shroud in a gesture of farewell. She couldn't allow herself to think of her crushing grief for Charles and Lee now, not while Simon needed her.

Meghann observed the rest of the stage, at first thinking nothing of the limp rag doll lying in an antique chair lined in horsehair. At first, she thought it some kind of macabre decoration but on closer inspection she realized it was a corpse— a boneless, shriveled, corpse with a knife planted in what was once a chest.

Nauseated and horrified by this new display of her son's phenomenal power (even if Simon wanted to, he couldn't have been responsible for the thing's condition), at first Meghann didn't realize she knew the dead woman. Then her eyes focused on the luxurious blond hair unaffected by the body's destruction and remembered where she'd seen hair like that. It was back in the fifties, at that horrible party Simon threw to introduce her to the vampiric society he'd formed over the centuries.

Meghann glared at the corpse, all traces of pity for the dead woman vanished. Meghann didn't know her name, didn't care to know it. She only knew that at that long forgotten vampire ball,

Meghann had balked when Simon began to feed from two helpless young girls to the delight of the slinky blonde who joined him after Meghann refused.

Meghann ground her teeth, remembering the other vampire's ecstasy as she stretched out beside Simon, trying to wrest him from Meghann by proving she was more debauched than Simon's chosen consort.

Meghann had turned on her heel and left the party in a huff, treating Simon to a display of icy nonchalance for several evenings before he finally laughed and threw her down on the nearest bed, telling her she couldn't blame him for being born four hundred years before her but Meghann had no reason to be jealous. Then, all night, he proceeded to prove Meghann was the only woman he wanted.

After that night, Meghann forgot about the vampire tramp but a grasp of her silver hair showed Meghann the creature hadn't forgotten about Simon at all. Meghann didn't feel herself blanch or her nostrils quiver with violent outrage when she saw the hand this awful woman had in harming Ellie. The psychic impressions Meghann received didn't tell her why Mikal inflicted such agony on his sole vampiric collaborator, but psychopaths were unpredictable. Maybe Mikal killed the woman out of some frustration he felt toward Simon or maybe he was simply bored and craved the thrill he got from causing pain.

Hidden speakers suddenly came to life all around her; the bass so strong the darkwave music with its frenetic, techno beat was distorted. Meghann jumped, her eyes wary and darting from side to side as she held her sword out in front of her the way Alcuin taught her to.

Meghann clenched her hands tightly around the balsa staff to keep them from shaking. She knew the howling music was invitation—Mikal was ready to properly introduce himself to his mother.

Meghann felt warmth on her back and knew she'd face blinding light the moment she turned around. Mikal meant to exploit her every vulnerability, starting with her a vampire's sensitivity to bright light.

Meghann turned around slowly, not intending to allow her son to blind her. She kept the naginata ready for attack and stared into the light, seeing beneath and beyond it as Alcuin had taught her to do.

Once her eyes adjusted, she could see that the tombstone bar was now illuminated by a clever lighting system hidden in the dome ceiling carved into the form of grayish-black storm clouds.

Meghann. . .

Her heart contracted at the telepathic cry and the dark, angry music swelled louder while a lighting effect crackled from the ceiling, the bluish-white light illuminating Simon Baldevar lying within the now open doorway, his arms and legs in cruciform position with a sword buried in his heart.

"Simon!" Meghann shrieked and her own sword clattered to the floor. She ran to him, moaning like a hurt animal when she saw how closely he resembled the hideous prophecy Alcuin had shown her the night before.

Meghann knelt beside him, her heart in her throat when she saw his chalk white skin already displaying the fatal blue tinge of cyanosis while his shallow gasps for breath revealed a death rattle. Simon was as close to death as a vampire could come. Unless the stake was removed and he received massive quantities of fresh blood, he would die before sunrise.

"Simon," Meghann sobbed, taking one of his icy hands in hers. "Simon, no!" For a moment, the hideous vision before her blurred, coalescing into the other night Meghann had seen her master impaled... the night she'd done this to him. Meghann went through a bewildering juxtaposition, remembering that one time she'd been glad to see Simon like this, spat on him, as he lay weak and helpless before her and living through the hellish present of seeing him near death again.

"I didn't mean it," she cried, covering the bloodless lips and white face in kisses. "Simon, I didn't mean it. I never told you that before. I never told you how sorry I've been for that night. I didn't want you to die, I didn't. I just wanted to get away from you... I was so young, so confused. I thought you were smothering me, I thought I hated you. But Simon, even then, those forty years I wasted, I missed you. I never let any other man take your place in my heart. I... I never told this to anyone else, but I dreamed of you during those forty years. I had dreams of you holding me, loving me, and I'd wake up with tears running down my face because I missed you and I wanted you back. Simon, I'm sorry... I've been sorry for so long but I never told you and now it's too late."

Distract him. Simon's golden eyes, glazed with pain but radiating steely resolve, focused on Meghann, urging her to overcome her panic and concentrate on his words.

Listen to me, Meghann, Simon continued and Meghann saw what the effort of speaking cost him—he started to shake and the cold skin beneath her hands grew even clammier. *Keep away from Mikal when he shows his face again. Just distract him and I will dispose of him.*

"You can't fight him now!" Meghann protested aloud but Simon's eyes had closed again. He wasn't dead, but he was gravely ill and would remain that way until Meghann took the sword out of his chest. But she couldn't do that unless she had fresh blood to offer. If Meghann simply yanked the sword out, Simon would die from blood loss. She had to get him out of here, find a mortal, and then remove the stake so he could drink as much blood as he needed to recover. She still didn't know how Simon had managed to remove the stake she had impaled him with and still had the strength to search out prey—it was nothing short of a miracle.

"But you're not alone now," Meghann whispered, kissing him before she grabbed his legs, prepared to drag him out of the room. She'd have to call out to Jimmy now so he could watch her back while she got Simon out of the house. "I'll help you, I'll get you out of here."

Meghann never knew what made her drop Simon and catapult over his inert form, spinning around in time to see Mikal lunge at her with a broadsword drenched in blood.

Meghann glared at her naginata and it flew into her hand at the same moment Mikal tried to knock it away. Meghann delivered a savage kick to his wrist and he leaped back in surprise, though he recovered quickly and began to advance on his small mother.

Mikal parried a thrust at Meghann's heart and she deflected it though she felt the impact of Mikal's sword clashing against hers all the way from her wrist to the ball of her shoulder. Her entire arm tingled unpleasantly and Meghann knew she was no match for her son's extraordinary physical strength. Her only hope lay in dodging his blows, dancing around him until he finally grew lax and she got a chance to attack.

"No!" This time Mikal went for her head and Meghann did a back flip, landing on top of the bar. Her new position at least gave her the advantage of being at eye level with him.

Mikal made a tentative swipe at her and Meghann answered by flipping a dagger she'd hidden in the small of her back at his heart. Mikal sidestepped the weapon and glanced speculatively at the stone floor beneath Meghann's feet. It began to tremble and Meghann knew Mikal meant to break the bar in half so she'd fall and lose her vantage point. Rather than deflect the attack, Meghann turned her attention to the liquor supply behind her and watched Mikal fall to his knees, squealing like a scalded cat when the bottles began hurtling themselves at him like missiles.

Despite the myriad cuts on her son's exposed skin, Meghann doubted the assault caused him much pain. It had simply been enough of a deterrent to make him think twice before he launched another telekinetic attack against his mother.

When the last bottle shattered against his skull, Mikal stood up, looking like a sulky teenager as he glared at Meghann. She stared back, impatient to end this battle so she could save Simon, but at the same time almost mesmerized by this child of hers she'd never had a chance to know and now had no desire to know.

No wonder he was able to fool Charles and me, Meghann thought as she inspected her son—he doesn't look like Simon or me at all. The jet black hair hadn't come from either of his light-haired parents and those nickel-plated eyes with their elongated pupils knew nothing of Meghann's green hue or Simon's amber color.

Try though she might, Meghann could find no piece of herself or Simon in this awkward-looking young man with his gaunt frame and beaky features that she couldn't recall in any member of her mortal family. The only area where Meghann saw a shadow of resemblance was in the great height Mikal had inherited from Simon and a certain wideness through his shoulders.

The longer Meghann stared, the harder it was to believe the stranger glowering at her was her own child. Meghann didn't have to worry about her feelings getting in the way during this confrontation. The silver eyes filled with a venomous mixture of seething, inexplicable fury, cold contempt and a nasty insolence killed any maternal feelings she might have had for Mikal.

Meghann forced herself not to look over his head and check on Simon. Mikal already knew how much his father meant to her; she was not going to give him a further edge by showing how afraid she was, how she knew that each passing minute brought Simon closer to death. But she had to destroy Mikal quickly... sunrise was only an hour and a half away.

Mikal frowned and cocked his head, standing well out of striking range, moving closer to Simon than Meghann would have liked. "How did you anticipate my moves?"

"You can't hide your thoughts from me . . . I'm your mother," Meghann said, hoping her sarcasm hid the alacrity she felt at discovering a chink in Mikal's armor. Like Ellie, Mikal wasn't used to anyone being able to read his thoughts. He'd never fought an opponent who could see into him; Meghann's psychic ability put her son at a definite disadvantage. "Mothers always know what their children are thinking."

"Do they indeed?" Mikal said with Simon's thin, mocking smirk. "Then look into my mind and tell me what you need to do to get your daughter out of here."

"Don't you mean what you force me to do?" Meghann countered. "You pose a great threat to your father and sister, as well as to me. Your need to destroy us all means I must kill you to guarantee our safety."

"Maggie," Mikal laughed with Simon's sardonic merriness. "Don't you look cute, trying so hard to be tough? You can't kill me anymore than you could kill him." Mikal used his sword to point at his unconscious father, careful to not take his eyes off Meghann. "I know all about your little spat now, how you almost destroyed him. But I am a far better marksman than you. Very sloppy aim, you missed his heart by several inches. You did have time to note my sword found the center of his heart?"

Meghann went rigid, blinking rapidly to keep the brutal shock of Mikal's words off her face. She hadn't been able to inspect Simon's wound but if Mikal were telling the truth, even fresh mortal blood wouldn't be enough to save Simon. A blow to the center of a vampire's heart was fatal, no amount of blood would heal the gaping wound. Ironically, the only thing keeping Simon alive was the sword in his chest. He'd die when it was removed.

"So you've lost your lover," Mikal taunted and Meghann thought he sounded more like a petulant grade-school bully than the mastermind that caused all this destruction. "What are you willing to do to save your daughter?"

Meghann ignored the question; she wasn't going to start a dialogue that gave Mikal any modicum of control over the situation. How could she kill him and get Ellie, as well as Simon, to safety? Meghann decided she'd take Simon out of here with the weapon lodged in his chest and keep him alive on blood transfusions until she could think of a way to heal him. If only Alcuin were here...

That was it! Alcuin! Meghann remembered her priestly mentor appearing to her after his death but before Meghann and Simon reconciled. He'd told Meghann she could kill Simon by invoking him, allowing his soul to possess her and infuse her body with his great strength so he could kill Lord Baldevar. Surely if Meghann called Alcuin now, he could destroy Mikal.

"No, no, Maggie," Mikal sighed in mock dismay. "Father already tried that. . . what do you think he was doing with the good doctor?"

"Alcuin inhabited Lee's body?" It wasn't really a question for Meghann realized immediately the perfect sense of Mikal's words. She felt a surge of admiration for Simon, calling forth his old enemy to use the body of a newly transformed vampire. And Lee... Meghann's throat closed with tears when she thought of that brave, final sacrifice Lee made for Ellie. Then her eyes clouded over with puzzlement. If Simon had invaded Mikal's stronghold with Alcuin at his side, what had gone wrong? Why was Lee dead and Simon grievously hurt while this monster boy was alive and unharmed? Why didn't she feel Alcuin's spirit nearby?

"Steel," Mikal said in response to the confusion on Meghann's face. "My lovely house is reinforced with steel beams... no spirits, be they angel or daemon, can enter my home."

"How is this your home?" Meghann demanded harshly and saw Mikal's inhuman eyes contract cautiously, plainly he hadn't expected her to take the offensive. "Simon paid for it and Ellie designed it. You contributed nothing.

"Isn't that what all this is about?" Meghann questioned ruthlessly, knowing she was on the right track when she saw Mikal's colorless lips tighten. "You know you aren't a match for your father in brains or looks. You're jealous of him, just like you're jealous of your own sister for being pretty, for being smart, for not having to terrorize people to get attention. You know you're nothing, that no one would ever notice you unless you hurt them. You can't build a fortune the way Simon did so you have to steal his money, and you haven't your sister's talent or imagination so this nightclub wouldn't exist if it wasn't for her. You don't hate your father, Mikal, you hate yourself. You hate yourself for the ugliness you see in the mirror and the emptiness you can't escape in your soul."

With a low, feral snarl, Mikal hurled himself at her and Meghann easily sidestepped him. He fell behind the bar and she leapt on top of him, sitting on his chest while she aimed the curved edge of the naginata at his vulnerable neck.

Mikal got his knees up and hurled Meghann off him before she could decapitate him. The force behind his blow was so strong Meghann crashed through the stone bar headfirst.

For a moment, her vision blurred and her head throbbed with the vicious pain of a concussion. Before Meghann could regain her equilibrium, Mikal fell on her, attaching his blood teeth to his mother's neck.

"I never got to breast feed," he snarled when Meghann lay weak and drained beneath him. Feebly, she tried to get her hand up and he broke it before tearing off her shirt and attacking a vein in her breast while his hands caressed the full globes of her breasts with obscene intimacy.

"Stop it!" she screamed, finding new energy to fight when she felt her son grow hard as he pressed himself against her. Meghann yanked on his hair with her good hand, the broken one wouldn't heal until she fed.

Mikal laughed at her attempts to defend herself and dragged her over to his semiconscious father, kicking him to make him more alert. "You cannot miss this, dear Father. I want you to hear her cry out, you must watch me take her... ow!"

Meghann managed to sit up and saw a thin line of scratches mar Mikal's face while Simon's skin turned an even more alarming shade of blue as his body began to convulse.

"Simon," she whispered and dragged herself closer to him. There was blood in her backpack; she had to get it in him before this new effort to save her cost him his life.

Mikal kicked her in the throat, catching the bloody puncture wounds, and Meghann fell back, blinking back tears from the pain while her son started tearing her clothes off, frenzied with the need to rape his mother while his father watched helplessly.

A deafening explosion rang in Meghann's ears and she felt something whiz by. Mikal, nearly inside her but not yet able to accomplish his vile intent, growled and swung her around so her body protected him from the gun Jimmy Delacroix had just fired.

"Drop her," Jimmy ordered at the same moment Ellie screeched, "Don't you hurt my mom!"

Ellie would have charged forward with her wooden stake, but Jimmy grabbed her hand—Not yet, Ellie. As long as Mikal had Maggie hostage with a sword at her throat, Jimmy wasn't going to make any sudden moves. The minute he or Ellie attacked, Mikal was going to kill Maggie.

He's just a kid was Jimmy's first thought as he glared at the weird, wild eyes and scrawny bare chest of Mikal. With all he'd done, it was easy to forget Mikal was Ellie's twin, the same age she was. But now, with his lank black hair dripping sweat and calculating but confused expression, Jimmy thought the monster that caused all this trouble looked like any rebellious teenager— albeit one with inhuman pupils and eyes the color of lead bullets.

"Jimmy," Maggie cried, squirming furiously to get away from her son. "Don't worry about me! Just take Ellie and get out of here!"

"No!" Ellie screamed before he could say anything. "I won't let him hurt you or Daddy!"

"This is Jimmy?" Mikal questioned and Jimmy thought the kid sounded just like his father—full of that same cold-blooded viciousness and mocking arrogance. "What a pleasure to make your acquaintance. You and I have a great deal in common. We're the only men in the world who've bedded Ellie and Maggie. But I think you're being selfish, Jimmy Delacroix. Why don't you take the one you've transformed and leave this one to me?"

Jimmy shuddered at the casual, lighthearted way Mikal acknowledged his incest. If only Maggie could get away from him, Jimmy would have a clear shot at his head. The Magnum would disable him long enough for Maggie to grab that sword by her side and take the kid's head off.

Daddy, Ellie whimpered and Jimmy was surprised when he didn't feel any happiness to see Simon Baldevar sprawled on the floor with a sword through his heart. If the kid could take Lord Baldevar out, how was Jimmy supposed to kill him?

First, we concentrate on getting Maggie away from him, Jimmy thought and Ellie nodded by his side, green eyes wide and full of terror as she stared at her struggling mother.

But, Jimmy, if I went over to Daddy and pulled the sword out…

No! That directive came from Maggie, still struggling wildly but focusing her gaze on Ellie. You'll kill him if you take the stake out… don't touch him! Ellie, please get out of here!

"I won't leave you!" Ellie screamed, her voice cracking with fear before she glared at Mikal. "Why are you doing this? Can't you leave us alone? Haven't you done enough?"

"I have not even started, dear Sister." Mikal tried for his father's sardonic edge and failed miserably. There was something too forced in his smile as he glared at Ellie, seeming to take her transformed condition as a personal affront.

"Look at her," Jimmy said coldly, thinking he'd found a way to put the sonofabitch off balance. "You failed, kid. Ellie's alive and well. . . there isn't one fucking mark left of what you did to her and what's more, she doesn't even remember what you did today."

Mikal's eyes bulged and knotted red and blue veins popped through his white face, turning it into a grotesque mask of thwarted spite and malice. If Jimmy had been Catholic, he would have crossed himself at the insane fury shining in Mikal's eyes as he glared at Lord Baldevar.

Goddamn you, Father!

Jimmy had no idea why Mikal focused his anger on Simon when he'd been the one to transform Ellie but Maggie had already told him the kid was out of his mind. Now Jimmy had to keep working on Mikal, get him so riled up he wouldn't fight with a clear head when Jimmy attacked him to get Maggie out of his grip.

"You're finished," Jimmy growled, seeing Maggie nod imperceptibly, approving of his strategy. "Maybe you can kill Maggie, but you can't deal with me and Ellie at the same time . . . one of us will get you. Why don't you release your mother and let us walk out of here? We won't hunt you down. You leave us alone, we leave you alone. What do you say?"

"I say there's fifty-seven minutes to sunrise, Jimmy Delacroix. You and my sister are going to have to hide from the sun. So you made a vampire out of her . . . too bad you two aren't going to have any anniversaries to celebrate. I'll find your resting place and dispose of you today. If you want, though, I'll handicap you to make the game more interesting. Take a running start. Flee my home now and let's see how far I have to hunt you down through the world before I slaughter you and my dear sister."

Jimmy didn't bother replying; he decided to take his chances and aim the Magnum at Mikal's head. Quick as a cat, Mikal lifted Maggie up so she covered him and the bullet wound up shattering her shoulder.

Maggie screamed in agony and Ellie hurled herself at Mikal before Jimmy could stop her. She ran forward and attempted to ram the stake through his unprotected crotch but Mikal tossed

Maggie to the side and grabbed Ellie's stake, using it to propel her across the room.

Ellie hadn't even landed in a heap by the smoked French doors before Mikal gathered Maggie up again, using her as a shield while he advanced on Jimmy with a sword in his free hand.

Jimmy was about to fire again when he heard a queer popping sound, the only noise in the still room. Mikal heard it, too, and whirled around in time to face his father, wobbling on his feet but advancing on his son with the sword he'd just forced out of his own chest.

Jimmy could see enough of Mikal's profile to identify the complete shock on his features, the wide open, startled silver eyes and gaping mouth that croaked out, "Father..."

That was all he said before Simon raised the sword in a clumsy but deadly arc, bringing it halfway through Mikal's neck before he fell to the floor; heavy, black blood poured out of his mouth while his body shuddered so violently he was almost lifted off the floor.

"No!" Maggie screamed and raced over to Simon. "No, no!"

"Maggie," Jimmy said gently while Ellie sobbed miserably at his side. "It's over."

"No!" Maggie yelled, glaring up at him and Jimmy didn't see anything resembling sanity in the metallic green eyes locked on his.

"I can save him," she said, her hectic gaze jumping from Simon to Mikal. Since Lord Baldevar hadn't fully decapitated him, the boy was still alive but barely. Jimmy hunched next to his body and saw the sword had severed his spinal cord; Mikal was paralyzed from the neck down. His eyes met Jimmy's and there didn't seem to be any pain or even fear in his expression, just deep surprise... as if his own mortality had just occurred to him.

"Bastard," Maggie hissed at her son and flipped him onto his back, her eyes cold and calculating when she handled the dying boy.

"Listen to me, Jimmy," she said urgently and Jimmy thought Simon Baldevar's impending death was pushing her into the breakdown that had started last night when she learned of

Charles's murder. She grasped Jimmy's hands with a grip like two anvils and her voice, normally so light and sweet, ripped through him like a razor.

"I can save him, I can," she babbled and glanced at Simon, still now with approaching death while blood continued to pump out of his chest in heavy spurts. "I know what to do now. One way, there's one thing that might work. But I need your help; I can't do it without you. Please, Jimmy. You have to help me!"

"Of course, Maggie," he said gently, willing to do anything to keep her from completely toppling over the edge. Let Maggie do whatever she wanted to try and save Simon Baldevar. Sunrise would arrive soon and she'd be forced to sleep. Tomorrow night would be time enough for him and Ellie to help Maggie start coping with Lord Baldevar's death. "Tell me what to do."

To his surprise, Maggie glared at the backpack they'd brought with them and it swung over to Jimmy's feet. Maggie ripped it open, threw him some of Lee's medical instruments, and then began barking out orders in the calm, concise tones of an experienced surgeon.

"Take the scalpel and slit open his chest," she said and hastily gulped down blood from the transfusion pack they'd brought. "I'd do it myself but I can't be so damned weak when I do the ritual. I have to feed and we don't have a second to lose."

Meghann drained the bag while she gave Jimmy the rest of his instructions telepathically. He did everything she told him to do, thanking God that Lee Winslow had given him some instruction in medicine over the years.

Jimmy sliced open Simon Baldevar's chest and used the wide retractor to snap his ribs. Only through a severe effort was Jimmy able to suppress the nausea and fear he felt when he stared at the heart. The sword had gone through the center of his heart, leaving a gaping, ugly hole. To his horror, Jimmy saw the edges of the wound were beginning to blacken and rot. Jimmy might not be a doctor or that learned in vampire lore, but he instinctively knew that once that black, mottled crud covered his heart completely, Simon Baldevar would die.

Maggie barked another telepathic order and Jimmy held Simon's heart while Ellie looked on anxiously. Jimmy was sure

Maggie would have preferred to ask her daughter to do this but she knew Ellie was liable to fall asleep at any moment, newly transformed as she was.

Jimmy wondered what Maggie had in mind to do next and watched her toss the empty transfusion pack to the side, placing both hands on Mikal's skinny chest. Jimmy noticed she never looked at her son, Mikal, who was still aware and made no effort which Jimmy could discern to reach her, to convince her to save him. With a chill, Jimmy realized Mikal hated so much and so senselessly he'd rather die than ask one of these people he'd done his best to kill to help him.

Maggie inhaled and Jimmy saw a strange calmness settle over her eyes. There was something withdrawn but expectant about her as she focused her blank green eyes heavenward and lifted her hands up.

Her lips moved, forming words that made no sense to Jimmy though Ellie gasped and then quickly shut her mouth, apparently not wanting to disturb her mother.

At her arcane words, a luminous black light formed between Maggie's upturned palms and it was Jimmy's turn to gasp, now knowing exactly what Maggie meant to do. He'd seen her do it once before—that time she meant to save his life by destroying a vampire Simon Baldevar sent to kill him. Now she meant to use this dark magic to help Simon.

The black light grew denser and lengthened in her hands until it was almost too much for Maggie to contain. When it took on a rounded shape, Maggie lowered her hands, bringing them back to Mikal's chest.

Mikal's eyes blinked a few times, for the first time appearing uneasy as his mother brought her fathomless light to his skin and her slender hands, bathed within the dark light, disappeared inside his chest.

Jimmy saw Maggie's pale skin whiten until she appeared ghostlike, almost a figment of the imagination instead of a real being. Large beads of perspiration formed on her forehead and dripped into her eyes and Jimmy knew Maggie was risking her own life to perform this magic. Despite the blood she'd drunk, she simply wasn't strong enough for this kind of sorcery. Jimmy almost called out to her to stop but held back, remembering the awful despair in her eyes when she pleaded with him to help her. Jimmy thought Maggie might well prefer death to life without Simon... or she might spend that life hopelessly insane if she failed tonight but didn't die with him.

Maggie's hands came out of Mikal's body, still bathed in black light and clutching his still beating heart.

Amazingly, Mikal was still alive, even as his helpless eyes focused on the heart that was no longer inside him. Now Maggie seemed to come out of her trance a little and there was pity in her eyes when she met those of her son, a helpless, frustrated pity warring with pure hatred as they stared at each other before Mikal finally closed his eyes, no longer able to look at the mother he hadn't been able to kill or dominate.

Jimmy never saw Maggie move, but suddenly she was kneeling over Simon, holding his son's beating heart above his own. Maggie's fangs, a startling white against the darkness all around them, descended and she bit into Mikal's heart, the blood pouring into the gaping hole in Simon's heart.

As soon as the first drops of purplish, thick blood hit, Simon's heart began to beat again with a furious intensity that made Jimmy yank his hands away in surprise. Awed and a little fearful, he watched the viscous black rot eating at Lord Baldevar's heart vanish.

A strangled moan broke Jimmy's shock and he turned to stare at Maggie, covered completely in that strange light she'd conjured. It bathed her and made every hair stand on end, as though she were caught in an electrical storm, but she didn't take her blood teeth out of Mikal's heart, determined that Simon should have every nourishing drop of blood even if the effort to give it to him killed her.

"Maggie," Jimmy said and grabbed her, determined to stop her before she destroyed herself but the black light she no longer controlled enveloped him the moment he touched her. Jimmy had the briefest sensation of an explosion roaring through him before he lost consciousness, not knowing if he, Maggie, or even Simon were going to live through this night.

Chapter Sixteen

White light, dazzling in its brilliance but so deadly . . . tried to pull away, knew the light meant death but there wasn't any pain, just warmth and an odd sense of renewal before exhaustion set in. Perhaps, Simon thought before he drifted off, this wonderful glow was the afterlife receiving him. But who would have ever thought a soul as dark as his would be welcomed so warmly?

The warmth must have been a last, desperate fantasy of life for there was no gentle, cocooning sensation the next time Simon woke up. In place of the all-encompassing glow, he felt bitter cold lodged deep within his bones and a dull, heavy, inescapable ache in his chest.

But perhaps he was not dead, Simon thought, *unless racking cold and relentless pain were the agonies of the hell he'd sold his soul to a thousand times over in the course of his immortality. No, he wasn't dead... he was simply too uncomfortable to be dead.*

But what force had saved him from death? Mikal was many things, but an inept swordsman he certainly was not... Simon remembered the icy feeling of steel cutting through his back and finding the center of his heart. A vampire could not recover if his heart was lacerated like that. Why was he still alive? There had been no mortal on the premises Meghann might pump for fresh blood to revive him . . .

Meghann! Simon strained mightily to open his eyes but the simple effort to part his eyelids was beyond him; it felt like they'd been sewn shut. Simon struggled to pull himself out of his stupor; he had to find out if Meghann was safe.

"Easy," a voice said softly and Simon felt a gentle pressure on his forearm. That light touch was the last bit of evidence he needed to convince him he wasn't dead . . . nowhere in hell could such a solicitous caress exist. "Don't strain yourself."

Simon thought he'd know that lilting voice anywhere. He forced his crusty, unwilling eyelids open and gazed into a pair of green eyes staring down at him with grave, loving concern.

"My love," he started to say but then his vision sharpened and the blurred paleness surrounding the emerald eyes gained definition, forming features too chiseled and sharp boned to be Meghann's. It was Elizabeth watching over him with eyes and a voice so like her mother's Simon mistook her for his consort.

Simon clamped down on the hand clutching his and croaked, "Meghann!" He was appalled when the urgent shout he'd intended came out as nothing more than the frail whisper of a very infirm or very elderly man. If he was left this weak after the encounter with Mikal, what possible chance was there that Meghann had survived? But if Meghann were dead, who had saved him and Elizabeth?

At her mother's name, Elizabeth looked uncertain and Simon felt his heart stop but then Elizabeth looked over her shoulder and screamed shrilly, "Mom! Mom, come quick! Daddy's awake... he wants you!"

The rushed footsteps began even before Elizabeth started to speak and Simon had the briefest impression of a red-and-white blur before warm lips started smothering him in kisses and Meghann yelped through her tears, "Simon, thank God! I thought I'd lost you. I was so scared you'd never wake up!"

Some of Simon's strength returned at the sight of Meghann and he was able to draw her down to him, crushing her small, dear body against him while he anxiously took in the half moon circles beneath her eyes and her white, sickly skin. "You aren't well, little one."

"Neither are you," Meghann sniffled and Simon felt another pain in his chest at her teary, bloodshot eyes peering at him from hollowed sockets. How sick and frail his Meghann was; she needed blood desperately.

Meghann nodded at his thought, bemusing Simon when he realized how weak he was, that she could peer into his mind with such little effort. She turned to Elizabeth and said, "Your father's

awake now so he doesn't need the stomach tube." Simon felt
Meghann tear uncomfortable tubing out of his nose while she
continued to address their daughter. "Can you go downstairs and
get us a few pints of blood? We both need to feed."

"Simon," Meghann said after Elizabeth left, stroking his
unshaven face tenderly, and Simon's arms tightened around her,
tilting her chin so he could give her a deep, lingering kiss now
that their daughter was no longer in the room.

For one delicious moment, Meghann melted against him
before inexplicably stiffening and resisting his searching mouth.
Simon allowed her to wriggle away and glare at him with an
intriguing mix of love and reproach.

"You should have brought me to Mikal's, not Lee!" Meghann
shouted. "I could have summoned Alcuin into me and you know
it! If you'd left Lee here, we could have gone after Ellie together
and Lee would still be alive..."

"And you and I would both be dead now," Simon broke in,
grabbing Meghann's wrists and drawing her against him. "Lee
Winslow died because he wasn't able to defend himself when
Alcuin's spirit departed his body. Could you have recovered from
such a shock, one moment possessed and the next standing in the
mist of battle, or would you, too, have been easy fodder for
Mikal's blade? And what makes you think I could continue
fighting to save our daughter when I saw you dead before me?
Had I brought you to fight our son, he could very well have
managed to kill you, Elizabeth and myself. I was right to leave
you behind."

"Oh no, you weren't!" Meghann replied heatedly, the
inexorable logic of his words flying over her head, as usual. "If I
meekly sat at home, you and Ellie would be dead. You're only
alive because I arrived to fight Mikal."

"Partially true," Simon acknowledged, making Meghann
relax slightly though she continued to glare at him. "I am alive
because of some effort of yours. Tell me, little one, just how did
you make a punctured heart beat again?"

Meghann flinched as though he'd insulted her instead of
complimenting her, her eyes suddenly dark and troubled. Simon
started to divine her thoughts but the effort gave him a severe

headache. Before he could ask his consort what disturbed her so, Elizabeth came into the room with four transfusion packs he sniffed with distaste.

"What is that?"

Meghann took one of the packs, forcing the others into his unwilling hands and gave Elizabeth a grin that transformed her miserable expression. "Look at your father's scowl and remember one thing: Men never change. Even if they live four hundred years, they're still miserable cranks when they're sick."

"I am a miserable crank because I have no use for this swill?" Simon never drank from stored packs; he'd rather feed from a garbage can than force stale blood down his throat. "If you wish me to regain my strength, madam, I suggest you procure fresh blood."

Meghann's face colored angrily but Elizabeth quickly interceded between her parents. "We've all been drinking the packs, Daddy. No one wanted to leave the house while you were... ill."

While you were waiting to see if I lived or died, you mean, Simon thought and drank the vile tasting blood with no further argument. Of course Meghann wouldn't search for prey while he lay on his deathbed. Simon stroked her cheek, not sure if the sudden well being rushing through his veins came from contact with Meghann or the foul-tasting blood packs. But he wouldn't criticize Meghann any further about the poor meal; he was feeling better now and there was time enough later to seek out decent blood.

When he touched her, Simon felt the telepathic link between him and Meghann restored. Immediately he knew how his extraordinary consort saved his life and why she felt shame for her actions.

"You poured Mikal's heart's blood into me to close the wound?" In Meghann's thoughts, Simon saw the darkened hall, the spectral glow Meghann called forth to allow her to plunge her hands into their son's chest and pluck out his heart. There were hands cradling Simon's damaged heart while Meghann performed her magic, hands that kept him alive until the ritual was complete.

Simon smiled at his daughter, taking her hand while he kept his arm firmly wrapped around Meghann. "You helped your mother save me?"

"No," Elizabeth said, suddenly flushed and ill at ease. "Jimmy held your heart, Daddy."

"Jimmy Delacroix?" It was not so unexpected that Meghann brought the creature with her to Mikal's. After all, Charles Tarleton was dead and Meghann was not such a fool that she'd charge into their son's lair without any kind of assistance. But Simon was curious to learn what kind of pressure Meghann put on Jimmy Delacroix that he'd help her save the vampire that transformed him against his will and made effort after effort to destroy him.

Meghann bit her lower lip, not meeting Simon's eyes when she said, "He saved Ellie, too. When we got to the house, Jimmy and I split up. I found you and he found Ellie and . . . transformed her. It was the only way to save her life."

Simon knew that. He well remembered finding his bleeding, ravaged daughter on the verge of death. Shock and grief dulled his reflexes at seeing her young, promising life shattered so viciously and with such little remorse. In his distraction, Mikal had been able to sneak up and stab his father in the back before he could transform Elizabeth.

Simon pulled his daughter closer, noting that the honey color of suntanned skin had faded away. Now she had a vampire's glowing paleness, though she wasn't milk white like Meghann, with her fragile, redhead's skin that had needed protection from the sun even before Simon transformed her. Instead, Elizabeth had his more opaque skin, ivory toned but without any hint of Meghann's translucency.

A nerve twitched in Simon's jaw when he remembered the bruised, suffering heap he'd found at Mikal's, his precious daughter battered within an inch of her life with her glorious hair hacked off her skull by a jealous mortal. Simon ran his hands over Elizabeth's healed face, finding no trace of scars from the abuse Mikal had heaped on her. Best of all, Simon saw no shadow of humiliation or remembered agony in her sparkling eyes.

Jimmy Delacroix had done a fine job of transforming Elizabeth, Simon reluctantly admitted to himself. He was surprised that Delacroix, whom he knew had no previous experience with transformation, kept Elizabeth's mind intact throughout the process. Perhaps the strong link he had with Elizabeth because he'd been close to her from infancy allowed the amateur vampire to cling to Elizabeth's soul and keep her safe.

"Do you remember your time at Mikal's?" Simon demanded, breathing a sigh of relief when Elizabeth shook her head. So he'd at least been successful in wiping Elizabeth's memory clean before Mikal attacked him.

"The only thing I remember is waking up and being . . . you know," Elizabeth said, speaking of vampirism with her mother's diffident tones. "Then, Jimmy and I went looking for you and Mom."

"Elizabeth," Simon said firmly, "You must not be ashamed of your immortality. That you take blood from mortals is no sin; it is simply a matter of survival."

"I know," Elizabeth said but Simon saw the discomfort in her expression. "It's just... new."

Simon decided not to press. There was time enough later for him to tutor Elizabeth in her new life. Instead of lecturing, he smiled at both the women in his life and said genially, "Where is Jimmy Delacroix? I must offer him my thanks for his aid." He had no further grudge with Jimmy Delacroix, not if the man had saved his life, as well as his daughter's.

Simon thought his words would make Elizabeth and Meghann happy but a long, indecipherable look passed between them and then Elizabeth said haltingly, "Daddy, when Mom put that... Mikal's... blood... in your heart, something happened. It was almost like an explosion. Mom fell over you and Jimmy flew away from your body like he'd gotten an electric shock. After that, they were both unconscious until sunset the next evening."

Of course they were. Simon gave his consort a level stare, wondering if her reckless impulsivity came about because she'd been so young when he transformed her. Immortal almost a hundred years and there was still nothing sedate or careful about Meghann O'Neill. That she had a great gift for magic Simon never denied but she never approached the Arts with the proper caution. Simon had been enraged when he found out that Alcuin tutored his consort in sorcery—putting such dangerous knowledge in the hands of a thoughtless child! Meghann rushed into spells and summoning with no thought for consequence— many times her actions landed her in situations she couldn't control. Though Simon was, of course, thankful that Meghann saved his life, he knew she had no appreciation for how potent the force she'd conjured was, that she risked her life, as well as the lives of Elizabeth and Jimmy Delacroix to save him.

Well, no more, Simon vowed silently and tightened his grip on Meghann until she felt almost an extension of him. Now that he was restored and there was no secret son keeping him from her side, Simon would watch her carefully, make sure Meghann performed no dark rituals that put her in peril.

"You were all... out of it. So I carried everyone to Mom's car and drove like hell to get us to Southampton before sunrise," Elizabeth continued, giving her parents a smile of shy pride. "I just made it... the sun was peeking over the ocean when I shut the door and sealed the shutters with everyone safe inside."

The sun! With an effort, Simon kept his face impassive, not wanting to alert Elizabeth and Meghann to the drift of his thoughts. Was it possible the blinding light Simon felt before had nothing to do with death?

Meghann suffused him with Mikal's blood and had no idea of the enormity of her actions. Simon could tell that by the green eyes following him without a trace of concern or apprehension. Meghann merely thought to heal his heart; she had no idea that she might have given him a gift of even greater value when she poured Mikal's blood into his dying body.

They'd discuss it later, Simon decided and kissed Elizabeth's forehead, murmuring, "You saved us from the sun so I owe you my life as well as I owe Jimmy Delacroix and your mother."

"Daddy," Elizabeth said with a husked, strained quality to her voice, like she was holding back tears. "You don't owe me anything. You're the one who came charging after me when Mikal kidnapped me. Mom told me she and Jimmy might have died if you hadn't killed all of Mikal's henchmen and weakened him before they arrived."

"The bodies." Simon's amber eyes darkened and he stared anxiously at his wife and daughter. "You did not leave that mess at the estate? How long have I lain unconscious? Mikal's infernal club was supposed to open this weekend."

"It's all right," Meghann replied calmly. "First, you've been unconscious for seven nights but we've taken care of everything in the meanwhile. Ellie told me that Mikal's body disintegrated after I pierced his heart with my blood teeth. As for Lee, Ellie put his body in the trunk so we could have a proper burial for him later. You know my father bought a plot at Calvary cemetery for me. Now that you're awake, we're going to hold a memorial service there as soon as possible for Charles and Lee. I got a double headstone for them... I thought they'd like to lay together, under one banner."

Meghann's voice broke and Simon squeezed her hand while they all bowed their heads in memory of the brave friends they'd lost to Mikal's treachery. When Meghann raised her head again and met his eyes, Simon saw that though she loved him and would remain with him, she'd never accept his decision to transform Lee and bring him to Mikal's. Meghann would go to her own grave thinking she should have been the one sacrificed that Lee Winslow might live.

"The other vampire . . . that boneless woman," Ellie said, picking up the thread of her mother's explanation, "I just left her outside. I knew the sun would turn her to ash. As for the humans, I left them there but I set fire to Mikal's office. I didn't know if he had any incriminating documents. I figured the corpses would provide the authorities with an explanation for what happened and it did. Look, Daddy."

Ellie shoved some newspapers at him and Simon scanned the articles, seeing that the police were seeking the missing owner of Immortal Light, one Michael Hollingsworth.

Thank God the boy did not use any identity traceable to me, Simon thought as he read the papers, silently praising his daughter's intelligence. The mortal corpses and fire led the authorities to ponder a possible extortion scenario or drug deal gone sour. They believed Michael Hollingsworth was on the run or dead and they'd seized the estate while they launched a complete investigation.

Simon didn't worry about the authorities finding any incriminating vampire evidence. Even if Mikal had been foolish enough to leave written proof or perhaps some vial of his blood, nothing would point in the direction of him, Meghann and Elizabeth. They were safe and it did not matter if the authorities found disturbing clues. They would do as lawmen had done all the centuries Simon was alive—ignore what troubled them and go on with their lives, refusing to speculate that there could be immortals among them.

"So you got us safely home and made certain Mikal's actions would not come back to haunt us," Simon smiled at Elizabeth. "What has all this to do with bringing Jimmy Delacroix to me that I may thank him?"

Again Elizabeth and Meghann looked away from him before Meghann replied, "He is still weak after recovering consciousness. He's... uh... not well enough to see you now."

"Right," Elizabeth chirped, her voice sounding hurried and deceitful to Simon's sensitive ears. His eyes narrowed as he considered his fidgeting wife and daughter—just what were they attempting to hide from him?

"I'm going to go out for a while," Elizabeth said, leaping off the bed and scampering away from her father's scrutiny. "I mean, I'm sure you and Mom want to, uh... be alone for a little while. Okay?"

"Fine," Meghann said before Simon could reply and Elizabeth made a hasty departure.

Simon started to glance at Meghann's thoughts to see what she and Elizabeth were attempting to hide from him but then he saw the grief and pain welling in her eyes and knew there was another matter he had to address first.

"Look at me, Sweet," Simon said and pushed her into the pillows, positioning his body over hers protectively. "We will speak now of Mikal and then put the matter behind us forever."

"I don't want to talk about him," Meghann cried in a taut, tinny voice. She tried to push Simon away, but he only held her tighter and grasped her jaw so she had to meet his eyes.

"We must," Simon told her, kissing her forehead as gently and reverently as he'd just done to Elizabeth. "I won't have you punishing yourself with this baseless guilt."

"Baseless?!" Meghann gave him an incredulous stare and the tears in her eyes bubbled over, following earlier tracks still evident on her pale, strained face. "Simon, I killed our son! I took his heart out of his body while he was still alive and lo... look... looking at me... watching his own mother sacrifice him."

"Hush," Simon said and nestled her head against his heart while she wept. Simon stroked her hair, noting with a pang how dull her usually flaming red hair was. It wasn't just lack of fresh blood but grief and despair that had stolen Meghann's beauty from her. It was up to Simon to restore her, as she'd done to him. He had to make her see reason.

"Little one," he said as she continued to sob against him, "did Mikal leave you any other choice?"

"That's not the point—" she started to say and Simon put a finger to her lips to silence her, feeling an erotic thrill course through him from even that brief contact. He saw Meghann jump slightly and knew she'd felt it, too, though she looked horror struck that she could experience lust in light of the hellish experiences of the past week.

"It most certainly is," Simon said firmly. "What would have happened to our Elizabeth if you did not kill Mikal?"

"You don't understand." Meghann raised her head from his chest, beseeching him with tormented eyes that hurt his heart far more than Mikal's sword ever could. "I know I had to kill Mikal, that it was Ellie's life or his, what a danger he was to our existence with his plans to expose vampires to the world. But Simon, I didn't just kill him—I sacrificed him! I saw you dying before my eyes and my only thought was saving you. I ripped Mikal's heart out and never even thought about him being my son until it was over. How could I use my own son like that?"

"If you had not, I would be dead. Is that what you want?"

"Of course not!"

312

"Then forget your guilt," Simon ordered. "Mikal was misbegotten. His only aims were destruction and causing as much suffering as he could. The boy was mad, Meghann. He had to be put down . . . never doubt the rightness of your actions. My only regret is that the burden of his death fell on your shoulders. That is why I would not take you with me to rescue Elizabeth—I wanted to spare you the pain of seeing what our son was."

Meghann didn't look away but her eyes became thoughtful, mind turning inward while she analyzed his words.

"Was he always like that?" she finally said and gave him a searching glance. "Was there ever anything more to my son than that... that thing I saw?"

"What does that matter?" With an effort, Simon kept his voice calm and didn't snap at the nonsensical question.

"It matters!" Meghann turned on her side and grasped his hands, green eyes wide and imploring. "Simon, I never knew my own son and what I did see, in the moments before I had to kill him, horrified me. I'll never forget what it was like to look in my boy's eyes and see nothing but unthinking, lunatic malice reflected back at me. Please, Simon. Tell me there was more to our son than the monster I encountered. Tell me there were moments in his life when you were proud to have a son. I can't stand to think we... our blood... produced something with no good in him at all."

Now it was Simon who turned away, refusing to meet her gaze. An awkward silence spun between them before Simon spoke again, his voice raspy and hoarse. "Our blood did produce something wondrous, Meghann: Elizabeth. How could I not be proud to sire her, a daughter who reminds me so much of you? She is everything I ever wanted from a child. You ask me was there more to Mikal than what you saw. My answer is yes, there was. Had there not been, I should have destroyed him long ago. But there were qualities—his brilliant mind, the powers I could never dream of matching—that stayed my hand.

"Ah, little one, I could tell you of long nights spent in conversation with our son, the happiness I felt at finally having a companion that matched my intellect. I could tell you of the joy I took in Mikal on those nights, how much I looked forward to bringing you our son. But such moments were fleeting and in the end, Mikal's intellect was no match for the sickness rotting his heart and sanity. Meghann, there could be no treatment for our son and his hatred for us meant it was his life or ours. I chose ours... yours, Elizabeth's and mine.

"Don't ever ask me about Mikal again, Meghann. I will not break my heart or yours thinking of what might have been, or of the scant fond memories I have of the boy. It is better to forget there ever was a Mikal and concentrate on Elizabeth, on the life we can finally have together."

Meghann put her hand on his shoulder and Simon knew that was her way of telling him she accepted his request, she'd never bring Mikal up again. Neither of them would ever forget the strange, troubling boy that had been their son but to think of him would only break their hearts.

Simon turned around and Meghann didn't resist when he kissed her with a blinding intensity, for he couldn't forget those terrible moments at Mikal's when he lay alone and gasping for breath, certain he'd never see Meghann again, never again feel her arch beneath him and beg him to take her.

"You're sure you're well enough?" Meghann asked him as he pulled off the delicate silk robe she wore. Simon knew the question was a mere formality for Meghann was already drawing him closer, gently shoving him toward heavy, aching breasts seeking out the comfort of his hard-planed chest.

"If the time ever comes when I lack the strength to make love to you, I beg you to behead me," Simon murmured and bent his chestnut head down to suckle her, blood teeth teasing and nipping in a pattern that might be familiar but still had the power to knock the breath out of her and make her lie moaning and panting beneath him.

What an intoxicating armful she was, Simon thought as her hands and mouth devoured him with the same loving extravagance he'd spent on her. Long ago Simon lost count of the number of women in his bed, but none of them had ever pleased him the way Meghann did. Meghann's appeal for him wasn't based on great sexual expertise, for Simon had had that in the concubines he'd purchased when he was a mortal trader in the

Levant and in professional courtesans like Gabrielle that he used to satisfy sophisticated desires. They'd interested him, some he even kept for years at a time, but never had he felt the devouring passion he had for Meghann.

"Fairie queen," he murmured against the cool hollow of her throat and watched her smile impishly at his words. That's what Meghann was to him, an enchanting creature like the wood nymphs Adelaide used-to tell him stories of. It wasn't merely that she was the most passionate woman he'd ever had in his bed but that there was something... untouchable about her. Yes, that was it—even after all this time, Meghann still reacted to him with a core of innocence in her every gesture, and that had the power to drive him to heights of rapture he'd never approached with anyone else.

"Do you know the story of Diana?" Simon questioned when Meghann began to stir impatiently at the prolonged foreplay, very obviously ready for him to take her.

"The virgin huntress," Meghann said, attempting to force his mouth back to her breasts. "She rode through the night."

"As you will ride me, little one." Easily Simon swung her on top of him, firmly grasping her hips to guide her movements as they made love.

Meghann smiled her pleasure at the position and willingly bent down to allow him to capture her nipple as she thrashed about on top of him.

The voluptuous breasts swaying enticingly about his head and long curtain of bright red hair brushing his arms and chest made his blood hunger, which was not at all assuaged by the meager blood packs, roar to life—but Simon wouldn't feed from Meghann now; she was simply too weak and he could not have her sicken now. Instead, he brought his wrist to her mouth and husked, "Drink of me."

Meghann started to shake her head, no doubt as concerned for his health as he was for hers, but Simon shoved his wrist under her nose, knowing Meghann was too hungry for fresh blood to be able to resist the intoxicating scent much longer. Excited by the blood lust that made Meghann's green eyes turn to smoke, Simon forced her beneath him, driving into her eager, writhing body until her fangs finally emerged from dark red lips and she bit into him, sucking down his blood in a passionate frenzy.

As he'd expected, Meghann did not feed for long when her eyes suddenly bulged wide and her complexion took on an alarming, greenish tinge. Frantically, she tried to push Simon's wrist away and he felt her start to retch.

"No." Still inside her, Simon clamped down on her mouth with his hand, ignoring her miserable, pleading expression. "Keep it down, Meghann. Force yourself to keep my blood in you."

A choked whimper was Meghann's only response and Simon felt a moment of alarm when her eyes rolled back in her head—she seemed on the verge of fainting. But then color came back into her face and her eyes fluttered open weakly, looking up at Simon in bewilderment.

"It's all right," he whispered as he continued driving into her, kissing her and noticing that his blood tasted quite different—the iron taste much heavier than usual, along with an indefinable, pungent quality. No wonder Meghann got sick . . . but it had to be done. "It's all right, little one."

Meghann made no protest, the brief nausea apparently not dampening her passion as they rocked together, ending in a fierce explosion that made her tremble and cling to him afterward while he petted and soothed her.

"I'm hungry," Meghann finally sighed against his chest and Simon laughed, swinging her off the bed along with him.

"Then I must feed you—blood and food. Get dressed and we shall go out. Do you realize we have not shared a meal since I returned? Where is Elizabeth? She can accompany us."

Abruptly, Meghann paled and looked nervous again but gave Simon a coy smile before he could interrogate her.

"Silly man, Ellie left the house so we could be together." Meghann wrapped her arms around his neck, standing on tiptoe when she purred into his ear, "I don't want to share your company tonight. Can't we go out and forget... everything? Just enjoy each other?"

Coquette, Simon thought, knowing Meghann was hiding some anxiety beneath the cat's eyes and flirtatious grin curling on her lips. But he knew she wasn't being dishonest… Meghann did want to be alone with him, to have a chance to laugh and talk as they'd not been able to do yet.

"Of course we can enjoy each other," Simon said and kept smiling as Meghann bounded away from him to bathe, thinking he fully intended to find out what she and Elizabeth were hiding from him before the night was over.

Chapter Seventeen

After making arrangements for dinner, Meghann bathed with a scrutiny bordering on obsessiveness, counting the number of times her hands massaged her scalp as she shampooed and the number of strokes to pare her nails with the emery board. There was nothing eccentric about her behavior; it was simply the only way she could force thoughts of Jimmy and Ellie out of her mind.

She couldn't think about their relationship (even the word when applied to Ellie and Jimmy made Meghann cringe) now that Simon was awake and able to read her mind with his usual impunity. Of course, Simon was no fool—Meghann knew he already suspected she and Ellie were hiding something but because of his illness, he hadn't been able to wring the whole truth from either of them.

How long do you think that's going to last, her thoughts demanded after Meghann toweled herself dry and attacked the tangles in her hip-length hair. *You can't keep this from Simon forever.*

Meghann sighed, her brow furrowing as the hairbrush worked its way through a particularly nasty knot. No, she couldn't keep Ellie and Jimmy's secret forever, however much she'd like to.

It wasn't that Meghann approved of them seeing each other, but no matter how she felt about the matter, she still dreaded the confrontation between Ellie and Simon that lay ahead. Right now, their relationship was nearly idyllic, the long-parted father and daughter loving each other wholeheartedly and doing everything within their power to please each other. But what would happen to that bond when Ellie finally witnessed her father's darkest side, saw the ruthless way he eliminated his enemies? For it would not matter now that Jimmy Delacroix had helped Meghann save Simon's life. Once Simon discovered he'd been in Ellie's bed, he'd never see Jimmy as anything but an enemy who had to be destroyed.

Meghann bit her lip in exasperation—she couldn't stop thinking these dangerous thoughts no matter what she did! Slamming the door on the disturbing matter, Meghann finished combing her hair and entered her dressing room. She glanced through her closets, discarding various outfits before settling on an all-lace shirtdress with a revealing neckline and scalloped sleeves. The outfit was sensual as well as elegant, the perfect combination to keep Simon's mind off anything but her.

Meghann smiled at her naughty plans and took a seat at her vanity table. As a vampire, she had no need of makeup but she wanted to put her hair up in Simon's favorite style . . . the one he'd lovingly take apart at the end of dinner.

Meghann pulled open one of the cedar drawers and withdrew some antique jade and gold combs. Then she picked up a hairbrush and confronted the mirror for the first time since she sat down. What she saw made her give out a long, petrified shriek that brought Simon running into the room, half dressed, with track marks from the comb still visible in his damp hair.

"What is it, Sweet? What's the matter?"

"Look!" Meghann pointed a trembling figure at her mirror image, or rather the lack of a reflection that greeted her. Vampires cast see-through reflections but there was always some element of visibility. Now Meghann could barely make herself out.

Simon moved behind her, putting his hands on her shoulders and Meghann saw his reflection was as flimsy as hers. It was like looking into black water and seeing only the most blurred, general details of an image.

"What's the matter?" Meghann cried, feeling as frightened and confused as she had the first time she laid eyes on her vampire self. "What's wrong with us?"

Simon patted her hair, and with a qualm Meghann noted she could hardly make out the motion of his hand stroking her in the mirror. "It might be a positive sign, little one."

"A positive sign?" Meghann repeated disbelievingly and swiveled around, relieved to turn away from her reflection. "A positive sign of what?"

Simon knelt beside the vanity seat, taking her clammy hands in his dry, calm ones. "Sweetheart, you filled my heart with Mikal's blood—the blood of the only vampire ever to walk in daylight."

"Simon!" Meghann gasped as his words and their meaning dawned on her. "You're right... I gave you Mikal's blood. Does that mean you're going to be able to withstand the sun now?" With all that had happened, Meghann had almost lost track of the original reason behind their children's birth... so Simon Baldevar could walk in daylight for the first time in four hundred years.

"I think we will withstand the sun together, Meghann." Simon smiled at her puzzlement and twirled a long strand of damp red hair in his fingers "Did you not just drink of me?"

"And that's why I got so sick!" Simon's grin broadened at her comprehension but Meghann continued to look doubtful.

"I don't understand." Meghann pointed at the mirror, careful not to let her eyes fall on her reflection. "Mikal could see himself as clearly as a mortal in mirrors. If we're going to be able to withstand the sun like him, shouldn't our reflections have become stronger instead of weaker?"

Simon shook his head. "You forget, Meghann, that we were vampires before his blood entered us. I think his blood will enhance our vampiric attributes, make them stronger. Therefore, our images might fade but our other abilities—our magic—will have grown a thousandfold stronger."

"If that's so, we could have less resistance to sunlight."

"No," Simon argued. "The ability to resist sunlight is a survival trait, therefore more dominant than the disease that forces us to live in darkness. Our telekinesis, ability to fly the plane, mesmerizing ability—all of these are survival traits, necessary to prolong our existence. Therefore, they will become stronger... as will our resistance to sunlight."

Meghann considered that. "Maybe. The only sure evidence to support your theory will be whether we fall asleep at dawn and feel the pain of the sunrise as usual. But Mikal's blood was diluted the moment it encountered our own. You can't think we'll be as strong as him such as the ability to walk around at high noon."

"How do you know we will not, doubting Thomas?" Simon said and nipped her ear. "As you say, we shall simply have to wait and see. But you are right to be cautious. Even if we encounter the dawn with no ill effects, we shall not travel from the safety of this house and its shutters for days. We must be careful in our experiment."

Simon grinned and picked up the hairbrush that had fallen to the floor, quickly styling Meghann's hair into the modified pompadour he'd always favored. "I do hope you take your own good advice about the sunrise, Meghann, and not fret between now and then. Didn't Elizabeth gracefully withdraw so we'd finally have a chance to enjoy ourselves?"

Meghann's lips whitened and Simon stared at her thoughtfully but again the gods were kind, and the front bell rang before Simon could interrogate her.

"Dinner's arrived," she said with relieved brightness and shooed Simon back into his dressing room. "Meet me in the atrium in about ten minutes."

When Simon came downstairs, Meghann presented him with a room that shimmered and glowed by the pinpoint light of a dozen candles. In mere minutes, she'd transformed the garden room into a place fit for a romantic evening, with scented candles and hothouse gold and red roses swimming in large glass vases perfuming the air. The wicker dining table was covered by an elegant white linen cloth and set for dinner for two, with celadon-colored cloth napkins in gold rings, Waterford crystal glasses, antique silver, and Wedgwood china. On the rosewood sideboard a sumptuous buffet featuring fresh lobster, London broil, coconut shrimp fritters, and other mouthwatering entrees beckoned.

"Surprise," Meghann smiled while the two caterers hurriedly arranged the rest of the dishes. *I meant it when I said I didn't want to share your company with anyone tonight... not even a crowded restaurant of mortals. I want you all to myself.*

And you shall have me, Simon smiled and Meghann felt her knees grow warm and loose, as if her bones had gently dissolved.

But have you forgotten we must feed on something besides mere food?

Taken care of Meghann replied smugly and turned to the two caterers. Her green eyes, a perfect match for the napkins on the table, widened slightly and both women went rigid, their own eyes becoming glazed and unfocused.

"How very efficient," Simon complimented her and started to walk over to the hypnotized pair but a look from Meghann stopped him, making him raise one eyebrow in a quizzical gesture.

"You can't kill them," Meghann said warningly. "The Waterside Restaurant knows I called them over here."

Simon rolled his eyes and took hold of one of the girls, a plump but pretty brunette. The girl made no move to escape, so lulled by the pleasant daydream of a Hawaiian beach Meghann put in her head she didn't even notice Simon. "Mikal's sword didn't pierce my brain, Meghann," he said as he rolled up the crisp white sleeve of her catering uniform.

With no further words, Simon made the smallest wound to pierce the girl's skin and began to feed. Meghann did the same to her victim, knowing in these summer months a vampire's mark could easily be explained away as mosquito bites if the wounds were small enough.

Meghann brought the wrist to her mouth and wrinkled her nose in distaste at the cloying perfume her host used. She disliked feeding off members of her own sex, though she could see from the smoldering gold eyes fixed on her Simon quite enjoyed the tableau of her feeding off another woman.

Then the girl's youthful blood flooded her mouth and Meghann forgot everything but the hot, coppery substance pouring down her throat like the smoothest wine. How right Simon was to despise transfusion packs, cold, glutinous blood that was nothing compared with the fresh, vital liquid she reveled in now. Transfusion packs never made her feel like she could soar through the night. Only warm blood completely restored her power and took away the gnawing, vicious ache of blood hunger that nagged and nagged at her to drink all she could . . .

Banrion!

Meghann winced at the exhortation, not sure if Alcuin was actually reaching out to her or if his voice was the tone her conscience took on to urge her away from murder. Whatever, the effect was the same—Meghann let the woman's wrist fall away from her mouth and straightened up, using one of the napkins on the table to wipe her lips clean.

She saw Simon had finished feeding and started instructing his victim to forget the bloodletting. Meghann thought she saw a smug gleam in Simon's eyes as he compared her much paler host to the girl he'd fed from.

Meghann smarted under his look, thinking he was no doubt remembering the many times she lectured him on the virtue of leaving one's prey alive. Those amused amber eyes were sending an implicit message—Simon was far more capable of restraint toward humans than her when he chose to be.

Have you no sense of humor, Simon said and gave her a half smile. *I'm simply ruffling your feathers a bit, my little schoolmarm of a vampire.*

Meghann felt her mouth twitch and gave up the effort to look annoyed, laughing aloud to the delight of the two caterers, healthy enough and having no memory of anything but dishing out the food and receiving the five-hundred dollar tip Simon gave to each of them as he bid them goodnight.

With the caterers gone, Meghann went to take a seat across from Simon but one long arm wrapped around her waist and deposited her in his lap.

"If we dine privately, there's no reason to put any distance between us, is there?"

"None at all," Meghann agreed, her voice not quite steady as Simon plucked a long-stemmed red rose from the table centerpiece and rubbed the soft petals under her chin before he placed the flower between her cleavage.

"How thoughtless of me," Simon said when a thorn pricked the skin above her breast and a bright red droplet of blood appeared. Inclining his head slightly, his warm tongue licked the wound clean.

Now her mind was finally clear, clear of everything but the sharp pull of lust she felt as Simon used the thorns to stab lightly at her neck and then gently suck the minuscule wounds clean.

"Simon," she breathed and moaned as though she were in pain when he moved his head away from her breast.

"Now we must eat."

Meghann leapt to her feet and made her way to the sideboard without protest, knowing the game Simon had chosen to play tonight. They'd tease each other all the long, lovely hours between now and sunrise, until their passions rose to such a fever pitch they could no longer deny themselves.

Simon smiled at her acquiescence and opened the wine she'd selected, a rare vintage of Hermitage Blanc Cuvee de l'Oree '96 that Charles and Lee had presented them with for their wedding eighteen years earlier.

"To Charles and Lee," Meghann said softly, clinking her delicate crystal glass against his.

Simon nodded and a pall fell over the table, the two of them eating the sumptuous buffet in silence.

"May I propose another toast, little one?" Simon finally said, and Meghann looked up from the plate she'd loaded with London broil, grilled salmon, and watercress risotto. Grieving for her friends or not, Meghann still had to satisfy the ferocious appetite of a vampire.

"To a long and happy future together... you and I reunited at long last, along with our wonderful daughter at our side."

Meghann lifted her glass in agreement, knowing she, Simon and Elizabeth could have a bright future but it would always be tinged by the sadness she felt for her departed friends... particularly Charles, her mainstay for so long.

Determined to try and enjoy this celebration of Simon's recovery, Meghann clinked her glass against his, speaking with forced gaiety. "What's in this future of ours? Before everything happened, Ellie said something about you giving her the money to start her own firm."

"Establishing a talent like Elizabeth's is a pleasure I greatly look forward to. But first I think we deserve a bit of leisure, all of us. Don't you agree? Along with the business, I also promised

Elizabeth a Grand Tour of Europe. Naturally I assumed you'd come along."

"Simon!" Meghann glowed, her good mood genuine now. "She... I'll love it! I haven't been to Europe since before she was born, except for that brief trip Charles and I made to Ballnamore... and that was hardly pleasure. But I hope you understand..."

"Understand what, little one?"

Careful, Meghann told herself and imagined a thick brick wall shielding her thoughts. With blood in her, the exertion to block Simon no longer made her queasy and weak. "Well, Ellie's a young woman now. You have to provide her with her own quarters and understand that she'll be, er..."

"Wanting to see young men her own age instead of spending every minute with us?" Simon asked dryly. "Really, Meghann, I know our daughter is of an age and I've already selected suitable acquaintances for her."

"What kind of suitable acquaintances?" Meghann asked curiously, spooning up some of the delicious lobster bisque and feeding it to Simon.

He accepted the tribute with a smile before responding. "Men she can marry... young men of excellent families with great fortunes and bright prospects. A great many of my mortal acquaintances have sons in Elizabeth's class, attending or graduated from proper universities. Elizabeth may see any of them and when she chooses one to marry, it shall be my pleasure to transform him and make him a partner in my various business concerns... what the devil is the matter with you?"

"Oh, Simon!" Meghann panted out, red faced and breathless from her laughter. "Oh, you... oh, God, that's so funny! You went and picked out some MBA, prep school clones for Ellie. You wonderful, misguided idiot—Ellie can't stand boys like that! She's going to show your 'suitable acquaintances' the door!"She explained before more giggles erupted.

"What on earth is wrong with a good education and a desire for wealth?" Simon demanded, tight lipped and scowling in the face of Meghann's continued laughter, looking for all the world like an insulted hawk. "Please tell me you have not encouraged

Elizabeth to favor the kind of scruffy riffraff you gave yourself to during our separation. I won't have my daughter wasting herself on down-at-the-heels trash."

Knowing "scruffy riffraff" was a not-too-veiled reference to Jimmy Delacroix, Meghann backed away from the subject hastily. "Where do you want to start the tour? Italy will be miserably hot right now . . . what about York? Ellie's dying to see where you came from."

Simon reached for one of the shrimp, sautéed in a delicious garlic sauce, and moved it over her lips before he began feeding it to her. "It shall be my pleasure to show Elizabeth her heritage. Little one, you'll give yourself an aneurysm if you continue trying to deceive me."

She'd forgotten how Simon attacked—sudden and swift with as much forewarning as a lion diving out from cover. Caught off guard exactly as he'd wanted her to be, Meghann choked and tried to slide off Simon's lap, only to be kept still by an arm that was suddenly that of a prison warden instead of a lover.

"I don't know what you're talking about," she muttered, reaching for her wineglass to wash down the shellfish that was caught in her throat.

"Is that why you won't meet my eyes?" Simon inquired in the menacing cobra's whisper she hadn't heard in years. Meghann knew from past experience his next move would be to bleed her and then strike her as a reprimand.

"Don't you dare hit me!"

"What have you done, Meghann, which would cause me to want to hit you?" Simon grasped her chin in a punishing grip with his thumb and forefinger, forcing her eyes to lock on his. Meghann straightened on his lap and stared back at him, refusing to give Simon the satisfaction of seeing her shut her eyes to avoid him.

"If you ever hit me again," she said in a voice that didn't quaver and betray her inner turmoil, "I'll leave you forever. Now let me go!"

"You've been hiding something all night and I demand to know what it is," Simon said, unmoved by her threat.

"I'll tell you if you stop manhandling me. Now put me down!"

"So you can escape me via the astral plane? I think not."
Simon grinned nastily when she flinched... escaping this
argument by flying away was exactly what Meghann had in
mind. "It is only because I love you so that I have not peered into
your mind but I shall if you continue to try my patience."

"Simon, I... I can't stand it anymore. I don't want anyone else
to die... please!"

"Die? Enough of this! I shall not waste another moment on
senseless riddles and coy evasions."

"No!" Meghann could feel the invasive presence coursing
through her thoughts, violating her mind with the same brutal
force of a rapist.

"Stop it! Stop it!" Meghann did everything she could to block
him but Simon, damn his soul, was right about what the effort to
thwart him would cost her. Within seconds, her temples started to
pound, her vision blurred, and a thin trickle of blood fell from
one nostril. Knowing she'd have a seizure if she didn't relax and
Simon would get the information he wanted anyway, Meghann
stopped fighting... better to save her strength so she could help
Ellie and Jimmy.

No sooner had she thought their names than Simon let out an
inarticulate roar and dropped her from his lap like something
diseased.

"You let that odious creature put his hands on my child?"
Simon glared down at her, his face white as a sheet but for eyes
the same flat, pale yellow of an attack dog ready to strike.

"It happened while we were in Chicago . . ." Meghann started
to explain and Simon's hand lashed out to grab her by the hair
and yank her off the floor.

"Why is he still alive, Meghann?" Simon demanded and
Meghann, scalp smarting from the punishing grip on her hair,
landed a solid blow at his unprotected genitals.

A crack across the face sent Meghann flying into the French
doors. The force of her landing shattered the glass against her
head and back.

Painfully, Meghann pulled herself away, feeling hundreds of
small, bleeding cuts against her scalp and back. She knew they'd

heal within minutes but for now they stung mightily and she had no idea what else Simon had in mind for her.

Simon stalked over to her, giving her a look of scorn before he addressed her with an icy contempt unlike anything she'd ever heard from him before.

"Woman, you are a poor excuse for a wife and a sorrier one of a mother. All I ever asked of you was that you keep my daughter safe and you have failed utterly, actually giving your blessing to her fornicating with that scum..."

"He saved your life!"

Simon raised an eyebrow. "And you thought to repay him by prostituting Elizabeth's body?"

Meghann didn't have any impression of leaping up but she moved so fast even Simon couldn't stop her before she slapped him across the face with all her strength.

The shocking red imprint of her hand against his white cheek appeared and disappeared, but Simon made no move to hit her back. He only said coolly, "You have proven yourself an unfit mother but a ludicrously simple mind to read. I know you told my daughter and that cowardly lecher to hide from me. All I need to know now is where you sent them so I can attend to Elizabeth. After that, you shall never see her, or me, again."

"I never want to see you again!" Meghann screamed, infuriated by the hurt tears that threatened to spill out of her eyes. She'd wept over Simon's dying body, thought she'd die along with him if he left her and look what he was doing to her now! "How dare you call me an unfit mother when our son is dead because of what you raised him to be?!"

Simon struck her chin, breaking her jaw. "Tell me where my daughter is."

"You can't see it, can you?" Meghann demanded after her shattered bones healed. "Beat me all you want, it won't do you any good. I can't tell you where Ellie and Jimmy are because I don't know! They've gone someplace far away and they won't come back until I tell Ellie it's all right. And I'll never do that, no matter what you do to me . . . you won't have any chance to destroy Ellie through me!"

Simon's eyes didn't harden or narrow. Instead, rage gave them a transparent, glassy quality that made Meghann fear for her life as he leaned toward her.

And she suddenly found herself in New York City, standing in front of a town house she hadn't thought of in years.

Meghann looked around, unable to believe the busy Manhattan street and mellowed oak wood facade of the town house were real. Certainly, it was possible that terror gave her the ability to escape Simon via the astral plane but no vampire could travel from Southampton to New York City. Why, it was a distance of more than ninety miles—more than triple the maximum distance of thirty miles a vampire could fly!

Mikal's blood has given you greater power, Banrion.

"Alcuin?" Meghann said, not noticing the curious stares of passersby as she looked around for the ghostly mentor she could hear but not see.

Don't let Simon push you away, Banrion. He needs you so desperately. You must help him do right by your daughter and remind him of my promise.

"What promise?" Meghann asked but the otherworldly presence surrounding her had vanished. Now she felt all the sensations of the physical world it had forced back . . . the hot cement sidewalk beneath her flimsy summer shoes and soft light of the streetlight beaming down on her, the muggy staleness of the city air in contrast with the sharp ocean breeze of Southampton.

Meghann stared at the elegant town house, thinking that this was where everything truly began, far more so than the house on Long Island Mikal had appropriated to carry out his vicious battle against his parents.

Had Mikal known about the town house, Meghann wondered as she climbed up the smooth marble steps. Did he know this was where his father transformed his mother during World War II? Did he know thirteen years after that transformation Meghann thought she'd finally thrown off Simon's brutal rule over her body and soul by staking him and leaving him on the rooftop for the dawn of a new day to finish him off?

Right now, Meghann would heavily regret not killing Simon that long ago night if it wasn't for her daughter. It wasn't immortality but Ellie that was Simon Baldevar's one true gift to her. She should have left the ungrateful bastard to die the other night instead of risking her own life to save him.

But if his behavior tonight finally had made her see the error in loving him, why couldn't she get rid of the dull, tight ache in her heart? Why did she still shudder when she remembered that hideous night a week ago when she'd held Simon's dying body in her arms? She'd been out of her mind with grief and pain, knowing if Simon died she would too and it wouldn't be through suicide either. Meghann would have simply lost the will to live this life without Simon Baldevar in it.

Damn you, Simon Baldevar, Meghann thought savagely and glared at the mahogany front door with its stained glass panels and it swung open for her. *How can I love a monster like you when all you do is hurt me?*

Meghann stepped through the foyer with no thought of trespassing on some mortal's home. She knew Simon still owned the property, had reclaimed it around the same time he decided to come back from the dead and reclaim her.

Perhaps it was foolish to enter this house where Simon could easily find her; maybe she should use her head start to escape him more permanently. But Meghann knew Simon could probably find her wherever she went—damned if she'd give him the satisfaction of watching her run in fear. Better to remain here and face head on the confrontation she knew couldn't be far away.

Most of the priceless furniture Meghann remembered was packed away in storage. Only a few massive pieces remained, covered in huge sheets that made the large rooms seem desolate and abandoned as she wandered through the dark house.

Meghann paused at the steps leading to the basement, thinking of the bedroom that lay below and all she'd gone through there—everything from unimaginable pleasure to the utter disintegration of her ego as Simon bent her mind to his will with his humiliating mastery over her body.

Meghann let her hand trail off the forbidding black door. Even after all this time, she couldn't bear to reenter that room and remember her change from innocent undergraduate to concubine of a power-crazed madman. There was something else she needed to see here, so Meghann closed her eyes and flew up to the rooftop.

"Call Elizabeth."

Though the steely voice made her heart plummet, Meghann kept still and opened her eyes slowly, glaring at the fiend that awaited her in the precise spot where she'd left him to die.

"Never," Meghann said, not attempting to escape but staying well out of striking range. She didn't think Simon would kill her—Ellie would never come back if he did. On the other hand, Simon might torture her in the hopes her pain would bring Ellie running back to her mother's side.

"I should bloody well torture you for procuring your daughter to…"

"Shut up!" Meghann yelled, no longer frightened but enraged. "I did not procure Ellie to Jimmy Delacroix. I told you everything happened while we were in Chicago."

"So why did you not kill Delacroix the moment you discovered what he'd done to Elizabeth?"

"Because I needed someone by my side when I went to rescue you and Elizabeth. Since Charles was dead and you'd taken Lee for your own futile scheme, I had no one else to rely on but Jimmy."

Something flickered in the depths of Simon's imperturbable gold eyes when she reminded him what his strategy had cost Lee Winslow and his voice lost some of its hostility when he spoke to her again. "You used him so you'd have an ally when you faced Mikal. I understand that, but why is he still alive? You should have destroyed him for violating our daughter. Instead, you hand her to him. Your actions defy reason."

Meghann gave him a disgusted look. "I didn't give Ellie to Jimmy. A statement like that shows you know nothing about her and less about me. My God, you think I wouldn't take apart with my bare hands anyone who hurt Ellie? Jimmy didn't rape Ellie or take advantage of her—they love each other."

"Love?" It was Simon's turn to look disgusted. "What kind of love can there between an innocent child and that pathetic weakling?"

"Jimmy is not weak. He's withstood your every attempt to destroy him—I'd say that shows a great deal of strength." Meghann mentally shook her head, wondering how she'd been maneuvered into defending a relationship she in no way approved of.

"You do not approve?" As he divined her thoughts, Simon seemed less and less angry with her.

"No more than I approve of you reading my mind," Meghann snapped. "But what can I do?"

"What can you do?" Simon echoed incredulously. "You, with all your power, are telling me you could not dispatch that loathsome creature?"

"Your daughter loves that loathsome creature," Meghann said. "Have you thought of what it would do to her relationship with us if we kill her lover?"

Simon's face darkened when Meghann reminded him Ellie and Jimmy were lovers, but his voice had lost all its anger when he spoke to her. "So that is what you meant when you said you didn't want anyone else to die. You worry slaughtering Delacroix would cost us Elizabeth's love? Meghann, we must do what is right for Elizabeth . . . not allow her to destroy herself because we fear to correct her."

"Killing Jimmy Delacroix isn't right! What's right is realizing Ellie is an adult now, capable of making her own choices even if we don't approve of them. For God's sake, Simon. Do you really think Jimmy is going to hurt her? He transformed Ellie—successfully, I might add. That alone shows what a powerful bond there is between them."

Simon's eyes narrowed and Meghann thought she'd finally said something Simon Baldevar couldn't refute. "Don't you see that Jimmy proved what kind of man he is when he charged into Mikal's club to rescue Ellie? Throw away your ridiculous prejudices and jealousies and see Jimmy Delacroix for what he really is—a fine, brave man who loves Ellie with all his heart.

He'll never hurt her, and it's over his dead body that anyone else will hurt her. Isn't that enough for you?"

"Elizabeth could do far better than him," Simon replied but here was no heat behind his words. His flat, considering tone gave Meghann hope she might actually accomplish the impossible and get Simon to leave Ellie and Jimmy in peace.

"All Ellie and Jimmy are asking for is a chance. After everything that's happened, can't you at least grant them that?"

Simon turned his back to her, staring at the brightly lit skyline and dark trees of Central Park before he spoke to her again. "He will come before me as a man and ask for my daughter's hand before I consider this. I will not see Elizabeth with some spineless creature that cannot face me to ask for her."

Meghann let out the breath she hadn't even known she was holding, thinking this was as safe as Ellie and Jimmy could be from Simon's wrath. Meghann wondered if she should tell Simon that Jimmy was all for facing down Simon, that it had been her and Ellie who urged him to leave the house once Simon regained consciousness.

"Maggie," Jimmy had argued before Ellie finally got him to leave. "What are we accomplishing here? Me and Ellie going on the run from Baldevar like criminals while you fight my battles with him? This isn't right. Either I confront him head-on or I'm the chickenshit that dickhead likes to think I am."

"Vulgar, if accurately, put," Simon said and Meghann nodded an amused gleam in his eyes as he crossed the roof to come to her side. "Perhaps Mr. Delacroix has some small merits I was not aware of."

"Stay away from me," Meghann said coldly and started for the rooftop door. "I told you what would happen if you ever hit me again."

Meghann reached the heavy aluminum door, intending to leave Simon for good now that she'd gotten him to agree to leave Ellie and Jimmy alone. She grabbed the thin, rusty handle and then fell back in shock, transfixed by what she saw.

"Simon..." Her voice came out thin and reedy, devoid of fury or any emotion but astonishment. "Simon, look."

She heard swift footsteps behind her and made no attempt to resist when Simon wrapped his hands around her waist. Together, they stared at something neither of them had seen in countless decades—the shadow of the slowly lightening sky illuminating the cracked, rusty door handle.

When Meghann first came up here, the handle was bathed in darkness. Now there was enough light to show each crumbling flake of the rusty handle... light that should have been making her and Simon feel the exhaustion and pain of imminent sunrise. Meghann thought she'd never seen anything as beautiful as that chipping rust growing brighter and brighter with each passing second.

"Simon..." Meghann said again, his name almost sounding like a prayer as she turned to him.

Simon stared at the door, seeming as transfixed as she was, and then lifted his eyes to the sky, still dark but now deep blue instead of the black that was all vampires could stand seeing.

If careless about the time, a vampire could still be awake in this gray light of the pre-dawn hour, but they felt sluggish and ill, if not in actual pain. Just looking at Simon, Meghann could tell he wasn't experiencing any aches and pains any more than she was.

"Do you think..." she began.

"I don't know, Meghann." Meghann whipped around at the wonder and humility in his voice—two things she'd never expected to hear from cool, ironic, detached Simon Baldevar.

"I'm scared," she confessed. It wasn't the coming dawn that frightened Meghann but the possibility this was all she'd be allowed to enjoy of it. She couldn't bear to come so close to enjoying sunlight, only to be driven back into darkness once the fiery orange ball rose in the sky.

Simon didn't attempt to soothe away her fears with meaningless words. He merely turned her around and said, "My love," before gently kissing her.

Meghann responded to him, her anger over his behavior when he found out about Ellie and Jimmy forgotten. It was impossible to hate Simon now, to feel anything but cautious hope and a deep sense of thanks that there was someone here to share this moment with her. Only another vampire could understand her joy in watching the burgeoning light chase the shadows from the rooftop and the stars from the sky.

Simon broke off their kiss, and turned her around so they could both view the horizon. Then he opened the rooftop door so they could rush into the dark house should the need arise, and then they leaned against each other, waiting and hoping.

Meghann trembled violently and Simon grasped her tighter as they watched the sky go from purple to navy blue and finally the azure of a new day. Meghann had forgotten what a gradual process the sunrise was, each gradual step so subtle you could miss it completely if you weren't watching with the same avid attention she and Simon were.

She waited for the pain, the bone-deep agony that was the last step before her skin would burn from exposure to sunlight. But the pain never came and all Meghann felt as the sky lightened was the first natural light and warmth on her skin in seventy years.

Finally, the reddish-orange ball of the sun appeared and Meghann trembled from head to toe while her heart rocked in her chest. Every instinct within her screamed at her to run from the killer sun but she took comfort from Simon's hard body supporting her and stood her ground.

Meghann had been wrong about sunrise—it wasn't slow at all. One minute she saw a small ball climbing rapidly in the sky, and the next blinding light bathed the city. She watched the city burst into life and didn't know she was crying until the falling tears tickled her cheeks.

How could she not cry at the miracle she was witnessing, at knowing she could bear the sun as well as a mortal? But what mortal could ever feel as Meghann did, take such delight at seeing colors and life she'd long since forgotten? What mortal knew to appreciate the trees of Central Park, no longer dark sentinels but a brilliant mass of full, green leaves? Meghann had forgotten green, forgotten the natural color of the world that she hadn't seen in so long. At night, all the color went away. How conditioned she'd become to blurred generalities. She'd forgotten the texture and depth of a leaf that wasn't visible by night just as she'd forgotten the sharp gray of the skyscrapers standing impassive and proud against the bright sky.

Simon's hands grasped her shoulders in an almost painful grip and Meghann turned to him, seeing wetness on his face that indicated he must have cried his own tears when he saw the sunrise.

Meghann peered at him closely, looking for the black circles beneath his eyes and ghoulishly white skin that characterized vampires during daylight hours. But Simon looked just as he always did, giving Meghann hope she too looked presentable in the sunlight. All the sun showed her was a man with pale skin, somewhat paler than average but easily explainable as the result of a prolonged illness.

We can walk among the mortals in daylight and not be thought of as unholy monsters, Meghann thought and looked at Simon expectantly but he simply continued to stare down at her.

"You can't read my thoughts, can you?" she asked and he shook his head regretfully.

"I don't believe we'll have our full strength during the day," Simon said and Meghann nodded—she'd expected as much. Mikal had no more strength or power than the average mortal during the day... a few hours without her magic was a small price to pay for the privilege of seeing the world sparkle to life all around her.

"Ellie!" Meghann said and smiled brightly. "Simon, this is wonderful. I hated the thought of her missing the sun—now she won't have to at all!"

"No," Simon said firmly. "She will not drink of our blood just yet."

Meghann was about to ask why not when she realized why Simon wouldn't share the gift of daylight with his daughter—Jimmy Delacroix. To appease Meghann, Simon wouldn't harm Jimmy but withholding the gift of daylight was his way of expressing disapproval over Ellie's choice of lover.

"Are you going to keep Ellie in the dark until she breaks up with Jimmy?" Meghann demanded.

"Only until I am certain she... and perhaps Jimmy Delacroix, as well... deserves this gift. Besides, we do not know what drawbacks there are just yet. I am imploring you to wait, Meghann, and not allow our daughter to drink of you behind my back."

"Tell me what promise you made Alcuin and I won't let Ellie drink my blood until you're ready for her to experience daylight," Meghann said, remembering Alcuin's brief visit to her. Alcuin, Meghann thought with a pang. If only he, Charles and Lee could share the sun with her.

Simon gave her a sour grin, wide gold eyes still taking in the beauty of the new day all around them. "I should have known the pontiff would come to you in an attempt to dictate my behavior. The promise he attempted to extract from me was that I no longer slaughter my prey or anyone else except in the name of self-defense."

"Honor it," Meghann said and Simon laughed, an unpleasant, derisive sound.

"Why in the world would I do that?"

"Because we killed our own child," Meghann said quietly and for a moment the world was as dark as it was the night she chose to kill her son to save her husband. "How much more blood can you want on your hands?"

Simon didn't turn away from the sun when he said in a tight voice, "Have you any idea what you are asking of me—that I bend beneath the will of a priest that tried for centuries to control me?"

"What about you asking me to keep the gift of light from my daughter?" Meghann returned. "Please, Simon. At least honor Alcuin's oath while you deny Ellie the sun. Do that and I. . . I'll never bring up Mikal or what happened tonight again."

After a long moment, Simon turned away from the sun and stroked her face. "If you could only see how your hair glows in the sun. I never thought to have the privilege to look upon you in the light of day. Very well, Meghann. I give you my word I shall not destroy my prey while Elizabeth cannot walk in daylight."

Meghann accepted his promise with a nod, thinking Alcuin had been right. Simon did need her—to break that core of dark ruthlessness within his soul. But she needed him as well, needed his fierce strength and never waning love to support her through her immortality.

Meghann reached up to kiss Simon, feeling a sense of peace descend over her. For the first time, she was truly accepting of her vampiric state. No longer did she have to hide from the sun, her daughter was safe, and Simon would never threaten Jimmy Delacroix again. Certainly, she had regrets—namely the deaths of Charles and Lee. But with her new ability to walk in sunlight, Simon's love, and Ellie's safety, Meghann had as much as she'd ever dared dream of since the night she transformed.

All these thoughts raced through Meghann's mind while she and Simon kissed, their mouths and hands turning urgent with need.

"You know," Meghann said impishly when Simon started guiding her down the steep stairs toward the bedroom, "I've never made love during the day."

"And I have not in four hundred years," Simon laughed, scooping her into his arms. "I think we must do so straightaway."

Meghann melted against him in agreement, thinking for the moment of nothing but what it would be like to throw open the bedroom shutters and make love in the warmth of the sun.

Discover other fine publications at:

http://www.darkoakpress.com

CPSIA information can be obtained
at www.ICGtesting.com
Printed in the USA
BVOW08s1835300318
512056BV00002B/188/P

9 781941 754306